THE BEST IS YET TO COME

ESCAPE TO THE LAKES BOOK 3

JESSICA REDLAND

Boldw**o**d

First published in Great Britain in 2024 by Boldwood Books Ltd.

Copyright © Jessica Redland, 2024

Cover Design by Lizzie Gardiner

Cover Images: Shutterstock and Adobe Stock

A CIP catalogue record for this book is available from the British Library.

Paperback ISBN 978-1-83518-292-5

Large Print ISBN 978-1-83518-288-8

Hardback ISBN 978-1-83518-287-1

Ebook ISBN 978-1-83518-285-7

Kindle ISBN 978-1-83518-286-4

Audio CD ISBN 978-1-83518-293-2

MP3 CD ISBN 978-1-83518-290-1

Digital audio download ISBN 978-1-83518-284-0

Boldwood Books Ltd
23 Bowerdean Street
London SW6 3TN
www.boldwoodbooks.com

To Emma, Terry, John, Nicole and Jade at Alpacaly Ever After in the Lake District with tremendous gratitude for generously giving your time and sharing with me your incredible knowledge and passion for camelids

AUTHOR'S NOTE

The Willowdale series is set around Derwent Water in the Lake District National Park – an area I know and love from many wonderful holidays. When I started writing the series, I had a burning question. Is it Derwent Water or Derwentwater? As it happens, there's no definitive agreement, with the versions being used interchangeably. I have chosen to consistently use the two-word spelling of Derwent Water because both Ordnance Survey and the National Trust use this. Neither version is incorrect.

There are also variations in spellings of fells and other places (e.g. Cat Bells and Friar's Crag), in which case I have gone with Ordnance Survey's spelling.

The use of both Elter Water and Elterwater is not an inconsistency. The former is a lake, the latter is the nearby village.

Please further note that, while I've used Keswick as an anchor for the fictional setting of Willowdale and do mention several real places in this book such as Carlisle and Ambleside, any businesses, farms and schools mentioned are fictional.

PROLOGUE
2 SEPTEMBER

Rosie

It was a Monday morning in early September and I'd decided to use my day off to finally clear out his Lordship's bedroom at Willowdale Hall, enlisting Mam and my best friend Autumn to help me. *His Lordship* was the nickname Mam had given to our former boss and landlord, Hubert Cranleigh, because of the way he'd stomped around hurling out orders as though he was landed gentry from a different era.

So much had changed since his fatal riding accident at the start of this year. His estranged son, Oliver, had returned to the estate for the first time in eighteen years. Oliver and I shared a chequered history and had parted on very bad terms so seeing him again after so long was a challenge, especially when he dropped the bombshell that he was planning to sell the hall. Not only would that mean losing my job as the manager of Willowdale Hall Riding School & Equestrian Centre, it would mean Mam and I could no longer live in Horseshoe Cottage in the grounds of the estate, which would be disastrous. Since

Mam was knocked down in a hit-and-run accident on the road between the hall and village when I was fourteen, her physical scars had healed but her mental ones hadn't. She'd barely left the safety of the grounds so I was desperate to convince Oliver to change his mind for her sake. In the process of doing that, Oliver and I faced our difficult past and fell in love all over again. Actually, we'd never stopped loving each other but the timing and circumstances had never been right until now.

His Lordship's riding accident uncovered an unexpected secret. After looking into live organ donation, Oliver discovered that they weren't related, which left a huge question – if Hubert Cranleigh wasn't Oliver's father, who was?

Oliver's mam, Kathryn, had died after a short illness when Oliver was twelve so he couldn't ask her and, although Mam had been friends with her, Kathryn hadn't confided in her, so the identity of Oliver's biological father remained a mystery. It was a long shot but I wondered whether Kathryn might have kept a diary and it turned out she'd kept one every year since she was twenty-four. We found them in Hubert's bedroom and it was obvious from various ripped pages that he'd been reading them and hadn't liked what he found.

We'd been gathering everything together when we got distracted by a tree which had fallen onto the disused boathouse out the back of the hall during the previous night's storm. Checking out the damage, we discovered a sports car hidden inside which turned out to be the vehicle involved in Mam's hit-and-run. Although finding the car – and therefore discovering that the driver had been none other than Hubert Cranleigh – was extremely distressing for Mam, it was the catalyst she needed to seek professional help and check herself into a support facility, and she'd made tremendous progress.

While Mam recovered, I started on Kathryn's diaries.

Ploughing through page after page revealed that she'd been in an extremely unhappy, abusive marriage with a serial adulterer but that she'd found her own happiness through a long-term secret relationship with Oliver's biological father. The big problem was that he was only ever identified by the letter C and Oliver had no idea who C could possibly be. After a month of reading and getting no closer to solving the mystery, Oliver decided it was time we put the past to bed and focus on our future together – a future which included exciting new plans to develop Willowdale Hall – but I still hoped that one day we'd discover who his father really was. In the whole tree-on-the-boathouse kerfuffle, we'd forgotten about the ripped pages. Until now...

Autumn joined Mam and me on the floor of his Lordship's former bedroom, using tape to stick together ripped-up pieces from Kathryn's diaries, hoping that we'd find some clues to uncover the identity of Oliver's father – the mysterious C.

Eventually, we had a few intact pages. I picked up the longest entry and started reading it in my head. It was a bit awkward with the words split and the shine from the sticky tape, but I forged on.

Wednesday 21 June 2000

I don't think I've ever been so nervous in my life. H wasn't meant to be coming. He should have been working away but he came back a day early and got a bee in his bonnet that I'd sulk if he didn't come with me. As if! He's never shown interest in anything else school related so I was hardly going to be stroppy if he missed parents' evening. So off we go and he has a face on him like a slapped arse. The minute we arrived, Oliver couldn't wait to drag me over to his favourite teacher. Also my favourite.

Somewhat different reasons. C's face lit up when he saw me.

'Oh, my God!' I exclaimed as I got a little further.

'What?' Mam and Autumn cried together.

'This is it! This is the answer!' I looked at them, eyes shining. 'I know who C is.'

'Who?' Autumn asked.

'Let me just finish this to make sure.'

I continued reading.

Impressive acting skills when he realised H was behind me. Don't know how he managed to keep that same smile on his face when I bet he wanted to punch H instead. We sat down and C raved about what a brilliant student Oliver was and how he was convinced he had a future ahead of him in medicine. It should have been a really proud parent moment but all I wanted to do was cry because H got to play dad yet couldn't have been less interested in how Oliver was doing and that wonderful man would have done anything to step into his shoes. How H didn't spot the resemblance, I'll never know. But I guess you don't notice things when you're not looking, do you?

'See what you think,' I said, passing the page to Autumn and Mam to read. 'But I'm one hundred per cent certain from this that Oliver's biological father – C – is my old biology teacher, Mr Wynterson.'

Autumn's eyes widened as she looked up. 'I agree. Oh, my God!'

'I remember him,' Mam said. 'Wasn't he one of your favourite teachers?'

'Yes. Him and Miss Eccles.'

'Wasn't he Oliver's favourite teacher too?' Mam asked.

'Yes, and he was more than just a teacher. He got him back on track when he was failing at sixth form and he helped him when he had a breakdown at university so he became Ollie's mentor too.'

'But he's actually his dad,' Autumn said, scanning down the page once more. 'And it's clear from this that he knew. I wonder why he never said anything.'

'Only one way to find out.' I clapped my hands to my cheeks, shaking my head. 'I can't believe we've found out who C is after all these months.'

'How do you think Oliver will take it?' Mam asked.

'He'll be shocked but I think he'll be delighted. It's someone he knows and admires. I know he regrets that they lost touch.'

'Looks like he has the perfect excuse to get back in touch now,' Autumn said, handing me back the page.

I glanced down it again, heart pounding. We'd done it! We'd solved the mystery and I was absolutely certain Oliver would not only want to get in touch with Mr Wynterson but he'd want to do it pretty quickly too.

As for how Oliver would feel about Mr Wynterson keeping his identity a secret, that was another matter. Why hadn't he said anything? He must have known things were bad between Oliver and Hubert? I sighed, shaking my head. He must have had his reasons and I guess we'd find those out very soon.

1

SIX WEEKS EARLIER

Emma

'It's the last day of the school year, the students have gone, and I know you'll all be itching to get out of here and start your summer holidays...' Kelvin Patterson, principal of Corbeck School in Carlisle, paused as he looked round the teaching and support staff gathered in the staffroom, '...so the fact that so many of you have stayed late is testimony to how highly we all think of Emma.'

'And cake,' called one of my colleagues, making everyone laugh. The cooks had made an enormous slab of chocolate sponge cake which they'd iced with *Good luck Emma!* and a four-leaf clover.

My cheeks glowed as I felt all eyes on me and I swallowed down the lump in my throat. I always found the summer term emotional – saying goodbye and good luck to the GCSE students – and invested in a new waterproof mascara and large supply of tissues to see me through it. But this time it was me saying goodbye to my teaching family, which thrilled and terrified me in equal measures, especially after twenty-five years – nineteen of them at Corbeck School – devoted to a career I loved.

'Emma has been such an asset to this school. I could list all her amazing achievements...' Kelvin continued, all promises not to make a speech or a big fuss clearly forgotten. He laughed as he caught my eye and I shook my head vigorously. 'But I promised Emma I wouldn't embarrass her. What I *will* say is that I'm going to miss her and I know everyone here will too.'

Tears pricked my eyes as I took in all the nods. My lifelong best friend Rachael placed a reassuring hand on my arm and gave me a gentle squeeze, helping me hold it together for a little longer.

Kelvin focused his gaze on me. 'Emma, we wish you every success in your new venture on the farm. I'm not sure what's going to prove the most challenging – herding students or herding sheep – but you were brilliant at the former and I'm sure you'll be equally brilliant at the latter. There'll be a huge void when we return in September without you. Good luck to you and Grayson, thank you for everything you've done for us all and we hope you enjoy your leaving gifts.'

He led everyone in an enormous round of applause, accompanied by cheers and whistles as I was handed several gift bags and a huge bouquet of flowers. I couldn't hold the tears back any longer and what was the point anyway? My eyes were already red and itchy from saying goodbye to my students across the day with each lesson end bringing me closer to my final farewell.

'Grab yourselves a piece of cake,' Kelvin called as the applause tailed off. 'Have an amazing summer, everyone, and I look forward to seeing most of you back here in September.'

Everyone crowded round me, offering hugs and hand-shakes, which I accepted in a tear-sodden daze.

* * *

'It's like Christmas!' Rachael declared as she passed me the final gift bag to squeeze into my car later.

I closed the back door and the boot, shaking my head at how full my car was. 'I can't believe how generous everyone has been.'

'Because they all love you. Fantastic teacher, brilliant boss, amazing friend.'

Her voice cracked and I enveloped her in a hug as we both sobbed together.

'I was so determined not to cry today,' she said, wiping her eyes when we released each other. 'Nearly made it.'

'At least it's not a proper goodbye for us. After forty-seven years, you don't get rid of me that easily.'

My mum and Rachael's mum Gail had become good friends after meeting at ante-natal classes and, born just two days apart, Rachael and I had spent a lot of time together as children. As lifelong best friends, we'd been bridesmaids at each other's weddings and I was godmother to her twins, Cian and Maeve. It was hard to believe they were now twenty-five. Where had the years gone?

Rachael taught French and Spanish and was now Head of Modern Languages and I was Head of Sciences, specialising in biology. I loved how we'd ended up teaching at the same school.

'It's going to be really strange being back here in September without you,' Rachael said.

'It'll be strange knowing you're back here and I'm not.' I glanced wistfully towards the school building and sighed.

Rachael tucked her long auburn hair behind her ears and widened her pale blue eyes at me. 'I know that sigh! You're not regretting it, are you?'

I shook my head and smiled reassuringly at her. 'Just having a moment of nostalgia. It was a big, scary decision but it was the right one. Let's say I'm having a few wobbles but no regrets.'

'Completely understandable. New home, new career, new life – that's a lot of change at once so it's bound to feel a bit overwhelming.' She hugged me once more. 'I'd better let you get home to continue your packing, and I'd better get home and think about the holiday packing.'

'You and Cormac have an amazing time in Hawaii. I'm not jealous at all.'

'Thank you and good luck with the move. Looking forward to my farm tour once we're back.' She kissed me on the cheek then headed off to her own car with a wave.

I took one last look at the school where I'd made some lovely friends and worked with so many incredible, inspiring students. I pressed two fingers to my lips, kissed them, and threw the kiss in the direction of the building with a smile. What an amazing nineteen years I'd had here, but Grayson and I were starting a new chapter at Bracken Ridge Farm in the Lake District National Park and I was so excited about working on the farm alongside my fiancé, lapping up his extensive knowledge of Herdwick sheep, Belted Galloway cattle and environmentally friendly farming. I might be forty-seven years old but age was just a number and it was never too late to start completely afresh. Bring it on!

2

I'd not long finished unwrapping all my gifts and had them spread all over the dining table when I heard Grayson arriving home from work, prompting me that I really needed to get ready for our night out. We lived in Riverside Cottage – a two-bedroom home in the village of Halderbeck at the northern tip of the Lake District National Park. To celebrate my last day at school, we'd booked a table at The Hidden Fell – Halderbeck's only pub, a couple of minutes' walk from the cottage.

While Grayson was removing his boots in the hall, Monty ran through to the dining room to see me, bouncing around for attention. A five-year-old border collie, Monty worked with Grayson at nearby Petersgill Farm and I loved how he always sought me out the moment they arrived home.

Grayson appeared and did a double-take at the laden table, running his hands through his dark hair. 'Have you robbed a gift shop?'

I laughed. 'Looks like it, doesn't it?'

'How many mugs this time?'

'Twelve.'

'Duplicates?'

'A couple.' I'd built up an enormous mug collection over the years with *Best Teacher* being a common theme. 'I have some *happy retirement* ones this time.'

He raised his eyebrows. 'Retirement? Well, I suppose it is in a way.'

'Lots of farm animal mugs too,' I added, but Grayson just rolled his eyes. He was a creature of habit and would only drink from a pair of plain navy mugs he'd brought with him when he moved in with me three years ago.

'Look what I got from the staff,' I said, pointing to a pile of cushions on one of the dining chairs. 'They'll look lovely on our new sofa.'

Grayson glanced at the top one – a stunning watercolour illustration of a Highland cow – and wrinkled his nose. 'It's a bit fussy.'

'It's beautiful,' I said, picking it up to reveal a fox design by the same artist.

'I'm off for my shower,' Grayson said, clearly not interested in seeing the rest of the cushions. He left the room and I showed the other two – a hare and a stag – to Monty.

'You think they're beautiful, don't you?' I said to him in a sing-song voice which had him wagging his tail. 'What's that, Monty? They'll look so much nicer on the sofa than the boring plain navy cushions Grayson chose? I couldn't agree more.'

I stroked his ears before piling the cushions back up on the chair. Grayson's reaction didn't bother me one bit. He wasn't one for bright colours or patterns – whether that was in clothing or soft furnishings – so even a subtle check design would have been *a bit fussy* for him.

I surveyed the rest of my gifts – candles, stationery, smellies, soft toys, a couple of lovely scarves and enough chocolates to open my own sweet shop. One of the mugs in particular made me smile. It had a picture of a cartoon alpaca on it next to a suitcase, accompanied by the slogan, *New adventure? Alpaca my bags!* I adored llamas and alpacas. I've no idea what had triggered it because I'd never spent time around either animal, but I was always drawn towards any stationery or other merchandise I spotted my students with. I remembered mentioning my love for alpacas to the student who'd bought me the mug after admiring her alpaca phone case at the start of the school year. It was so touching that she'd stored that information to buy me a meaningful end-of-year gift.

'I think I'll leave these here for now and pack them straight into a moving box tomorrow,' I told Monty. 'We're eating out so it's not like we need the table tonight.'

Before Grayson moved in with me, I could count on two hands the number of occasions when the dining table had been used for eating. Even though the second bedroom was set up as a home office with a desk and bookshelves, I preferred to spread out when I was marking homework so I used the dining table and ate off a lap tray in front of the television. Both those habits irritated Grayson, who was a neat-freak and a traditionalist with meals. 'What's wrong with your desk upstairs?' he'd ask. 'Why do you need to take over the dining table and half the floor too?'

So I'd embraced eating at the dining table and found I liked how the formality gave us the opportunity to talk about our days – something we probably wouldn't have done with the TV on.

Monty followed me into the kitchen where I filled his bowl with food and changed his water, leaving him to eat while I went upstairs to get ready.

* * *

'So, how was your last day?' Grayson asked when we'd settled at our table in The Hidden Fell and placed our food and drinks order. 'Did you cry?'

'I went through a full box of tissues. It wasn't pretty.'

'You didn't have to leave,' he said, his voice gentle.

'We both know I did. There was no way I could have done that commute.' Bracken Ridge Farm was a few miles outside Coniston and the drive to school would have been a minimum of ninety minutes each way.

'Agreed, but you didn't have to pack in the career you love. There are schools nearer the farm, you know.'

'I know, but I'm ready for a complete change. I know this started off as your dream but I've fallen in love with the farm and it's my dream now too. Can you believe that, a fortnight today, we'll be celebrating our first full day there? It's been a long road but it's going to be so worth it. I'm so proud of you for keeping going, despite the setbacks.' I raised my glass. 'To never giving up on your dreams.'

He smiled and clinked his glass against mine.

Bracken Ridge Farm was a very special place – one of fifteen farms in the Lake District which the author, illustrator and conservationist Beatrix Potter had left to the National Trust. It was the third tenancy Grayson had attempted to secure. The selection process was rigorous and tough, which was understandable as the National Trust Lettings Team needed to ensure they found tenants with the relevant experience and aligned mindset to continue Beatrix Potter's legacy. Grayson's first application hadn't made it past the pre-viewing questionnaire. Second time around, he'd passed the questionnaire and been invited to the viewing day – a chance to tour the farm, meet the outgoing tenant farmer and ask questions. Those who were still interested after the viewing day submitted a formal application and tender process with those passing that invited to a selection event. Grayson progressed to that stage but made *an absolute balls-up* of the interview – his words, not mine. Nerves got the better of him, his mind went blank and he barely answered any of the questions.

When Bracken Ridge Farm came up, he wasn't sure he could face going through the process for a third time but I convinced him to give it another try. He had a massive wobble on the morning of the interview and was close to pulling out but I talked him round and, thankfully, he composed himself and aced it.

I was a firm believer in things happening for a reason and the previous disappointments had been worth it because Bracken Ridge Farm had turned out to be the one most ideally suited to Grayson's skills and interests and it was also my personal favourite.

'Hamish has asked if I can work right up until the end of the month,' Grayson said. 'He's got a hospital check-up on the Wednesday. I know it's not ideal, but...'

'It's fine,' I said when he tailed off, his expression apologetic. 'I've made good progress already.'

'You'll do a better job than I would,' he said, smiling at me.

He might be neat and tidy but Grayson's ability to pack was shocking. I'd ordered a large supply of boxes, tape and bubble wrap and had already started working systematically through each room so I was confident of being ready ahead of moving day, even without Grayson's help.

Our tenancy would start on the first day of August and we'd timed completion on the sale of Riverside Cottage for the same day. I'd known I'd be on my own packing next week and had hoped that Grayson's boss Hamish would release him early to help me the following week, but it wasn't a crisis that he hadn't. I'd be on my own unpacking at the other end too as Grayson's priority had to be the farm. While he settled in, I'd committed to the mammoth job of painting all the rooms in the farmhouse. The outgoing tenants, Jack and Teresa Gaskill, had favoured bold, dark colours like maroon, navy and forest green, which made the rooms appear small and dark. My aim was to get the bedroom, lounge and kitchen sorted first and then fit the rest around helping Grayson on the farm.

'Will you miss Petersgill Farm?' I asked.

'I suppose. Hamish has been good to me, especially keeping me on after he recovered, but running someone else's farm isn't the same as running your own. That was always the plan and it should have happened a long time ago.' His jaw tightened and he shook his head as he shuddered. 'Let's not go there tonight.'

Our food arriving gave a natural pause in the conversation anyway. I really felt for Grayson and everything he'd been through. When I met him at a New Year's Eve party seven and a half years ago, he'd been running Low Fell Farm in the Cumbrian countryside north of Penrith with his parents. He'd devoted his whole life to that farm, working on it unpaid while at school and, after finishing agricultural college, he'd ploughed his wages back into nature-friendly sustainable projects. His investment was on the understanding that his parents would retire when his dad turned sixty-five and pass the farm down to Grayson, just like it had been passed down from Grayson's grandfather and great-grandfather. Being a lover of animals and spending time outdoors myself, Grayson's passion for farming and nature was what had attracted me to him in the first place and I'd loved hearing all the ideas he had for further changes when Low Fell Farm became his.

During those early years of our relationship, there'd never been any question mark over Low Fell Farm becoming Grayson's. His parents had mentioned it when I first met them and they'd shown me the unused barn which they were getting converted into a new home for them so that Grayson could have the farmhouse as his own. I'd seen each stage of the barn conversion and had even been shopping with Grayson's mum for soft furnishings. All the while, there were constant references to Grayson taking over. And then they'd completely shafted him.

Just before Easter three years ago, they announced that they'd sold Low Fell Farm and would be moving to Corfu where the warmer climate would be kinder to his mum's arthritis. No warning, no discussion – just a done deal a year ahead of his dad's planned retirement. They couldn't understand why Grayson was so upset, especially when they'd done him *a huge favour* by arranging with the new owner for Grayson to stay on as a farmhand. A farmhand! As if that came close to compensating for taking his future home and livelihood away from him.

I was devastated for Grayson that his parents could do something so devious and not actually see how wrong it was. He was a kind man and empathetic to his mum's health conditions so he'd definitely have found a way to make their move abroad possible – perhaps by selling the barn conversion or some land – but they hadn't given him that opportunity.

The new owner of Low Fell Farm had agreed that Grayson's parents could rent the barn conversion from him while they searched for a property on Corfu. They extended the invite to Grayson but he was so angry and disappointed with them that he moved in with me instead. We'd been a couple for over four years by that point and had talked about moving in together on the farm when he took over so it wasn't like it hadn't been on the cards for us but it was a shame that, instead of being able to celebrate it as a key moment in our relationship, it had become a reactive, rushed necessity.

Grayson turned down the job with the new owner and took on some temporary labouring work while thinking about what he wanted from the future. Six months later, he secured a temporary role managing Petersgill Farm while Hamish took some time out for cancer treatment. Being temporary made it perfect for Grayson to work towards his new dream of becoming a tenant farmer on one of Beatrix Potter's farms, although it had meant that he'd needed to step back into the role of farmhand rather than manager when Hamish was well enough to return to work, which hadn't been nearly as demanding or fulfilling for him. But it had been a bit of short-term pain for long-term gain because, in a fortnight's time, he'd finally be living his dream. The best things came to those who waited and Grayson had done more than his fair share of waiting. I was so lucky to be part of that dream with him.

3

On the two occasions I'd been to Bracken Ridge Farm – visiting day in January and over the Easter holidays in early April shortly after Grayson accepted the tenancy offer – it had been drizzling. Low cloud had shrouded the fells, preventing me from seeing it at its best but, as Grayson pulled onto the farm track on Sunday morning, my heart soared. The sun was shining in a cornflower-blue sky and I could finally take in the beauty of the setting.

'Impressive, eh?' Grayson said, giving me a sideways glance.

'It's stunning.'

The whitewashed farmhouse itself was picture-perfect – double-fronted with a wooden porch, climbing roses round the door and windows, and an attractive lawn enclosed by a drys-tone wall – but it was the backdrop that took my breath away. The fells were higher than I'd expected, curving protectively around the farm. There were approximately a thousand acres of land consisting of fields to the front and side of the house and the fells beyond and I couldn't quite believe that it would soon be all ours to nurture over a fifteen-year tenancy.

The track opened out into a large parking area opposite the side of the house, flanked by barns and various outbuildings. Several hens were strutting around so Grayson carefully manoeuvred his 4x4 around them.

Teresa, a warm, gentle woman in her early sixties, crossed the track, arms outstretched in welcome.

'So lovely to see you both again,' she said, taking my hands and kissing my cheek before doing the same to Grayson. 'I've radioed Jack and he's on his way down on the quad bike. Do you want to come in for a cuppa, Grayson, or would you rather get straight out?'

'Straight out, if that's okay with you.'

It was their final handover session and Grayson wanted to make the most of it. Jack had said he was welcome to ring him after we'd moved in but Grayson didn't think that was fair, especially when Jack was retiring so should be given the opportunity to fully let go.

'Jack thought you'd say that,' Teresa said, smiling at him. 'I'll see you later.'

She led me through the side door which was used as the main entrance to the house, through the boot and cloakroom, and into the large kitchen. I smiled at the piles of newspaper and boxes.

'Please tell me your house looks as chaotic as ours,' she said as she removed a couple of mugs from under-cupboard hooks.

'It does. Boxes everywhere.'

'Are you excited about moving here?' she asked as we settled in the lounge a few minutes later with mugs of tea.

'Very, but I'm nervous too.'

'Aw, you'll be fine. It's a wonderful farm and we've both been very happy here. Wish we could have stayed but retirement calls and, to be honest, we're both ready for it. Did you manage to secure a teaching job locally?'

'Slight change of plan. Moving to a farm is a big change in lifestyle and I decided I wanted to fully embrace it, so I'm going to help Grayson out.'

'Oh, how lovely! Have you worked on a farm before?'

'Never, but I love animals and I'm an enthusiastic learner. I might not be quite so enthusiastic when it's bucketing it down, but I'll give it my all.'

'Good for you. And if you don't like it, at least you still have teaching to fall back on.'

'Do you ever help Jack out?' I asked.

'I collect the eggs each morning, but that's as far as it goes. I was happy to live on a farm but I never wanted to be a farmer and Jack knew that from the outset. I've got my sewing business and I wanted to keep that going.'

I'd already discovered from my previous visit that Teresa made soft furnishings. One of the spare bedrooms was her sewing room and I'd been fascinated by the floor-to-ceiling shelving units packed with colourful bolts of fabric, crates full of yarn, and small sets of drawers full of thread and sewing paraphernalia.

'Most of the time, it's a one-person job,' Teresa continued, 'but there are key times of the year when lots of help is needed. We've got three grown-up children who help out and the neighbouring farmers all lend each other skills and equipment. I think Jack's already introduced Grayson to them.'

'He has.' I paused to sip on my tea, frowning. 'You don't think there's going to be enough for me to do here?'

'Oh, goodness, please don't think that. There's *always* something to do on a farm so I'm sure Grayson will be able to keep you busy. If he doesn't, there are plenty of other things you could do to keep busy and bring additional income in.'

'Such as?'

'It depends on your time and inclination. There are minimal-effort activities like selling eggs. We've had eggs and an honesty box at the end of the track for years. Of course, minimal effort means minimal income but, as the eggs would go to waste otherwise, it was a no-brainer. Not that you can do that with Grayson not wanting to keep the hens.'

I hadn't been too pleased when he'd made that decision as I loved the idea of checking the henhouse each morning for fresh eggs. *We're not running a poultry farm* was his unhelpful response. A handful of hens was hardly that but it wasn't worth debating. He was, after all, the animal expert and in charge of the farm.

'For more effort and more income, you could run a bed and breakfast using the spare bedrooms,' Teresa continued. 'I did that for a couple of years when we first took the farm on and the income was welcome although, for me, the downsides eventually outweighed the positives and I packed it in.'

'Downsides?' I prompted.

'Constantly washing sheets and towels, no-shows, feeling like I couldn't go anywhere in case guests arrived early...' She laughed lightly. 'I'm not selling it very well, am I?'

I smiled at her. 'Not really. Any other suggestions?'

She sipped on her tea, evidently thinking about it. 'Oh, I know! It's not something I actually actioned but I did all the research several years back. Come with me.'

Intrigued, I followed her up the stairs and into her sewing room which also had boxes everywhere. She pulled open a drawer in a tall filing cabinet, shaking her head after riffling through it.

'It's not in there,' she muttered, standing up after going through all the drawers. 'Where could it...' She looked around the room, brow creased. 'Maybe... wait here a minute.'

She dashed out of the room and I looked around me. The bolts of material had gone and all that remained on the shelves were several crocheted animals. I took a step closer. Was that...? I moved aside a giraffe to reveal two adorable white llamas. I picked them both up, admiring the pastel-coloured rugs over their backs and the scarves round their necks. One was wearing a bobble hat and glasses and the slightly smaller one sported a jaunty beret.

'Found it!' Teresa announced, returning to the room with a ring binder clutched to her chest. She nodded towards the llamas in my hands. 'You like them?'

'Oh my gosh, Teresa, I *love* them. These are amazing. I have a thing for llamas and alpacas.'

'Then you must have them.'

'Oh, I couldn't. They must have taken you ages to make.' I studied their adorable expressions and knew I'd regret it if I didn't keep them. 'Let me pay for them at least.'

'Absolutely not. Consider them a housewarming gift. And, if you love camelids, you're going to love this.'

She handed me the ring binder. An A4 page was inserted into the cover pouch with the words *PROJECT CAMELID* written at the top in thick marker pen capitals and a picture of a herd of llamas beneath it.

'After I stopped doing the B&B, I was planning on running a llama or alpaca walking business on the farm,' she said, smiling at me.

My heart leapt for the second time that morning. A business walking my favourite animals around the farm? I couldn't imagine anything more perfect. I opened the binder and started flicking through the pages, excitement bubbling inside me.

'The costings will be out of date but everything else should be helpful. Let's go back downstairs to our drinks and I'll tell you more about it.'

* * *

'You want to do what?' Grayson asked, stopping at a T-junction halfway home and staring at me, eyebrows knitted.

'I want to set up an alpaca or llama walking business,' I repeated. 'Or rather I want to look into it. Teresa gave me contact details for two places she visited when she was doing her research.'

'Is walking llamas or alpacas even a thing?'

'Yes, and it's really popular.'

'Why? I don't get it.'

'That's probably because you're not the target audience.'

He shook his head before pulling away. 'How much does a llama cost?'

'Probably nothing. The ones that Teresa was looking into were rescues from someone whose circumstances changed. If I was a breeder or wanting to show them, we could be talking significant money, but that wouldn't be the plan. What do you think?'

'I think I don't like the idea of the general public traipsing all over my land.'

I rolled my eyes at him. We'd already had that conversation many times. There were several rights of way across the farm so he was just going to have to accept the idea that he couldn't completely escape from people.

'If I did start walks, I'd stick to the lower parts of the farm out of your way so there's no need to panic. And it's not like it's going to be several times a day every day with stacks of people.'

'Where would you keep them?' he asked, the hard edge to his tone suggesting to me he really wasn't keen.

'Teresa would have used the front field opposite the house and reconfigured that stone barn which backs onto it to give them shelter. Jack doesn't use the field or the barn so presumably you won't either.'

'Probably not, but...'

'But what?' I prompted when he tailed off.

'I don't know. It's not something I was expecting.'

'Me neither and I'm not saying I'm definitely doing it but it is something I *really* want to look into.'

He sighed. 'Sod it! I suppose there's no harm in doing some research but if you did want to go ahead, you're on your own with it. I don't have the time or the interest.'

'Okay. That's fine by me.'

'I mean it,' he said, his tone a little more forceful, as though he wasn't convinced he'd made his point clear. 'Any work needed in the field or barn would have to be done without me. I'm here for the Herdies and Belties, not some stupid llamas.'

'They're not stupid,' I said testily.

He glanced at me, eyebrows raised, clearly surprised that I'd snapped – something I never did. But what did he expect? Just because it wasn't his thing didn't mean he needed to be rude about it.

'What's your next step?' he asked, his voice softer, although still laced with disinterest.

'I'm going to get in touch with the owners of the farms Teresa visited and see if I can have a tour too. She says they're completely different set-ups which helped her focus on how she wanted to run her business.'

I filled Grayson in on the rest of the conversation I'd had with Teresa. He made all the right noises but it was obvious he wasn't engaged. Not that I minded because I liked the idea of being in charge of something of my own rather than working all the time for Grayson. He had an incredible amount of knowledge and expertise about Herdwick sheep and Belted Galloway cattle which I could never hope to match but it would be lovely to build up my own area of expertise. As soon as we got home, I was going to contact those two farms and see if I could organise visits for next week in between packing. I'd already been excited about the move but the idea of my own business with my favourite animals had taken it to a new level.

4
_____

On Thursday morning, I was in high spirits as I drove forty-five minutes from Riverside Cottage to Butterbea Croft in the Yorkshire Dales National Park for my second research visit of the week. Windows down, I sang along to the Birthday Bangers – a playlist of *banging tunes* Rachael and I had created years ago for the car journey on our annual birthday weekend away together. If I was feeling low it never failed to lift me as, not only were all the songs upbeat, but the memories they evoked were too. And if my mood was already sunny like today, the playlist maintained that happiness.

A couple of days ago, I'd travelled to Haltsby Farm over the border into Lancashire. It was a large family-run business with the husband and son managing the farm and the wife and daughter running a farm shop, café, and animal-handling experiences. Visitors could pet and walk llamas, feed playful goats, stroke rabbits and guinea pigs, and bottle feed lambs in the spring. There were also walking trails round the farm to see sheep, pigs and cows. It was an impressive set-up, albeit on a much grander scale to what I'd be running at Bracken Ridge Farm.

Today's destination of Butterbea Croft, run by sisters Ruth and Lizzie, was a former working farm but now operated as a sanctuary for unwanted animals and I was looking forward to seeing the contrast. They had alpacas rather than llamas and I had a feeling they'd be the way I wanted to go. I'd loved meeting the llamas at Haltsby Farm but I was keen for my walks to appeal to all ages and couldn't help thinking that younger children might be less intimidated by alpacas, which were about half the size of their cousins.

I'd had an exceptionally busy week, working my way through Teresa's Project Camelid folder in between packing up the cottage. She was a woman after my own heart – very organised and thorough with her research – and I'd learned so much already from that and my visit to Haltsby Farm.

Grayson and I had barely spent any time together as he'd been working longer hours at Petersgill Farm helping Hamish finish off a couple of projects and I'd spent my evenings packing to catch up on the two days lost to research. Thankfully, he hadn't made any more *stupid llamas* comments, although he wasn't exactly brimming over with enthusiasm either. But that was fine because I had enough enthusiasm for both of us.

Ruth had told me she'd meet me in the farmyard and, as soon as I pulled in, a woman in khaki combat trousers and a maroon vest top smiled and waved.

'Great to meet you, Emma,' she said, shaking my hand with enthusiasm as soon as I got out of my car. 'How was your journey?'

'Really good, especially in this gorgeous weather.'

'Isn't it divine? Lizzie's with the alpacas now so let's go and meet them. We've got four boys – Bart, Magnus, Percy and Clyde – who were all rescues from the same place two years ago...'

'They're absolutely gorgeous,' I said after Lizzie introduced me to the four boys. Magnus was light grey but the other three were all white.

'Don't say that too loud in front of Percy,' Lizzie said, laughing. 'He's the alpha and he knows he's a very handsome fella, don't you, Percy?' She stroked his neck and he nuzzled his head into her neck.

'Most alpacas don't really like their faces being touched but Percy loves it,' Ruth said. 'He loves a kiss on the side of his nose. When he nuzzles into Lizzie's neck like that, that's exactly what he's after.'

Lizzie kissed him and stroked his ears.

'Is it just because he knows you or is he like that with everyone?' I asked.

'Everyone,' they said together.

I gently put my hand out and stroked his face and, moments later, he nuzzled into my neck, inviting a kiss from me too.

'I'm in love,' I said, stroking his neck.

'He charms everyone he meets,' Ruth said.

I stroked the other three on their necks and shoulders. Although I'd read loads and studied stacks of photos to understand the differences between the two animals, nothing beat seeing them in the flesh and interacting with them like this. While I loved llamas too, the smaller alpacas were the ones which had completely captured my heart. I loved how they had more hair – often quite fluffy – on their faces and how they had a more smushed-up appearance compared to longer-faced llamas. Their ears were different, with alpacas having smaller spear-shaped ears and llamas having longer banana-shaped ones. The longer I spent with them, the more I could see the personality differences emerging that I'd read about, all of which convinced me that they were the better animal for my walks.

Just like Teresa had found from her own visits, it was really helpful to see two completely different set-ups. Ruth and Lizzie invited volunteers to help rather than being open to the public like Haltsby Farm. They also ran a special programme for schools and clubs, which was something I might like to consider much further down the line.

Spending the day with the sisters was inspiring and not just because of the amazing work they did with the wide range of animals they cared for but because they were inspirational women in their own right. I'd discovered that Ruth was a year younger than me and Lizzie was a year older and they'd both tragically lost their husbands within three months of each other shortly after Lizzie turned forty. The farm had belonged to Ruth and her husband but she hadn't wanted to run it on her own so she and Lizzie had decided to live there together, sell off some land and livestock, and run an animal sanctuary instead. We shared the same outlook and had so much in common that I felt like I'd found two new friends after only a short time in their company.

'It's been a great day,' I said to Ruth and Lizzie as I prepared to leave late that afternoon. 'You've both been so helpful.'

'It's been lovely having you here,' Ruth said. 'You're welcome back any time and you can call or email with any questions.'

'If you do decide to go for it, let us know,' Lizzie added. 'The next time we hear about llamas or alpacas in need of rescue, you might want to take them yourself.'

'If I do go for it – which I'm fairly certain I will – I think alpacas will be best.'

All the way home, I couldn't stop smiling at the thought of my own herd of alpacas. It was a big decision and, as it affected Grayson as well as me, I needed to be one hundred per cent sure it was right for both of us. Or maybe ninety per cent right for Grayson as I was fairly sure he'd never be fully on board.

5

THREE WEEKS LATER

'Oh wow, Emma, it's absolutely stunning.' Back from her holidays and looking relaxed and refreshed, Rachael turned in a slow circle in the farmyard on Thursday morning, taking in my new home. 'How's it going?'

'Good, but tiring. I've spent most of the past fortnight painting.'

'The walls or yourself?' she asked, smiling at me.

'Have I got it in my hair again?' I put my hand up and felt the crusty paint between the choppy layers of my long dark hair and, as I moved my hand away, I noticed a couple more patches of paint on my arm and rolled my eyes at Rachael, who laughed.

'I've got a few gifts to congratulate you on your new home and new adventure.' She opened the back door to her car and removed a beautiful bouquet of flowers in assorted shades of pink – my favourite colour – and a large sparkly pink gift bag. 'Happy housewarming!'

'Aw, Rachael, you shouldn't have. Thank you.' I breathed in the scent of the flowers and peeked into the gift bag, spying a bottle of Prosecco and a card along with some wrapped gifts.

'You're welcome. I'm gasping for a cuppa so you can open those while we have a drink and then I need the grand tour, inside and out.'

While Rachael explored the kitchen, opening drawers and peeking in cupboards, I flicked the kettle on to boil and filled a vase with water for the flowers. When we sat down at the kitchen table with our drinks, she instructed me to open my gifts – a box of my favourite chocolates and a cerise-pink boiler suit for working on the farm which made me laugh and which I couldn't wait to wear. The final gift was a beautiful wooden house painted white with a pair of sheep beside it and the words *Our New Adventure* written on the plinth.

'This is gorgeous,' I exclaimed, twisting it round to take in the detail. 'I'll find somewhere special to display it.' I carefully wrapped it back up in tissue paper and returned it to the gift bag. 'Do you want the inside tour now?'

'Good plan. Although if it's all as lovely as your kitchen, I might never leave.'

I led her upstairs to the master bedroom at the back of the house.

'What a view!' she declared, heading straight for the dual-aspect windows looking out over the fells and fields. 'How amazing to wake up to that every day.'

She frowned as she looked round the rest of the room. 'This isn't your bedroom furniture.'

'We needed a new mattress which led to a conversation about a new bed—'

'Which led to you ordering an entire new bedroom suite,' she said. 'It's not your usual taste. I like it, but it's...'

'Quite dark,' I finished for her. 'Grayson chose it.'

I'd been torn between white and pale grey-painted furniture and, when I asked Grayson his opinion, he looked up from his iPad and declared they were all a bit bland. A few minutes later, he thrust his iPad under my nose, saying, 'I like this. Completely different to what we had before.' I couldn't argue with that. The deep midnight-blue furniture was certainly a contrast to the cream furniture at Riverside Cottage but, as this was the first time Grayson had ever shown the slightest smidgen of excitement about anything house-related, it didn't feel right to object.

I showed Rachael the two double bedrooms at the front which were separated by the bathroom.

'We'll probably put my old bedroom furniture in one of these but, for now, most of my stuff is in one of the barns. It's been easier painting and putting up blinds and curtains without furniture in the rooms.'

I showed Rachael the final bedroom at the back of the house, which contained my desk.

'I started unpacking in here,' I said, pointing to a quarter-filled bookcase, 'but I realised I have no sense of how I want to use the space now that I'm not teaching so I decided to leave it for now.'

'It's another lovely room,' Rachael said, peering out the window. 'I'm not sure I'd get much work done in here. I'd be stopping every few minutes to gaze at the fells. Why don't you turn it into a crafting room?'

'Because I don't think a one-day workshop painting plant pots with you makes me a crafter.'

'An artist's studio then,' she said, 'and don't say you can't draw anymore because a talent like yours doesn't just disappear when it isn't regularly used.'

I laughed at how well she knew me because I had been

about to protest that most of my drawings from recent years could hardly be called 'art' – illustrations of Bunsen burners, microscopes, test tubes and bacteria. Drawing had been a big passion of mine since my teens. I'd continued to sketch over the years and, in my thirties, as I'd struggled to come to terms with my marriage to Matthew ending, art had been my salvation and my therapy. I'd poured out my emotions onto huge canvases filled with dark, angry, sweeping brushstrokes or charcoal sketches of a solitary figure battered by stormy weather. It took a long time but eventually colour and variety returned to my work.

Since meeting Grayson, I'd picked up my sketchpad from time to time when something captured my imagination and I suspected I'd dig it out again soon because I was surrounded by inspiration at the farm. I was so thankful that I hadn't felt the need to lose myself in my art like I had done back then and I hoped I'd never feel that way again.

'Ooh! New sofas!' Rachael observed when we went back downstairs and into the lounge. 'I didn't think you liked leather suites.'

'It's that tan colour I'm not a fan of but I like the chocolate brown. And don't my leaving cushions look gorgeous? Although Grayson choose the navy ones behind them and he keeps swapping them to the front.'

'Yours are so much nicer,' she said. 'His are a bit...'

'Boring?' I suggested, and she nodded, laughing.

'There's still a lot to organise,' I said as we returned to our drinks in the kitchen, 'but the big job was the painting. Mum and John helped last week and I finally finished it this morning.'

John was my stepdad who Mum had met when I was eight, a year after splitting up from my dad.

'It's going to be just as gorgeous as Riverside Cottage when you're finished,' Rachael said. 'How did it feel closing the door for the last time?'

'There were tears.'

She placed her hand over mine. 'I thought there might be.'

My beautiful home had been my sanctuary after the unexpected breakdown of my marriage fifteen years ago. Matthew had given me the option to buy him out of our home but I couldn't bear the thought of staying there surrounded by memories and regrets. Riverside Cottage belonged to Rachael's grandma, who'd just gone into a care home with rapidly progressive dementia, so I rented it from her and bought it a year later after she passed away. Throwing myself into my career during the week and refurbishing the cottage during weekends and holidays gave me a much-needed focus and, along with my art, helped me heal.

'Ready for the outside tour?' I asked Rachael after we'd finished our drinks. 'Did you bring your wellies with you?'

'I couldn't find them but I've got my hiking boots.'

'Good, because it's still boggy.'

After several days of rain, summer had returned with bright blue skies and a few lazy clouds. It was good to venture out in shorts and a vest top again instead of being bundled up in a waterproof, but sensible footwear was still essential. Although *sensible* might be a stretch for describing my gorgeous sky-blue wellington boots covered in cartoon sheep.

'I love those wellies,' Rachael said as I shoved my feet into them by the door. 'They're going to look great with your new boiler suit.'

'They were the first purchase I made when I heard we'd got the farm. And if it wasn't so hot today, I'd have put that boiler suit on with them. I love it. I can't wait to show it to Grayson.'

I locked up while Rachael put on her hiking boots by the boot of her car. Joining her, I pointed out a toilet and laundry room in an extension, both accessible from the farmyard, and an external door to a large office which Grayson used.

'So tell me all about Hawaii,' I said as we set off along the track deeper into the farm.

'It was amazing. We were expecting the islands to be beautiful but they blew us away. It's probably best if I talk you through my photos when we've done the tour because I'm not going to do justice to it with words. You need to see it. Might have cost us a small fortune but you only turn fifty once so it has to be done in style. Now that the bar's been set so high from Cormac's big birthday, I need to think hard about what I want to do for mine. Can't believe it'll be us two turning fifty in two years. Where's the time gone?'

'Crazy, isn't it? By the way, I've settled the balance for our Northumberland weekend. Can't wait.' Grayson and I had needed to cancel a week in Crete as it had clashed with the start of the tenancy so, with no holiday happening this year, I was especially looking forward to my birthday weekend away with Rachael – something we'd done every year for the past two decades.

'Me neither. Favourite weekend of the year!'

'We've got about a thousand acres,' I told Rachael as we passed the last of the outbuildings and went through a gate into one of the empty fields. Some of our large flock of Herdwick sheep were grazing in the field beyond so we leaned against the next gate watching them. I pointed out where our boundaries were and told her more about the livestock and Grayson's plans for the first year on the farm.

'Have you done much to help on the farm?' Rachael asked.

'Not yet, although we did agree that I'd focus on the house

while he found his feet. I'll start working with him at the weekend. In the meantime, I've been looking into running my own business.'

As we walked back to the farmyard, I told Rachael about Project Camelid, stopping by the field I proposed to use. It was predominantly flat with a spattering of trees and several rocky areas round the eastern side.

'How would it work?' Rachael asked. 'Is it just about walking and being with the animals or would they learn things too?'

'The latter. I think I'll go with what Teresa was planning – start with a safety briefing and short talk, introduce the ones they're walking, then take a circular route round the farm giving more information to those who want it. Every time I look at this field now, I picture alpacas in it.'

'This is so perfect for you. You love alpacas, you love the outdoors and you love teaching. What better way to combine all three? What does Grayson think?'

I wrinkled my nose. 'Not convinced. He said it's ultimately my money and my call but I'd have to do it on the complete understanding that I go it alone without his help.'

'That's very supportive of him.'

I laughed at Rachael's sarcastic tone and could completely understand why she'd reacted that way as what I'd shared really didn't paint Grayson in a great light, especially when I'd been so supportive of his dream.

'It's not that bad and I do see where he's coming from,' I said. 'He's got a full-time demanding job and the last thing he needs is another animal distracting him from the livestock he already has.'

'I suppose that's fair. So what's next?'

'I want to get into a routine of working with Grayson before

I make any final decisions. I'm ninety-nine per cent certain I want to do it but it needs to work with rather than against what Grayson's doing with the farm. That is, after all, why we're here.'

'It's why Grayson's here,' she said, holding my gaze, her expression earnest. 'But it's not just about him. If I was in Grayson's shoes, I'd be so flattered that you were willing to give up your career and sell your beloved cottage to support me with my dream that I'd be bending over backwards to make sure you get something special from this huge life-changing move. I'd be hitting the road, picking out alpacas with you.'

I put my arm round her shoulders, laughing at her passionate speech. 'What would I do without you?'

'You'll never have to find out.'

We rested against the fence, looking out over the field in silence.

'It's so peaceful here,' Rachael said after a while, 'but I'm going to burn if I stay out much longer. Should we retreat inside and I can show you my holiday pics?'

We sat at the kitchen table and Rachael gave me a running commentary as she scrolled through her photos but, all too soon, we'd reached the last one and she had to leave for a dental check-up. I walked her back to the car, gave her a hug goodbye and thanked her once more for the amazing house-warming gifts.

'Get those alpacas,' she said. 'Your eyes lit up when you spoke about them. That's Grayson's dream.' She swept her arm across the fells before pointing to the front field. 'And that's your dream.'

I smiled at her, nodding. Yes, it was.

6

I heard the door open at 6 p.m., signalling Grayson and Monty's return, and smiled as the dog rushed through to greet me.

'What's that smell?' Grayson asked, joining us, curling his lip up as though he could smell something disgusting.

'Lasagne?' I said, my hackles rising. I'd made it this morning between finishing the painting and Rachael arriving and I didn't appreciate the suggestion that it didn't smell good.

'No, not that. Something else.' His eyes flicked round the room. 'Those!'

He was pointing at the vase of flowers Rachael had brought me which I'd arranged and placed on the kitchen table.

'I hate lilies,' he declared.

'Since when?'

'Since always.'

Lilies were one of my favourite flowers, especially the pink ones like in the bouquet from Rachael. I'd frequently had them in the house over the years and Grayson had never expressed a dislike for their scent.

'Can't you smell them?' he asked, scowling at me.

'I can only smell lasagne.'

He grabbed the vase and held it at arm's length as though it was radioactive and headed into the hall with it.

'Where are you taking my flowers?' I called, following him into the hall.

'Dining room.'

'That's better,' he said, slamming the dining room door moments later. 'Hopefully the stench will be contained in there. I'm going for a shower.'

And with that, he disappeared upstairs. With a heavy sigh, I returned to the kitchen and dished up Monty's tea into his bowl.

'Hi, Emma, how was your day with Rachael?' I muttered. 'How lovely of her to bring you flowers.'

Grayson was easy to get along with the vast majority of the time but, every so often, he'd arrive home in a foul mood and be really picky with me about the most ridiculous things. I'd learned to let it wash over me because it was never about me and he'd usually open up later about whatever had happened to upset him – anything from injuring himself to finding one of his flock ill or even dead. I didn't appreciate him taking his bad moods out on me and always told him so once he'd calmed down, which procured a promise not to take it out on me next time. But then the next time arrived and we went through the cycle again. It was frustrating but no relationship could be perfect all of the time and, when you loved someone, you accepted their bad habits and personality peculiarities. I had my own. I wasn't prone to bad moods or sulking but I knew I drove Grayson to distraction in other ways.

I glanced at the kitchen table and sighed. The Project Camelid folder was on there along with a pile of paperwork I'd been sorting through after Rachael left. If Grayson was in a bad mood, it would only escalate if we ate off trays tonight. He'd just put the lilies in the dining room so we could hardly eat in there. Best clear the kitchen table to try and keep the peace.

The shower must have done Grayson the world of good as, when he appeared half an hour later, he looked a lot more relaxed and he even smiled when he saw the table was clear and set for dining.

'Tea will be ten minutes,' I said.

'Okay.' He opened the fridge, removed a can of cola and took several glugs. 'I was ready for that. It was hot today.'

'I was thinking of you out in it. Rachael could feel her shoulders burning so we couldn't stay outside for long.'

'How was the holiday?'

'They had an amazing time. She showed me her photos and told me about all the places they'd visited. Hawaii is definitely on my bucket list now.'

He shook his head. 'Nope. Doesn't appeal at all.'

How could he be so dismissive when he knew nothing about the islands? I wanted to challenge him on it but that bad mood was obviously still simmering beneath the surface so it wasn't worth it.

'Rachael brought us some chocolates,' I said, indicating the box of milk and white chocolates on the worktop and realising too late that they wouldn't appeal to Grayson. He didn't have a sweet tooth and if he did eat chocolate, it was dark – the more bitter, the better. I didn't mention the Prosecco as he wouldn't be interested in drinking that and he wasn't one for sentimental nick-nacks so I wouldn't show him the ornament either. Even though it said *Our New Adventure*, it could go on the shelves in my office where I'd appreciate it.

'She got me this too,' I said, pulling the pink boiler suit out of the bag and holding it up against me.

'What is it?'

'A boiler suit. For working on the farm.'

'It's bright pink.'

'I know! Isn't it amazing?'

'It's hideous,' he said, the disgusted expression on his face matching the way he practically spat out the word.

'Grayson! Don't be so mean.'

'I'm not being mean. I'm being truthful. You're not seriously going to wear that around the farm?'

'I don't see what the problem is,' I said, keeping my tone light as I folded it up and placed it back in the bag. 'You wear boiler suits all the time.'

'Yeah, and they're navy or black.'

'Which happen to be your favourite colours. Pink's mine.'

'And I suppose you'll be wearing it with those ridiculous wellies.'

I winced. He hadn't called them *ridiculous* before although it was obvious he'd been unimpressed with them.

'Yes, I will,' I stated defiantly.

'Not around me, you won't.' And with that, he called Monty and strode out of the kitchen, slamming the door behind him.

I stared after him, mouth agape. What just happened? Had he really just told me what I could and couldn't wear?

The buzzer sounded on the oven and I turned the heat off but left the lasagne bubbling away on the shelf. I didn't feel quite so hungry anymore. I'd had such a lovely day with Rachael and, in the space of about half an hour, Grayson had ruined it. Why did he do that?

7

'Emma! You're doing it wrong!' Grayson cried, flinging his hands up in exasperation a couple of days later. Tutting, he removed the five stones I'd just added to rebuild the damaged drystone wall and dropped each one onto the ground.

'I'm doing what you told me to do,' I responded in a tone much calmer than I felt.

'If that was true, why do you think I'd be saying you're doing it wrong?' he demanded.

Because you're being childish and petty and impossible to work with! But I didn't say that. *Deep breath!*

'Will you show me again, please?'

I clenched my fists as I watched him put the same five stones back in exactly the same places.

'See! Much more stable.'

A sigh slipped out as I picked up another stone.

'Not that one!'

'You don't even know where I was going to put it,' I protested, finally snapping.

'Show me, then.'

'No.' I dropped the stone on the ground. 'Drystone walling obviously isn't my forte so I'll leave you to play with your stones your way.'

'It's not playing. It's work.'

'Then stop being so childish about it. You removed my stones and put them back in exactly the same position. What's that all about?'

'I did not.'

'You did. You've done nothing but pick at me all day. Anyone would think you don't want my help.'

My heart pounded as I glared at him, challenging him to admit to what I'd begun to expect from a horrendous day of working with him, but he averted his gaze. Bending down, he picked up the stone I'd just dropped and put it in the exact place I'd been aiming for.

'See you later,' I muttered, blinking back tears of frustration as I stormed across the field, back to the farmhouse. I'd been so excited about our first day of working together but I'd hated every single moment. The work itself was fine but doing it with Grayson was not. I liked to brainstorm ideas and chat while I worked but Grayson preferred to plough through tasks in methodical silence. He wasn't a patient teacher either and I couldn't seem to do anything the way he wanted me to, despite me following his instructions to the letter. I hadn't got to the bottom of why he'd been in a foul mood on Thursday evening so presumably his attitude today was still connected to that and all would be well once he finally opened up about whatever was bothering him. But, if what was bothering him was the two of us working together, we were in trouble.

8

'Are you all right, love?' Mum asked, pushing her lock of grey hair behind her ear as she looked at me with concern on Monday morning. 'You've barely touched your cake. That's not like you.'

I didn't feel like me today. I should be on top of the world but I felt completely deflated after a second disastrous day of working with Grayson yesterday. Mum had been planning to visit me at the farm this morning but, following four evenings and three days of tension, I was desperate for a change of scenery. I'd phoned her saying I needed to go shopping so could I meet her in Ambleside for morning coffee and cake instead.

Not wanting to worry Mum, I cut off a forkful of coffee and walnut cake and shovelled it in my mouth, but it took several gulps of latte to force it down thanks to the tightness in my throat.

'You can talk to me about anything, you know,' she said, her voice soft with understanding.

I put my fork down on my plate with a sigh. 'It's Grayson.

Rachael bought me a bright pink boiler suit to wear around the farm and he was really rude about it. I know he's never been a fan of pink so I wasn't expecting him to go into raptures, but I wasn't expecting him to tell me I can't wear it around him.'

Mum's eyes widened. 'He actually said that?'

'Those exact words. I'm nearly forty-eight, for goodness' sake, but he made me feel like a little girl being told off.'

'I'm so sorry. When was this?'

'Thursday. He stormed out in a huff, barely spoke to me on Friday and then I've had the weekend from hell trying to help him out on the farm. I couldn't seem to do anything right and all we did was argue.'

She looked bewildered. 'All because Rachael bought you a pink boiler suit?'

'And some lilies. Apparently he doesn't like the smell of them so he shoved them in the dining room.'

'I'm not defending him,' Mum said. 'But could this be him reacting to too much stress? He's never run a farm completely on his own before. What if he's realised he's taken on too much and is worried he can't cope?'

I mulled over the idea but it didn't ring true. Grayson was extremely capable and his behaviour towards me at the weekend hadn't felt like it was the reaction to stress – it had felt more personal than that.

'I honestly don't know,' I said, shrugging. 'But let's change the subject. Have you and John decided what you're going to do for your wedding anniversary?'

'It's not a special one, or rather it's not a big one. Every anniversary with John is special.'

I loved how, after thirty-nine years together, Mum's eyes still sparkled every time she mentioned John. They had the same divorce solicitor and had met when they somehow got triple-booked for the same time slot with him. When the third person kicked off about how disgraceful and unprofessional the mix-up was, Mum and John let him take the appointment, grabbed a coffee together and had been inseparable ever since. They affectionally referred to the incident as *the world's greatest admin cock-up*.

'We'll probably go out for a meal,' Mum continued. 'We're thinking we might do something special next year as we'll have been together for forty years then. That deserves a big holiday, don't you think?'

'Definitely. And, after seeing Rachael's photos, I highly recommend Hawaii.'

'It's one of the places we're considering so we'll have to invite her and Cormac round one evening. It's ages since we've seen them, although we had a lovely night out with Gail and David on Saturday...'

The next ninety minutes flew past as we chatted about Rachael's holiday, Mum and John's catch-up with Rachael's parents, Project Camelid, and the latest news from my sisters and their families. I was eleven when Mum and John married. Stacie was born a year later and they had Laura in the November of the following year shortly after I turned fourteen. We were all really close despite the big age gap and me having a different father. Biologically, they might be my half-sisters, but they were full sisters as far as I was concerned and I was a full auntie to Stacie and her husband Charlie's three children – eight-year-old Sawyer, six-year-old Ashton and three-year-old Eden – and Laura and her boyfriend Dillon's two-year-old daughter Anna.

'The kids can't wait to see the farm,' Mum said.

It had been Stacie's birthday the day after we moved in and we'd gone out for a family meal to celebrate, so it hadn't been too long since I'd seen them all but they hadn't actually visited the farm yet. It would have been too chaotic while I was painting, but me finishing it had clashed with both families going on holiday.

'It would be lovely to have everyone over for a barbeque before the kids go back to school and nursery,' I said.

'What about August bank holiday weekend?' Mum suggested.

'Sounds good. Hold it in your diary and I'll have a word with Grayson when he snaps out of his grump.'

We walked back to Mum and John's house where I'd left my car. My early childhood home had been in the pretty village of Willowdale on the north-west side of Derwent Water. When my parents separated, Mum and I stayed there while Dad moved into a rented flat above a gift shop in Keswick town centre. John moved in with us about a year after he and Mum got together and the three of us had moved to Ambleside the summer they wed, coinciding with me starting senior school. They still lived in the same house now – a beautiful detached property in an elevated position on the outskirts of the town with a large back garden sloping down to the River Rothay.

We found John sitting on the deck under the shade of a parasol, doing a crossword puzzle.

'How was cake?' he asked, putting his pen down as we approached.

'Delicious,' I said, smiling warmly at him, 'although not as good as yours.'

My stepdad had never baked a thing in his life but after he'd retired, handing over his conveyancing solicitor practice to Laura, he'd found an old recipe book of his mum's. Telling us that her sponge cakes were like a slice of heaven, he'd decided to recreate one. He hadn't been lying about how divine they were so, every time we had a family event, we begged him to make a cake or two. He'd fallen in love with baking so was happy to oblige.

'I'm thinking about inviting everyone over to the farm during the bank holiday weekend. I need to run it by Grayson but, if it works for him, it'd be amazing if you could whip up a couple of cakes for then.'

'Consider it done. Are you stopping for some lunch?'

'I need to head off – shopping to do – but I'll see you both soon.' I gave them each goodbye hugs and set off down the lane.

With shopping only being an excuse to escape from the farm, I felt at a loss as to what to do next. It was lunchtime but, as I'd barely touched my cake earlier, there was no way I could manage something more substantial. What I really fancied was a cool drink and a sit by a river or lake. I'd try nearby Elter Water – a small lake fed by the River Brathay.

The traffic through Ambleside and around the northern tip of Windermere was busy but it was distinctly quieter as I turned off onto the road alongside the river, past the lake, through the bracken-clad heathland and into the chocolate-box picturesque village of Elterwater.

I stood for a moment near the car park entrance looking around me. The picnic benches outside the pub were full and there were people milling about, taking photos of the slate houses and the backdrop of the Langdale Pikes. I'd forgotten how beautiful it was here.

After purchasing a cold bottle of fizzy orange from the café, I returned to the track running alongside the car park. It was an easy flat walk past the tree-flanked lake then beside the river. Finding a quiet spot along the riverbank, I sat down, sipped my drink and marvelled at the view.

I hadn't been here in decades but memories flooded back of

a family picnic the summer I finished my GCSEs. Stacie had just turned four, Laura was a few months off her third birthday and I could vividly recall the pair of them wearing bright red wellies, each clinging onto one of my hands, as we paddled in the shallows where the lake and river met. Once they found their footing, they let go and chased each other through the water but Laura slipped and tumbled onto her side. In seconds, I'd scooped her up and soon had her giggling again. It was such a strong mothering instinct and I knew at that moment that I wanted children of my own. But we don't always get what we wish for. That nurturing role had come in other ways through my hugely rewarding teaching career, being an auntie to Sawyer, Ashton, Eden and Anna, and a godmother to Rachael's twins but, every so often, I was hit with a pang of longing for the family of my own that I'd never had.

Pushing thoughts of children aside, I focused on the Langdale Pikes. They would be so lovely to draw. I rummaged in my bag and found a small notebook I used for shopping lists. A biro and lined paper weren't the ideal tools but it wasn't like anyone was going to see the finished product – this was just for me – and I felt a tremendous sense of satisfaction as I looked at the finished article. Not bad at all.

A golden Labrador raced past me and bounded into the water, chased by a girl of about six and a boy who looked a couple of years older. She squealed as the dog shook its coat over her and I waited patiently for them to move on and leave me to my quiet contemplation. A man and woman joined them and the woman declared it a lovely spot. To my surprise, she shook out a picnic blanket less than two feet away from me and settled down onto it, shouting to the children to keep watch on the dog and not to get too wet, while the man had a very loud conversation on his mobile phone.

With my peace destroyed, I sighed inwardly, put my drink and notepad back in my bag and returned to the car park. As soon as I started the engine, I tutted, reprimanding myself for acting too much like Grayson, who couldn't bear to be around squealing children. Although, to be fair, the family had unnecessarily invaded my personal space when there'd been ample space to spread out.

As I drove back to the farm, I considered what Mum had said about Grayson being stressed as a result of taking on too much. Could she be right? Over the weekend, I'd wondered if his bad attitude towards me had been because there wasn't enough for both of us to do but what if he'd been pushing me away because he didn't want me to see that there was too much and he was already struggling to keep on top of it all? This was a dream he'd pursued for several years and if it wasn't turning out as expected, that would be difficult to admit. I'd have to speak to him about it, but finding the right time to do that could be a challenge.

9

It was half past two when I arrived back at Bracken Ridge Farm. I pushed open the kitchen door and the first thing that hit me was the smell of lilies. The vase containing Rachael's flowers was in the middle of the kitchen table, the lilies all fully open now. Grayson found it difficult to say *I'm sorry* because he struggled to admit he was in the wrong, so apologies were often shown rather than spoken. Could the moving of the flowers mean he was sorry? He certainly should be.

Bang on six, I was emptying the dishwasher when Grayson returned. Monty ran in first as usual and I crouched down to give him a fuss.

'Thanks for moving the flowers,' I said, looking up at Grayson when he appeared.

He glanced at the table and frowned. 'Where are they?'

'I put them back in the dining room. If you don't like the smell of lilies, it isn't fair to have them in here.'

Without a word, he went into the hall and returned moments later with the vase.

'I don't dislike the smell of lilies,' he said, placing them gently on the table. 'It's just that they were my mum's favourite flowers. The day they told me they'd sold the farm, Dad bought her a large bunch. I'd forgotten about that and, when I smelled these ones last week, it took me right back. I shouldn't have taken it out on you and I should have been honest about what the smell had triggered.'

'Aw, Grayson, I'm so sorry. I thought securing the tenancy here had helped you move on from what they did.'

'It has and I'd choose this place over Low Fell any day. I think it just hit me that it was all over. I've now got what I was always working towards – my own farm – even if that's as a tenant rather than an owner. It's the perfect farm for me, but what price did it come at? I don't have my parents in my life because they didn't care enough to involve me in the biggest decision of our lives. You know I'm rubbish at talking about feelings, but I'm sad that we're not in touch and that they have no idea I've secured this. My dad would've loved this place.'

I slipped my arms round his waist and hugged him. 'It's not too late to reach out to them if that's what you want.'

'To be honest, I'm not sure it is. This is a fresh start and I don't want to contaminate it with the past.'

He kissed the top of my head and we stood there for several minutes holding on to each other.

'I'd better hit the shower,' he said eventually, letting me go. 'Another hot one today so I must stink.'

I winked at him. 'I wasn't going to say anything.'

Stepping back, I willed him to also acknowledge his appalling attitude to my work across the weekend which, for me, had been far worse than his strop about the flowers, but he headed upstairs without a word.

Sighing, I dished up Monty's tea. 'Fancy him being triggered by the smell of lilies. I'll have to remember that one in future.'

As I finished preparing our meal, I reflected on what Grayson had said about his parents. Was it really too late for him to make peace with them? They were both in their early seventies and would hopefully be around for many years to come, but what if something did happen to one or both of them? Would Grayson be able to forgive himself for not reaching out? I wasn't going to instigate that conversation tonight and trigger another bad mood, but it was worth raising at some point. My list of things to talk to him about was building.

I twiddled my engagement ring round my finger. Grayson had proposed to me two years ago. Recognising that we'd never properly celebrated him moving into Riverside Cottage because of the circumstances, we'd gone to The Hidden Fell to celebrate one year of living together. It had been a brilliant night but we'd had far too much to drink. On the way home, he'd repeatedly thanked me for being so supportive through all the crap with his parents.

'I don't know what I'd have done without you,' he'd slurred as we approached the cottage. 'You're the best thing that's ever happened to me. I love you so much.'

'I love you too.'

'I lost the farm and I lost my parents but I don't ever want to lose you.'

'You're not going to lose me,' I assured him. 'I'm not going anywhere.'

He stopped and studied my face for a moment. 'I know how to make sure I don't.' Next minute, he'd dropped down onto one knee but the combination of the sudden movement and too much alcohol made him unsteady and he ended up on both knees but it didn't deter him from asking me to be his wife.

The following day, I'd expected him to have either forgotten he'd popped the question or to have passed it off as a joke because it had been the last thing I'd expected from him, but he drove me into Carlisle to go ring shopping. Over a celebratory lunch, we agreed not to set a wedding date until he'd got his farming career back on track. But now that his career was sorted, was it time to think about wedding plans? Unless Grayson's career hadn't been the only reason he'd wanted to delay our wedding. What if he'd been holding back because of the difficult decision as to whether or not to invite his parents and their reaction to whatever choice we made? The more I thought about that now, the more it made sense.

Even though Grayson hated being the centre of attention, I knew he wanted a traditional wedding ceremony, although perhaps not as big as the one he'd been planning with his ex-fiancée Chrissie, who'd broken off their engagement a year before Grayson and I met. Everything had been good between Grayson and his parents when he'd been with Chrissie so the 'traditional' ceremony would have been straightforward but ours wouldn't be if his parents weren't there.

I loved Grayson and wanted us to get married but, if the delay was connected to his parents and he was feeling melancholy about their fractured relationship at the moment, it wasn't the time to mention weddings. There was no rush. Our wedding was not a priority but I couldn't help thinking that getting Grayson to reach out to his parents should be, although tact and timing would be everything.

10

'That's not what I showed you!' Grayson flapped his arms a few days later, shooing me out of the way, and took hold of the sheep. 'You need to hold him like this.'

My jaw clenched as he put his arms round the Herdwick in exactly the same hold I'd just relinquished.

'How's that different from what I was doing?' I demanded, frustration bubbling over after a long morning of sighs, tuts and being made to feel useless.

'It just is.'

'I don't see how.'

'Emma! Just hold the damn sheep so I can cut it loose.'

I've never wanted to prolong an argument more than I did now, but it was heartbreaking seeing the sheep so tangled and I didn't want to delay releasing it any longer than we already had.

I took over from Grayson. His mutter of, 'That's better,' was barely audible and I bit back the urge to snap, *It's not better, it's the same as before!*

He snipped the long piece of plastic sheeting wrapped around the sheep's legs and gave it a once-over to check there were no injuries before sending it on its way. But the joy at seeing the Herdie bounding unimpeded across the fell was short-lived.

'Why can't you just do as you're asked?' Grayson sounded as frustrated as I felt as he stuffed the plastic into a bin bag attached to his quad bike. 'That took four times as long as it needed to.'

It was obviously a rhetorical question begging for an apology but there was no way I was going to say sorry when I'd done nothing wrong.

'Monty! Up!'

At Grayson's call, Monty obediently jumped onto the back of the quad bike. It was time to go back down to the farmhouse for lunch but I was so annoyed with Grayson that I didn't want to be near him right now. I certainly couldn't bear the thought of sitting so close to him on the back of the quad bike, arms wrapped round his waist.

'In your own time,' he said, his voice dripping with sarcasm.

'I'd rather walk.'

He shrugged. 'Suit yourself.'

'And I won't be helping this afternoon.'

He didn't even attempt to hide his smile at that news.

Hands on hips, I watched the bike heading down the fell and sighed heavily. I really wasn't in the mood for an hour's walk but it was the lesser of two evils.

After returning the lilies to the kitchen on Monday and opening up about what had triggered his strange reaction, the tension had lifted and everything had been back to normal, although I could see now that us doing our own thing over the past two days had massively contributed to that. Grayson and Ted, our neighbouring farmer, had been sheep-dipping together – a process of dipping the flock in a special solution to kill parasites. They'd done Ted's flock last week and ours this week. As Ted had a son and daughter already helping with the process, I'd have been surplus to requirements. I'd therefore spent Tuesday on more alpaca research and had visited Butterbea Croft again yesterday, spending a lovely day with Bart, Magnus, Percy and Clyde as well as deepening my friendship with Ruth and Lizzie.

Last night, Grayson had seemed relaxed and happy so I'd sounded him out about my family joining us for a barbeque at some point over the approaching bank holiday weekend. I loved a big family get-together and my highlight of the year was when we all gathered at Mum and John's on Easter Sunday. I knew Grayson was never keen on it. He never came out and directly said that but I could read him like a book most of the time and his discomfort was obvious. It wasn't that he didn't like my family. The struggle was having everyone in the same place at the same time and I could completely understand it as we could be loud and somewhat overwhelming, especially for someone who spent most of their days in peaceful solitude and thrived on it. He had no idea how to interact with children either. He'd never wanted kids – something he'd made clear right from the start of our relationship – and he was an only child so there were no nephews or nieces on his side of the family. He must have been desperate to make amends after the lilies incident as his response to the suggestion was really positive and he even offered to give the two older ones, Sawyer and Ashton, a ride on his quad bike. I really thought we were back on track.

Until this morning happened.

Before moving to the farm, I'd thought Grayson and I made a pretty good team so it would be fun to work together, but this was the furthest thing from *fun* I'd ever experienced.

By the time I made it down to the farmhouse, Grayson had already eaten and driven off again, as anticipated. Just as well as I had nothing to say to him right now.

* * *

Early that evening, I was measuring the barn which I wanted reconfiguring for the alpacas when I heard Grayson returning on the quad bike for tea. The tension I'd spent all afternoon trying to release immediately returned and my stomach churned.

My unexpected lunchtime walk had given me a lot of thinking time and, even though I'd have loved to learn all about farming and help out as much as possible, it was obvious that Grayson didn't want my help and I didn't want to give it if it made me feel this lousy. Jack and Teresa had said that running Bracken Ridge Farm was a one-person job most of the time and I should have listened to that instead of getting carried away with thoughts of a dramatic career change from teacher to farmer.

I loved Grayson the fiancé but I couldn't stand Grayson the boss. This didn't need to be the end of me working on the farm but it had to be the end of me working with him. My focus would be the alpacas. The additional research this week had got me even more fired up about it and I was one hundred per cent sure I wanted to go for it, leaving Grayson to run the rest of the farm how he wanted without me. My plan was to tell him that over tea. I couldn't imagine he'd try to talk me out of it. Our working relationship was not a match made in heaven.

* * *

'How was your afternoon?' I asked, placing our plates of food on the kitchen table half an hour later.

'Really good,' he said.

Without you, I silently added.

'I think it's best if we don't work together again.' I'd aimed for light and breezy but it came out strained, and I didn't miss the brief tug of a smile at the corners of his mouth.

'Not what you expected?' he asked, gently.

I wasn't going to dignify that with a response. 'I'd prefer to devote my time to my alpaca business. I've done enough research now to convince me I want to go for it.'

'Up to you, as long as you know I won't be helping.'

'You've made that *very* clear. The alpacas will be my thing, the Herdies and Belties will be yours and never the twain shall meet.'

'Wouldn't it be simpler to go back to teaching?'

'Probably, but I'm not after a simpler life – I'm ready to do something new and exciting and the alpacas fit the bill perfectly.'

This afternoon, I had briefly entertained the idea of returning to teaching and had even logged on to a job site but my heart hadn't been in it. If the alpaca walking business didn't take off and bring in some income, I might have no choice but, if I did teach again, I wanted to do so knowing I'd given the alternatives my best shot. I'd already done that for my little fantasy world where Grayson would train me up, and running the farm as a duo would bring us even closer together, but it hadn't turned out as hoped. I had everything crossed that the alpacas wouldn't be another misguided fantasy.

11

'Are you still okay to take Sawyer and Ashton out on the quad bike today?' I asked Grayson when he returned from his early rounds on August bank holiday Monday.

I'd anticipated a retraction of the offer so I hadn't actually told Stacie about it – no point courting disappointment. However, Grayson surprised me by nodding.

'They won't muck about, will they?' he asked as he put a capsule into the coffee machine.

'They'll be good as gold, especially if they're told it'll be their first and last ride if they do anything silly. I can run alongside you if you want.'

'It's fine. I don't mind taking them out on my own. Will the girls be upset about not having a go?'

'Anna's too young, but Eden might want a try. Maybe you could sit her in front of you and have a ride round the yard?'

'I'll think about it.'

I'd told everyone to arrive for about 11 a.m., which gave me plenty of time to chop the salad and prepare the kebabs. Mum brought a huge bowl of her speciality – homemade potato salad

– which was to die for and I could happily eat a whole plate of it to myself. John brought a large Victoria sponge and a white and dark chocolate marble cake which looked incredible.

The weather couldn't have been more perfect, meaning we could spend the day outside. There was the ideal entertaining space outside one of the outbuildings in the farmyard – a built-in barbeque with a double grill and a couple of wooden picnic benches and parasols which Jack and Teresa had left behind, saying they wouldn't have space for them at their new home. I'd set up my table and chairs from Riverside Cottage there, creating just enough seating for the full family and plenty of shade from the sun for those who wanted it.

While Grayson took Sawyer out on the quad bike, John asked if I'd mind him taking a walk round the farm. The adults were all keen to join him but Ashton was eagerly awaiting his turn on the quad bike, Eden was preoccupied wheeling a couple of soft toy cows round the farmyard in a toy wheelbarrow and Anna was asleep in her buggy in the shade, so I offered to stay back with the kids.

Anna, snuggled under a lemon blanket Mum had knitted for her when she was born, looked so adorable with one fist against her mouth, her fingers curled round a Piglet comforter. Her other hand was poking out from beneath the blanket and I lightly placed my index finger across her palm, my heart melting as she wrapped her fingers around it.

'You're so beautiful,' I whispered. 'I'd have loved a baby like you.'

Sniffing, I blinked back the tears blurring my vision and turned my gaze to where Ashton had joined his sister and the pair of them were giggling as she chased him round the farmyard with one of her soft cows, mooing loudly. What would it have been like having my own children running round the farm? It would be such an idyllic childhood learning all about animals and having so much room to play.

Some things weren't meant to be and even if I'd had children, they'd be grown up now. Although they might have had children of their own so...

Feeling like I was heading down the dark path of regrets, I gently released my finger from Anna's grip and sipped on my drink.

Eden raced over to the table, breathless from chasing her brother, grabbed her juice bottle and took several greedy gulps. She plonked it down and scrambled onto my knee for a cuddle, still clinging onto one of the cows. She felt sticky from her exertions but I didn't mind.

'Are you a farmer now?' she asked.

'No. Uncle Grayson's the farmer. I just live on a farm. I thought you'd have gone for a walk to see the cows.'

She twisted round to look at me, eyes wide. 'You have cows?'

'Yes and, even better than that, they're your favourite type.'

'The stripy ones?'

'That's right. They're called Belted Galloways.'

I'd learned all about Belties in the early days of seeing Grayson as they'd had a herd at Low Fell Farm. Petersgill Farm hadn't had any so he was delighted to be working with them again here. With their origins in the region of Galloway in south-west Scotland, the 'belted' part of the name came from the distinctive wide white belt around the cow's middle, with the rest of the body being black, red or a light brown colour called dun. They were a hardy breed with a double hair coat, making them ideal for fell life, and they were mainly bred for their high-quality beef.

'I *love* stripy cows!' Eden exclaimed. 'Can I see them?'

'Not right this minute but how about I take you for a walk after we've eaten? Would you like that?'

'Yes, please, Auntie Emma.'

She tucked herself in for a tighter cuddle and I kissed the top of her blonde hair. Beside us, Anna murmured as she changed position, but she didn't wake up. Once more, my thoughts drifted to what it might have been like to be a mum. I'd been delighted for my sisters having their children but I'd taken myself off somewhere quiet after each pregnancy announcement and after each birth, sobbing for my missed opportunities. I'd shed many more regretful tears over the years because, with Mum and Stacie both being midwives – Mum now retired – babies were a frequent topic of conversation in our family. My family were caring and sensitive and they'd never have discussed babies so often in my company if they'd known how I really felt about being a mother.

'Your necklace is pretty,' Eden said, tugging gently on the silver pendant necklace I'd treated myself to. 'What is it?'

'It's an alpaca. I'm going to get some alpacas and take people on walks around the farm with them.'

'Are they big?'

'Bigger than Herdies but not as big as Belties.'

'Can I cuddle them?'

'Depends if they like being cuddled or not but you'll definitely be able to stroke them.'

She released a small squeal of delight and kissed me. 'I love you, Auntie Emma.'

'I love you too, sweetheart.'

I kissed her head once more and cuddled her tightly. Being an auntie and godmother was the next best thing and I couldn't be sad about that. Wistful, perhaps, but not sad. Or at least, I'd try not to be, just like I'd been doing for a very long time.

* * *

A couple of hours later, after the leftovers and plates from the main course had been cleared away and slices of John's cakes distributed, Mum stood up and tapped her knife against the side of her wine glass to get everyone's attention.

'I just wanted to thank you, Emma and Grayson, for inviting us all to spend the day in this beautiful setting. I know it hasn't been easy securing a tenancy but we're so proud that you've got your own farm now.' She raised her glass in the air. 'Congratulations, Emma and Grayson.'

The rest of my family followed the toast as Grayson and I smiled at each other.

'Emma and Grayson aren't the only ones with exciting plans for the future,' Mum continued. 'Laura?'

My youngest sister stood up and I glanced at Stacie. Could Laura be expecting a second baby? The curious expression on Stacie's face suggested that, whatever Laura's news was, she was as much in the dark as me.

'As you all know, we finally completed the renovations on Mill House in time for the Easter holidays,' Laura said. 'It's been nice having a few months off but now Dillon and I are getting all twitchy. We've been looking around for another project...'

A collective gasp came from the adults. They couldn't possibly want to move. Their home – a former water mill – had been a wreck when they'd bought it seven years ago and they'd painstakingly brought it back to life. They both already had demanding jobs, Dillon as a property developer and Laura running John's former solicitor practice, so Mill House had been a real labour of love with most of the work done on evenings and weekends.

'You should see your faces,' Laura said, laughing. 'Don't panic! Mill House was always intended as our forever home and we're staying put. Our new project isn't a property. It's our wedding.'

I'm not sure whether it was Stacie or me who squealed the loudest. We rushed at Laura and Dillon with hugs and congratulations. A couple of bottles of bubbly appeared from somewhere and we all toasted the newly engaged couple and admired the ring which she'd been keeping in her bag so nobody would spot it.

'We need the proposal story,' Stacie said.

Laura and Dillon exchanged loving smiles.

'There isn't one,' Dillon said. 'Anna was asleep one evening, we cracked open a bottle of wine and were discussing how strange it was having nothing to plan. I joked that we should get married and we both looked at each other and said, *Actually, why not?*'

'So romantic,' Stacie joked, clapping her hand over her heart and pretending to swoon.

'That might not have been,' Laura said, 'but I still got my romantic moment. After we picked up the ring, Dillon took me to Waterhead and properly proposed to me on the jetty at sunset.'

We all knew the significance of Waterhead – the area by the northern tip of Windermere where the cruise boats docked, just south of Ambleside. Laura and Dillon had met there for their first date, it was the place where he'd first told her he loved her, and it was where she'd revealed to him that she was pregnant with Anna.

'I'm so pleased for you both,' I said, feeling all choked up. 'When's the big day?'

'Next December,' Laura said. 'We're having a Christmas wedding.'

I smiled at her, already picturing her and Dillon in their wedding finery posing in front of a Christmas tree. 'I've never been to a Christmas wedding. It'll be lovely.'

'Ooh, and a big question for you two,' Laura said, looking from Stacie to me. 'Will you both be my bridesmaids?'

'Yes!' Stacie cried, punching the air.

'I'd love to,' I said. 'Thank you.'

Laura and I had been bridesmaids for Stacie when she married Charlie nearly a decade ago. I'd never have assumed Laura wanted the same, but it was touching that she did. I certainly wanted them both as my bridesmaids when Grayson and I finally tied the knot.

As we tucked into our cake, Laura and Dillon told us which venue they'd booked and who else would be in the wedding party. Even though the wedding was over a year away, Laura admitted that she was dying to go dress shopping and asked if Stacie and I were free on Saturday, which we both were.

I was about to put the final forkful of Victoria sponge into my mouth when Charlie said, 'So, Emma and Gray, when's the big day for you two?'

My stomach plummeted to the ground. For a start, Grayson detested his name being shortened. Secondly, he hated being the centre of attention so a question like that in front of the whole family wasn't going to go down well. And, thirdly, I still hadn't found the right moment to ask if the date-setting delay was because of his parents so a public discussion was far from ideal.

'No plans, Charlie,' I said, trying to sound jovial. 'The priority was always to secure one of Beatrix Potter's farms before we even considered setting a date.'

I'd hoped that would be sufficient to refocus the conversation back onto Laura and Dillon but, much as I loved my brother-in-law, Charlie had never been great at taking a hint.

'Big tick in that box,' he said, indicating the farm with a sweep of his hand. 'So will Laura and Dillon beat you down the aisle?'

I glanced at Grayson, expecting him to say it was highly likely because we needed time to settle in and establish a routine, but he put his fork down with a clatter, mumbled something indecipherable, and left the table.

'Charlie!' Stacie hissed, giving her husband a sharp jab with her elbow.

'What did I do?' He looked genuinely perplexed.

'Don't worry about it,' I said, giving him a half-smile, not wanting him to feel uncomfortable.

The sound of the quad bike starting up didn't surprise me. Grayson obviously needed some space away from prying questions. While I did understand that, I wished he could have just made a joke about it or avoided the question and excused himself saying he needed to work. Storming off like that was a little childish, not to mention embarrassing.

Charlie grimaced. 'Have I put my foot in it? Is the engagement off?'

'Good grief!' Stacie put her hand over Charlie's mouth. 'Know when to stop talking!'

I couldn't help laughing at that. 'We're still very much engaged and everything's fine but you know Grayson doesn't like being the centre of attention so being put on the spot like that'll have made him squirm.'

'And you know he hates being called Gray,' Stacie added, staring pointedly at Charlie as she removed her hand.

'Sorry, Emma,' Charlie said.

'It's okay, but it's too early into our new life on the farm to switch our focus to wedding plans. When we do, you'll be the first to know. Right, let's get these plates cleared and the kettle on.'

Mum, Laura and Dillon helped me carry the plates and left-over cake into the kitchen. Mum put the kettle on and I loaded the dishwasher while my sister and her new fiancé went back outside to gather drinks orders.

'Is everything really all right between you and Grayson?' Mum asked after I'd set the dishwasher away, her expression full of concern.

'He's a nightmare to work with,' I admitted, 'so that's the end of that. He's going to be the only farmer here and I'm going to get myself some alpacas.'

'You're definitely going for it?' she asked, eyes lighting up. 'I'm so pleased for you.' She drew me into a hug. 'But if you ever want to talk about anything else, you know I'm here for you. No matter how petty it might seem.'

'Thanks, Mum, but there really is nothing to worry about.'

Or at least I hoped there wasn't. Since agreeing not to work together, the past couple of days had been really good but now Grayson had stormed off in front of my family. I couldn't keep up with his mood swings at the moment. It was like living with a hormonal teenager.

Over drinks, I told my family about my proposed new business venture, which they all loved the sound of. Dillon joined me in the barn I was hoping to use as a shelter. He confirmed that a reconfiguration for access from the field shouldn't be too difficult and he'd be happy to squeeze in the work if I did proceed with my plans.

There was still no sign of Grayson when we returned to the group and I didn't want to end the family get-together prematurely by searching for him as they'd definitely take that as a cue to leave as well as a suggestion that there was something to worry about. Besides, I'd promised I'd take Eden to see the Belted Galloways and I wasn't going to renege on that.

It ended up being a girls' trip out. Eden took Anna's hand and encouraged her cousin to walk as much as she could, with Mum, Stacie, Laura and I taking it in turns to carry her over some of the rougher terrain. I couldn't see any sign of Grayson or Monty.

When we returned from seeing the Belties, it was time for everyone to head home. They gathered their belongings together and, after hugs all round, made a mass exodus. They all asked me to say goodbye to Grayson for them and I didn't know how to respond except to smile and nod. Storming out on me was bad enough but doing it in front of my family – and staying away – was rude and humiliating.

12

It was dark, my family had long gone and I was half-heartedly watching the television when Grayson and Monty finally appeared.

'The quad bike had a flat,' Grayson said, as though that was a sufficient explanation for storming off, staying away, and not making contact.

'Radio flat too?' I challenged as I scratched behind Monty's ears. Mobile signal could be patchy on the fells but the Gaskills had left us their radio system which Grayson always had with him for safety.

Grayson didn't respond but he did at least have the decency to look guilty.

'I'm going for a shower. Can you feed Monty?'

He headed upstairs and I led the dog into the kitchen with a frustrated sigh.

* * *

'I should have radioed you about the flat tyre,' Grayson said, joining me in the lounge after his shower.

'And?'

'And I've repaired it now.'

'And?'

He looked at me, face blank, and shrugged.

'And I'm sorry for storming off in front of your family,' I suggested, eyebrows raised.

'I didn't!' His tone was incredulous. 'I had work to do.'

'You didn't say that. You just walked off mumbling.'

But he'd grabbed the remote control and had switched his attention to scrolling through the TV listings. Feeling too weary to drag it into an argument, I headed for the door.

'I'm going to read in bed.' I paused in the doorway to give him a final chance for an apology, but he simply nodded and lifted his hand in a half-wave and I wasn't convinced he'd even heard what I said.

'Good conversation,' I muttered under my breath as I ascended the stairs, unable to decide whether Grayson genuinely thought he'd done nothing wrong or whether he didn't care.

The fresh air had clearly wiped me out as I didn't wake up when Grayson came to bed or when he rose the following morning. Our paths didn't cross until he came home for tea at six. While we ate, it was as though a switch on his mood setting had been flicked to *extremely good*. He barely paused for breath as he talked animatedly about something he and Ted had been discussing about the Belted Galloways. I loved this side of him – when he got all passionate about the animals – and I was happy to see him so excited, but I didn't like the way Monday had been swept under the carpet and, much as I didn't want to bring his mood down, it needed discussing. I'd suggest we have a talk over a post-meal cuppa.

'I'll see you tomorrow,' he said, pushing his chair back once he'd cleared his plate.

'Why? Where are you going?'

'Ted invited me to the pub to continue our discussion about the Belties. I'll leave Monty with you.'

And then he was gone and I looked at the dog and shrugged. 'Looks like it's just you and me tonight. Nice of him to warn us.'

While I was happy enough in my own company, I'd spent the entire day on my own in the farmhouse without speaking to a soul and the isolation suddenly hit me. Feeling like the kitchen walls were closing in on me, I had to get out.

'Come on, Monty, let's go into the yard.'

I grabbed his ball and launcher stick and took him into my alpaca field. I tossed the ball several times, gulping in the fresh air between throws, but I was still craving a two-sided conversation so I FaceTimed Rachael.

'Do you think my mum could be right about him finding it too stressful?' I asked when I'd brought her up to speed with Grayson's mood swings. 'Or have I made it more stressful than it needed to be by trying to create a job where there isn't one?'

'You're doing nothing wrong,' she said, shaking her head vigorously. 'Grayson's definitely the one at fault here.'

'You're not just saying that because you're my best friend?'

'No. You've done everything for that man at the pace he's wanted it and what's he done for you in return? You never pressured him about moving in together but opened up your home to him when things fell apart with his parents. You supported him through that and you were by his side every step of the way while he went after the Potter farms, picking up the pieces after the first two fails and encouraging him when he nearly pulled out of the third attempt. You were prepared to change your home and job to fit around whichever farm he secured and, now that he's decided he doesn't want you working on the farm with him, you've found a new focus. I personally don't think running the farm is stressful for him and neither is working with you. You're the easiest person in the world to work alongside. The only stress in his life is what he's causing.'

I loved the resounding passion in her voice as she listed off each point and it did ring true that Grayson was at the root of all the angst lately.

'You've even furnished the farmhouse according to his taste,' she added. 'Which I know for a fact isn't the same as yours.'

'He's hidden my cushions behind the plain ones again. It's become like a game. He hides them, I liberate them.'

Rachael rolled her eyes. 'What a child.'

I shrugged. 'Maybe he thinks the same about me. The plain cushions were there first.'

'Perhaps, but that lounge is so masculine. Everything in there is his choice so the least he could do is let you have a few pretty cushions to brighten up the place.'

Monty had lost interest in his ball and was lying down on the cool grass panting so I clambered onto the gate.

'Can I ask you a question? Do you actually like Grayson?'

A pause and a wince. 'Not when he's treating you like this.'

'What about the rest of the time?'

Rachael ran her hand through her hair and shrugged. 'Do you want me to be honest, even if you don't like the answer?'

'Yes, please.'

'Are you sure because, if I say certain things, I can never un-say them?'

My stomach did a loop-the-loop. Rachael would never have said that if there wasn't something bad coming.

'I'd rather hear the truth,' I admitted, bracing myself for whatever she had to say and wondering if I'd agree with her.

'Okay. Do I like Grayson? If we're talking as a friend for me...' She scrunched her nose up and waggled her hand from side to side, palm facing down to show her indecision. 'I don't mind an evening in his company but I think I'd struggle with any longer. I don't find him particularly easy to talk to but that's because about the only thing we've got in common is you. But this isn't about me. Do I like him as a partner for you?'

My stomach lurched once more as I awaited her verdict.

'I did at first,' she said. 'Matthew hurt you so badly and I feared you were never going to let love in again and then you met Grayson and it was like somebody had switched the light back on, although it was one of those dimmer switches and it was low at first but, the more time you spent with him, the brighter it got. I loved that he didn't try to rush you into anything or try to change you in any way. You both kept going with your own interests and you found a way to be together in the meantime – two separate lives blending together effectively.'

'But?' I prompted when she fell silent.

'You really want me to say it? Okay. My *but* is that I think he's been really selfish since your move. He's pushed you away when you've tried to help him and he hasn't been particularly supportive about the alpacas. It's as though all he wants you to do is look after the house for him. And...'

She paused, grimacing, and I steeled myself for more bad news.

'...it's as though that dimmer switch has been turned down again.'

I exhaled slowly, processing everything she'd just said.

'I'm sorry, Em. Are you mad with me?'

'Gosh, no. I appreciate you being honest.'

She gave me a weak smile. 'Thing is, what I think isn't important. He's not my fiancé. What's important is how you feel. Do you still love Grayson?'

'Yes.'

'Do you still want to marry him?'

'Of course!'

'Then you'll work this out. The pair of you are dealing with a lot right now so there are bound to be disagreements. You've moved house, taken on a new business, left your job and are planning to add a second business into the mix. One of those things in isolation would be stressful and you've got four. The dust will settle soon.'

'I hope so. Thanks again for the honesty. It's exactly what I needed.'

'You know where I am if you want to talk some more.'

We said our goodbyes and ended the call. I sat on the gate for a few more minutes but my hands and cheeks were bitterly cold so I clambered down, retrieved the ball, and returned to the house with Monty. Rachael had made a good point about how much change we were individually and collectively going through right now and that could be why Grayson's mood was so up and down. We were strong and we'd be fine. Once I found a herd of alpacas and showed him I could look after them on my own, he'd come round and support me in my new venture. I was certain of it.

13

My phone rang shortly after 9.30 a.m. a couple of days later and I smiled as I saw Ruth's name on the screen.

'We might have some alpacas for you,' she said, sounding a little breathless. 'Would you like to join us on a rescue today?'

'Oh, my gosh! Yes! Where?'

'To a smallholding in Northumberland. There's seven alpacas and we thought you might like to make them your herd.'

My heart raced. 'I'd love to but I'm not ready yet. The barn needs work and I haven't got any food in or checked whether the local vet can—'

'Don't worry about any of that,' she said, cutting across me. 'We can keep them at Butterbea Croft until you're ready. The main thing is we're getting them out of harm's way. So, do you want to join us? If you're coming, I'll wait for you and Lizzie will go on ahead to start the ball rolling but, if you're not coming, I'll set off now too.'

'I'm coming. Give me five minutes to get organised.'

'Excellent. See you shortly.'

As soon as I'd disconnected, I rang Grayson but there was no answer. It wasn't unusual as he tended to keep his phone on silent when he was working. I tried the radio but he didn't answer that either so I sent him a text.

TO GRAYSON

> Unexpected change of plans. I'm off to Northumberland to help Ruth and Lizzie rescue some alpacas. Not sure when I'll be back but I'll text you when I know more x

* * *

Ruth was leaning against her 4x4, talking into her phone when I arrived at Butterbea Croft an hour and a quarter later. She waved as I parked the car.

'I was checking in with Lizzie,' she said as I approached her. 'She'll be there in fifteen minutes. Are you all set?'

'Yes, good to go.'

'Thanks for inviting me,' I said as we set off down the track. 'I'm excited, but I'm worried too. You mentioned getting them out of harm's way? Are they in danger?'

'Possibly. The call was from a woman called Debbie. Her parents have recently split up and it's very hostile. The alpacas belong to the dad but they're kept on the mum's land. The mum refuses to look after them and won't let the dad near them unless it's to take them away but he has nowhere to put them. The mum started making comments about *accidentally* leaving the gate open and, as they're not far from a main road, Debbie's been scared of what could happen to the alpacas or the general public if they got out. She visited first thing this morning and found the mum standing by the alpaca enclosure with the gate wide open. She was wearing a nightie, had nothing on her feet, and she was carrying a penknife.'

'Oh, my God! Did she intend to...' I couldn't bring myself to finish the sentence.

Ruth shrugged. 'I dread to think. Debbie called an ambulance and they've admitted the mum to hospital. The dad's there now checking on the herd but, as he hasn't got any land and couldn't afford to rent any even if he found some, Debbie wants us to take them.'

'It's lucky they didn't escape when the gate was open.'

'Very lucky. Either they were at the far end of the field and didn't notice or it had only just happened when Debbie turned up.'

As we travelled across to Northumberland, Ruth told me more about the different circumstances under which they'd taken in animals. There were a couple of cases of neglect but most were changes in circumstance such as owners dying, going into care facilities, falling ill, being injured, or struggling financially.

'We've had owners in tears when we've collected animals from them,' she told me. 'It's distressing to see them so upset and it's additional stress on the animals too. Some want to stay in touch but we have a clause in the handover agreement stating that handing them over means fully letting go and trusting that we'll care for and make all the right choices for their well-being. It might seem harsh but it's best for all parties that way. We learned that the hard way after a couple of former owners couldn't let go and went overboard with their demands for constant updates.'

How fortunate that there were wonderful people like Ruth and Lizzie who devoted their lives to taking care of animals in need and ensuring they lived out their days in a safe and happy environment.

We were about forty minutes into the ninety-minute journey when Lizzie rang.

'The alpacas are ours,' she said. 'Debbie's dad, Mitch, has signed a release form.'

'That's a relief,' Ruth said. 'What sort of state are they in?'

'Not too bad, considering. Debbie has clearly done her best to keep them fed and watered but the poor things haven't been sheared.'

I winced at that. They should have been sheared earlier in the summer. They'd have been really uncomfortable wearing their thick fleeces during the hotter weather.

'They haven't had their toenails trimmed either,' Lizzie continued, 'and I think there's one with a foot infection. Other than that, I think we have a healthy herd, although we'll obviously get the vet to give them a thorough check.'

'Is Mitch still there?' Ruth asked.

'No. He left about ten minutes ago with his tail between his legs. Can you believe this? He wanted us to buy them for a grand each.'

Ruth gasped. 'A grand each? Didn't Debbie say he got them for free as rescues himself?'

'Yes, and she reminded him of that in no uncertain terms. They had a right barney about it, Ruth. The language! The upshot is we've rescued them without charge and Debbie has said we can have the halters and leads for free too. The halters are really posh ones with their names embroidered on them and they're in great condition.'

'That's a bonus,' Ruth said, glancing at me after the call ended. 'You can pick up basic ones for a tenner but if Lizzie says they're posh ones with their names on, they could have been anything from thirty to fifty quid each so that's saved you a nice outlay. If you want the alpacas, that is.'

The way she said that last statement made me smile as it was a definite *I know there's no way you're going to say no* tone.

'If I didn't take them – and we both know that's a fairly unlikely *if* – you do have space to keep them?'

'We do, so don't worry about that. You have to make a decision that's right for you because, if it's not right for you, it's not right for the alpacas and they've already had a rough time of it.'

As soon as I saw the seven alpacas huddled together in their enclosure, any small doubts I might have had about doing this vanished. Those beautiful animals would absolutely be making Bracken Ridge Farm their home and I couldn't wait to take over their care.

I wished I could ask Ruth and Lizzie to take them straight there, but I had to be practical and ensure that they only moved to the farm when I was ready. Transporting them twice wasn't ideal as moving animals could be stressful for them, but it would be better transporting them twice than moving them straight to an environment that wasn't right for them, especially after they'd already endured several months without proper care and attention.

Lizzie was on her own as Debbie had accompanied her mum – who the paramedics believed had suffered a stroke – to hospital.

'One of our more dramatic rescues,' Lizzie told me. 'Although thankfully not the most traumatic. As I said on the phone, the main visual concern is the lack of grooming and toenail trimming. I haven't looked too closely as I want to keep them as calm as possible before we travel. Are you ready to meet them?'

I couldn't be more ready. I already knew from my research that alpacas came in five main colours – white, fawn, grey, brown and black – although there were further common shade variations. The herd comprised of two white alpacas called Bianca and Florence, two light fawn ones called Charmaine and Camella, a dark brown one called Jolene, a light grey alpaca called Barbara and a rose grey one (grey with a reddish tint) named Maud. Lizzie wasn't sure whether Mitch had chosen the names or whether they'd been named by the previous owner, but they all really suited them.

'Everything's all right,' I said to Maud, stroking her neck. 'We'll look after you.'

Charmaine gave my elbow a gentle nudge and I stroked her neck too with my other hand.

'They like you already,' Ruth said, smiling at me.

At the start of every school year, as I surveyed each class I was allocated from the brand-new intake of eleven-year-olds, I always felt a buzz of excitement. At that moment, we were strangers who knew nothing except each other's names but the possibilities for the year ahead stretched out before us. Who'd be the star student and who'd be the joker? Who would lead and who'd follow? Gazing at the seven alpacas before me, I felt that same tingle of anticipation as to what lay ahead. But they weren't just my students. These seven animals would become my job, my family, my life and I'd do everything within my power to ensure they lived their absolute best life at the farm.

'Let's get them loaded into the trailers,' Ruth said. 'Lizzie's trailer is bigger so she'll take four and I'll take three. This weather's great for transporting them – cool and overcast – so we don't need to worry about them overheating. The journey's short enough not to need a water stop but I've got buckets and a container of water in my boot just in case.'

Bianca, Florence, Barbara and Maud were all led into Lizzie's trailer. Florence and Barbara were relaxed about the whole thing, lying down at the far end as though they were seasoned travellers. Bianca and Maud were both a little hesitant but it didn't take too long to coax them in and they settled beside the other two.

'You see how they're lying down on their bellies with their legs tucked under them?' Lizzie asked me. 'That's known as cushing. It's the perfect position for travelling as they're not going to fall over. They'll settle down to sleep like that too, sometimes close together.'

The relative ease of moving the first four had lulled us into a false sense of security because the remaining three – Camella, Charmaine and Jolene – were having none of it and it took about twice as long to get them into Ruth's smaller trailer. Although I hated that the situation was stressful for the alpacas, it was really helpful to see the techniques and noises Ruth and Lizzie used to calm and encourage them. I'd read textbooks, websites and blog posts as well as watching a stack of online videos, but nothing beat seeing the alpacas handled in real life and being an active part of it.

Lizzie set off while Ruth secured the trailer and I closed the gate to their former enclosure, taking one last look around. It was a good space, but it was quite small with just one tree to provide shade and a three-sided structure at the far end for shelter. They'd have something far superior at Bracken Ridge Farm.

'You're a natural with them,' Ruth said when we'd joined the main road back towards the Yorkshire Dales. 'How are you feeling about it all?'

'Excited. Raring to go.'

'Does this mean you want to take them?'

'Definitely. I'll need to double-check it with Grayson but he did say it was up to me what I did.'

'Excellent! I'm so pleased for you, Emma. Welcome to your alpaca adventure. You won't regret it.'

14

———

It was late afternoon when we arrived back at Butterbea Croft and after six by the time we had The Magnificent Seven, as I'd christened them, disinfected and settled in their new temporary home.

'I'm starving,' Lizzie said as the three of us rested our forearms on the barred metal gate, watching the alpacas exploring and munching on the lush grass.

I hadn't thought about food until now but realised we'd skipped lunch so, when they invited me to join them for an Indian takeaway, I'd have been daft not to accept.

Grayson had replied to my text at some point during the afternoon with nothing more than 'OK'. I tried phoning him to tell him I'd be staying for food but there was no answer so I texted him again.

TO GRAYSON

> That was an exciting day out. So much to tell you! We've just got the alpacas settled at Butterbea Croft. Skipped lunch so I'm staying here for a takeaway. Will let you know when I leave x

Twenty minutes later, the only reply was a thumbs up reaction, although that wasn't unusual for Grayson. He wasn't a big talker and he was a man of even fewer words over the phone.

It was nearly half eight by the time we'd eaten and my eyelids felt heavy.

'You look shattered,' Ruth said as she cleared my plate away.

'I feel it. I think it's the excitement of my first rescue. I could happily drift off into the land of dreams right now. Time to hit the road.'

'Have you got any plans for tonight or first thing?' she asked.

'I'm meeting my dad in Keswick in the morning. Why?'

'Because I don't like the idea of you driving when you're tired. We've got a spare bedroom here and I can loan you some clothes for tomorrow. You could drive straight to Keswick from here in the morning. It's closer.'

If home had only been half an hour away, it wouldn't be too much of a problem but an hour and a quarter was a long drive when feeling sleepy. It would be in the dark too with a significant part on winding country lanes so it wasn't worth the risk and I gratefully accepted the offer.

TO GRAYSON

> Another change of plan. I'm struggling to keep my eyes open so I've been invited to stay overnight. I'll drive straight to Keswick in the morning to meet Dad so I probably won't see you until you finish work tomorrow. Missing you x

I wasn't hopeful of more than another thumbs up or an 'OK' but he actually managed an additional two words, although there was no kiss. There was *never* a kiss.

FROM GRAYSON

> OK. Sounds sensible

As I settled beneath the covers in the spare bedroom a little later, I checked my phone in case Grayson had been in touch again, but there was nothing. I frowned at his last message. I was used to the lack of kisses – it was actually a standing joke between us that, if ever he put a kiss in his texts, I'd know he'd been kidnapped. But why couldn't he say he was missing me? Or tell me to sleep well or drive carefully – something to suggest that he actually cared about me because, right now, I was beginning to wonder whether he did.

Feeling a strong desire to get some sort of reaction from him, I sent him another text.

TO GRAYSON

> The alpacas are gorgeous and I've told Ruth and Lizzie I'd like to take them. You said it was up to me what I did but I'd appreciate that final thumbs up from you before I say a definite yes x

The thumbs up reaction came through, followed by a text.

FROM GRAYSON

But I want nothing to do with them

Clenching my teeth, I angrily typed in a response to that. In capitals.

TO GRAYSON

YES, I KNOW!

I switched my phone to silent and sank back onto the pillows with a frustrated sigh. I really didn't understand why this was such an issue for Grayson or why he felt the need to repeatedly hammer home his message of disinterest. Rachael was right about him not being very supportive, especially after everything I'd done for him over the years. Right now, our relationship didn't feel very balanced, with Grayson doing a lot of taking and no giving. I prayed that would change once he fully found his feet.

15

I'd arranged to meet my dad outside Derwent View Café in Keswick at 10 a.m. the following morning. A large café by the commercial end of the lake, it was one of my favourites because they made the best flapjack I'd ever tasted, drizzled with caramel sauce and white chocolate and topped with pumpkin seeds. Just thinking about it made me drool.

I'd been up early with Ruth and Lizzie to help them with their rounds and, in particular, to say good morning to The Magnificent Seven. The proceeds from the sale of Riverside Cottage were sitting in my savings account so, before leaving, I made a bank transfer for an initial £1,000 towards vet bills, transportation, foot treatment and grooming. As we were coming to the end of the summer, they wouldn't need a full shear but they'd definitely need some of their fleece removing.

'It's my way of confirming that I'll definitely be taking the herd as soon as the barn's ready,' I told the sisters when they insisted it wasn't necessary to make any payment yet. 'I'll transfer the rest once you have the final vet bill through.'

They both hugged me goodbye, thanked me for my help

yesterday and said they'd keep in touch with photos and videos until I was ready for the transfer to Bracken Ridge Farm.

After yesterday's overcast weather, it was a beautiful sunny day. The car park near Derwent Water would have been heaving over the bank holiday weekend and hopefully wouldn't be quite so packed today but, as it was still the school holidays, I wasn't taking any chances and arrived an hour early to guarantee a space. It gave me the perfect opportunity to enjoy a walk alongside the lake.

When I'd lived in Willowdale and the weather was warm enough, weekends and school holidays had typically been spent sailing or kayaking on Derwent Water, out on my bike or walking in the fells. When I moved to Ambleside, the much larger Windermere was close but not quite on the doorstep so I didn't spend as much time on the water as I used to. By the time I was fourteen, I'd secured a part-time job in a café for Saturdays and school holidays so all my time was taken up with work, homework, friends and family and I never went out on the water again. Grayson and I hadn't found time yet to visit Coniston (the lake rather than the village) despite it only being a few miles from the farm, so it was lovely to be beside a body of water today.

Although the boat trips hadn't started for the day, there were already quite a few people on the shingle beach, feeding the ducks, geese and swans and posing for photos on the wooden jetties. I continued along Lake Road towards Friar's Crag. A large group were crowded round both the main bench and the rocky area which afforded the best views of the lake and, judging by the stack of photos they were taking with different people in each, they weren't going to move away any time soon. I backtracked and continued clockwise round the lake past Strandshag Bay, along the boardwalks, and as far as the Centenary Stone. I only had a few minutes to drink in the view of Cat Bells to my right and the Borrowdale Valley ahead of me before retracing my steps to Derwent View Café to meet Dad.

If I was asked to describe my relationship with my dad, I'd struggle to put it into words. It wasn't a great relationship, but it wasn't a bad one either. We saw each other reasonably regularly and occasionally spoke on the phone in between times, but I always felt like there was something missing between us and had struggled for a long time to put my finger on what it was.

When I was little, I was really close to both of my parents. At the start of the summer holidays when I was seven, we went to Blackpool for a week and stayed in a static caravan and I still have memories of donkey rides on the beach, jumping the waves in the sea, feeding money into the penny falls in the arcades, and screaming on the ghost train at Pleasure Beach. And, most vividly, I remember walking along one of the piers between my parents, one hand holding Mum's, the other holding Dad's, and feeling so happy that I could burst. The day after we got home, the thing that burst was the bubble around our happy family unit when my parents announced that they'd wanted me to have a lovely holiday as a family of three but it would be the last time we'd all go away together because they were getting divorced. I didn't understand what that meant and, because Dad moved out that same day, I believed that he didn't want to be with Mum or with me anymore. I thought he didn't love either of us and I spent much of the rest of that summer in tears.

Mum had suggested Dad give me some time and space to come to terms with it – something I discovered much later – but that well-intentioned idea made things worse. To me, Dad staying away confirmed what I believed – that he didn't want anything to do with me. I was angry with him for a long time and I put my hands up to being a petulant child and then a stroppy teenager in his presence but, to give him his due, he never gave up on me. After that initial bit of space, he saw me regularly and was exceptionally patient with my moods.

A thaw from my end came when I wanted his advice about my A level choices and a teaching career. He arranged for me to undertake work experience at the school where he taught and was honest with me about the highs and lows of the profession. His support was invaluable and I started seeing him as someone who genuinely cared about me and my future instead of the person who'd abandoned me and broken my heart.

After that, our relationship improved but we still weren't close like I was with Mum and John. Spending time with Dad was a little like spending time with a distant relative or a friend of the family – all very pleasant with lots of polite chitchat but no depth. I used to wonder whether it was me holding back, harbouring some residual resentment from the divorce but, after we'd been married for a couple of years, Matthew had expressed concern that he didn't think Dad liked him. When I asked whether Dad had said or done anything to make him think that, his response was, *He's always pleasant but there's this distance. It's like he's on his best behaviour and holding something back.* And that was the light bulb moment. My dad was guarded. There was a wall between us and I wondered if it was my fault for pushing him away for so many years. Was he always careful and considered around me, not wanting to say or do anything that might push me away once more and had that distance projected onto my husband? So we had an afternoon in the pub together and I instigated a heart-to-heart about my parents' divorce and how it had affected me. It was good to get it out in the open and deal with a few issues. Except it made no difference. The wall was still very much present, leaving me with only one conclusion – its existence was actually nothing to do with me.

Over the years, I'd tried to break through the wall but not knowing why it existed made that impossible. I asked Mum but she didn't want to get involved, not even confirming whether she knew the reason Dad was so guarded. So I let it go and decided it was better to be on polite terms with my dad rather than find out why the wall existed but have no dad in my life because I'd pushed too hard.

I spotted Dad from some distance away, locking his bike to a cycle rack opposite the café. A couple of years after Mum married John, Dad moved out of town and into a house in Pippinthwaite, the next village over from Willowdale, and it would have been a lovely ride from there this morning.

'Oh, hi, Emma,' he said, when I joined him. 'I was expecting you to come from the other direction. Have you been for a walk?'

There was no offer of a hug, although I didn't move to give him one either. I was a tactile person, always hugging my family and friends, and it saddened me that I didn't have that level of closeness with my own dad.

'I got here early to bag a parking space,' I told him, 'so I've been to the Centenary Stone.'

We headed inside and ordered drinks. I hesitated, gazing at the delicious cakes, but went for flapjack as usual while Dad chose lemon drizzle cake.

'How's your farm training going?' he asked after we'd settled at a table for two outside with views over the lake.

'It isn't. Grayson doesn't need my help to run the farm and, even if he did, we've discovered we can't work together.'

'Oh! Sorry to hear that. You were really excited about it.'

'Maybe a bit too excited. I got carried away in my little fantasy world and it turned out to be just that – absolute fantasy. But I have a new plan...'

I explained how Teresa had planted the camelids idea which was now happening following yesterday's Northumberland rescue.

'I haven't heard you sound this enthusiastic about something in a long time,' Dad said, smiling at me. 'If there's anything I can do to help, let me know. I'm pretty useful with a power saw and a hammer these days.'

'Thanks, Dad, I will. So what have you been up to?'

We chatted about the cycle rides Dad had completed over the summer. He'd retired from teaching almost three years ago just after turning sixty-five and, from what I could gather, spent most of his time walking, cycling or working on DIY projects around the house. I'd asked him several times how he was finding retirement and always got a smile and a non-committal comment like *I've never been so busy*. He had friends with whom he went hiking and he had others in the cycling club he'd joined but I wished he had someone special in his life. Forty years was a long time to remain single, but perhaps he was happier in his own company. Plenty of single people were that way through choice. I certainly had been after my split from Matthew. After he broke my heart, meeting someone else was the last thing on my mind for many years. For Dad, I wondered if remaining single had hit differently since he'd retired and had so much more time at his disposal.

'Have you seen much of your mum recently?' Dad asked. They didn't stay in touch but they always enquired after each other.

'A couple of times. I met her for coffee and then I had the

whole family over for a barbeque on Monday. There's big news. Laura and Dillon are engaged. They're having a Christmas wedding next year.'

'I thought they didn't want to get married.'

'We all did, but they had a change of heart and decided it's time.'

'Any more thoughts on a date for you and Grayson?'

My stomach lurched. It was an obvious question but it made me uncomfortable as, with Grayson's erratic behaviour lately, it was challenging enough getting through each day, never mind planning for the future.

'Getting the farm needed to take priority and now Grayson's settling in while I've got the alpacas to focus on.' I somehow managed to sound brighter than I felt. 'I can't see it being next year but maybe the year after. We'll see. There's no rush. We have all the time in the world.'

'All the time in the world,' Dad repeated as he stared into his empty latte cup, a frown creasing his forehead.

'Everything okay?' I asked.

'Hmm?'

'I said is everything okay? Dad?'

He looked up and shook his head slowly. 'Sorry, Emma. Miles away for a moment there. Please give Laura and Dillon my congratulations. That's great news.'

The smile was bright but it didn't reach his eyes.

'Are you sure you're okay?'

'Couldn't be better.' He glanced at his phone. 'Your parking ticket will expire soon so we'd best head off.'

I wiped the crumbs off the table onto one of the plates and stacked our crockery together on the tray – still a habit despite it being decades since I'd worked in a café – and headed outside with Dad.

'Great to see you as always,' he said, giving me a hug. 'Let me know about the barn. I'm serious about being able to help out.'

'Okay. Enjoy your cycle home.'

He wandered over to his bike and I headed back to my car. That had been strange in the café just now. Even though there'd always been that wall, that distance between us, I couldn't remember him ever drifting off like that before and it worried me. Was there something he wasn't telling me? Could he be ill? As soon as that idea popped into my head, it took hold and I stopped dead, heart pounding. What if he'd had an ill-health diagnosis and he was worried that, if Grayson and I didn't get our act together really soon, he wouldn't be around to see us get married?

I spun round and spotted him in the distance, astride his bike, fastening the chin strap on his cycling helmet.

'Dad!' I shouted, sprinting across the car park, but he'd already set off. By the time I reached the cycle rack, he was halfway across Crow Park. I bent over, hands on thighs to catch my breath, but kept my head up, my stomach churning as he disappeared from my view.

I returned to the car with one minute to spare on the parking and set off back to the farm. Hopefully it was nothing but it did make me determined to find a way to break down that wall and properly get to know my dad.

Another thought struck me. What if it was nothing to do with illness at all or about being around for my wedding? What if him repeating *all the time in the world* was to do with how he was finding retirement on his own? Teaching had been every-thing to him. I was already feeling a little lost about not returning to the classroom next week after a career spanning twenty-five years so a three-year absence after more than four decades in the profession was bound to have had an impact. I'd often wondered if Dad could be lonely but I'd never pushed him on it. From now on, I was going to. I'd do my bit to bridge that distance between us whether he was ill, lonely, or there was something else going on and I'd start by seeing if Dillon could use him as a labourer for the barn changes. The three of us would make a great team together. Unlike Grayson and me.

16

When Grayson and Monty returned to the farmhouse after work that evening, I was at the kitchen table on a FaceTime chat with Laura discussing the final arrangements for tomorrow's wedding dress shopping trip. Spotting me on the phone, Grayson pointed upstairs to indicate that he was going up for his shower so I stroked Monty while I finished up with my sister.

I was dishing up our meal and wondering which version of my fiancé would be joining me tonight when he came back down. I hoped spending last night on his own would have given him ample time to reflect on how difficult he'd been recently. Surely things had to improve now that we had our own separate activities.

'Good day?' I asked brightly, sitting down at the table.

'Yeah. Got loads done.'

He didn't sound particularly enthusiastic and I sighed inwardly. Was that it? Conversation over?

We ate in uncomfortable silence for several minutes. I was

on the verge of slamming my cutlery down and demanding he tell me what his problem was when he spoke.

'So tell me all about the rescue yesterday. How many alpacas are there and why did they need rescuing?'

I stared at him, stunned by how interested he sounded.

'Or don't tell me and we can continue eating in silence.' He gave me a mischievous smile and I finally relaxed.

'There are seven of them...'

He listened and gave off a very good impression of someone who was genuinely interested and excited for me until he asked *that* question with a curled-up lip and doubt in his eyes.

'You're really sure you want to do this?'

'Never been more certain.'

'It's not going to pay you a patch on what you earned as a teacher.'

'I know that but it's not about the money. It's about doing something new and exciting.'

'You think picking up alpaca poo is going to be exciting?'

'That's a small part of it. You have messy stuff to do too but it's not the whole job, is it?'

He shrugged. 'Good luck to you. I think you're going to need it.'

It was said in a joking voice accompanied by a wink as he cleared the plates, but I knew that wasn't how he meant it. That was the moment when I realised I might have his approval to bring the alpacas to Bracken Ridge Farm but I'd never have his full support or understanding and I wasn't sure how I felt about that.

* * *

Laura had invited Mum, Stacie and me to join her and her best friend Alisha – also a bridesmaid – at Mill House for breakfast the following morning before heading out for our shopping expedition. She'd planned a tour around several bridal shops in Cumbria, ending the day with drinks and a takeaway back at hers. John would be Mum's and Stacie's taxi service home afterwards but Alisha and I were staying overnight.

I'd risen shortly after Grayson left on his rounds and was therefore ready far too early so I wandered over to the alpaca field with my coffee, reflecting on last night's conversation. Forearms resting on the gate, my alpaca mug cradled between my hands, I still wasn't sure how I felt about Grayson's final comments. Was having his blessing the main thing and it didn't matter that he didn't get it? Or should I expect him to support me whether he got it or not?

When I set off to Mill House a little later, I pulled up the Birthday Bangers playlist, determined not to let Grayson's lack of encouragement bring me down. I wanted to approach my sister's special shopping trip with a positive head on.

Even if the music hadn't raised my spirits, it was impossible not to be lifted when I was with my mum and sisters. Mum and John both had bubbly personalities and exuded warmth so it was no surprise that Stacie and Laura were the same. I'd inherited those traits from Mum too and they came out most strongly when I was in my comfort zone – doing something I loved and was good at like teaching or when I was around the people I loved who excited and inspired me. But I was also my dad's daughter and, when tested, my instinct was to retreat and close down. I hated anyone seeing me like that so I did my utmost to hide it. Rachael was the person who'd seen me at my lowest but, even then, she hadn't known everything. Nobody had.

* * *

Laura looked stunning in all the wedding dresses she tried on but she found the winner in the second shop we visited. As soon as she emerged from the changing room, tears rushed to my eyes and I clapped my hand to my heart.

'It's perfect,' Mum whispered.

'I think it's the one,' Laura said, beaming at us as we all enthusiastically agreed.

The ivory lacy bridal gown shimmered when she moved. Wide sheer sleeves fastened round the wrists with satin buttons made it wintry rather than summery, as did the addition of an ivory cape with a faux fur trim round the hood and hem.

With no doubt in anyone's mind that Laura had found *the one*, she encouraged us to look at bridesmaid dresses while she placed her order. Stacie, Alisha and I shared similar tastes and quickly agreed on beautiful deep heather gowns with soft grey faux fur stoles from the same shop. The manager told us that, as our bridesmaid dresses came from the same dress designer as Laura's gown, the lining of her cape could be made from the same material. They could also use that colour for pocket squares, ties and cravats depending on what Dillon wanted and a sash and petticoat for winter white flower girl dresses for Anna and Eden.

'Alisha, why don't you try on some wedding dresses in the next shop?' Laura said when we drove towards the next town in search of a mother-of-the-bride outfit.

'You wouldn't mind?' Alisha asked. She was also engaged and getting married in Fiji next year with Laura as her bridesmaid.

'Of course not! You missed out on the fun with your auntie making yours so why not?'

Alisha laughed. 'Okay, I'm game, but only if you try on more too.'

'You're on!'

'And let's try on some really ugly ones.'

I sank back in my seat, hoping nobody would suggest that, because I was engaged too, I should join in. When they didn't, I couldn't help wondering if they'd all agreed – and warned Alisha – that it was a no-go area for the moment on the back of Grayson's strange reaction at Monday's barbeque.

At the next bridal boutique, while Alisha and Laura tried on wedding gowns, Stacie and I searched through an extensive range of mother-of-the-bride outfits with Mum. She found a gorgeous dress in soft green and cream with a matching hat and jacket which would perfectly complement the heather of the bridesmaid dresses and took it into the changing room. Stacie was distracted by the shoes, so I took a time out, resting on an elegant silver chaise.

The first couple of dresses Laura and Alisha tried on were hideous. Alisha's looked like several poodles had been knitted together and Laura's was an over-the-top mess of flounces and feathers. I could still hear their peals of laughter as they tried on something less flamboyant.

When they emerged from the changing rooms in their third even more toned-down choices, my breath caught. Alisha's dress was exactly what I'd have chosen for myself – a simple but elegant off-the-shoulder design in cream tulle. I stared at her, tears burning behind my eyes. Would I ever get to wear a stunning dress like this and have the big wedding day I'd always dreamed of?

Matthew and I had married at a registry office followed by a pub meal with my family and our closest friends. Like Grayson, he'd had a falling out with his family, albeit for very different reasons. He didn't want them at our wedding but couldn't face the abuse he knew he'd get if we had a big event and didn't invite them.

I'd known Matthew from the year above me at senior school and had really fancied him but, despite considerable encouragement from Rachael, was too shy and insecure to give him any indication that I was interested. We'd say 'hi' and smile if we saw each other around school but that was as far as it went until I bumped into him in the Post Office queue when I was twenty-two. I mean quite literally bumped into him, having tripped over the laces on my trainers which I hadn't noticed had come undone. Matthew steadied me in the nick of time before I face-planted the floor and I couldn't believe it when I looked up at the former object of my affection. The years apart had done nothing to dampen that teenage crush and, when he asked me if I was free for a coffee and a catch-up after I'd posted my parcel, my heart sang with joy. Coffee led to drinks the following night and he admitted that he'd really liked me too back in school but had never asked a girl out before, was scared of messing it up, and didn't think I'd be interested in him anyway because he was so geeky. It was really endearing to hear that he'd been as insecure as me and we agreed we'd be honest with each other about what was going on in our heads from that point.

When he told me he wanted to marry me but was afraid he couldn't give me the type of wedding he knew I wanted, I appreciated the honesty and told him I'd run off to Gretna Green with him if it meant we could be together because an enduring marriage to the man I loved was far more important to me than the wedding day. I loved him even more when he told me that Gretna Green would be his preferred option but, knowing how important my family were to me, he wouldn't dream of asking me to say *I do* without them present. If only he'd remained honest with me throughout our marriage. If only he'd stayed willing to compromise.

So I hadn't had my dream wedding day with Matthew and I wasn't convinced it would happen with Grayson any time soon but, as I watched Alisha and Stacie placing a sparkly tiara on Laura's head, I realised I was at peace with that. What I'd said to Matthew all those years ago about an enduring marriage versus one special day still applied, more now than ever before. It was the marriage I wanted with Grayson and I didn't need to wear a big white dress to prove how much I loved him or a commitment to grow old together. Even though the past month had been up and down, my feelings for him hadn't changed. It would be the first day of September tomorrow and I had my fingers crossed that it would be kinder to us than August had been.

17

After a light breakfast at Mill House the following morning, I drove to Mum and John's for Sunday lunch.

'Sounds like you had a great day out yesterday,' John said as I helped him peel the vegetables.

'It was lovely. Has Mum tried on her outfit for you?'

'She has and she looks incredible in it, although your mum could wear a potato sack and she'd still light up the room.'

Mum had been searching for something in the fridge but she closed the door, crossed the kitchen, slipped her arms round his waist and pressed her head against his back.

'You two are so adorable,' I said, smiling at them.

In all their years together, all I'd ever seen was love, support, and warmth. They never bickered and I'd once asked Mum whether they were just on their best behaviour in front of us and had disagreements behind closed doors but she said there was very little they disagreed on and, if there was something, they respected each other's opinion too much to turn it into an argument. I imagined their natural sunny dispositions helped keep things on an even keel.

'Are you pleased with your dress?' John asked me.

'Delighted. It's a gorgeous colour. Shame I have to wait until next year to wear it.'

Over our takeaway last night, I'd told everyone about The Magnificent Seven. Alisha, an assistant in a veterinary surgery, proclaimed that alpacas were her spirit animal and she'd definitely be booking onto a walk as soon as I was open for business. I'd asked if she'd like to go on a trial walk once they were settled and ready, so she joked that Laura was ditched and I was now her new best friend.

'Would you like to be in my trial?' I asked John over lunch.

'I'd love to be.'

'You have to promise to give me your honest opinion. If my talk and tour need work, I want to know.'

'I'm sure you'll be brilliant but I solemnly promise to be honest.' He placed his hand across his heart and fixed me with an earnest expression which made me smile.

'I'm not sure how soon it'll be. Ruth and Lizzie say they need a bit more practice walking on a lead and, of course, they'll need to get used to me and their new surroundings.'

'Just give me the shout when you're ready and I'll be there,' he said. 'Unless it's while we're on holiday.'

'You're going on holiday?' I asked, looking from John to Mum.

'Last-minute decision,' Mum said. 'We couldn't remember the last time we went away on our own so we've booked a fortnight in Malta, flying from Manchester a week on Monday.'

'Aw, you'll have an amazing time. And when you come back, you need to organise a big holiday for next year to celebrate forty years together.'

'On it already,' John said. 'We've ordered some brochures.'

I was so pleased to hear that. Mum and John did so much

for us all and a significant proportion of their time went on looking after Sawyer, Ashton, Eden and Anna while my sisters were working. They loved being grandparents and I knew they cherished that time, but it did mean that time on their own was a rarity. I was craving a holiday myself but, given a choice between going away and getting my alpacas, the alpacas definitely won. I couldn't wait to welcome them to the farm.

* * *

The following week was extremely productive and, to my relief, argument-free. Grayson wasn't brimming over with enthusiasm about my alpacas arriving but he was at least showing an interest in my preparations. Now a month into life at Bracken Ridge Farm, it seemed he'd found his stride, which had considerably lifted his mood. He'd also developed a strong relationship with Ted, and talked passionately about the joint projects they'd been exploring.

On Wednesday, I drove across to Butterbea Croft to see Ruth, Lizzie and The Magnificent Seven. The herd had been sheared and they looked so different and so much thinner without their fleeces. The vet had been and had confirmed Ruth and Lizzie's initial visual assessment that they were in good condition, but they were awaiting their test results to make sure all was well internally. Charmaine was the only one who needed some specific treatment for a foot infection, although it was only a mild one which should clear up quickly.

Dillon confirmed Tuesday and Wednesday next week for the work on the barn so I enlisted Dad to help out on both days. He sounded surprised and pleased that I'd taken him up on his offer of help, which made me determined to include him more. Ruth, Lizzie and I arranged an alpaca handover date of Friday next week, allowing a couple of extra days for the building work in case of bad weather or unexpected problems.

The manager at the veterinary practice with which Grayson was registered confirmed that one of their vets had experience of working with camelids so would be happy to take on my herd, so that was another task ticked off on my enormous to-do list. I placed an online order for feeding and water troughs and a long list of other essentials including buckets, a large poop scooper, a rake for their bedding, disinfectant mats and disinfectant to prevent the spread of anything nasty as the alpacas and my customers moved in and out of the enclosure. I placed another order for bales of straw for their bedding, good-quality hay to eat, and various supplements they'd need to take to keep them healthy, all of which would arrive early next week.

My final bit of preparation was to pull on some heavy-duty gloves on the Friday – the last dry day before a weekend of rain was forecast – and comb every inch of the alpaca field searching for litter.

Saturday brought the forecast downpour. It remained dark all day as the rain hammered against the farmhouse and the wind chased leaves from the trees. I felt for Grayson out in it but bad weather was part of the life of a farmer and those who farmed in the Lake District were fully prepared for an above-average rainfall, which was the reason we had the landscape we did. On days like this, I appreciated the genius of an external laundry room, allowing Grayson to hang his waterproofs up to dry rather than have them dripping all over the kitchen floor.

The new academic year had already started with two staff training days at Corbeck School before the students returned and it had felt very strange not being part of it. Rachael had messaged me saying how weird it was being there without me and how many of my colleagues had asked after me, expressing sadness that I'd gone. It was a lovely boost to hear how much I was missed. She asked if I was free for a catch-up over the weekend so I suggested afternoon tea today at a gorgeous café in Coniston.

'I hate being at school without you,' she said as soon as she arrived at the café, shrugging off her wet coat. 'It doesn't feel right.'

While we waited for our food to arrive, Rachael ran through some of the details about the start of term. It was a little surreal hearing it all – what the new intake of students were like, which staff members had changed their hairstyle over the summer break, and the structural changes around the building – when I was no longer part of it.

'Does it feel weird hearing all this?' Rachael asked, as in tune with my thoughts as she'd always been.

'Very. There's part of me that feels like I'm missing out and I want to be part of it but I'm so excited about the alpacas that I know it was the right decision for me to leave.'

'Dare I ask about Grayson's opinion of them?' she asked, wincing slightly.

'He seems to have accepted it and he thankfully hasn't made any more comments about me being on my own. That message was definitely received loud and clear.'

'I still think he should be more supportive after everything you've given up for him.' She laughed lightly. 'Sorry. I think you got that message loud and clear too.'

I gave her a reassuring smile. 'I honestly didn't mind you saying it. In fact, I'm glad you did. It helped convince me that I needed to do something for me, even if he wasn't fully behind me.'

'Good for you.'

'I'm sure that, when he meets them, he'll love them and be begging me to let him help.'

Rachael nodded. 'And, when he does, I hope you remind him he wanted nothing to do with them.'

We laughed but nervous butterflies flitted in my stomach. Grayson was a stubborn man and the reality was that he probably wouldn't change his mind about the herd. Him falling in love with them like I'd done was another moment spent in fantasy land. But that was fine as that meant the full responsibility for the herd and the business lay with me and I was more than ready to embrace it.

18

I stood by the bedroom window on Sunday morning but couldn't see the fells for the low cloud and rain. Today's rain was a steady patter rather than a torrential downpour like yesterday, but it left me a bit stuck. There was nothing else I could do to prepare for The Magnificent Seven, the house was clean, the washing complete, the shopping done and the only task left on my to-do list was unpacking my office.

I crossed the landing and leaned against the doorframe, frowning at the unopened boxes. I had stacks of science books which I'd need if the alpaca business didn't work out and I had to either return to teaching or do some private tutoring, but having them on the shelves presented an expecting-to-fail vibe which wasn't how I felt about my business. Shaking my head, I closed the door, went downstairs and placed my pretty cushions in front of the plain ones with a sigh.

I'd have picked a fell and gone for a walk if the weather had been decent but I was a fair-weather hiker only, seeing no joy in trudging to the top of a fell, muddy and drenched, without the reward of the stunning view. The view was surely the whole point.

A knock on the side door made me jump. I was surprised to see Dad on the doorstep and ushered him inside, out of the rain.

'I'm sorry for turning up without phoning first,' he said, hanging his jacket up. 'Am I interrupting anything?'

'I'm at a loose end today so your timing's impeccable. Tea? Coffee?'

'Tea, please.'

'Okay. Make yourself comfortable in the lounge while I make it. Won't be long.'

When I took his mug through, Dad was looking out of the window with his hands clasped at the back of his head, his elbows cradling his face. His strange reaction to *all the time in the world* came flooding back to me. Dad had never paid me an unexpected visit and news of illness was just the sort of thing that would warrant showing up unannounced.

'Everything okay?' I asked, my voice a little squeaky as nervous butterflies chased each other round my stomach.

He dropped his arms and turned round to face me. 'There's something I need to tell you.' The serious expression and matching tone filled me with dread.

'Okay.' I placed his tea down on a side table.

'I probably should have said something before now, but I wasn't sure how to break it to you.'

My legs felt shaky and I sank down onto the sofa, still holding his gaze.

'This isn't easy to say.' He perched on the sofa beside me. 'It's probably best if I just come out with it and then I'll explain.'

'Okay,' I repeated at barely a whisper. My lips and throat felt very dry as I braced myself against the message I feared was coming: *I've got cancer. I'm terminally ill. I've got three months left.*

'I have a son,' he said.

I stared at him, my brain struggling to compute those words which bore no resemblance to what I'd anticipated. Had I heard him right?

'Which means you have a half-brother,' he continued.

Half-brother? Who? When? How? But I couldn't seem to spit out any of those words and just kept staring at him, eyes wide.

'I appreciate that'll have come as a bit of a shock. Do you need a moment?'

'I'm... I...' I gulped. 'I thought you were going to tell me you were seriously ill.'

'Ill? Why would you think that? Do I look ill?'

'No, but when we met last week and we were talking about weddings, I said Grayson and I had all the time in the world and you repeated that and drifted off. I thought you'd had a serious diagnosis and was worried that you *didn't* have all the time in the world left.'

'No, nothing like that. I never thought... It was that phrase. It takes me back to...' He shook his head. 'It'll become clear in a bit. But I'm absolutely fine. Fitter and healthier than I've ever been thanks to all the walking and cycling since I retired.'

I exhaled loudly. 'That's a relief.'

'Sorry for alarming you.'

My mind was whirring. He *really* had a son? Had he been having an affair? Was that why my parents split up? Or could this be a recent thing – a new much younger girlfriend I knew nothing about?

'How old is he?' I asked.

'Thirty-six.'

Not a recent thing, then! I normally excelled at maths but

my mind had gone completely blank. I couldn't even focus on my own age, never mind work out whether Dad had been having an affair.

'It was after your mum and I had split up,' he said, as though realising what was puzzling me.

'Thirty-six,' I repeated. 'So why am I only finding out about him now?' I gasped as a thought struck me. 'Have you only just found out?'

Dad winced. 'I've always known but he hasn't. He only found out at the start of the week. We met up yesterday.'

'Oh! Erm...' So many questions! Where to start? 'What's his name?'

'Oliver.'

'Does Mum know?'

'I've just come from her house. I wanted her to hear it from me.'

He paused to sip on his tea while questions raced round my head and I fought not to spill them all out at once. Who was the mum? Had they been together for long? Why had he been keeping it secret for all these years? Why didn't his son know until now? How had he found out? And questions aside, I had no idea how I felt knowing that I had another half-sibling, especially one who wasn't much older than Stacie and Laura and who could have been part of my life for thirty-six years if he hadn't been a big secret.

'I understand it's a lot to take in,' Dad said gently.

'You're not kidding.'

As I gazed at his face, trying to work out what I wanted to ask first, it struck me that this was it. This was the wall between us. The distance I'd felt was because he'd spent my teen years and the whole of my adult life keeping a huge secret from me.

'How about you start at the beginning?' I suggested.

19

It was still chucking it down when Dad left. I made another mug of tea and sat at the kitchen table, reeling from his news. I wanted to speak to someone about it. Not Mum as she was too close to it and likely still processing it herself. Grayson wouldn't appreciate me dragging him away from his work for something that was a shock but certainly not an emergency. Rachael was having her in-laws round for lunch and I didn't want to ring her in case they were still there, so I sent a message.

TO RACHAEL

Can you give me a ring when you have a moment? Dad has just revealed a big secret and I could do with someone to talk to about it. Thanks x

My phone rang moments later and I went through to the lounge to curl up on one of the sofas.

'What sort of secret?' Rachael asked after assuring me her in-laws had gone and I wasn't disturbing anything.

'A thirty-six-year-old son called Oliver.'

'No! Oh, my gosh! That's... wow! I wasn't expecting that.'

'Me neither. You can see why I wanted to speak to someone.'

'Who's the mum?'

'Her name was Kathryn and she was Dad's girlfriend when he was at college but they had a big falling out...' Dad hadn't wanted to go into the details this afternoon and I wasn't sure I'd have taken them in even if he had. 'Mum and Dad got married and had me and Kathryn got married too but apparently he never got over her and that's why my parents split up.'

'They had an affair?'

'Not while he was with Mum. They hooked up again a couple of years after the split but Kathryn wasn't sure whether Oliver was Dad's or Hubert's – her husband's. As Oliver got older, the resemblance to Dad was unmistakeable so they both knew.'

'Did the husband know?'

'Supposedly not, although he was having flings left, right and centre and rubbing Kathryn's nose in it. Didn't sound like a very nice man.'

'So why didn't she leave him for your dad, especially if her son was his?'

I'd asked Dad the same question. 'Dad said Kathryn owned Willowdale Hall and there was a fear she'd lose it if they divorced but, when Oliver was twelve, she decided she'd had enough and was willing to take that risk. She wanted absolute confirmation that Oliver was Dad's so had their DNA tested but she died suddenly after a short illness before the results came through. They arrived at Dad's house the day after she died and he's kept it secret ever since.'

Dad's voice had cracked at that point and he'd needed to take a moment before continuing. Even though he'd only given me the salient points this afternoon to give me a chance to process the headline news, I'd been left in no doubt that Kathryn had been the love of his life.

'Oh! That's heartbreaking. And Oliver never knew until this week, but your dad's known all his life? That must have been difficult.'

'I said the exact same thing.'

I pictured the sad expression on Dad's face when he told me that Oliver had been one of his students.

'I didn't know what to do when Kathryn died,' he said. 'I wanted to go to the funeral but I couldn't. I wanted to comfort Oliver but, as far as he was concerned, I was his biology teacher. How could I break it to him that I was really his father?'

'You actually taught him?' I asked. 'So you saw your son every day at school and you couldn't say anything? That must have been difficult.'

'It was, but it was also a blessing because it meant he was in my life, even if he had no idea what his presence meant to me. He was naturally gifted at science and we often spoke about his career choices. He wanted to be a surgeon but he fell in with a bad crowd at sixth form and his grades massively slipped so I was able to give him a fatherly talking to, even though he didn't know that's what it was. He got back on track and went to university and I resigned myself to not seeing him again but he lost his way once more and needed a push so he reached out to me. I helped him with a change of direction – GP instead of surgeon – and we stayed in touch for several years after graduation. We sent Christmas cards and met up every so often, but it fizzled out eight or nine years back. I was gutted but what could I do?'

'Couldn't you just have told him who you really were?' I asked.

'Every time I saw him I tried to pluck up the courage but I just couldn't find the words and, the longer I left it, the harder it became, especially after I found out he'd also had a horrendous relationship with Hubert Cranleigh and had severed ties with him when he left for university. I imagined Oliver being angry with me for not taking Kathryn and him away or for not coming back for him when she was gone. I imagined him hating me for not being at her funeral and not opening up to him about who I was. I'd already lost Kathryn and I was so scared of losing Oliver out of my life that I took the coward's way out and said nothing. I lost him anyway because, when work and life got too demanding, what logical reason was there for him to stay in touch with a former teacher when he had access to new experts and mentors who were following the same career path as him?'

'What a predicament,' Rachael said when I'd summarised the conversation for her. 'It's easy to say he should have told Oliver but who knows how you'll react until you're standing in the same shoes? I feel so sorry for your dad right now.'

'Me too.'

'Imagine keeping something like that secret for thirty-six years. I don't think I could do it.'

I wished I could respond with *me neither*, but that would be a lie. I'd been keeping my own slice of the past hidden from everyone I loved and Dad had been right – the longer you leave it, the harder it becomes to share it. My secret wasn't quite on the same scale as Dad's but it had still impacted significantly on me and I'd faced it alone. Dad had talked about being a coward but I knew he'd been far from that. He'd been incredibly brave.

20

Talking to Rachael had been really useful for helping me take in Dad's news but I found myself pacing the kitchen, clock-watching, waiting for Grayson's return so that I could spill it all out to him.

Even though I knew Grayson hated it when I delayed him from taking a shower, I thought he'd agree with me that this was important.

'You're never going to believe what I've found out,' I blurted out, the moment he opened the kitchen door. 'Dad came round this afternoon and—'

'Was he expected?' he snapped, cutting across me.

'What? No!' I said, bewildered by the interruption. 'But that's not the point. He came to tell me I've got a brother.'

'What are you talking about?'

'Dad's got a thirty-six-year-old son who he's been keeping secret from everyone including Mum.'

I garbled out some of what I'd learned this afternoon, barely pausing for breath.

'So how did this Oliver find out that your dad's his dad if your dad didn't tell him?'

'He and his girlfriend found a load of his mum's old diaries and hoped his biological father's identity would be in there but Kathryn only used Dad's initial letter, C, so they were none the wiser. Then earlier in the week, Rosie found—'

'Who's Rosie?'

'Oliver's girlfriend,' I said, exasperated by another interruption. 'She found some ripped-out pages which talked about this C being at a school parents' evening and they worked it out. Dad taught Oliver and Rosie so they both knew him.'

'I'm guessing you'll want to meet this Oliver and his girlfriend,' he said.

'At some point, yes. It's a lot to take in for now.'

'Is it just them or are there kids and cousins and Uncle Tom Cobley and all?'

'I don't know. I don't know anything about that side of the family but I guess I'll find out over time. Exciting, though, isn't it?'

'Thrilling,' he deadpanned. 'I'm going for my shower.'

When he came back downstairs, he announced he was meeting Ted at the pub, would warm up his tea when he returned, and left leaving me completely flummoxed by his lack of reaction.

While Grayson was at the pub, Mum FaceTimed me to check I was holding up all right after Dad's revelation.

'I could ask you the same,' I said. 'Did you know?'

'I had my suspicions.'

'Dad said you and Kathryn were friends.'

She nodded. 'I met her when I took riding lessons.'

'And you introduced her to Dad?'

'Yes. She was having a big party for her seventeenth

birthday and she wanted to meet some new people. Your dad and I had been friends for years but I wanted more and thought he felt the same. I hoped going to Kathryn's party together might be the moment it happened.'

My heart sank for her. 'But he fell for Kathryn instead.'

She smiled ruefully. 'The moment he saw her, I knew I'd lost him to her. I was so upset but what could I do? They were great together. On paper, it shouldn't have worked. In reality, it was a match made in heaven. But it's okay because I found my perfect match in John.'

He must have been nearby as she looked to one side, smiling.

'I'm a bit confused about what happened next,' I said. 'Dad glossed over how it ended and how you and he got together.'

'He probably didn't want to bombard you with too much background detail when he had such a big piece of news to share. I'm sure he'll be happy to explain when you're ready to hear more. And I do think it's your dad you should hear it from rather than me.'

'I'm sorry you got hurt.'

She smiled and shook her head. 'It was a long time ago and I have no regrets about any of it. When your dad and I did get together, I was never in any doubt that he cared deeply for me, but I was also never in any doubt that the love of his life was Kathryn. I was there the moment they met, I was friends with them both in the eighteen months they were together and I was the shoulder he cried on when it ended. While I was picking up the pieces I knew that, even if Christian somehow did come round to seeing me as more than a friend, we'd never have what the pair of them had but we can't control what the heart wants and I wanted your dad. Always had. And even though my head was screaming *run! He's in love with someone else!* I didn't let it shout loud enough to make me see sense. We *did* have a good marriage, Emma, but it wasn't real, no matter how much I tried to kid myself that it was. We might not have been meant for each other but that lapse in judgement on both our parts gave us you and, no matter how much it hurt to accept that I was always going to be second best, I'd do it all again to have you and I know your dad would too.'

There was so much warmth and love in her voice, making me feel tearful.

'Also, John and I would never have met if I hadn't been going through a divorce and, without him, there'd be no Stacie, Laura or our gorgeous grandchildren. There was a lot of pain and sorrow but I wouldn't change a single thing because it was worth it to have all of you in my life.'

'As long as you're okay,' I said, my voice coming out a little squeaky.

'Don't worry about me. I'm more than okay. Your dad and I had a really good long overdue talk and made our peace over a lot of things. You know, I did worry about him after Kathryn died and I thought about reaching out but...' She shrugged.

'You had your own life, Mum. I'm sure Dad wouldn't have expected you to be there for him.'

'He didn't, but it doesn't stop me wondering whether he could have used a friend back then. He's kept a lot locked up inside for so many years and I'm glad it's out in the open now, but I think he might need your understanding and support over the coming weeks. I know that's a lot to ask when you've had a shock.'

'I'm okay. Having another half-sibling – especially a brother this time – is exciting news and I'm not angry with Dad or anything like that. I'm just a bit shocked.'

Mum gave me a gentle smile. 'I know we're off on our holidays tomorrow but, if it does hit you while we're away and you want to talk, you must phone me. You don't have to go through anything alone.'

'Thank you but there's no way I'm going to disturb your much-deserved break. We can talk when you're home. And, on that note, I'd better say goodbye and wish you both a wonderful time.'

'Thank you,' John called from somewhere off camera.

'One final thing,' Mum said. 'I know you've not had the easiest of relationships with your dad over the years and, given what you now know, it would be easy to think of him as the one who broke my heart and therefore the bad guy in all of this, but the truth is I let him. I knew what I was getting myself into. I knew Kathryn was the one. If we're talking blame, it's fifty-fifty. And even though I was the one who ultimately ended the marriage, we did have a lot of happy years together first because we were good friends and that counted for so much.'

We said our goodbyes and I sat for a while reflecting on what Mum had said. She hadn't given much detail but it had been so interesting to hear her take on things. Deep down, I *had* always thought of Dad as *the bad guy* and it had influenced my attitude towards him. It was clear now that there'd been so much that I hadn't known and not only was I now seeing their relationship in a completely different light, I was seeing Dad differently too. And part of that picture included a heartbroken person hiding the truth from the world. Hard relate.

21

I didn't wake up until after nine o'clock on Monday morning, which wasn't surprising considering my mind wouldn't switch off until well into the early hours. It wasn't just Dad's news I had to process and my subsequent conversation with Mum. It was that his secret had pushed open the door to my past and whether I should have told the truth about Matthew and me. And, as if that wasn't enough to keep my brain awake, I also had that strange reaction from Grayson to try to get my head around. He'd definitely seemed more concerned that Dad had turned up out of the blue and whether there were other members of Oliver's family who'd want to visit the farm, which was weird.

I still felt thrown by it as I showered and dressed this morning. That final word – *thrilling* – had been so odd, delivered in a tone that suggested it was exactly the opposite. How could he be so disinterested in something that was such a major thing for me?

Needing some fresh air, I took my coffee over to the alpaca enclosure and sat on the gate to drink it, trying to clear my mind of everything except The Magnificent Seven arriving on Friday. My lovely herd. I closed my eyes, thinking about the adorable sounds they made, how it felt to sink my fingers into their fleece, the caring instinct that burned inside me when I was near them.

Feeling much calmer, I walked back to the farmhouse. Grayson appeared round the corner on his quad bike and, as soon as he drew it to a halt in the yard, Monty jumped down and raced round me.

'Bit early for lunch,' I called, glancing at my phone.

'We need to talk,' he responded, his tone flat.

'Everything okay?' I asked. He was looking at me so intently and it was making me nervous.

'We need to talk,' he repeated. He instructed Monty to get a drink of water from the nearby bowl and, instead of going into the farmhouse, he headed for the picnic benches.

'Do you want a drink?' I asked.

'No. I want you to sit down and listen.'

It was stated like an order. Feeling thoroughly chastised, I plonked my empty mug on the picnic table and sat down opposite him, my stomach in knots.

'I can't do this anymore,' he said eventually.

'Run the farm?' I asked gently, thinking maybe Mum had been right about sole responsibility for the farm being too stressful for him.

He scrunched his face up, looking bewildered. 'No. Why would you think that?'

'I just...' I shrugged. If not the farm, then what?

'I can't do *this*,' he stated, with strong emphasis on the last word. 'Us.'

My stomach plummeted to the ground and I opened my

mouth to speak but no words came out. He couldn't possibly be ending it, could he?

'You must realise it hasn't been working for a while.'

'There've been a few niggles,' I managed, my voice coming out hoarse.

'Understatement of the year. It's been more than a few.'

'Maybe, but that's only because we've been dealing with so much change all at once.'

'We didn't need to have that much.' His voice was cold. 'We could have just had the move but, oh no, you had to go and throw a whole lot more into the mix and mess everything up.'

'Like what?'

He ignored my question. 'This is *my* dream, Emma. *Mine!*'

I winced at the volume, heart pounding.

'I've been working hard for it for so long but you couldn't just let me have it. You *had* to be part of it.' There was so much bitterness in his tone and his words made no sense to me. Moving to the farm might have started off as *his* dream but it had become *ours*.

'Of course I'm part of it. I'm living here.'

'Which would have been fine if you'd stuck with teaching, but you went and threw your career down the toilet to work on the farm despite me repeatedly telling you there wasn't a job for you. And when you finally got that into your head, you decided it would be a good idea to waste our time and money on an alpaca invasion.'

'Invasion? Seven alpacas, Grayson. *Seven.* And in a field and a barn you don't use, looked after by *me* and paid for by *me*.'

'That's not the point. The point is that it's not what I planned. I don't want them here and I...' He looked down and lowered his voice, 'and I don't want you here either. I'm sorry to be so blunt, but we're through. I thought I could get over the alpaca thing but when your family quizzed us about when we were getting married, the answer that came into my head was *never*.'

I stared at him, mouth agape, stomach churning. Had he really just said *never*?

'That was two weeks ago,' I said, my voice way too high. 'That was before I committed to the alpacas. Why didn't you talk to me about it?'

'I thought I was having a wobble because of all the arguments but yesterday was the final straw.'

'How?'

'Because your dad turned up unannounced. Because your family keeps expanding. Because I don't like being around people all the time and you do and it's not the life I want. I don't want to be taking your nephews and nieces out on my quad bike. I don't want to spend every Easter Sunday at your mum's with your entire family, or for your family to—'

I raised my hand in a stop gesture, shutting him up. It was bad enough him attacking me but I wasn't going to hear a negative word spoken against my family when all they'd ever done was be kind to Grayson.

'And I don't want to hear any more of this,' I said, my voice strong and determined. 'Have you heard yourself? I, I, I, me, me, me.' I lowered my voice to mimic him as I quoted him. '*This is* my *dream. Mine! I've been working hard for it for so long but you couldn't just let me have it. You had to be part of it.*' Fixing him with a hard stare, I reverted to my own voice. 'Yes, I did have to be part of it because I thought it was *our* dream and that *we'd* been working hard for it but apparently this is all about you. So you can have it. Have it all to yourself and I hope you'll be happy here on your own. When the winter hits and the farm is cut off, I hope your bitterness towards your parents is good company.'

I rose from the picnic bench and snatched up my mug. 'I'll pack up as much of my stuff as I can now and I'll come back later this week to get the rest and to clear my furniture out of the barn. I trust that's okay with you.'

The moment I mentioned my furniture, Rachael's words came back to me about the new bedroom furniture and the leather sofas being Grayson's taste rather than mine.

'Oh, my God! It was over for you way before any of that stuff you just mentioned. You were planning this from before we even moved in. That's why you chose that furniture. You *knew* I wouldn't be staying long term.'

The shocked expression on his face confirmed that for me and I felt sick. He'd played me. He'd got me to clean and decorate his house, help him with the two-person jobs around the farm, cook for him every evening while he settled into a routine and, all the while, he'd been planning to cut me out of his life. No wonder things had been so bad between us since we'd moved in. It was because he wanted me gone and the farm all to himself. Had he been hoping he'd push me to the point where I'd had enough and I ended it, saving him the bother?

'I guess that answers that,' I snapped. 'You absolute...' The urge to spew out a bunch of expletives and call him every derogatory name under the sun was strong, but I was better than that. If I was leaving, I was doing it with dignity and grace.

I stood a little taller and said in a calm voice, 'I'll arrange a removals van as soon as I can.'

'As long as you're not too long. And make sure you cancel the alpaca invasion.'

His voice was as cold as his eyes, giving me a scary moment of clarity. Grayson didn't love me and it was quite possible he never had. Why hadn't I noticed this before?

'Don't worry,' I said, my voice as cold as his. 'I wouldn't dream of inflicting you on those gorgeous creatures.'

It was a cheap shot but I had to say something. I added a curl of my lip and shake of my head to convey my disgust with him before turning and heading back towards the house.

I'd almost reached the door when Monty nudged against my legs. I looked down into his warm brown eyes and my heart broke. This wasn't just goodbye to Grayson. It was goodbye to Monty too and I loved that dog so much. I crouched down and wrapped my arms round his neck, breathing in his doggy smell blended with mud from the farm. Tears dripped onto his fur and I wished I could bundle him into my car and take him away but he wasn't mine.

Grayson whistled loudly and I bristled. Could he not have given me longer to say goodbye? Selfish piece of... As Monty tried to wriggle free, I kissed his fur then released him and he scampered across the yard to his master. I couldn't bring myself to raise my gaze to Grayson. I never wanted to lay my eyes on him again.

It felt cold in the kitchen and I realised I was shaking. Presumably the shock. I zipped my fleecy jacket right to the top, sank onto one of the chairs and pulled out my phone. I had to get out of here but I needed help. I pulled up Mum's number, releasing a frustrated cry when I realised she'd be at the airport. I wasn't going to drop this on her and ruin her holiday. There was only one feasible alternative and it was someone I'd never reached out to before. It didn't feel right but what choice did I have?

'Dad?' I whimpered as soon as he answered. 'Can you come to the farm? Grayson's dumped me. I need help moving my stuff.'

'Oh, Emma. I'm so sorry. Are you okay?'

'Not really. Didn't see it coming at all. Erm... is there any chance I can stay with you for a few days until I can work out what to do next?'

'You can stay for as long as you need. There's plenty of room in the house and garage to store your furniture.'

'Thanks, Dad. You're a lifesaver.'

'I'm on my way.'

After disconnecting, I sank my head into my arms on the table, tears soaking into my fleece. What was wrong with me? Why did I keep falling for emotionally unavailable men who didn't want me to be part of their dreams?

22

———

I couldn't sit there forever. I'd no doubt shed plenty more tears of pity, frustration and embarrassment over the days and weeks to come but, for now, I needed to pull myself together sufficiently to crack on with some packing before Dad arrived. I sat up and wiped my tears but, as I gazed round the kitchen, they refused to subside. I loved this room, this house, this farm and I loved Grayson but the feeling clearly wasn't mutual. How could he do this to me? How could he stand back and say nothing while I gave up my home and career for him, already knowing he didn't want me in his life? It wasn't like I'd done any of those things on a whim. We'd talked about them all first and he could have spoken up at any point.

'Not worth it,' I muttered. 'Get packed and get out of here.'

Between our two cars, Dad and I would be able to take a lot of my stuff but nothing big. The thought of coming back for the rest made me feel nauseous. I needed to get away from Grayson and never return. Was there any way I could make that happen today? There was only one person I knew who had a van.

'Hi, Emma, how's it going?' Dillon asked when he answered his phone.

'Not so good. Grayson has decided he doesn't want the alpacas at the farm so I need to cancel the work this week. I'll still pay for the materials.'

'Don't worry about that. I'll be able to use them on other projects. But why doesn't he want the alpacas there?'

'Because he doesn't want me here either. Apparently this is *his* dream and I'm messing it up so I'm moving out.'

'No way! What a knob! Are you okay?'

'I've been better. I have a huge favour to ask. Grayson said I can keep my furniture here but only for a short time and I know what he's like. He's going to pester me every day to collect it and I can't deal with that. I need to sever all ties to him. There's no way I'll be able to get a removals van quickly. I don't suppose there's any way you can move my furniture to my dad's house in Pippinthwaite today? I know it's a big ask but, as you've now got the next two days free, I was hoping—'

'Give me half an hour to rearrange a few things and I'll be over with a van, a flatbed for the bigger furniture, and a couple of the lads. We'll definitely get you moved out today.'

Feeling relieved to have that sorted, I went onto the WhatsApp group which Mum, John, Laura, Dillon, Stacie, Charlie and I all shared. I didn't want Laura to hear the news from her fiancé before she heard it from me.

TO THE FAMILY

Hi everyone. Bit of unexpected news today.
Grayson has decided that Bracken Ridge Farm
is his dream but I'm not so we've split up.
Obviously I'm shocked and upset but my focus
for now is getting out of here and trying to find
a new home for my alpacas. Dad's on his way
and Dillon's bringing some vehicles and muscle
so we can shift my belongings to Dad's. I know
you'll be concerned about me and I really
appreciate that but please don't call as I need
to crack on with the packing so I can get out of
here ASAP. I'm okay(ish) and will catch up with
you all later xx

I copied the message and pasted it into my thread with
Rachael, who immediately replied.

FROM RACHAEL

Typing this muttering expletives under my
breath. How dare he? Are you free on
Wednesday night after school? Call me if you
want to scream/talk/cry/vent in the meantime
xxxxxxxxx

Her reply made me smile and I responded to confirm that
Wednesday was fine and I'd probably survive until then but
appreciated the concern.

My final task was to ring Ruth at Butterbea Croft.

'That's low,' she said when I'd briefly explained what had
happened. 'I know you'll be hurting right now but it sounds
like a lucky escape to me.'

'It probably is,' I admitted, 'but it's too raw to feel like that
just yet. I'm so sorry about messing you about with the alpacas.'

'Don't worry about them. They can stay here as long as you
need them to. You focus on getting moved out and settled and

we can talk about the herd when you've had a chance to catch your breath.'

'Thanks for being so understanding.'

'That's what friends are for. And, just to throw in some further assurance, Lizzie and I know what it's like to have the rug pulled out from under you and the future you were expecting snatched away. It might be different circumstances but, like us, you'll be mourning for the future you should have had. You had a home and a job and now you need to rethink both. If that rethinking means that you can't take the alpacas, please don't think for a moment that you've let them or us down. If we hadn't met you, we'd have taken them ourselves so if Butterbea Croft needs to become their permanent home, so be it.'

I was so choked up with gratitude for her understanding and kindness that I only managed a whispered, 'Thank you.'

'Take care of yourself, Emma, and don't rush into anything until you're absolutely ready.'

It was a weight off my mind that she could keep The Magnificent Seven for as long as was necessary and, much as I hoped that it wouldn't be the outcome, it was a relief to know that they could stay permanently at Butterbea Croft if it came to it. I'd never have left teaching or sold Riverside Cottage if I'd had the tiniest inkling that this was on the horizon and I couldn't believe that Grayson was so heartless that he'd allowed this charade to get that far. Had I known him at all?

'Delicious and just what I needed,' I said, wiping my greasy fingers.

It was 7 p.m. and Dad had treated us to a chippy tea which we'd eaten with our fingers straight from the boxes at the breakfast bar in his kitchen. It had been an exhausting afternoon but Dillon had turned up with three of his team and, between the six of us, we'd managed to move everything. Grayson would get a shock when he finished work for the day and tried to make himself a drink because I'd taken the kettle and coffee machine. I'd also taken the toaster, microwave, pans, crockery and cutlery because they were all mine, bought before Grayson moved into Riverside Cottage. Dillon had even disconnected the washing machine – also mine – although Teresa had left the one in the external laundry so Grayson disappointingly still had a machine to use. I'd removed his pair of navy mugs from the cupboard and left them in the space where the coffee machine had been and dropped my engagement ring inside one of them.

Dad's double garage and both his spare bedrooms were now full of my furniture and belongings. Thank goodness I hadn't got around to selling or giving anything away.

'Thanks again for letting me stay,' I told Dad as I made us both a mug of tea.

'It's no problem at all. I've got the space and it'll be nice to have some company. As I said on the phone, you can stay here as long as you need.'

He gave my hand a gentle squeeze and I blinked back the tears that rushed to my eyes. That wall between us had started to crumble with Dad's revelation yesterday and it felt like another layer of bricks had been smashed away today. Hopefully some time together would smash it down completely. Silver linings.

But as I settled down in the larger of the spare bedrooms

that night, my gaze resting on a couple of suitcases and a pile of boxes, I didn't feel nearly as positive. Warm tears trickled down my cheeks and soaked into my nightdress and pillow. I'd given up everything for Grayson and he'd thrown it back in my face. What was I going to do now?

23

The day after I moved in with Dad, the heavens opened again, the dark skies and torrential rain mirroring my mood. I'd slept surprisingly well, muscles aching from lugging boxes, but I'd woken up early feeling extremely low. I wanted to stay hidden under the duvet pretending my whole world hadn't just fallen apart, but I had far too much to do.

My first task was to contact the two companies who were supplying my alpaca feed and equipment with a request to put the orders on hold due to an *unexpected change in circumstances*. I didn't think *my fiancé kicked me out* sounded very professional. Fortunately, nothing had been dispatched yet but putting the request in made me feel even lower. I wanted my alpacas. I wanted to start my business and Grayson had taken that away from me.

As I unpacked the contents of my suitcases into my new bedroom, I cast my mind back over the past weeks, months, years searching for any indication that Grayson had been about to end our relationship. Had there been signs I'd missed or perhaps had chosen to miss? Had the thrill of moving to that stunning farm and beginning an exciting new chapter together made me blind to how badly wrong things had gone? Things hadn't been great between us since moving to the farm – and I now knew why – but Grayson had clearly been planning to end things from way before then and I really hadn't seen it coming.

One side of a dress slipped off a hanger and, when I tried to hook it back on, the other side slipped off. In a fit of frustration, I screwed the dress into a ball and tossed it into the bottom of the wardrobe, sinking down the side of my bed into a heap on the floor.

'Who does that?' I cried, thumping my palms on the stripped floorboards, glad that Dad had nipped to the supermarket and couldn't hear my meltdown. 'Who uses another person like that?'

I snatched at my phone and scrolled through all the photos I had of us together. So many memories of days and nights out, weekends away, holidays. I thought we were happy. I thought it was for life. Knowing he'd been planning this from way before our move and considering his behaviour around me hadn't changed until we arrived at the farm, I had to conclude that our whole life together had been a lie. Seven and a half years! Wasted.

I tossed my phone onto the bed in disgust, convinced now that he'd only moved in with me because he had nowhere to live. Then he'd stuck around because it had benefited him – rent-free, half a share of food and bills, someone to share the chores, not to mention the emotional support I gave him as he applied for a Beatrix Potter farm tenancy.

But why ask me to marry him? That didn't make sense. Burnt by my experience with Matthew, I'd never expressed a strong desire to walk up the aisle again so why had he proposed? I slapped my head against my forehead. Of course!

How stupid was I? He'd asked me to marry him to keep me sweet, to make me believe there was a future for us and he'd protected himself from it ever happening by suggesting we make the Beatrix Potter farm tenancy the priority. In fact, he'd been even cleverer than that because I was actually the one who'd suggested we delay setting a date until after he'd secured a farm. He must have been congratulating himself on a situation well-handled.

I sank my head back against the mattress and looked up at the ceiling, trying to empty my mind. Every so often the wind redirected the heavy rain so it lashed at the window, making me jump. I've no idea how long I sat there, torturing myself for letting someone so heartless into my life and into my heart, but my backside was numb by the time Dad shouted up the stairs that he was back and would heat up some soup for lunch.

Heaving myself up, I shuffled across the landing to the bathroom and splashed some cold water onto my face before going down to see if Dad needed any help. I stirred the pan of soup while he buttered chunks of freshly baked bread.

'How are you holding up?' he asked.

'Not great,' I admitted. 'We should have been working on the barn today ready for the arrival of my alpacas on Friday. Instead, I've had to put my food and equipment orders on hold because my whole life's on hold.'

'Anything I can do to help?'

'You're already doing so much by giving me a place to stay and store my stuff. I really appreciate it. I'm not sure what I'd have done without you.'

As my voice cracked, Dad drew me into a hug. It wasn't forced or unnatural and I sank into his arms – an unfamiliar but welcome place.

'I'm not going anywhere,' he said. 'I'm here for you.'

* * *

Mid-afternoon, the rain let up and Dad suggested we take a walk around the village. Pippinthwaite was a fair bit bigger than Willowdale with a couple of housing estates on the edges, but it didn't have many more amenities. We passed a pub which Dad told me did a fantastic carvery on a Sunday, a small café, a butcher's, a hairdresser's and a playground.

'Have you heard from Grayson?' he asked.

'No, and I don't think I will now.' I'd half-expected an angry text from him when he discovered I'd removed everything except his precious mugs from the kitchen but I hadn't heard a peep out of him.

'How are you feeling about it?'

I sighed. 'Blindsided, confused, devastated, stupid.'

'Why stupid?' Dad asked.

'Because I thought he was one of the good ones.'

'If it's any consolation, I thought he was too.'

'That's what Mum said.' She'd called last night from her holiday to offer her condolences and check I was holding up okay, especially with the break-up coming so soon after the news that I had a half-brother. I'd reassured her I'd live but I might have some serious trust issues for a while.

'How's your mum doing?' he asked. 'I realise my timing wasn't great. If I'd known she was about to go on holiday...'

'I think your timing was spot on,' I said, linking my arm through his as we walked. 'It's good that she's got some time away to mull it all over. And that's not me saying that. She said it herself last night.'

'That's good to hear. Your mum's an amazing woman and I never wanted to hurt her now or back then.'

We walked in silence for a while.

'Why did things end with you and Kathryn?' I asked. 'Mum said it was your story to tell so she didn't give me any details.'

We wandered aimlessly round the village several times as Dad recounted the story of how he and Mum had been friends at school and, when they started sixth form, they became closer and he started wondering whether it could be more, so Mum had been right about him feeling the same way as her. Kathryn went to Borrowdale Heights – a private school in the area – but, as Mum had told me, she knew her through going riding.

'The minute I saw Kathryn, it was like a thunderbolt hit me,' Dad said, his voice warm. 'I'd heard people talk about that but I'd never believed it until it happened to me. We were inseparable after that. She was doing her first year of A levels, just like us, but she wasn't enjoying any of her subjects and dropped out at the end of the first year. Her dad had died a few years earlier but the estate belonged to her mum's side of the family. Her mum wanted to prepare her to take over but Kathryn was going through a rebellious phase. She didn't like being tied to the hall, didn't like the Lakes anymore, wanted to spread her wings and see the world and she wanted me to go with her. I couldn't. I didn't come from money like she did. I had a summer job lined up and the second year of sixth form to complete. Kathryn said she'd stick around until I finished my A levels and we could take a year out and travel then, which would have been a brilliant experience but there was no way I could afford it.'

He paused and sighed. 'She wouldn't take no for an answer. Kept saying she'd pay, but I couldn't let her do that. She didn't seem to understand that it wasn't just the cost of travelling that was the issue – it was the time. I needed to work every holiday to save up for university.

'Kathryn met me after my final exam and we went to the

pub. She gave me a card to congratulate me on finishing my exams and, when I opened it, there was a plane ticket inside for the first leg of our round-the-world travels. She was so excited and reiterated that it wasn't a loan and she wouldn't expect me to ever pay her back – just being together was all the payment she needed.'

I could picture the scene and how uncomfortable it must have been when she'd done something generous but really hadn't grasped why Dad had repeatedly said no.

'We had this huge argument,' Dad continued. 'It was awful. I accused her of not listening or understanding me and she threw the same accusation back in my direction. I called her spoilt and selfish. She called me boring, said she wished we'd never met and that she was fuming that I'd made her wait for a year when I'd known all along that I was never going to travel with her. Thing is, I'd been honest with her about that every step of the way so I hurled not listening back at her and we went round in circles until the landlord asked us to leave because we were disturbing the other customers. As a parting gift, Kathryn poured my pint over my head.'

We sat down on a bench overlooking the village hall.

'Next year, it'll be fifty years since that happened but I can remember every moment. I can even feel the drink trickling down my face and neck, stinging my eyes and that smell.' He shook his head. 'So that's the tale of how we met and how we split up. Kathryn took off on her travels as planned and, every couple of weeks, she sent me a postcard telling me what an amazing time she was having and all about her latest boyfriend. It hurt a lot but your mum was such an amazing friend. I don't know what I'd have done without her. She helped me pick up the pieces and that friendship I'd wondered about did become something more.'

He ran his fingers through his hair and tilted his head back, looking up at the darkening sky.

'Looks like rain's on the way again. Best head back.'

We stood up and set off back to his house.

'I did love your mum,' he said. 'But...'

'But not in the same way you loved Kathryn,' I finished for him.

He nodded. 'I tried to make it work. We both did. But she knew she didn't fully have my heart and she was right to end it. She deserved so much better. I'm so glad she found John and, in him, everything I couldn't give her.'

I linked my arm through his once more and gave him a squeeze. 'Life can be really complicated sometimes, can't it?'

'You're not wrong there.'

24

I drove into Carlisle to meet Rachael after school the following day.

'I can't believe he did that to you!' she cried, meeting me outside the city centre pub, arms outstretched. 'Are you okay?'

'Still processing it all. Let's get a drink and order food and then I'll give you the whole sorry story.'

'What a tool,' Rachael said, shaking her head after I'd brought her up to date. 'Actually, tool doesn't cut it but there are families around so I won't go any stronger. No, I will...' She muttered a string of expletives in French and Spanish. 'That's better. Urgh! This is so rubbish. He wasn't my top of my friends list but I'd never have thought him capable of this.'

'Me neither. I'd have put money on him being a decent human being but how wrong was I?'

'Makes you wonder about all that stuff with his parents. We always believed they were the bad guys but maybe it was the other way round.'

'I never thought of that but you could well be right. I liked his parents. They were warm, friendly people who were always nice to me. But if he made all that up...' I shook my head. I wasn't sure I wanted to know the full extent of his deception.

Our food arrived – a large shared tray of tapas – and we hungrily tucked in.

'I need you to promise me one thing,' Rachael said when we'd finished eating and ordered a round of coffees. 'Stop blaming yourself. I know you'll be analysing every single aspect of your life, wondering how you could miss that he's a lying, scheming arse and it's not good for you. He fooled everyone including me. I genuinely believed he loved you and his intention was to marry you and I bet your parents and sisters will say the same.'

'They all have.' I'd spoken to Laura and Stacie last night. 'I just feel so stupid.'

'He's the stupid one for not realising what a gem he had. So what happens now?'

I shrugged. 'I honestly don't know. I have no home and no job. Do I try to find somewhere to rent and do some supply teaching while I work out what the hell to do next? Do I try to find a full-time job and get back on the housing market no matter where that job takes me? Or do I stay with Dad, find a field to lease and see whether I can make a go of it with The Magnificent Seven somewhere else?'

'What does your heart want to do?'

'I still want to make a go of it with the alpacas.'

'And what does your head want?'

'The same, but my head's telling me it's a no-go zone. I know that the main attraction is being with the alpacas but I can't help thinking that the setting for the walks is just as important. The farm was ideal because it's surrounded by fells and is beautiful. I can't imagine some random field having the same pull so now I'm scratching my head trying to think of what my USP could be when I don't have the land or funds to do anything like what they offer at Haltsby Farm or Butterbea Croft. What can I offer that's unique?'

'You've already answered your own question. Your USP is your setting, so you need to find another spectacular one. I don't mean buy yourself a farm but what about seeking out a field next to a castle, at the base of a fell, next to a lake, underwater, on the moon? Okay, so the last two might be a bit tricky but do you get my point?'

I picked up my phone and pretended to tap something in as I spoke. 'Just googling fields-with-spectacular-views dot com. Oh! There's one available in Atlantis and another on Saturn. Interesting.'

'It's good to see you smiling,' she said. 'Although you can ditch the sarcasm.'

'Ditching it. And you're right. The location *does* need to be my USP. There must be somewhere available in the Lakes. It's not like there's a shortage of stunning views. Although whether it's affordable is another matter. The money from selling Riverside Cottage is now under considerable unexpected pressure – getting some land, running the business *and* getting me a new home.'

'You'll find somewhere,' she said. 'I bet it'll be even better than Bracken Ridge Farm.'

I held up crossed fingers on both hands. 'Let's hope I find it quickly cos I could really do with something going right for me.' I lowered my hands.

'And you'll find somewhere to live too but you don't have to worry about making that your priority while there's plenty of space at your dad's. Get the business side sorted and the rest will come along later or maybe even together. A farm's financially out of reach but a smallholding or a cottage with a paddock might not be.'

Rachael's confidence that it would all work out was reassuring.

'Tell you what, Rach, I'm looking forward to our birthday weekend away this year more than ever before. I've never been more ready for a holiday.'

'One month to go and I'm sure that you'll either be set up with your new venture by then or you'll be well on your way. The best is yet to come, Em. I can feel it.'

I hoped so. I hated feeling so directionless.

25

I woke up the following morning feeling a lot more positive after an evening with my best friend who never failed to lift me. Talking to her helped me realise that, not only had Grayson and I not been in a loving relationship, but we hadn't been friends either. Friends were there for each other through the good times and bad. They supported, encouraged and cared. I could place thousands of ticks in all those boxes for Rachael but none for my ex.

When I met Grayson, I'd already dealt with the baggage from my break-up with Matthew. Well, most of it. I had, after all, had eight and a half years to do it and the help of Rachael and my family. Across those early dates, when we'd shared our stories, I hadn't needed to lean on him but he'd still been hurting from his break-up with his fiancée Chrissie a year earlier so I'd helped him move on from that. We'd then had the situation with his parents selling the farm and his relationship with them falling apart which affected so many aspects of his life as well as (allegedly) knocking his confidence. I was there for him every step of the way, emotionally and financially. I'd encouraged him as he struggled with being a labourer until he found the temporary management role at Petersgill Farm and I championed him throughout his tenancy applications. I couldn't think of a single occasion where he'd been there for me in return.

Hearing Dad clattering in the kitchen, I went downstairs to join him for breakfast.

'Good morning!' I declared.

'Good morning to you too,' Dad said, handing me a mug of coffee. 'You sound brighter today.'

'I feel it. A few hours with Rachael is always good for the soul and she's helped me get something clear in my mind about my alpaca business.'

I told him what Rachael had suggested about the place I walked the alpacas being my unique selling point.

'Makes sense,' Dad said. 'And I might just know the perfect place where there's lots of land. It's by Derwent Water so you've got the lake and the fells. There isn't a castle there but there is a beautiful old manor house steeped in history so there'd be loads of stunning and varied photo opportunities for your customers.'

'It *does* sound perfect. Where is it?'

From the pause, I knew there was going to be a catch.

'Willowdale Hall,' Dad said, looking at me uncertainly.

'Oliver's home,' I said, mulling over the catch. 'But he hasn't even met me yet. We've only just found out about each other.'

'And?'

'And the first time I meet him, I can hardly say, *Hi, I'm Emma, the half-sister you didn't know existed. Can I use some of your land for my homeless herd of alpacas and can I walk all over it with them and a bunch of strangers?* How awkward would that be? You don't just meet your half-sibling for the first time and ask for a huge favour like that.'

'Why not? I hear what you're saying and, yes, it is a big ask but do you have any alternative options at the moment? If Oliver was willing, this could solve all your problems. Not only is it the perfect setting for your business but it's local and in an area you know and love. You can stay here – a short drive or bike ride away from the herd or you could even settle back in Willowdale.'

It sounded very tempting and I'd love the opportunity to live in Willowdale again with easy access to the lake for kayaking but it was a huge liberty to take.

'Should I arrange for you to meet Oliver?' Dad asked. 'I'm sure he'd be eager to help out a family member in need.'

I wanted to say yes but I shook my head. 'I *do* want to meet him but it's too cheeky to do that and throw this at him.'

'I really don't think Oliver would see it like that.'

'Possibly not, but I don't know him yet and I don't feel comfortable about it. My fiancé turned out to be a user and it hurts being on the receiving end. I want to get to know my brother but I don't want to start off our relationship taking advantage. I can't be anything like Grayson.'

'It wouldn't be like that,' Dad insisted, 'but I respect your decision and I'd never push you into anything that makes you uncomfortable. If you change your mind, let me know.'

'I will do.'

'So, what's on the agenda for today?' he asked.

'Not sure. Some trawling online to see if I can find a home for the alpacas. What about you?'

Dad glanced towards the window. 'I might go out for a bike ride while there's a break in the rain. It's forecast to start again this afternoon. I don't suppose you fancy joining me? A bit of fresh air might be good for clearing your head.'

'Where are you thinking of going?'

'Into Keswick? If you want to join me, I'll treat you to a hot chocolate and a piece of your favourite flapjack from the Derwent View Café.'

'You've convinced me! Give me half an hour to get sorted.'

* * *

Dad was right about it feeling good to be out in the fresh air, cycling through Pippinthwaite on one of his spare bikes. We left the main road and paused at the start of Cumbria Way – a walking and cycling pathway through the fields in the direction of Keswick town centre.

'Check out those puddles,' Dad said, pointing along the track. 'We'll get filthy and drenched if we do that route. How about Willowdale instead? You haven't been to The White Willow yet. They do good cakes there – all homemade – and I'm fairly certain they have flapjack.'

'Okay. That won't be much of a ride out, though.'

'We can cycle through the village towards Cat Bells and turn back when you're tired. Sound good?'

I nodded. 'Lead on.'

I took a quick look around me before we set off. The sky was grey and the rapid movement of the clouds meant the fells were illuminated one moment and bathed in shadows the next. It was mesmerising to watch. To me, every part of the Lake District was beautiful, but I probably hadn't fully appreciated quite how amazing the scenery around Keswick was with being so young when I'd lived in the area. Returning after so many years had given me a fresh perspective.

Dad was already well down the lane and had stopped, presumably wondering what was keeping me. I waved at him and set off. We cycled alongside the River Derwent, crossing over the metal bridge and through the outskirts of Willowdale. I'd had no reason to visit the village since moving to Ambleside when I was eleven so it was quite a trip down Memory Lane. The houses looked familiar – some slate, some whitewashed and others a mixture of both – but I noticed many had small key safes by the door, indicating that they were holiday rentals rather than private homes. What had once been a large hotel had become self-catering holiday apartments.

We approached a junction onto the main road through the village and I called to Dad to stop so I could take it in. There was a bench by a bus stop so we wheeled our bikes over to it and sat down. On the corner opposite was the village green.

'That willow tree has certainly grown,' I said. I remembered it being large from childhood but nothing like this. There was a wooden bench in front of it, a post box, and several planters bursting with flowers. It looked like a lovely place to sit.

'That's where we'll go for cake,' Dad said, pointing out The White Willow beyond the village green. I imagined that the terrace area with metal chairs and tables would be very popular on sunny days, giving customers a lovely view across the road to the lake.

'It's strange being back after so long,' I said. 'It's hard to tell what's really changed and what I've forgotten over time.'

We set off once more, cycling past The White Willow on the right, the marina on the left and houses either side, these ones mainly detached and individually designed. The houses became sporadic, replaced by woodland and we soon reached the edge of Willowdale Hall's grounds. I followed Dad past the riding stables entrance but he stopped a little later as we reached the main gate and dismounted.

I looked at him warily. 'Don't tell me you've arranged to meet Oliver.'

'I wouldn't spring that on you and he'll be at work anyway. I just thought there was no harm peeking through the gate while we're passing.'

I dismounted too to humour him. The wrought-iron gates were quite beautiful with interwoven flowers and vines and, although I could see a fair way down the drive, there was no sign of the house from here. The drive was flanked by trees and the gentle rustle of the leaves accompanied by birdsong was extremely calming.

'How does it feel being here?' I asked Dad, wondering if the estate brought back difficult memories for him.

'I never went to the house. There was too much of a risk of someone seeing us and Hubert finding out, although we did sometimes meet at the stables.'

'Do you still miss her?' I asked after a while.

'It's hard to say. Other than those eighteen months in our teens, we never had a proper relationship again. It was all stolen moments and dishonesty which never sat well with either of us but it was the way it had to be. I do miss her but, just as much, I miss the possibility of the life we could have had.'

Even though I hadn't known the story behind their split until now, I'd always believed that Mum was the one who'd been hurt the most and I'd never stopped to consider how much Dad had missed out on. It was clear now that he'd missed the chance to be part of a family, perhaps to have other children, to have someone with whom to grow old. Although he'd frequently told me how pleased he was that Mum had found happiness with John and had Stacie and Laura, that also had to have hurt. He loved children but he hadn't been able to be a regular hands-on dad to either of his because I'd pushed him away and Oliver hadn't known who he was.

The sound of dogs barking drew our attention away from the gate and an excitable cocker spaniel with a beautiful reddish-gold coat bounded up to us followed by a much larger red dog whose breed I didn't recognise.

'Toffee! Chester!' a woman called as she approached us. The dogs obediently returned to her and she clipped them onto leads.

'They're gorgeous,' I said, as she drew closer. 'What's the bigger one?'

'He's a Hungarian Vizsla. Handsome lad, isn't he? He's soft as anything – they both are.'

I crouched down to stroke each of them.

'Were you calling at the hall?' she asked.

'Just being nosy,' I admitted. 'I used to—'

But I didn't get to finish the sentence as the woman exclaimed, 'Mr Wynterson? Oh, my God! It *is* you.'

'Rosie Jacobs? You haven't changed!'

I stiffened at the moniker I'd heard so recently. Rosie? That was the name of Oliver's girlfriend. I glanced up at Dad, eyes wide. Had he engineered this?

26

'Rosie, this is my daughter Emma,' Dad said. 'Emma, this is Oliver's girlfriend Rosie and I promise you I didn't plan this.'

He'd evidently read my mind!

'Lovely to meet you,' Rosie said, smiling warmly at me, revealing cute dimples. 'You know about Oliver, then?'

'Dad told me on Sunday. Bit unexpected.'

'I hear you. For us too. Oliver would love to meet you but only as and when you're ready. We do appreciate it's a lot to take in.'

'I want to meet him too,' I assured her. 'It's just that I've had a horrendous start to the week and my head's all over the place.' I realised what I'd just said and grimaced. 'That sounds awful. Just to be clear, the horrendous start to the week was *not* the news about Oliver.'

'I'm sorry it's been a tough one,' she said, her voice and expression sympathetic. 'Would a cuppa and some homemade shortbread help? My mam's been baking this morning and her shortbread is melt-in-the-mouth delicious.'

I glanced at Dad and he shrugged. 'Fine by me but completely up to you, Emma.'

I looked back at Rosie. She seemed really nice and it would be rude to blank her. Dad had said the decision was mine but I knew he'd be keen to catch up with her after so many years, so I nodded. 'That sounds great.'

Rosie tapped a code into the keypad by the gates and they opened with a creak.

'Every time I open these gates, I make a mental note that they need oiling and then it goes straight out of my head,' she said.

We followed her through the gates, pushing our bikes as the dogs ran on ahead.

'Welcome to Willowdale Hall,' Rosie declared. 'Have you been here before, Emma?'

'Never. I lived in Willowdale until I was eleven but I only ever walked past the estate.'

'In that case, we'll take the long route round via the big house.' She laughed lightly. 'Mam and I live in a small cottage in the grounds and we've always referred to it as *the big house*. Even though I spend half the week living in it now, I still can't break the habit.'

I liked Rosie instantly and couldn't imagine anyone meeting her and not warming to her. If Dad hadn't already told me she was the same age as Oliver, I'd have put her at thirty, possibly even a couple of years younger. She was fresh-faced with long dark hair worn in a fishtail plait and dark eyes which sparkled when she spoke.

Toffee and Chester chased each other along the gravel driveway and past a sizeable slate cottage which looked like it had seen better days.

'That's the former gatehouse,' Rosie said. 'Needs a fair bit of

TLC, as you can see. Hubert Cranleigh completely let it go – a theme throughout the estate – which is a huge shame.'

She suggested we leave our bikes in the gatehouse garden, assuring us that nobody could get onto the premises without her letting them in through the gate.

'We've got big plans for bringing this place back to life,' she said as we set off again.

We turned a corner and the mansion came into view.

'It was built in the late nineteenth century,' Rosie said. 'It has three storeys and more rooms than we know what to do with so the plans include turning part of the hall into holiday accommodation, although we haven't commissioned an architect yet. Oliver moved out when he was eighteen so we need time to live in it and find out what works for us before we rush into any major changes.'

Like the gatehouse, the hall was made from local slate, but sandy-coloured stone features and window surrounds softened what could have been an imposing building.

'I love old buildings,' I said. 'It's stunning.'

'We think so. I'd take you inside but I don't have the keys on me.'

Rosie led us down a track through some trees, telling us it would take us to Horseshoe Cottage where she said she'd lived all her life with her mum, Alice.

'Has the end of your week been better than the start?' Rosie asked me.

'Each day's an improvement.' Rosie was so warm and friendly and I didn't want to appear aloof by avoiding the subject. She might as well know. 'My lousy start was that my fiancé told me he didn't want to be with me anymore which meant I also lost my home and job. On a positive note, it can only go up from there.'

'Aw, that's awful,' Rosie said. 'I'm so sorry. One of those things would be bad enough but all three together is a lot to cope with.'

'It is, which is why I haven't made arrangements to meet Oliver yet.'

'Oh, gosh, no! Completely understand that. No pressure from us.'

We walked a little further.

'So did you work with your fiancé?' Rosie asked. 'Sorry. Just say if you'd rather not talk about it.'

'No, it's fine. I taught science and biology, like Dad, and Grayson's a farmer. He secured a tenancy on one of Beatrix Potter's farms and I left teaching to run it with him. Not the best decision I've ever made.'

'That sucks. What will you do now?'

'Not sure. Lots of thinking to do.'

'Emma!' Dad said, giving me a gentle nudge in the ribs.

'Ssh!'

'Ask her!' he murmured.

Rosie stopped and glanced from Dad to me and back again, looking amused. 'What's going on?'

I rolled my eyes, knowing there was no way I could dismiss it as nothing. I didn't have a problem opening up to Rosie about my horrendous week but I still didn't feel comfortable asking about land when I hadn't even met Oliver.

'I was going to run a business from the farm and now I can't,' I said.

'Tell her about the alpacas,' Dad prompted.

'Dad!'

'What alpacas?' Rosie asked.

I couldn't avoid it. 'It was going to be an alpaca walking business. I helped some friends rescue a herd of alpacas recently and they were due at the farm tomorrow. Fortunately my friends can keep them but...' I shrugged as I tailed off. What more was there to say?

'I thought there might be some space to keep them here,' Dad piped up. 'It would be a stunning place to walk them.'

I shook my head at him. 'And I told Dad that I was *not* about to meet my brother for the first time and immediately ask for a huge favour like that.'

Rosie looked thoughtful. 'I've not come across alpaca walking before. Do you mind telling me more?'

'Alpacas are gorgeous. They're friendly, gentle, docile but they also have these amazing individual personalities.' I felt my spirits lifting as I spoke about them. 'We rescued a herd of seven females and the plan – once they were settled in and ready – was to offer ninety-minute sessions for small groups. I'd give them a safety briefing, introduce them to the alpacas and we'd go for a walk round the farm, stopping for various photo ops and snippets of information from me about alpacas and caring for them. They'd be able to stroke them and take selfies and generally just enjoy being around my favourite animal.'

'Aw, that sounds amazing. I'd love to do something like that.'

'Everyone I've mentioned it to has said the same so I'm sure it'd be popular. I'd imagine some customers would come just because they love animals and it's something a bit different to do, but I think others would come because they need to get away from their day-to-day life and their problems. Because alpacas are so gentle, you can switch off from all your troubles and just be in the moment with them. But I have nowhere for anyone to do that. It's not just about finding a field, it's about finding a backdrop so that everything combines to make the walk really special, almost magical.'

'Which is why I suggested here,' Dad said, clearly determined to get Rosie's approval. 'There's no better backdrop than this – lake, fells, hall.'

Rosie's smile was wide. 'I completely agree. Obviously, I'd need to talk it over with Oliver but I think he'll love the idea as much as I do.'

'Oh, Rosie, I don't expect you to—'

'I know you don't, but we've got a really strong vision for the estate and, from what you've just described, alpaca walks would one hundred per cent fit with that.'

'You're not just saying that?'

'Absolutely not! The house is enormous and the estate is huge but who needs to live like that these days? The holiday accommodation is the starting point. That needs a big outlay but will soon earn a good income to invest back into the rest of the estate. We want to build a café to attract day visitors and we'll be developing the gardens and creating woodland trails. The overall vision is to create a place where people come to relax and find their happy. During the First World War and for several years afterwards, the big house was used as a place of convalescence for officers who'd been wounded serving their country. We've got old letters from patients who directly attribute their healing to the surroundings. Isn't that amazing? During World War II, it was used as a boarding school for evacuees from Tyneside and, again, we've got thank you letters and know of children who were so captivated by the place that they later settled in the area with their own families. We want to draw on that legacy of providing a safe space to heal and to escape and make Willowdale Hall a place for happiness, healing and wellness.'

'That's a lovely vision,' I said. 'There's so much scope.'

'That's what we thought. We've already got the riding stables and I'm exploring what we can do beyond regular riding lessons like using horses for therapy. So, as you can tell, alpaca walks would fit brilliantly with that vision. It'd be sooner than we might have liked but sometimes opportunities present themselves which are too good to turn away. I can even think of the perfect enclosure for them. I'll show you it on our way out.'

We'd reached the end of the track and stepped out onto a lane where Rosie pointed out Horseshoe Cottage, a pretty ivy-clad slate cottage surrounded by trees.

'Mam loves animals,' Rosie said as she led us up the drive-way. 'Have you got any photos of your alpacas?'

'Stacks of them. And videos. You really mean it about running the business here?' I was still reeling from what she'd just said.

'Definitely. We'd never have thought about it ourselves but now it doesn't seem right not to have it. What you said about customers just being with them and it feeling like an almost magical experience is so aligned to everything we want to do.'

She opened the door and the two dogs pushed past her.

'Mam!' she called. 'We've got a couple of visitors.'

A slender woman with long dark hair appeared, wiping her hands on a tea towel.

'This is my mam, Alice,' Rosie said, not that introductions were needed. The family resemblance was unmistakeable. Alice was basically an older and slightly shorter version of Rosie.

'Mam, this is Oliver's dad, Mr Wynterson.'

'Christian,' Dad said. 'I recognise you from parents' evenings when I taught Rosie.'

'I recognise you too, although it's been a long time.' Although Alice was smiling, I couldn't help noticing her wringing the tea towel and wondered whether unexpected visitors made her anxious.

'And this is his daughter, Emma,' Rosie finished. 'Oliver's half-sister.'

'Hi, Emma. Lovely to meet you.'

'I spotted them outside the gates and invited them back for a cuppa. Is that all right, Mam?'

'That's fine, love. You've timed it perfectly for homemade shortbread.'

We sat round a large wooden table tucking into buttery, crumbly shortbread and talking about my alpacas. As Rosie had predicted, Alice loved the idea and agreed that the walks would perfectly align with Oliver and Rosie's vision for a happy place promoting wellness.

'They are so gorgeous,' Alice said as she and Rosie scrolled through my phone, cooing over the photos of The Magnificent Seven. 'Tell you what, I could have done with a few relaxing alpaca walks over the years.'

'Mam hasn't been well,' Rosie explained. 'But you're doing so much better now, aren't you?'

Alice placed her hand over Rosie's. 'Thanks to you, Oliver and Xander.'

'Xander's my dad,' Rosie explained.

When Alice removed her hand, she nodded towards the plate. 'Help yourselves to more shortbread.'

I didn't need to be asked again. 'This is so delicious, Alice.'

'Oliver's mam, Kathryn, taught me everything I know about baking. This is her recipe.'

'Did you know Kathryn well?' I asked.

'I thought I did. I thought we were friends but, over the years, I've realised we were more like acquaintances. She was lovely to me and we spent a lot of time together baking and riding, but she never let me in. I didn't know about you, Christian, and I had no idea that things were as bad with Hubert as they were. They both put on a good front.'

'She wanted to tell you about us,' Dad said, 'but we agreed to keep it our secret. The more people who knew, the more likely it was that Hubert would find out. She thought the world of you, Alice, and she loved it when you baked together. She'd be so happy knowing you're still using her recipes. They were passed down from her great-grandmother although Kathryn had put her own spin on most of them.'

As Dad spoke about Kathryn his face lit up and it struck me again how much he'd clearly loved her. A part of me had feared he'd never dated after Mum because I'd made things so hard for him after they separated and it was a relief to discover that wasn't the case at all and there had been someone he loved, even if they hadn't been able to properly be together. I could finally let go of that guilt.

Rosie told us she'd need to get back to the stables soon to prepare for an adult beginners' class this afternoon so, if we wanted to see the field she had in mind for The Magnificent Seven, we'd need to do that now.

'You're both welcome back any time,' Alice said. 'And, Christian, if you ever want to spend some time reminiscing about Kathryn, I'm here.'

I could see from the sparkle in his eyes that the offer had really touched Dad. 'I'd love that,' he said. 'Let's swap numbers.'

'It would be amazing if you and Mam did get together to talk about Kathryn,' Rosie said to Dad as we set off back across the estate without the dogs. 'What you said about Kathryn thinking the world of her will have been music to her ears. She genuinely did think they were close until my best friend Autumn moved here last spring and she saw what really close friends are like together. After that, she was worried she'd perhaps failed Kathryn in some way.'

'It'll be good to chat to someone who knew Kathryn,' Dad said. 'And I can give her plenty of reassurance that she never let Kathryn down. Completely the opposite.'

Rosie gave him a grateful smile. 'Thank you. If you do meet up, can I suggest that it's here or The White Willow? She doesn't venture far. It's connected to how poorly she was but, as I said, she's getting a lot better.'

She turned to me and clapped her hands together. 'Let's talk alpacas. The field is near the entrance so I'll show you that last. I know nothing about alpacas but if they're anything like my horses, they'll appreciate the opportunity to stand in the water at the edge of the lake so I'm thinking you could do a circular route from their enclosure, past the big house, through the gardens, down to the lake for a mid-point rest, round the back of the house and return to the start. I'll quickly show you the beach that'll probably be best.'

We followed her along a pathway through the woods with the hall on our right.

'Most of the estate has been left to grow wild and while that's a good thing in some respects – wildflowers, wildlife and so on – it's not great overall. It should have been much better managed. Hubert used to employ a gardening contractor each spring but he didn't take anyone on to do it last year and, this year, there was a massive question mark over the future of the estate so another spring has passed us by. Xander recommended Killian Buchanan, who is phenomenal and totally aligned to what we want to do here. He's a gardener, a tree surgeon, and also really useful with wood so he's going to do a load of repairs on our boundary fences. If you do want to set up your business here, and if Oliver approves, we can get Killian to work on the enclosure as a priority. He'd work to your exact spec and he'll probably have a million other genius ideas. He's such a quick thinker.'

The track continued through woodland but suddenly Rosie stepped aside, giving me a clear view ahead of a grey pebbly beach and Derwent Water.

'Wow!' I said, turning in a slow circle, taking in the 360-degree spectacular views of the lake surrounded by fells, the islands, the estate grounds and Willowdale Hall itself.

'What happened to the jetty?' Dad asked, pointing to a wooden jetty which was in a sorry state with slats missing and a big twist in the middle where some of the supports into the water were sticking out in peculiar directions.

'Big storm years ago. Looks amazing, doesn't it? I have no idea how it didn't smash to pieces. I love it like that but, if we're going to let the public into the grounds, we'll need Killian to repair it.'

I could just imagine the jetty in the background of alpaca photos, adding an element of peculiarity to the lakeside scene, but I could understand the health and safety implications of such an unsafe structure.

'Would it be a good stop-off?' Rosie asked.

'It's perfect. I can picture my alpacas here, standing in the lake or even lying down in it.'

I'd have happily stayed on the beach for ages, drinking in the views and absorbing the serenity of such a beautiful place, but I was conscious Rosie had said she needed to prepare for some riding lessons so I suggested we head off. As we made our way back through the woods and past the house, Rosie asked me about the rescue circumstances.

'Sounds like it was fortunate timing before neglect set in,' she said after I'd told her the story. 'Makes me all the more eager to give them a home here. And, speaking of home, we're nearly there.'

Opposite the gatehouse, we veered off to the left along a track which, with the hedges trimmed back, would be wide enough for a vehicle. We rounded a corner and came to a wooden five-bar gate.

'Ta-dah!' Rosie declared, unlatching the gate.

We entered a paddock enclosed by trees with a group of three large beeches towards the middle which would provide plenty of shade for the alpacas as well as somewhere for dust baths. They liked to rub at the bark to create dust in which they'd roll around.

'It was the paddock for the riding stables for years until his Lordship – sorry, I mean Hubert Cranleigh – did a major refurbishment of the stables including creating a new paddock. I've been renting it out to a riding customer who had a couple of Shetland ponies but she sold them in May and I decided not to re-advertise until we were clear what our plans were for the estate. What do you reckon, Emma? Would this suit The Magnificent Seven?'

'Honestly, Rosie, it would be perfect but...'

'I get it. You don't want to get your hopes up in case Oliver says no, but I'm sure he won't. I won't actually see him tonight. I go to the quiz at The Hardy Herdwick and Oliver plays squash so he stays over at his place near Penrith, but I'll give him a call when we've both finished work.'

As I gazed round the paddock, a lump lodged itself in my throat and tears pricked my eyes. The field itself was no more or less suitable than the one at Bracken Ridge Farm but it was the setting that made the difference. The farm was beautiful but the estate was incredible, spectacular, special, awe-inspiring... so many adjectives. I could already picture the social media posts and the gorgeous photos for customers with the variety of backdrops. Rachael had definitely been right about the land being the USP and Willowdale Hall had that in spades and, even more important, there was something magical about this place. Yes, it had been neglected and was in a sorry state in parts, but it oozed potential. I loved Rosie and Oliver's vision and my head was buzzing with how I could promote the health benefits of switching off and being at one with the alpacas and nature.

'We'd better let you get ready for your lessons,' Dad said to Rosie, 'but it's been great to see you again after all these years.'

'You too, and it was so lovely to meet you, Emma. Welcome to the family, both of you.'

She briefly hugged me and then Dad, setting off a swirl of emotions inside me. I loved being part of a big family and it was growing again. I'd lost a fiancé but I'd gained a brother, his girlfriend and her parents. It wasn't a bad trade at all.

27

Dad and I were relaxing in front of the television early that evening when a call came through from Rosie. I stepped into the kitchen so I wouldn't disturb Dad.

'I can't talk for long as I'm nearly at the pub but I've just spoken to Oliver and he's all over the alpaca idea. He agrees that it's a perfect fit with what we're doing here and we both can't wait to go on our first alpaca walk.'

My heart soared. 'You've just made my day. That's brilliant news. Thank you both so much.'

'It's a pleasure. Killian's around in the morning but he's got the afternoon off so do you want to meet us both at the field at ten to go through what you'd need from him? The sooner we can get the work done, the sooner you can be reunited with The Magnificent Seven and the sooner I can stroke my first alpaca.'

'No plans for the morning so that all sounds great. I can't thank you and Oliver enough for doing this for me.'

'We're both really excited about it.'

She rattled off the code for the gate and told me I was

welcome to arrive earlier to explore fully and make an assessment as to what I might need before I met with her and Killian.

'Good luck in the quiz,' I said.

'We need it! We have the occasional moment of glory but, typically, we're second from last every week.'

When the call ended, I released an excited squeal. Finally something was going my way. Everything happened for a reason and, as far as my alpaca adventure was concerned, Grayson refusing to have an *alpaca invasion* on *his* farm was looking like it could be the best thing for the business. Willowdale Hall presented a more beautiful and inspiring walk, it was in a more accessible location, and the plans that Oliver and Rosie had to develop the estate should create a symbiotic relationship. Guests in their luxury holiday accommodation spotting alpacas being walked round the grounds would hopefully be interested in booking a walk themselves and any holidaymakers discovering the hall through my alpaca walks might consider the accommodation for future visits to the area.

I felt so lifted that I had a solution for The Magnificent Seven – a better one than I could ever have dreamed of and one that would happen quickly. Much as I wanted to let Ruth and Lizzie know the great news, I decided to be practical and hold off for now in case a closer inspection revealed any problems with the paddock. I also needed to understand what sort of timescale Killian could work towards as I'd hate to suggest a couple of weeks to the sisters only to find that Killian needed double or triple that.

Sadly, one aspect of my life being back on track didn't automatically make everything else better. I'd been struggling all week to come to terms with what Grayson had done. Despite the encouraging phone calls from Mum, Stacie and Laura, my meal with Rachael and the outpouring of love and support from them and the rest of my family, I couldn't seem to stop my emotions bouncing around all over the place. One minute I'd be so overwhelmed with hurt that I could barely breathe, the next I'd be shaking with anger and feeling like such an idiot. No matter what Rachael and my family said about Grayson fooling them too, it didn't bring me much comfort. They'd seen him intermittently for short bursts of time but I'd lived with him. We'd been out on dates, spent holidays together, talked for hours, shared a million kisses, made love, made plans for the future and never once had I had even the teeniest tiniest inkling that, for him, it was all fake. Which all left three big questions which repeatedly haunted me. Why had I spent over seven and a half years with a man who'd pretended to love me? How could I have been fooled twice? How hadn't I learned after what happened with Matthew?

Standing by the kitchen window, looking out over Dad's back garden, I could feel myself spiralling again, so I summarised today's incredible news in a WhatsApp message to Rachael, knowing that any response from her would lift me.

FROM RACHAEL

> YAAAAAAYYYYYYY!!!!!! This sounds perfect.
> Send me some pics tomorrow if you can.
> Brilliant news x

She accompanied her message with several GIFs of llamas and alpacas, making me smile. Moments later, another message appeared.

FROM RACHAEL

> I hope you're celebrating the beginning of an
> exciting new adventure and not mourning for
> what you had before. Focus on this and not
> him. Never him. He really isn't worth it x

He definitely wasn't worth it. The start of this week had been horrendous but things had turned around very quickly and I did need to celebrate those wins. Fingers crossed they kept going on an onwards trajectory. As Rachael had said in the pub the other night, the best was yet to come and, with the prospect of a beautiful new home for my herd, it felt like that might be true.

28

I was up early on Friday morning, eager to get to Willowdale Hall and explore The Magnificent Seven's new home more thoroughly and, if Rosie didn't mind, walk the circular route she'd suggested so I could start thinking about how to describe the experience on my website.

Rosie messaged me while I was eating breakfast.

FROM ROSIE

Just spoken to Killian and he's asked if we can push the meeting back to 11. Would that still work for you?

Dad and I had planned a picnic lunch and walk round Buttermere. It was only half an hour's drive south-west of Pippinthwaite so that still gave us plenty of time.

TO ROSIE

That's fine by me. How did the quiz go?

FROM ROSIE

Usual position – second from last!

She'd added several laughing out loud emojis.

TO ROSIE

Better than being last! Would you mind if I do the walk you mentioned before our meeting? I can remember the route

FROM ROSIE

Explore as much as you'd like! See you at 11

'I'll make the picnic while you're out,' Dad said after I told him about the slight change of timing. 'We can set off as soon as you're back. Assuming you're still okay for our walk?'

'Definitely. I'm looking forward to it.' I downed the last of my coffee. 'Thanks again for making yesterday happen. You knew it would be too muddy on Cumbria Way, didn't you?'

'Me? I have no idea what you could possibly be suggesting!'

I laughed at his feigned innocence. 'Yeah, right.'

'Okay, you've got me. I thought if you could just see the estate, you wouldn't be able to resist the temptation because it's perfect for what you want. But I genuinely had nothing to do with Rosie being there and inviting us in. That was serendipity.'

Serendipity? I loved that idea. It had a magical quality about it, just like Willowdale Hall.

Breakfast finished, I packed a notebook and pen in my bag and drove to Willowdale Hall. I parked by the track to the paddock, kicked off my trainers and slipped my feet into my sheep wellies. A wave of sadness passed through me as I thought about the moment I'd bought them, full of excitement about the new chapter Grayson and I had ahead of us at Bracken Ridge Farm.

I missed the farm and I missed Monty so much that it hurt. I missed Grayson too, which infuriated me because he didn't deserve for me to feel that way after what he'd done. I wished it had been as easy for me to walk away as it clearly had been for him but it felt like there was a massive void in my life, having lost my home, job, dog, partner and the future we had planned all at the same time. Even though I was excited by the alternative future unfolding in front of me, I couldn't shift the feeling of loss. And it wasn't just because of Grayson. This break-up had stirred up so many memories of my split from Matthew and I really didn't want to venture down that road again.

I closed my boot with a thud, trapping my pain inside. Today was a good day and the start of a new chapter and I wasn't going to let thoughts of Grayson or Matthew blight it in any way. Looking around me, I breathed in deeply a few times and stood still for several minutes listening to the birds chirping overhead. It was wonderful being back at the estate. What must it have been like for Rosie and Oliver growing up here with such enormous grounds to explore? Would it have been exciting or could it have been lonely, separated from the village and hidden from passers-by? I looked forward to finding out more as I got to know my brother and his girlfriend.

Once I'd finished the walk, pausing at regular intervals to scribble notes and take photos, some of which I sent to Rachael, I returned to the paddock and added a note about cutting the hedges back.

The grass on either side of the gate had been worn away but, despite all the recent rain, wasn't particularly muddy, although that was probably down to lack of use recently. With alpacas and customers traipsing in and out, there was potential for it to become messy so I'd seek Killian's opinion as to whether it would be better to have an area that was hard-standing.

I set off in a clockwise direction round the paddock, pausing every so often to take photos and make further notes.

Alpacas needed the same sort of perimeter fencing as sheep. Four foot was sufficient height to contain them – they wouldn't attempt to jump over that – and it could be made in a few different ways. The field already had standard stock fencing of wire between wooden posts and it was mainly in good condition. If my herd had been llamas instead, I'd have needed double that height as the alpaca's larger relatives were curious creatures who were prone to jumping over fences, especially the males.

Once I'd completed my perimeter check and noted down five sections which needed attention, I zig-zagged across the paddock from top to bottom, searching for any nasties in the ground, but there was nothing that gave me any cause for concern. The grass was lush, just as I'd have expected if Rosie had been using it for those Shetland ponies. Although not a priority for now, I'd have to ask Rosie about a second field. Once a year, I'd need to move the alpacas and rest the paddock for three months, allowing the grass to grow and all the parasites to die off. If the Shetland ponies had moved on in May, it had fortunately already had that rest this year.

I was finished with about ten minutes to spare so I clambered onto the gate but, as soon I was settled, it struck me that the last time I'd sat on the top of a gate like this had been at Bracken Ridge Farm when my life had been very different. I wanted to be at my bubbly best when Killian appeared – not feeling melancholy – so I climbed back down. Rosie had told me that Killian would be able to drop everything he was currently working on to meet my needs but that didn't mean he'd be pleased about it. He'd have a project plan for works around the estate and having my alpacas unexpectedly becoming top priority was going to knock it all out so a strong first impression was positive.

Before long, I heard voices along the track and turned expectantly. Rosie appeared walking beside an extremely tall, broad man. I was five foot nine and Rosie was the same height as me but Killian towered over her. I reckoned maybe six foot six. Everything about him appeared to be plus-size from the grey T-shirt straining across his pecs and impressive biceps to his thick dark hair tied back in a messy man-bun, from the tattoos covering every exposed inch of his arms to the pair of enormous hands which encased one of mine when he shook it after Rosie introduced us.

He glanced at the time on his phone before shoving it in the back pocket of his jeans. 'I've got fifteen minutes absolute max. What do you need from me?'

His voice was deep, velvety and extremely engaging, but I didn't feel engaged. I felt extremely nervous. It wasn't his physical presence giving me butterflies – I knew from all my years in teaching never to judge a person by their appearance. It was the lack of smile and the intensity in his eyes that intimidated me along with the immediate declaration of limited time. Dropping everything for me evidently had inconvenienced him, just as I feared, although it was a bit harsh him limiting the discussion when he was the one who'd pushed our meeting back an hour. Thank goodness Rosie was here, smiling encouragingly at me.

'I, erm, I was thinking...' I flicked through my notebook but couldn't seem to focus on anything I'd written. All I could think about was how daunted I was by the prospect of working together, although that was likely a hang-up from the bad experience of working with Grayson. *Pull yourself together, Emma! You don't need your notes. You know what needs doing.* I straightened up and closed the book.

'The fencing that's up is ideal for alpacas but there are five places where it's damaged, including two where the posts have come down, so I'll need those repairing. Do you want me to show you them?'

He shook his head. 'I'll do a walk-around on Monday.'

'Okay. The hedges along the track are really overgrown and it would help if I could drive a vehicle down so that—'

'Agreed. I can soon cut those back. What else?'

'Erm...' I ran my fingers through my hair, feeling flustered. Killian's tone wasn't impatient, but the words and the interruption conveyed urgency. 'The main work will be in this entrance area. This is where I'll bring customers to meet the alpacas, give them a safety briefing and show them how to hold the lead but it'll also be the place they get fed.'

'They don't eat the grass?' Killian asked, looking surprised.

'They do – and they can munch away on that as much as they like – but they'll also eat hay and special supplements. The supplements need to be controlled to ensure they all get what they need and that there isn't one alpaca who scoffs the lot. I want to enclose this section of the paddock with more fencing and another gate.'

'How big an area?'

'About fifty or sixty foot squared. It needs to house a wooden shelter – twenty-four by eight foot – for feeding and sleeping, although they won't always...' I stopped myself. If Killian was in a rush, he really didn't need me wittering on about their sleeping habits. 'I also want to create a holding pen between the paddock and this part.'

I ran through a few more details while Killian kept his eyes fixed on mine, nodding solemnly. I wished he'd take notes. It always threw me when waiting staff didn't write orders down but perhaps they and Killian had much better memories than me.

'I'd also welcome your thoughts on the immediate entrance into the field.' I explained my concerns about it getting too churned up – messy for my herd and customers. 'I don't know whether we need to create a solid surface.'

He studied the area around him and stamped on the ground in a few places. 'A few different options spring to mind.'

But he obviously wasn't going to share them with me. He ran his hand across his beard, looking thoughtful as he scanned around him once more.

'Anything else?' he asked, returning his gaze to me.

'I've got water and feeding troughs on order which will need installing in this area. I noticed there's already one in the paddock but—'

'It's definitely on its last legs,' Rosie said. 'Best to replace it. Killian, could you look into whether we can keep a constant water supply going to both troughs? That would be better than worrying about manually keeping them topped up on a hot day.'

'Yep, I can look into that. If that's all...?'

If something else had sprung to mind, I'm not sure I'd have shared it. It was obvious to me that Killian Buchanan had better things to do. Hopefully the work would be straightforward with limited further discussion required and it would also be quick.

'I'll see you on Monday, Killian,' Rosie said. 'I hope the weekend goes well.'

'Thanks.' He turned to me. 'I'll have a proposal for you by Wednesday at the latest.'

'Okay. Thank you.'

He left and Rosie gave me one of her huge smiles. 'Isn't he fabulous?'

Not from what I'd seen but I smiled politely, not knowing

Rosie well enough to say anything against someone who could, for all I knew, be one of her best friends.

'I've got a few things I need to crack on with at the stables but Mam's around if you want a cuppa before you head off, or you're welcome to stay in the paddock for longer.'

'Thanks, but I need to shoot off,' I said. 'Dad's making a picnic and we're going for a walk round Buttermere.'

'Ooh, lovely. I haven't been there for ages.'

'Me neither. As a kid, it was a family favourite because of the tunnel. I'd walk through with my sisters making these deep villainous laughter noises – *mwah ha ha ha* – seeing who could create the loudest and longest echo.'

'It has to be done,' Rosie agreed, laughing. 'You have sisters?'

'Yes, but they're on my mum's side. She remarried four years after splitting up from Dad.'

'I see! Aw, I was getting excited about more family to meet.'

The disappointment in her tone was touching. 'They might not be related to Oliver but they're lovely and they'll definitely want to meet you all and treat you like family.'

'I've always wanted to be part of a big family,' she said after I'd given her an overview of names and ages. 'And thanks to Kathryn's diaries revealing your dad's identity, I've got my wish.'

'I completely agree,' I said.

I felt very blessed to have so many new extended family members but a little voice at the back of my head whispered *Just a shame you didn't add to the numbers yourself.* Every time I thought I'd made peace with it, the disappointment and regret gave me a little nudge.

29

Dad and I arrived at Buttermere at half twelve. There were stacks of walks starting from the car park, appealing to all levels of ability and ambition. Those wanting a long low-level walk could go round Buttermere and Crummock Water. The two lakes had once been the same body of water but were now separated by lush meadows. More ambitious hikers could head into the surrounding fells and enjoy stunning views looking down over the two lakes. Dad and I were sticking to Buttermere – a fairly easy four-and-a-half-mile circuit with only a few gentle inclines.

We set off anti-clockwise, crossing the wooden footbridge over the beautifully named Buttermere Dubs – a small river connecting Buttermere with Crummock Water – and the less sweetly named but more impressive Sourmilk Gill – a stream which tumbled down from the hillside. Our initial conversation was fairly standard – observations about the weather, the beautiful surroundings, and the people around us – before moving on to reminiscing about previous visits.

'You mentioned being here with your mum and John, but

can you remember your mum and me bringing you?' Dad asked as we travelled along the pathway through Burtness Wood. 'You'd have been six at the time.'

'I don't think so.'

'You had this soft toy alpaca called Fraggle that I'd bought you for Christmas when you were a toddler. Your mum hadn't wanted me to get it because it was really big but I insisted, thinking you'd love it. You didn't. You barely looked at Fraggle for years but, when you were six, you became obsessed with him and insisted on taking him everywhere, including our walk round Buttermere.'

'Fraggle,' I said, casting my mind back. 'I *do* remember him. Wow! Blast from the past!' Could Fraggle have been the cause of my fondness for llamas and alpacas?

'Your mum kept saying you'd get bored carrying him after two minutes and you had to leave him in the car but you started crying and I couldn't bear to see you upset so I promised I'd squeeze Fraggle into my backpack if he got too heavy for you. To be fair to you, you managed longer than two minutes – I think you made it to five before telling me Fraggle wanted to ride in my backpack. You were worried about him not being able to breathe so I had to leave the top open which was just as well as I'd have had to bend his neck right over to fit him in otherwise. I got some funny looks that day! Although that could also have been because I looked like a packhorse. There wasn't room for much else in my backpack with Fraggle in there so I had to wear all the spare jumpers and waterproofs tied round my waist. I've got a photo of it somewhere.'

'Aw, Dad, that's so sweet of you. I hope you can find the photo. I wonder what happened to Fraggle.'

Dad winced. 'You didn't want anything to do with him after your mum and I split up. You knew I'd chosen him and, well…'

'I was angry with you and it was another thing to lash out about,' I finished for him. 'I'm sorry.'

'Don't be. You were young and it was confusing for you. We talked this over before and you know I've never held it against you. You did nothing wrong.'

We continued in silence for a while, with me mulling over how difficult it must have been for Dad back then. I was struggling now with everything I'd lost at the same time and Dad had been through something very similar, losing his home, his marriage, his best friend and his daughter in one fell swoop. It was an eye-opener to walk in his shoes.

'So what did happen to Fraggle?' I asked eventually. 'Did you give him to a charity shop?'

'I couldn't bring myself to part with a soft toy you'd loved so much. I had so many happy memories of you and that alpaca so I still have him. He stands in the corner of my bedroom.'

I stopped walking and stared at Dad, eyes wide. 'You've seriously kept him for forty-odd years?'

Feeling all emotional, I launched myself at him and we stood in the middle of the woods, holding each other as tightly as our backpacks would allow. I'd never thought of Dad as being particularly sentimental but that was one of the most touching things I'd ever heard.

Over Dad's shoulder, I spotted a large crowd of hikers approaching us and was conscious of us blocking the path so I released him and we set off again.

'I'll have to reacquaint myself with Fraggle when we get home,' I said. 'If that's okay with you.'

Dad smiled at me. 'Of course it is. He'll be pleased to see his best friend again, although he says his adventuring days dangling out of a backpack might be over.'

As we both laughed at that, it struck me how much our relationship had changed across the past week. It wasn't only because he'd shared his long-held secret and let me in. It was because I'd let him in too. All this time, I'd believed he was the one who'd maintained the distance between us, on my high horse that I'd done my bit years ago by addressing my negative reaction to him splitting up with Mum, but I'd kept a barrier between us. I'd never turned to him when I needed help and I hadn't opened up to him about anything of consequence. He wasn't the only one who'd kept our conversations superficial. When Grayson pulled the rug from under me on Monday and I needed help, I'd cursed him for his horrendous timing while Mum and John were heading off on their holiday. I'd briefly considered using my spare key and staying at their place but I'd reached out to Dad instead and it was the best thing I could ever have done. Having him come to my rescue, welcoming me into his home, and spending so much time with him had already broken down more barriers than revealing his secret had. If I was searching for reasons why I'd been with Grayson, here was another one – my break-up with him had helped repair my fractured relationship with my dad.

We passed another waterfall and, soon after, the tip of the lake. The path continued on through a further field before skirting the top edge where four beautiful red-coated Highland cows were lying down on the grass, not at all fazed by the passers-by pausing to take photos.

'After horses, these were Kathryn's favourite animals,' Dad said as we watched them. 'She wanted to keep some at Willowdale Hall but Hubert told her she was being ridiculous and you don't keep Highland cows as pets so I bought her a soft toy one instead. She christened it Sunny and it became a thing for us. She'd have built up quite a collection.'

'What was she like?' I asked as we set off walking.

'As a teenager, she was exciting, exuberant, energetic, enchanting and often exasperating. I'd never met anyone like her before. She had so many ideas and dreams and it was intoxicating being around her but I was far too practical for my own good. I couldn't share those dreams with her and it frustrated me that she couldn't seem to understand that. Although I'm sure I frustrated the hell out of her too.'

'What about as an adult?'

He sighed. 'After the way Hubert Cranleigh treated her, she could have retreated and been a shadow of her former self but all those things were still there, although somewhat toned down. She'd have moments where it all got on top of her but she was determined he wouldn't destroy her. If she enjoyed something, she tended to be really passionate about it like riding, reading, baking and looking after the hall. She grew herbs and vegetables and it gave her a buzz to cook with what she'd grown herself. She loved sunflowers. They were our other thing. I gave her a packet of seeds one year and seeing them grow made her so happy that I bought her seeds every year after that. She gave the flowers names and talked to them. Hubert used to tell her she had a screw loose but that made her do it even more.'

There was so much warmth in that memory, just as there had been when he'd talked about my walk round Buttermere with Fraggle. Dad was capable of so much love and I'd never given him credit for it before.

'Her husband sounds horrendous. Did he...' I tailed off, not sure I wanted to go where that sentence was potentially leading.

'She used to talk about his affairs and emotional abuse but she was adamant he never laid a finger on her,' Dad said, his expression darkening, his voice gruff. 'It was only when we made the decision to get Oliver's DNA tested that she admitted he'd physically hurt her too but she refused to give me any details. Said it was best I didn't know.'

My stomach churned, thinking about what she must have gone through at the hands of the person who was meant to love her.

'Did she say why she hid it from you?'

'It was complicated. She was worried about me confronting Hubert and getting into trouble, the police not believing her, the impact on Oliver, what Hubert would do to her in the meantime, the future of the hall... Much as she wanted it to end, the fear of making things worse stopped her from saying anything. Also, the more he hurt her, the more determined she became that he wouldn't take her family's home from her. She had an exceptionally strong determined streak.'

We'd reached the halfway point at the tip of the lake, so Dad suggested we stop for our lunch. There was a gravelly beach and the path ran alongside it with a few grassy patches to sit on. We took swigs from our metal drink bottles before starting on our food.

'Did she ever tell you why she finally decided to leave him?' I asked, biting into my first sandwich.

'End of her tether with it, I presume. I've wondered about it a lot but I'll never find out so it's not worth the brainpower.'

'Could there be an explanation in her diaries?'

'There could be, but I'd prefer to let sleeping dogs lie.'

I could understand why Dad would feel that way but I wasn't sure I'd feel the same in his shoes. If I had questions and there might be a way of getting answers, curiosity would get the better of me.

We sat in silence for a while, eating our picnic and enjoying the view. The sky was the palest blue and laden with clouds, although they weren't threatening rain today. A light wind made shadows dance upon the fells and created ripples across the water. When a sudden gust made me shiver, Dad suggested we pack up and continue our walk.

'I wish I'd met Kathryn,' I said after we set off. 'I think I'd have liked her.'

'I think you would too. She desperately wanted to get to know you but she didn't think it was fair on your mum. She hated that we'd hurt Liv, especially when they'd been friends. It was one of the reasons she held back with Alice, worried she was the type of person who somehow managed to unintentionally hurt her friends. She could be really thoughtful like that.'

I mulled over all the things Dad had said about Kathryn and the mixture of personality traits, passions and random quirks like naming and talking to her sunflowers. If he'd thrown the original question back at me, asking what Grayson was like, what would I have said? Passionate about farming and the environment would have been top of the list along with love for farm animals, but what else could I share? What were the aspects of his personality or random quirks that had made me love him? My pace slowed as my mind whirred, desperately searching for examples. There had to be something!

'Are you okay?' Dad asked, evidently aware that I'd fallen behind.

'I've kicked a stone into my boot,' I said, crouching down with one foot out in front of me. 'I'll catch you up.'

He set off again and I straightened up, frowning. I had nothing. Absolutely nothing I could cite as a reason why I loved Grayson. It had to be because I was too annoyed and hurt by his actions to pull something to mind because I had loved him with all my heart. Hadn't I?

I caught up with Dad. 'All sorted. Another question for you.

We're a week on from Oliver coming back into your life. How are you feeling about it all?'

'Relieved,' he said. 'And not just because Oliver knows and is okay about it, but because you and your mum know too and neither of you reacted negatively.'

'Did you think we would?'

'Over the years, I've imagined every conceivable scenario – positive and negative – for all three of you. I can't tell you how much I appreciate how brilliant you've been, Emma. I know it can't have been easy for you, especially with everything else you've got going on right now. I probably should have said this much, much sooner but I'm so proud of you – not just for the way you've handled the news about Oliver but for everything you've achieved and the wonderful person you are.'

Dad had never said anything like that before and I only just managed to force out a *thank you* around the lump in my throat. What a special moment.

* * *

As Dad drove back to Pippinthwaite a little later, I was still buzzing from the walk and from his compliment. I loved how close we'd become. Our conversations these days couldn't be more different from the polite chitchat of old and it was so lovely to be able to hug him and it not to feel forced and awkward.

During our final stretch of the walk, I'd asked Dad what Oliver had been like as a boy and what he was like now. He spoke about our similarities in appearance and various person-ality traits we shared, which had been lovely to hear but also made me eager to meet him. Dad and I were heading over to Butterbea Croft tomorrow so I could introduce him to my alpacas. If Oliver didn't have plans already, perhaps he'd like to join us.

'I think it's time I met Oliver,' I said. 'What do you think about inviting him on our road trip tomorrow?'

Dad glanced across at me with a smile. 'I think that would be a wonderful idea.'

* * *

We hadn't been home for long when Dad disappeared into the dining room. He had a desk in there with his computer and a printer on it, and the dining table was covered in files and text-books from his teaching days. He was gone for quite some time and I could hear the sounds of him moving things around. Then he ran upstairs and back down moments later before joining me in the lounge.

'Oh, my gosh! Fraggle!' I cried as he handed my childhood soft toy to me. 'He's bigger than I remembered.'

The light beige alpaca – which had to be about two feet high from toes to ears – had stumpy legs, curly fleece and the most adorable cream face with pink cheeks.

'How on earth did you squeeze him into your backpack?' I asked, hugging Fraggle to my chest.

'With great difficulty,' Dad quipped, handing me several photographs.

He looked just like the packhorse he'd described earlier with all the spare clothing draped around him and Fraggle peeking over his shoulder. There was another photo taken from behind showing the backpack with Fraggle bursting out of it and one of me cuddling Fraggle by the entrance to the Butter-mere tunnel. The rest of the photos were other occasions where I was with my furry friend, stirring long-forgotten childhood memories of me pushing him down the slide and on the swing in the back garden and making a sandcastle with him on Blackpool beach, recognisable from Blackpool Tower in the background.

'Was this taken on our final family holiday?' I asked.

'I wasn't sure whether to show you that one,' he said, looking uncertain.

I studied it a little longer and ran my finger down the picture. 'I'm glad you did. It *was* a great holiday. I'm sorry it was the last one you ever went on with me.'

Dad had asked me to go away with him – several times – but I'd refused and nobody had made me do something I didn't want to. I felt sad about that now but I could make it up to him. I was here now and, from the way he'd opened up to me so far about Kathryn, I couldn't help thinking that he needed me as much as I needed him.

30

'I'm so nervous,' I told Dad as he locked up the house the following morning. 'My palms are sweating.'

'I bet Oliver's nervous too,' he said, giving me a reassuring smile.

Considering I was older than Oliver by over a decade, it seemed a silly thing to admit to. I suppose it was because it wasn't just about me meeting my half-brother now. It was about meeting the person whose mum my dad had loved so much that his relationship with my own mum – or anyone who might have come along in more recent years – hadn't stood a chance. And it was about meeting the person who held my livelihood in his hands. No matter what Rosie had said, there was a trickle of fear that he might have been pushed into having the alpacas on his estate by an overly enthusiastic Rosie and it wasn't really what he wanted.

'Bear in mind I haven't seen Oliver since last Saturday,' Dad added as we walked towards his car. 'He might be nervous about seeing me again too. I know I am.'

It was my turn to give the reassuring smile. 'It'll be fine. We've got this.'

Dad had told me they'd spent five hours in the pub last Saturday but the time had flown and there was still so much to explore. Although that first meeting had been really amicable, it didn't mean there wouldn't be uncomfortable times ahead while they unpacked the past.

We'd arranged to pick Oliver up at Willowdale Hall and drive over in Dad's car as it was bigger than mine and therefore more comfortable for the backseat passenger.

The main door to the house was a double wooden one with wrought-iron furniture. I was about to reach for the knocker but Dad had spotted a doorbell and pressed that. Moments later, one side of the door opened and we came face to face with a man who bore such a striking resemblance to my dad that he could only be Oliver. Although I'd been nervous about meeting my half-brother, I hadn't felt particularly emotional about it until now. Tears rushed to my eyes and my breath caught in my throat. I searched for something profound to say but all I could manage was, 'Hi.'

'Hi,' Oliver responded, his glistening eyes suggesting he was finding this as emotional as me.

'Come in for a minute,' he said, stepping back.

I wanted to look around me but I couldn't take my eyes off Oliver as he shook hands with Dad and they clapped each other on the back in a kind of man-hug.

'Handshake?' he asked, glancing at me uncertainly.

'Hug?' I offered instead.

His smile widened. 'Much better.' He put his arms round and held me tightly for a few moments.

'I can't believe I've got a sister,' he said when he released me. 'It's so good to meet you.'

'And you. I guess we've got a lot of catching up to do.'

'Just a bit.'

Last night, I'd been thinking about all the things I wanted to ask him but, standing here opposite him now, all I could do was smile and think *I've got a brother!*

'Should we hit the road?' Dad asked.

* * *

As Dad drove to Butterbea Croft, Oliver and I sat in the back like children, chatting non-stop. With the journey being just forty-five minutes, we only managed an overview of our careers and where we'd been living but it was a start to getting to know each other.

Oliver talked about losing his way when he was taking his A levels and how much support Dad had given him. He also spoke about reaching out to Dad after a breakdown during his first year at university. I'd never thought about being proud of my parents before but I could have burst with pride hearing how influential Dad had been in Oliver's life, supporting him through a couple of challenging times and helping him get back on a path to success.

'It would be easy to think that you went out of your way to help me because you knew you were my father...' Oliver said, directing his comment to Dad, '...but I think you'd have done even if there was no connection at all, wouldn't you?'

Dad nodded. 'I'd never let anyone struggle when it cost me nothing except time to help them.'

Even if he hadn't said all those lovely things about my dad, I'd still have liked my brother. He had a gentle, calm way about him and I could see how he'd make a great doctor. I bet all his patients felt reassured after a consultation with him. The conversation flowed so easily that I wondered why I'd wasted any energy on being nervous.

Listening to Oliver talking about how important my dad had been to him made me think again about how difficult it must have been for Dad to be in Oliver's life for all those years but not really part of his life. Just like it had been with me. Well, we were both an active part of his life now and I certainly wasn't going to miss out on any more time with him.

* * *

'Rosie's so envious of me getting to meet your alpacas first,' Oliver said after I'd introduced him and Dad to Ruth and Lizzie. 'I've been instructed to take lots of photos.'

'I hope you like them,' I said, feeling a wobble of nerves in my stomach that Oliver could, in theory, change his mind about them coming to Willowdale Hall.

'No doubt about that,' he said, smiling at me. 'I love animals. I was brought up around horses and I always wanted a dog. Hubert would never allow one but my mum defied him and got me this gorgeous West Highland Terrier after I left primary school, although I didn't have him for long. Hubert sent me on this horrendous summer camp thing and, when I came back, Angus had allegedly run off.'

'You don't sound convinced by that,' I said.

'Hubert hated Angus and I think it was a little too convenient that he disappeared while Hubert was walking him.'

'I have a confession to make,' Dad said. 'Angus was from me. I always wanted to get gifts for you but it was too risky. Hubert wouldn't have known that they were from me but Kathryn said it would be hard for her not to say anything. She told me how much you wanted a dog and a neighbour of mine had a litter of Westies for sale so I couldn't resist.'

'Thank you for doing that,' Oliver said, sounding a little choked up. 'He was a lovely dog. He meant so much to me.'

We'd reached the alpaca enclosure and I pointed out who was who. Ruth had left three containers of feed near the gate so we could easily entice them over to us. Seeing my herd interacting with Dad and Oliver gave me my first insight into how my business would work and it gave me a warm glow. The alpacas were curious and seemed eager to meet their visitors – once they'd eaten, of course. Food was always the top priority!

We spent the morning with the herd. At my request, Ruth and Lizzie hadn't mucked out the shelter or scooped the poop from the field – something with which Dad and Oliver willingly helped.

After lunch, we set off back to Willowdale Hall and I felt another warm glow inside me at how enthusiastic Dad and Oliver were about their time with The Magnificent Seven, already making observations about their different personalities.

'We haven't talked rent for the paddock,' I said to Oliver. 'Do you have a figure in mind?'

'Nothing. I wouldn't dream of charging you rent.' He looked and sounded surprised that I'd even asked.

'You have to. It wouldn't be fair on you, especially when you were earning an income from the Shetland ponies being there.'

He shook his head. 'We weren't planning to do anything with the paddock for the foreseeable future so you're not depriving us of any rental income. Plus, you're family and we want to help you.'

'But I don't want to take advantage.'

'You wouldn't be. This is something Rosie and I want to do and, besides, starting a new business is tough. There's stacks of expenditure and no income so we'd rather you have a proper chance to get the business up and running and turn a profit without worrying about rent. When the business is a success – and Rosie and I know it will be – we can maybe have another discussion about it but, for now, it's non-negotiable. We're not charging you a penny.'

Tears pricked my eyes. Until this morning, this man had been nothing more than a name to me. Until a week ago, he'd been a complete stranger. Now he was my brother, the kindest landlord ever and I could see us becoming really good friends.

'I'm so grateful to you and Rosie for doing this for me,' I said.

'Same to you for letting your herd live at the hall. I love the thought of being able to visit them any time I've had a bad day.' He frowned as he looked at me. 'Just made a big assumption there. Would that be all right with you?'

'Of course! You'd be welcome to visit them any time you want.'

I moved the conversation on to asking him how long he and Rosie had been together. I'd already told him about Grayson and Matthew – a heavily edited version – while we'd been with the herd.

'About eight months,' he said, 'but we dated for a while when we were teenagers. It's a long and complicated history which I'm sure Rosie would love to tell you about over a bottle of wine at some point.'

* * *

When we arrived back at Willowdale Hall, Oliver led us down a hallway to the right of the entrance hall. 'I'll take you to our favourite room before I make the drinks,' he said. 'As you can see, the hall needs a lot of work. We've done some cleaning and sorting but it's barely made an impact.'

He pushed open a door on the right.

'It's a library!' I declared, my eyes immediately drawn to the floor-to-ceiling shelving packed mainly with books. When we'd walked round Buttermere, Dad had mentioned that reading had been one of Kathryn's passions so I suspected she'd spent a lot of time in here.

'Mum's two favourite rooms were this one and the kitchen,' Oliver said. He took our drinks orders and said we were welcome to explore while he made them.

'Kathryn used to tell me about this room,' Dad said as he wandered round the bookshelves peering at the various photos and ornaments. 'I never came inside but it's exactly how I imagined it from her descriptions.'

He picked up an ornament of a Highland cow – presumably one of the collection he'd built up for her – and smiled as he showed it to me. 'This room is so Kathryn. I can picture her in here. I can almost feel her in here.'

'Does that make you sad?'

He appeared to consider that before replying. 'Actually, no. It brings me comfort to know that, despite all the challenges she had being trapped here with him, she had rooms that made her happy that were completely her and nothing to do with him. He never came in here and he never ventured into the kitchen either. The great thing about a mansion like this is that there's more than enough room to shut yourself away from someone you want to avoid – not seeing them and not even hearing them.'

He continued his circuit of the room, intermittently picking up photo frames and smiling at other items. He'd made it as far as the door when Oliver returned with our drinks.

'Mum loved her Highland cows,' he said, joining Dad as he picked up another ornament, smiling at it fondly.

'I bought her this,' Dad told him. 'I bought her most of the cows in this room. She told me Hubert never came in here but, if he had, she'd have told him she'd treated herself.'

'There are a couple more in the secret room,' Oliver said, crossing the room. 'Want to see them?'

'There's a secret room?' I asked, fascinated.

Oliver stopped where he was. 'It's on the far wall but I won't tell you any more than that. See if you can find it.'

'Kathryn mentioned it but she never told me how to access it,' Dad said, joining me in front of the bookcases.

'Got it!' he declared after a while, confidently reaching out and pressing his thumb against the wood.

'It's just a knot,' Oliver said, laughing.

'Is it one of the books?' I asked as my tactic so far had been to move a few leather-bound books, but Oliver shook his head.

When Dad and I announced that we gave up, Oliver stepped forward and tipped a candle holder to one side. There was a click and then he pushed on the whole bookcase, which twisted round by 180 degrees.

'That's so clever,' Dad said.

Oliver indicated with his hand that we could go through the gap.

Inside was a miniature library, still with books all around it. In the middle were two high-backed armchairs with a standard lamp and coffee table between them.

'We discovered from Kathryn's diaries that, when Hubert was in an especially foul mood and she couldn't face him, she hid out in here,' Oliver said. 'He had no idea it existed and she loved the idea of him knowing she was in the house but not being able to find her.'

Dad picked up a beautiful sculpture of a mother and baby Highland cow with a heart-shaped balloon rising above them and the words *I love you* across it. 'This was one of her favourites. I gave her it for Valentine's Day one year. If Hubert Cranleigh didn't know this room existed, that's probably why she kept it in here.'

He didn't need to expand any further on that. It wouldn't be so easy for Kathryn to make out she'd treated herself to an *I love you* ornament.

We returned to the main library and Oliver closed the secret door behind us. I stood for a moment admiring the woodwork. Even though I knew where it opened, I couldn't see any joins.

'There are priest holes and various other secret passages and panels around the house,' Oliver said. 'Mum used one for her diaries. They were in a secret drawer in the wood panels in her bedroom. Speaking of which, do you want to look at Mum's diaries?'

He directed his question to Dad and I registered that he'd avoided directly addressing him all day and could understand that dilemma as to what to call him. It was early days for Oliver and it had to be hard enough to break the Mr Wynterson habit, never mind deciding between Christian or Dad.

Dad clasped his hands behind his head, elbows out to the side – typical thinking mode for him – then dropped them by his side, shaking his head.

'I'd find it too strange reading her words but not being able to hear them directly from her and I don't want to read things that she might not have wanted me to. I've no objection to you and Rosie reading them if you want to understand Kathryn more, but it's a strong no from me.'

'Completely understand,' Oliver said. 'Rosie and I felt really intrusive at first and, if it hadn't been for trying to solve the mystery as to who my real father was, we'd never have delved in. Rosie did all the reading at first.'

Dad glanced at me. 'You wouldn't want to read them, would you?'

'I didn't know Kathryn so it wouldn't feel right,' I said, shaking my head. 'Out of curiosity, where do you keep them?'

'You probably didn't spot them but they were on one of the shelves in the secret room. It was Mum's sanctuary so it felt like a good resting place for them.'

We'd only just settled on the sofas and armchairs surrounding a grand fireplace when the doorbell rang so Oliver went to investigate.

'Enjoyed your day with your half-brother?' Dad asked when he'd gone.

'Loved it!'

I heard voices in the hall and the scamper of paws on the tiles. Next minute, Toffee and Chester raced into the library, tails wagging, and dashed between Dad and me. Alice appeared with Oliver and an attractive man who bore a strong resemblance to Brad Pitt.

'This is Xander, Rosie's dad and my good friend,' Alice said. 'We were walking the dogs and saw you were back so we wanted to hear how it had gone.'

I swelled with pride as Oliver waxed lyrical about the alpacas and showed Alice and Xander the photos and videos he'd captured for Rosie. My favourite was one of Barbara humming. Alpacas had a wide repertoire of sounds including making a humming sound, the pitch of which typically varied depending on whether they were doing it because they were really happy, in need of attention, curious or anxious. They made clucking sounds, similar to chickens, to communicate with each other as well as various grumbling and snorting sounds to warn other alpacas to get out of their space.

We stayed for another hour and, even though Alice had introduced Xander as *Rosie's dad and my good friend*, it was obvious to me from the adoring glances and the frequent touches that their feelings for each other extended beyond friendship. I had no idea what their story was but, to me, they seemed perfectly suited and I hoped that they could find a way to push aside whatever was holding them back and just go for it. It would be easy to think they had all the time in the world but who knew how long we all had left? That thought jolted me. Dad had never explained why he'd disappeared into his memories when I'd said that phrase. We'd unlocked the door to the past and found a half-brother which had been quite a distraction, and hadn't returned to it. Could it simply be that he and Kathryn had thought they'd have all the time in the world to be together and it was snatched from them before they did? I must ask him about it, but not now. Maybe on the way home.

As we prepared to leave, I crouched down to say goodbye to Toffee and Chester. Stroking their ears, I experienced a pang of longing for Monty and wondered whether he was missing me.

It had started drizzling so we gave hugs goodbye and I raced Dad across the gravel to the car. On the way back to Pippinthwaite, the steady swiping of the wiper blades made me feel sleepy and I gazed out of the window, reflecting on the day. I'd seen and felt so much love around me since discovering this new branch of my family. Oliver was clearly besotted with Rosie and it was obvious it was reciprocal from the short time I'd spent in her company. Alice and Xander were the same, no matter how much they might claim just to be friends. Dad had shared how he felt about Kathryn and that little list that I couldn't have replicated for Grayson had been an eye-opener. Grayson had never looked at me the way Oliver and Rosie or Alice and Xander looked at each other. How could I not have noticed that when I'd been surrounded by love with Mum, Stacie, Laura and Rachael all being so happy with their partners?

I thought about my reaction when I'd stroked the dogs goodbye. I'd longed to stroke Monty but I hadn't longed to reach out and touch Grayson. He'd been a liar but could the same accusation be levelled at me? Had I fallen out of love with him somewhere along the way? Or, even worse, had I never really been in love with him and had, instead, found him to be safe and easy? Had staying with Grayson been a habit rather than a genuine desire?

31

Over breakfast on Tuesday morning, a WhatsApp notification came through from an unknown number.

FROM UNKNOWN

Hi Emma, Killian here. Hope you don't mind me getting your number from Rosie – realised I forgot to ask you for it. I've got a proposal for your alpacas. Are you free at any point today to meet me at the paddock?

TO KILLIAN

A day early! Can't wait to see it. I'm free all day. Would 10am suit?

FROM KILLIAN

That's great. See you then

Killian was at the paddock when I arrived, using a tape measure. I was about to ask him if he needed any help holding it but he'd evidently finished what he was doing as he retracted it and clipped it onto his pocket.

When he looked up, I couldn't help noticing how tired he looked, with dark shadows between his eyes and his hair dishevelled.

'Hi, Emma,' he said without smiling. The words were cheery enough so maybe he was just one of those people who didn't smile. 'I've done you a rough sketch. Is this what you were thinking?'

He passed me a sheet of A4 and *rough* was the operative word. My eyes narrowed at the shelter.

'The shelter's too small,' I said, trying not to sound critical.

'It's not drawn to scale. It's more for checking I've got things in the right place.'

'That's fine, but you've got measurements on here and the shelter is too small.'

He took the sketch back. 'Twelve by eight like you said.'

'*Twenty-four* by eight,' I said, placing a strong emphasis on the larger number.

'That's not what you said.'

'I promise it is.' I'd brought my notebook with me and I flicked it open to where I'd written the word *shelter* followed by 24' x 8' in large letters. 'Seven alpacas need to be able to lie down in there with space around them.'

'Oh. Sorry. I was sure...' He took his phone out and tapped it in. 'Got it. Sorry about that.'

I glanced at the sketch again. 'The troughs are fine but what about the holding pen?'

He looked at me blankly and I fought back a frustrated sigh. What had been the point of Friday's meeting if he hadn't been paying any attention? Why couldn't he have written it down at the time? I bit back the urge to point that out and explained once more about the holding pen, but teacher mode kicked in when he didn't take any notes yet again.

'Are you sure you don't want to write it down?' I asked.

'No. I've got it now.'

Nevertheless, I asked him to run through everything he thought he needed to do. He did seem to have taken it in this time. I just hoped the information stayed there.

'I promise I'm normally on top of things,' he said. 'Friday wasn't a great day.'

'I wouldn't have minded if you'd rescheduled.' It came out a bit harsher than I'd intended and I was about to apologise but he got in there first.

'I should have done. I'm sorry for wasting your time but I've definitely got it now and this is my top priority.'

'It's okay. Sorry if that sounded like a criticism. I'm just anxious to be ready. My friends don't mind looking after the herd but I feel guilty about that when I should have taken over already so I'm conscious that every day counts.'

'No need to apologise. I'm the one who messed up. I'll be in touch as soon as possible.'

* * *

A message arrived a few hours later.

FROM KILLIAN

Apologies again. I assure you I do normally listen and promise that what I'm working on now will be what you want. Are you free at 9am tomorrow?

TO KILLIAN

Yes. See you then and no need to apologise again. Thank you

Another message came through containing only smiley and

llama/alpaca emojis which was unexpected considering my first impression of someone very serious.

32

The following day was clear and bright but it had rained heavily overnight so, when I was leaving the house, I grabbed my wellies. I was about to put my foot in one but hesitated, wondering whether Killian might make a derogatory comment about them. Shaking my head, I pulled them on anyway. Despite his aloof manner across our two meetings so far, Killian was *not* Grayson and I shouldn't judge everyone by his behaviour. Who cared what he thought anyway? I bought my wellies because I loved them and to hell with anyone else's opinions. Besides, I'd worn them for our last meeting and he hadn't reacted. Not that he'd been paying the slightest bit of attention. If I'd sported my cerise-pink boiler suit, he'd probably not have noticed that either.

I arrived roughly ten minutes early and Killian was already in the paddock with his back to me, looking down at something on a clipboard in front of him. He evidently sensed my presence as he turned round.

'Morning!' he declared brightly. 'Wow! Those wellies are awesome.'

'You like them?' I asked uncertainly, wondering if he was being sarcastic.

He smiled – actually smiled – and it transformed his face. 'I love them and so would my two little girls.'

I decided not to point out that I'd been wearing them last time. The less said about our shaky start, the better. I'd focus on something positive instead.

'You have girls?' I asked. 'How old?'

'Lyla's nine and Elsa's just turned six.'

'Aw, lovely ages.'

'You've got kids?' he asked.

'No, but I have six- and eight-year-old nephews and a couple of younger nieces.'

'And now you're an alpaca mum,' he said, still smiling.

The change in temperament was unexpected but extremely welcome and I was more than happy to go with it. 'I am indeed,' I said, smiling back at him. 'So what do you have for me today?'

'Something which actually meets your brief this time. Or at least I hope it does. I really am so sorry about the mess up. It's not like me to...' He broke off with a sigh. 'Let's just say I had a tough weekend and I brought it into work with me, which I shouldn't have done. You have my full focus now.' He smiled as he tapped the clipboard. 'I'm a visual thinker so I like to sketch my ideas. The one I gave you yesterday was poor. I think you'll like this one better.'

He passed me the clipboard and my eyes widened at the A4 drawing clipped to it. It was still rough but it was brilliant, showing the entrance to the paddock and the shelter – the right size, this time – with stable-style doors at either end and feeding stations. What really brought it to life was the addition of three cute cartoon alpacas. There was one at the water trough, one peeking over the stable door with hay hanging out of its mouth and another grazing on the grass.

'You can't tell from the sketch but I'd suggest another stable door inside the shelter,' he said. 'That way, if you need to segregate any of the herd due to special dietary needs or illness, you can completely shut off one side.'

'That's a brilliant idea,' I said, impressed by his insight.

'Thank you. Also, I was trying to think practically in terms of the public experience so, to avoid queues, I've suggested a row of sinks rather than just one. I've also added some benches so they can sit down while you're giving your safety briefing – ideal for anyone who struggles to stand for long.'

'Both great suggestions,' I said, cursing myself for not thinking of them.

'And I also thought that you might have people who turn up with big backpacks because they're incorporating this with a wander round the lake or a hike up Cat Bells. Rather than lugging their bags on the alpaca walk, I've suggested a waterproof storage unit which you can lock up and leave.'

I smiled at him. 'Have you designed something like this before?'

'No, why?'

'You just seem to have thought of everything.'

'This time,' he said, smiling ruefully.

I smiled back. 'I wasn't going to say that, but I do appreciate that you haven't just met the brief – you've exceeded it.'

'Which I should have done before. I really am sorry.'

There was such sincerity in his eyes and I wanted to ask about the tough weekend but that was way too intrusive for someone I'd only just met.

'How about we forget it ever happened?' I said, gently.

'Imagine this is our first meeting. Hi, I'm Emma Wynterson and I'd love to discuss the plans for Casa Alpaca.'

He laughed as he shook my outstretched hand. 'Killian Buchanan and I'm loving that name. Bear with...' He took the clipboard and scribbled something on it before returning it to me.

I smiled at the addition of a wooden pub-style sign by the entrance with the words *Casa Alpaca* on it and an alpaca beneath it.

'Are these the plans?' I said, feigning surprise. 'Oh, wow! They look wonderful.'

'They do now.' He rolled his eyes at me. 'And that's the last time I'm going to mention it. Pity party over. I'm glad you like the additions.'

He talked me through the rest of his sketch and why he'd placed certain items where they were before finishing with a recommendation for paving slabs across the area the customers would use, telling me that the shelter needed to go on slabs anyway, they'd be better for wet weather and easier to clean. He suggested recycled rubber matting for the track side of the gate, inside the holding pen and around the food and water troughs in the paddock which would avoid a churning-up of the areas the alpacas most used. It would also be better for the herd's cleanliness and more aesthetically pleasing.

I was so impressed with the detail he'd gone into. 'You've obviously done some research.'

'I've got one of those minds that's always on the go. Whenever I have an outing with the girls, I'm constantly evaluating what could make it even better. Can't seem to help myself. It's the small touches that can really make a difference to the customer experience. And, of course, there are many online rabbit holes...' He shrugged, smiling at me. 'I like to get things right first time where possible. That means lots of thought and research initially but that's nearly always time well spent. Not that you'd think that from yesterday's disaster.'

'Killian! What did you say literally five minutes ago?'

He laughed. 'Sorry. I'm just annoyed with myself.' He drew in a deep breath and shook his arms out. 'Letting it go. Okay. It's done. So, what do you think? Anything you'd like to change?'

'It's a yes from me to everything you've suggested and big thanks for putting in all that effort. Kicking myself for not thinking of it all myself.'

'I usually find it's easier to spot improvements when you're fresh to a project rather than someone who's already emotionally invested in it.'

I loved how gracious and understanding he was being and was struggling to align this version of Killian with the one I'd met on Friday and even yesterday. It was as though he'd had a personality transplant, moving from curt and quiet to warm, engaging, and humorous.

'I love your cartoon alpacas.'

'We've named one each. This one's Humphrey.' He pointed to the one by the water trough. 'I've no idea where Lyla dug that name from. The one peeking out the shelter is Elsa. I suspect you'll be able to guess who named her. This little fella here with the really shaggy hair is my choice – Boris.'

'Great names,' I said, laughing. 'If I expand the herd at some point, I might have to give you all naming rights.'

'What are yours called?'

'We've got Barbara – she's the boss – Maud, Bianca, Jolene, Charmaine, Florence and Camella.' I carefully pronounced the last name, wondering if he'd pick up on the play on words.

'Camella rather than Camilla?' he asked. 'As in camelids?'

'Exactly! Isn't it clever?'

'That *is* clever. I like it. Nicely done!'

I shook my head. 'Thank you, but I can't take credit. They were already named.'

Killian took the clipboard back and turned the page to a spreadsheet of costs for me to look down.

'You haven't included labour,' I said.

'Oliver has that covered.'

'No! He's already been too generous giving me the paddock rent-free. What's your day rate?'

He shook his head. 'I'm salaried while I'm here. It worked better for me to have a Monday-to-Friday job so I can spend weekends with the girls. So, if you want to pay, you'll have to take it up with the boss, although I doubt you'll get anywhere.'

'You and me both.'

'You can be my labourer if you like. I had a lad lined up for work experience this week but he fell off his bike and broke his collarbone at the weekend. You'd get your herd here sooner and Oliver would benefit because I can move on to my next job quicker.'

'You're on! I was going to help my brother-in-law create the original shelter so I'd love to help with this one. I don't have many skills but I'm a quick learner.'

'And I'm a patient teacher,' he said, his eyes twinkling as he smiled at me. 'I think we'll make a great team.'

I'd seriously had my doubts on Friday but now I believed we would, which was a lovely thought after the disastrous attempt at working with Grayson.

'I'm looking forward to working with you,' Killian added, making me feel warm and fuzzy inside. Again, a complete contrast to Grayson, who'd made me feel so unwanted.

'When do you think it'll all be ready?' I asked. 'I'd like to let my friends know how much longer they'll need to keep my herd.'

'We can start tomorrow and I reckon we'll be done in a fortnight max so I'd tell them...' He took his phone out of his jeans and opened a calendar. 'Tell them the herd can move to their new home any time from the first Friday in October. That gives us a full fortnight plus a bit of leeway just in case.'

We agreed a start time of nine in the morning and Killian handed me the sketch and costing, telling me he had copies for his use.

'Rosie says she's at the stables if you want to drop by but no worries if you have things to get on with.'

I needed to phone Ruth and Lizzie with a moving date for the alpacas and confirm a revised delivery date for the feed and equipment, but I had nothing else planned so I said I would see Rosie. Killian told me to follow the road past Horseshoe Cottage where I'd pick up signs for the stables.

The intermittent chirping of birds accompanied me on my walk and sunlight filtered through the trees. I smiled contentedly. What a stunning place. What a privilege it would be to keep The Magnificent Seven here. They were going to have such an amazing home thanks to Killian's brilliant ideas. I couldn't wait to get started tomorrow.

33

The riding stables were bigger than I'd expected, with an enormous American-style barn and another smaller stable block. The sliding door on the barn was partially open so I stepped through it, calling, 'Hello?'

I'd never had an interest in learning to ride – the water and the fells had called to me far more – but I still loved horses and smiled at the beautiful animals peering out from the stalls.

'Hello?' I called again, a bit louder this time.

Rosie appeared from a side door with some bridles draped over her arm. 'I thought I heard a voice,' she said, smiling at me. 'Have you finished with Killian?'

'Yes. I've seen his sketches, gone through the costs and enlisted myself as his labourer for the next fortnight.'

'You're helping? Aw, that's fantastic.' She hung the kit up on a hook outside one of the stalls. 'Killian's such a sweetheart. You'll have so much fun working with him.'

'I hope so. If you'd said that to me before today, I wouldn't have been convinced, but he was lovely just now.'

Rosie's smile fell and she grimaced. 'I'm so sorry. I should have given you a heads up that Killian might not be on top form on Friday. He wasn't rude, was he?'

'No! Not at all. He just wasn't particularly warm and I was worried he might be miffed with me that my alpacas had pushed his other priorities down the list.'

'He's really excited about the alpacas and can't wait to get started so I promise you it was nothing like that. Last Friday was a strange one for him. Remember I said he had the afternoon off? He was going to a memorial service for his late brother and sister-in-law.'

'Oh no! That's awful. When did they die?'

'Five years ago. Such a tragedy. So if he was out of sorts, it'll have been purely down to going to that and nothing at all to do with you and the alpacas. Thinking about it, I should have left it until this week but I got carried away wanting to get things moving.'

I wanted to ask more but it wasn't right to question Rosie. If Killian wanted to tell me what had happened, he'd do so in his own time.

'Killian said to drop by if I had a moment so this is me dropping by. Have you got lessons this morning?'

'Only with my best friend, Autumn. She usually comes on a Monday when we're closed but it was so wet and miserable that we went to The White Willow for cake instead and shifted her lesson into a cancelled slot today. She should be here in about fifteen minutes and I'd love to introduce you if you have time. I can give you a quick tour of the stables in the meantime if you like.'

'That sounds great.'

The stalls faced each other and we worked down one side and back up the other as she named the different horses and ponies. Most belonged to the riding school but there were some which belonged to clients. She paused by one of the stalls and released a gentle sigh.

'This was Zeus's home,' she said.

There was a small framed pencil drawing of a black horse hanging beside the stall.

'What happened to him?' I asked. 'Did he die?'

'Gosh, no. He was his Lordship's stallion and such a magnificent horse but we made the tough decision to sell him over the summer. Stallions can only be handled by experts so they're no good for teaching – even ones with a wonderful temperament like Zeus. I miss him so much but his new owner is so good to me. He's completely captivated by him and sends me photos and videos so I still get my Zeus fix.'

'It must be hard letting them go.'

'It's the worst, but selling them on and, sadly, losing them is all part of working with animals.'

'That's the one thing I'm dreading with my alpacas,' I admitted. 'The expected lifespan is anywhere between fifteen and twenty-five years and my oldest girl is eight so hopefully it won't be something I have to deal with for a long time, but you never know.'

I wasn't particularly superstitious but I touched the nearest wooden stable door for safety and appreciated Rosie crossing her fingers on both hands for me.

'It's a beautiful drawing,' I said. 'Did you do it?'

'I wish! I can't draw for toffee. Autumn's the artist. Before she moved here, she was an illustrator for a greetings card company. She still does a bit of that for her old boss on a freelance basis but her main thing is writing and illustrating children's books.'

'Wow! That's impressive. Anything I'd have come across? I've read stacks of books to my nephews and nieces.'

'Not yet. She wanted to get several books written before she tried to secure a publishing deal but she's about to start submitting now.'

'That's so exciting. Hope it goes well for her.'

Autumn arrived shortly afterwards and the affectionate way they greeted each other reminded me of my friendship with Rachael.

'So lovely to meet you,' Autumn said after Rosie introduced us. 'Gosh, I can see the resemblance to Oliver.'

'I agree,' Rosie said. 'I can see it more now with your hair tied back, Emma.'

I hadn't even thought about it but my first reaction on seeing Oliver on Saturday had been how much he looked like Dad and people often told me I looked more like Dad than Mum so I guess it followed that Oliver and I looked similar.

'I'm so excited about meeting your alpacas.' Autumn was shorter than Rosie and had long blonde wavy hair with honey tones which she pulled back into a low ponytail as she spoke. 'If you need to go on any practice walks, give me a shout. Very willing volunteer here. I've conquered my fear of horses so alpacas definitely won't give me the fear.'

'You were scared of horses?' I asked.

'Very. It was irrational as I'd never had a bad experience but they just seemed so enormous. Fortunately Rosie's a wonderfully patient teacher and she got me used to them gradually and taught me to ride. I couldn't imagine not riding now.'

'Speaking of which, let's get Leaf tacked up.'

'I'll leave you to it,' I said. 'The alpacas should be here in a few weeks' time and I *will* be looking for trial walk volunteers so I'll let you know, Autumn.'

I said goodbye and Rosie wished me all the best with my first day as Killian's labourer. Ambling back to my car, I couldn't stop thinking about Autumn's drawing of Zeus and what a talented artist she was. She might be willing to draw the alpacas for me. I stopped short, tutting at myself. What was I thinking? If anyone was going to draw The Magnificent Seven, it would be me. We were only a few days away from saying goodbye to summer and I could clearly visualise each of the herd brought to life in a painting – or maybe through coloured charcoal – wearing scarves in autumnal colours and with seasonal flowers and leaves. I hadn't felt the urge to draw for a very long time but it was strong now. My pace quickened in my haste to get back to the car and, before I knew it, I'd broken into a run.

I didn't know which box my charcoals were packed in and, even if I did, they were probably past their best. It was time I treated myself to some new ones and I knew exactly where to go for them – the shop at the Derwent Pencil Museum in Keswick which stocked the most incredible range.

Several hours later, I rolled my stiff shoulders and looked through my creations in the brand-new sketchpad I'd also treated myself to. I'd scrolled through my stack of photos and selected three different-coloured alpacas to focus on at first – Bianca with her white fleece and bright blue eyes, Barbara who was light grey and Camella who was light fawn. I'd need a lot more practice with blending to get the rose grey colour right for Maud and to ensure Jolene's dark brown didn't look like a solid lump of mud. They were very rough – just practising techniques and ideas – but they weren't bad as a starting point.

'What do you think?' I asked Dad after I'd put my charcoal

pencils away and washed my hands. 'They're only rough ideas for now but I'm quite pleased.'

He flicked through the pad, a huge smile lighting up his face. '*Rough? Quite pleased?* Emma, these are fantastic. If this is rough, then polished is going to be off the scale. I didn't realise you could draw this well.'

'I haven't done it much over the years but I haven't really had a reason to draw and now I do. I was thinking I could have a sideline business selling some alpaca merch with my drawings on – postcards, greetings cards, maybe even notebooks.'

'That's a brilliant idea,' he said. 'But with your talent, you could take it even further than that. T-shirts? Baseball caps? An online shop could be good for supplementing your income in the winter when I'd imagine the weather will mean the walks aren't quite so popular.'

'It's worth looking into,' I agreed, my mind racing with ideas following Dad's positive reaction. 'An alpaca tote bag would be cute.'

'Have you decided on a name for your business yet?'

'I think I've settled on My Alpaca Adventure. I thought about just having Alpaca Adventure but I think adding the *My* to the start makes it a bit more special as this is *my* personal adventure and, for those who go on the walks, it becomes their personal adventure so it works on both levels.'

'My Alpaca Adventure?' Dad nodded. 'I love it. Works for me.'

He returned my pad and I flicked through my sketches again, a sense of pride flowing through me. Just over a week ago, things had felt completely hopeless as I woke up on my first morning in Dad's house, weary from everything I'd lost. Now I had a home for The Magnificent Seven, an incredibly supportive and generous brother and his lovely girlfriend, and some clear plans in place to move my business forward. Ruth and Lizzie had been delighted with the update and had confirmed they'd transport the alpacas on the first Friday in October. I'd rescheduled all my deliveries and was looking forward to working with Killian to break ground tomorrow. Also, I hadn't given Grayson any headspace since putting my wellies on this morning as my focus had been completely on the future instead of regretting the past. Definite progress.

Settling down to sleep a little later, my thoughts turned once more to the sketches I'd done and how much I'd loved drawing. At that point, I did afford Grayson a little headspace. When I'd split up with Matthew, I'd spent hours pouring out my heart and soul into dark and disturbed images but I hadn't done that after Grayson ended things. My first foray into art post-Grayson couldn't have been more different to how it had been post-Matthew. Today I'd spent hours engrossed in creating beautiful, colourful, calming artwork instead of losing myself in tortured paintings. It was another reminder of how different things had been and that my suspicions from Saturday afternoon – that I might not have fallen as deeply for Grayson as I'd believed – might well be true.

34

Killian straightened up and dropped his rubber mallet into his toolbox. 'Lunch time!' he declared. 'What do you think of your new patio so far?'

'It's looking brilliant! I can't believe we've got so much done in two and a half days.'

'It's amazing how quickly you can get work done with enthusiasm, good equipment and the right team.'

'And a patient teacher,' I responded, smiling at him.

I'd learned so much, had worked muscles I didn't know I even had, and had loved working alongside someone who actually wanted me there. Working with Killian couldn't have been more different from working with Grayson. He was patient, explained things clearly, encouraged, praised, gave pointers for improvement in a constructive way and generally made me feel like I had an important role. Grayson had made me feel stupid for not immediately understanding what he meant when he pointed angrily at something instead of explaining what he needed from me, and he'd given me a clear message that I was a hindrance rather than a help, despite some of the jobs being ones he couldn't physically have done on his own.

Killian had hired a mini digger to clear the area and had shown me how to operate it, which had been so much fun. We'd installed the pipework for the sinks and water troughs and Dad joined us to lay the sub base on top of the heavy-duty weed control fabric. I swear we must have clocked up several miles between us pushing wheelbarrows back and forth between the paddock and the mountain of stones dumped at the end of the track. It had then taken hours to compact the sub base down with a plate compactor before starting on the patio.

'We'll definitely get it finished today,' Killian said.

We were downing tools at 3 p.m. and I was driving to Butterbea Croft. I'd have gone across earlier in the day but when Killian offered to work today – Saturday – because his daughters had been at a sleepover last night and wouldn't be back until half three, I shifted my plans. No way was I leaving him to do the work on his own when he was giving up his Saturday for me.

'Do you want to have lunch beside the lake?' Killian asked.

I swiped the back of my hand across my sweaty forehead and nodded appreciatively. 'That sounds great.'

Rosie had given Killian the keys for the old gatehouse and, being only a short walk from the enclosure, we'd been using the kitchen and bathroom in there. The rain had held off across the past couple of days but it had been cool and overcast – ideal for working but not for eating outside. Today we'd been treated to sunshine and blue skies – not quite so ideal for working, hence wiping the slick of sweat from my forehead, but perfect for a spot of alfresco dining.

'I'm sure I saw some deckchairs somewhere,' Killian said as I removed our lunchboxes from the fridge. 'In the hall, maybe.'

He left the kitchen and appeared moments later with a couple of rusting metal sprung deckchairs with faded striped material. 'How long do deckchairs last?'

'I'm not sure,' I said, giving them a dubious look. 'Might be a plan to test them before we lug them down to the lake.'

'And that's my job, right?' he asked, smiling.

I held a lunchbox up in each hand. 'I'm holding the food. Wouldn't want to risk dropping it.'

He rolled his eyes at me. 'Okay. Here goes nothing.'

The first deckchair took some force to prise apart and gave a loud creak as it finally opened and snapped into place. Killian placed it in the middle of the kitchen floor and slowly lowered himself onto it, crossing his fingers. It stayed intact, even when he wriggled around a bit. He pressed down on one of the plastic arms to push himself up and there was a loud crack as the arm splintered across the middle.

'Oops!' he said, scrunching up his face as he picked up the broken pieces. 'But it's still workable without the arms.'

'I'll let you have that one,' I said.

'Oh, I don't know. I think the brave tester gets to choose.'

'Then the brave tester had better try the other one too in case it's even worse.'

He did the same with the second deckchair but, when he wriggled around, there was a ripping sound and, next minute, the fabric had split clean across the middle, his backside had plummeted to the floor and the whole chair had half-folded in on him.

I watched in horror for a moment, scared he might have hurt himself. 'Are you okay?'

His expression was serious as he fixed his eyes on mine. 'I think I *will* take that first one after all.'

Reassured he was all right, laughter bubbled up inside me

and came out in a high-pitched squeal. Watching him attempting to extricate himself from the collapsed deckchair was even funnier. I tried to offer him my hand but the pair of us were laughing too much.

'I might just keep it on,' he said, waddling round the kitchen with the deckchair attached to him. 'It makes a certain style statement.'

My sides were aching by the time he was finally free.

'I declare that match as deckchair two, brave tester nil,' he said, raking his fingers through his dishevelled hair and pulling it back into a fresh bun.

'I keep a picnic blanket in my boot,' I said. 'We can grab that.'

Ten minutes later, we'd settled on the nearest of several pebbly beaches around the grounds.

'Be honest with me,' I said. 'Did you hurt yourself?'

'I might have a few bruises but I'll live. What about you? I thought you were going to do yourself a mischief with laughing so hard.'

'I'm so sorry. I couldn't help it. It genuinely was one of the funniest things I've ever seen.' Even the thought of it was setting me off again. 'For me, it's just topped off a brilliant week which I absolutely needed after the shocker of the previous one. I've really enjoyed working with you.'

'I've enjoyed working with you too. I love having work experience kids and apprentices but it's been nice to work with someone who's about my own age for a change.'

I'd wondered about Killian's age across the week and really couldn't place it. Him having six- and nine-year-old daughters didn't really help because he could have had them young or later in life.

'How old are you?' I asked, thinking it was too good an

opportunity to miss.

'Forty-four.'

'Bit younger than me, then. I'm forty-eight next month.'

'Really? I'd have put you younger than me.'

The compliment gave me a little fizz of pleasure. I wasn't someone who'd ever fish for compliments but it was lovely when they came along unexpectedly.

'It'll be the sheep wellies making you think I'm about twelve,' I said, smiling at him.

He laughed. 'Best wellies ever. Seriously, if they did them in giant feet sizes, I'd have a pair.' He stretched his legs out and twisted his feet which were, like the rest of him, plus-size.

'Size fourteens,' he said. 'Can't see me getting them in a pair of sheep wellies any time soon. I told Lyla and Elsa about your boots and they both want some.'

'I'm pretty sure they had them in children's sizes so I can send you a link if you like.'

'They need new wellies so that'd be brilliant.'

We continued to eat in silence for a moment, looking out over the lake. The improvement in the weather had brought out kayakers and paddleboarders and I closed my eyes for a moment, trying to remember how it felt to kayak on the lake when I was younger. It wasn't the time of year to be renewing my interest in water sports and I had too much to do with the business anyway but, next year, I'd try it again. I definitely fancied giving paddleboarding a go. I could imagine it being so peaceful, gliding through the water on a beautiful day like today. Opening my eyes, I took in the reflections of the fells in the gently rippling lake, feeling a sense of calm.

'You look deep in thought,' Killian said.

'I was remembering how much I used to love kayaking on this lake and what a shame I stopped. I was also thinking how beautiful it is here and how relaxed I feel now that everything's coming together so nicely.'

'Casa Alpaca's going to be great. If I was an alpaca, I'd think I'd made it to millionaire's row.'

'I really appreciate you dropping everything to work on this for me.'

'It's no bother at all. My work here is fluid because the weather can affect so much of what I do. I took the job with Oliver and Rosie knowing that things would chop and change all the time and that suits me. I adapt well to change.'

He looked so earnest as he said it and I felt the need to be honest with him about knowing something which he hadn't personally shared with me. This was my route in but I needed to choose my words carefully as I didn't want to cause any offence.

'I was worried at first that you might have been a bit frustrated with me for suddenly going to the top of your to-do list as you were a little quiet last Friday and then there was the first design which, of course, we don't talk about anymore. You said you'd had a tough weekend and Rosie mentioned you'd been to a memorial service so your mind was likely elsewhere.'

He grimaced. 'Was I rude on the Friday?'

'No.' The word hadn't come out very convincingly.

'I was, wasn't I? I'm so sorry.'

'No, honestly, you weren't rude. You were maybe a little short with me and I now know that's not your style having spent so much time with you this week.'

'I thought about suggesting we meet on Monday instead but Rosie was so excited and it made sense for me to crack on with it. I thought I'd be okay but, as it got closer to finishing time, it got to me more. Did she tell you who the memorial was for?'

'Your brother and sister-in-law but that was all she told me.'

He sighed and pulled his legs up to his chest, wrapping his arms round them as he looked out across the lake.

'You don't have to tell me anything,' I said. 'I wasn't fishing.'

'I know, but if we're going to be colleagues, it's good that you know. The memorial was for my younger brother Patrick and his wife Hattie, organised by her obsessive parents, and I was dreading it. I'd love to say it was better than expected but it was actually worse.'

He paused, scratching at some mud on his work trousers with his thumbnail and I waited silently for him to continue.

'They died five years ago on their honeymoon in Turkey. Carbon monoxide poisoning from a faulty oven in their apartment.'

My stomach flopped. 'Oh, Killian, that's awful. I'm so sorry.'

'The cleaner found them and raised the alarm. They were only thirty-four. Thankfully they hadn't taken Lyla and Elsa with them – they were staying with me. Elsa was only just a year old so she has no memory of her parents. Lyla was four but she just had a couple of really vague memories. I'm really all they've known.'

'I didn't realise they weren't your daughters.'

'Technically they are. I've adopted them and they both call me Daddy. Obviously they know about their parents but, as far as they're concerned, I'm Daddy, Hattie is Mummy and Patrick's their other daddy. My fiancée would have been Mummy too but, after Patrick and Hattie's written wishes came to light for me to adopt the girls if anything ever happened to them, she didn't stick around for long.'

'I'm sorry,' I said. 'Your brother and his wife were very young to leave instructions like that.'

'It was Hattie's influence. She had a chaotic childhood

with parents who moved home constantly, were always building businesses then going bankrupt and who'd change their plans at the drop of a pin. Understandably, she developed the need to be more in control of her own life. She was a major planner and, as soon as she started earning, she was properly adulting – savings plans, life assurance, pensions, a will. My brother was ex-army – same as me – and all that structure worked well for him. The only problem was that they'd never spoken to any of the family about their wishes for the girls, which I completely get because who expects to die so young? Having me as the chosen one was a shock for everyone – me included – and Hattie's parents didn't respond well to it.'

'They thought it should be them?'

'Exactly, which was a joke when they'd barely shown any interest in the girls before Hattie died. They kept going on and on about how they should have won the girls – won being the exact word they used, as though they were prizes in a raffle. Truth is, I know Ken and Joan well enough to know it was effectively about winning. They wanted the money, not the custody, and they'd have blown through Lyla and Elsa's inheritance just like they'd done with all the profits from their past businesses. When Patrick and Hattie made their wishes legal, they knew exactly what they were doing – what was best for the girls and their future.'

'What about your parents?' I asked.

'Not an option. My dad drifted in and out of our lives for years but, when I was eight and Patrick was three, he finally decided that being a parent was too much like hard work and an interruption to his drinking, so he cleared off for good. My mam's a fantastic woman but her health isn't great. She adores the girls and she'd have done everything she could to raise them well, but it would have taken a toll on her. Doting grandma is how it should be.'

'That must have been a big change for you.'

'Oh, massive, but you take what life throws at you and there wasn't a single moment when I wanted to contest Patrick and Hattie's wishes. I loved those girls when they were my nieces and I'd always been a hands-on uncle, so I had no hesitation in stepping up to give them a home and a future. The pair of them have given me so much back – little pockets of sunshine when the world turned dark.' He smiled, presumably picturing his little family. 'Anyway, the memorial was back in Barrow – that's where I'm from – and was something Patrick and Hattie would have hated. I told Joan that when she first mentioned it but she and Ken were adamant that they had to do something to honour Patrick's and Hattie's memories. I think about them every day, I miss them, I wish they were still here but they're not and I personally don't need some big, sad event to show that I cared. However, I do understand that people grieve in different ways and, for the briefest of moments, I wondered whether this was something they both really needed. And then I reminded myself who we were talking about here. Ken and Joan don't do anything unless there's something in it for them, although I couldn't imagine what. Even during the service, I still wasn't sure what the motivation was and I wondered if I'd turned into a cynic. Then a mate of mine sent me a photo of the front page of Tuesday's local paper. Another new business and a chance to garner some sympathy by raking over the tragedy again and lying about the amazing relationship they'd had with their only beloved daughter when the reality was that they barely spoke to her.'

He didn't sound bitter – just resigned. Clearly Hattie's parents had done a lot over the years. And the arrival of the newspaper explained why he was still off on Tuesday when we went through the first set of plans.

'They wanted me to take the girls to the memorial but that was a resounding no from me,' he continued. 'Why would I subject them to what was effectively a second funeral for their parents who'd died five years ago? Joan wouldn't accept my decision and kept pestering me. She must have convinced herself she'd broken me and I would take them because she went mad with me when I got there, demanding to know where they were. Of course, I now know she only wanted them for a photo opportunity.'

'She sounds like an, erm, colourful character,' I said, grimacing.

'That's a generous word. I can think of a few other more appropriate ones.' He released his legs and leaned back, resting on his forearms. 'I don't know why I blurted all that out. Suffice to say, last Friday was difficult but it's over and I'm hoping we won't have a repeat of it at year ten and fifteen.'

'Do they ever see their grandchildren?'

'No. They've only seen them three or four times since they were born. It's not up to me to cut them out of the girls' lives, no matter what I think of them, so I phone up occasionally and try to organise a visit but I'm always fobbed off. The sad truth now is that Lyla and Elsa don't even remember them. Ken and Joan did that – not me. It's a shame but at least they have one grandparent who cares. Mam lives in Cockermouth now. Puts her a bit closer to us in Keswick than when she was in Barrow, but far enough away that she gets her own space.'

Barrow, short for Barrow-in-Furness, was at the tip of a coastal peninsula at the southern end of Cumbria, about ninety minutes' drive from Willowdale. I'd visited the beach a couple of times but it wasn't an area I knew well.

'What about the rest of your family?' Killian asked. 'Are they local?'

He already knew that I was staying with Dad in Pippinth-waite and that my parents had divorced when I was young, so I gave him a potted history of my various house moves and an overview of the family tree.

I got the impression Killian knew Oliver and Rosie well but would they have shared the news about Oliver being my half-brother? Killian hadn't given any indication that he knew.

'Are you aware that Oliver's my half-brother?' I asked.

He sat straight up, eyes wide. 'Seriously?'

'Yeah, it's new information and a bit of a surprise for us both but I'm looking forward to getting to know them all better.'

'You couldn't be related to better people. So you and Oliver have the same dad?'

I gave a brief outline, not feeling it was my place to share too many details.

'I wondered if Rosie might have told you,' I said when I'd finished.

'She probably didn't want to say anything until you and Oliver had actually met and I've barely seen her this week. I'm dead chuffed for you. As I say, they're great people.'

'They seem to be and I'm so grateful to them for letting my alpacas have a home here. And a magnificent home it's going to be, thanks to you.'

'Teamwork,' he said, giving me a big smile. 'We're creating a magnificent home together.'

The way he looked at me gave me a warm glow inside. After everything that had happened at Bracken Ridge Farm, it was so good to feel like part of something again.

'The girls can't wait to meet The Magnificent Seven.

They've never seen an alpaca so we've been looking them up online and comparing them to llamas.'

'If you get your phone out, I can Airdrop you some photos of the herd if you like.'

'That'd be great.'

I selected several photos and Airdropped them to his phone with a promise to message him later to tell him which alpaca was which.

'What are those?' he said, pointing to the most recent photos I'd uploaded on my phone.

'Photos of some sketches I've been doing.'

'Can I see?'

I handed him my phone and he scrolled through. 'You drew all these?'

'Yes. They're a bit rough around the edges at the moment but I'll keep working on them and the hope is, down the line, I'll be able to use them on a range of merchandise.'

He returned my phone with a whistle. 'Artist, scientist, teacher, alpaca rescuer, digger operator and builder of patios... is there any end to your talents?'

'That might be it and artist is definitely a work in progress.'

'Artist is a major talent. I'm a little embarrassed by my cartoon alpacas now.'

'But they were adorable. I think you're really talented.'

'They were doodles, but thank you. I'm glad you liked them.'

We smiled at each other in a moment of mutual admiration and I had another warm glow inside. Not only was I now part of a team but I was surrounded by people who thought I had talents, who appreciated me, who thought I added value. I hadn't realised how badly that had been knocked out of me over the past couple of years. Or was it even longer than that? Did it go back as far as Matthew?

35

Later that afternoon, Ruth and I joined The Magnificent Seven in their temporary enclosure at Butterbea Croft. She'd told me that they had a local youth group volunteering for the day so Lizzie was with them but would drop by later.

'Less than a fortnight to go,' Ruth said. 'How excited are you?'

'Close to bursting. How have they been?'

'Such good girls. It's been a pleasure giving them board and lodgings. We're going to miss them. Most have been brilliant on their leads so it's as though they were always destined for their new life as part of your business.'

'I've got a name for it now,' I said. 'My Alpaca Adventure.'

'Aw, that's so perfect. Love it.'

All seven of them had been at the far end of the field but a quick shake of the treat bucket and they were making their way towards us now, led by Barbara.

'I swear she swaggers rather than walks,' I said to Ruth.

'Lizzie and I were just saying the same thing the other day. That's an alpaca with attitude.'

'Hi, Barbara,' I said as the light grey alpaca came closer and gave my arm a gentle nudge to get better access to the food.

Camella and Jolene were right behind her and soon the whole herd were surrounding us and I had that same feeling of warmth I'd had on the beach with Killian earlier. These seven beautiful animals were my future and I couldn't be happier about it. I'd already fallen completely in love with their personalities and quirks from only a handful of visits and soon I'd be able to spend every day in their company in the most stunning of settings.

'Shall we take a couple of them on a walk so they can show off their skills?' Ruth asked. 'Camella adores being with Barbara so I'd suggest we take them together although Babs will, of course, want to be the leader.'

We attached their halters and leads which didn't seem to bother them at all, and set off on a circuit round the farm. The setting was very pleasant in gentle rolling countryside but it didn't compare to the varied dramatic setting I could offer at Willowdale Hall. There'd have been nothing to stop Ruth and Lizzie offering alpaca walks – it was, after all, the time with the alpacas that customers wanted – but I could see that the location made the farm better suited to being a rescue centre than a business like mine.

I was really impressed with Camella and Barbara on their walk. I'm not sure how much their previous owner Mitch had done – or perhaps even their owners before that whose history we didn't know – versus how much Ruth and Lizzie had done but it all boded extremely well for My Alpaca Adventure.

'They seem really comfortable on their leads,' I said as we returned to the enclosure.

'We'll take Florence and Charmaine next, but it'll be a tad different,' she said with a mischievous grin.

Neither Florence nor Charmaine showed any objections to having their halters on and they walked nicely at first, Florence at the front with me, but suddenly she lurched to the left and rubbed herself up against a hedge.

'Ah! I see what you mean!' I said, laughing as Florence continued to scratch. 'She's like Baloo in *The Jungle Book*.'

Florence's other tricks included pulling on her lead, swapping sides and basically having a mind of her own as to which route she wanted to take.

'Barbara's definitely in charge when they're all together,' Ruth said, 'but I think Florence would like to be. She respects Babs too much to contest her for leadership so she tries to show us her leadership skills when they're apart. I'm sure she'll settle down the more walks she does but she's probably one to partner with a strong, confident customer. And, as you can see, Charmaine is really demure and will happily follow Flo's lead and not give you any trouble.'

We walked the final three together as alpacas like company so walking one on their own would cause unnecessary stress. Jolene and Bianca had no problem with their halters but Maud needed quite a lot of coaxing into hers. She was then reluctant to set off walking and generally seemed unsure of the whole thing.

'I don't want to distress her,' I said to Ruth when Maud stopped for a third time. 'Let's go back and we'll walk Jolene and Bianca without her.' I scratched Maud's neck and gave her gentle words of reassurance as we waited for Ruth to circle back with Jolene and Bianca so we could follow behind. As though sensing she was returning to 'safety', Maud showed no resistance as we walked back to the enclosure.

'Has she been like this all the time?' I asked, recalling that Maud had been a little hesitant when we'd rescued them but that it was Camella, Charmaine and Jolene who'd travelled in the second trailer and had been much harder to coax onboard.

'She has, but it's nothing to worry about. Some alpacas take longer to train than others. It's possible that she was a later addition to the herd and never got trained before, in which case she's doing brilliantly.'

Maud joined the others grazing while Ruth and I took Jolene and Bianca back out.

'Lizzie and I reckon Bianca's deaf on her left side but has some hearing on her right,' Ruth told me. 'She does seem to respond to noises if you're stood on that side of her.'

Bianca was a very special alpaca. Known as a blue-eyed white, she was a semi-albino. Deafness was believed to affect about eighty per cent of blue-eyed whites which meant there were some breeders – particularly those who bred for the show world – who weren't be interested in them. As that wasn't something I ever planned to do, I was delighted to have Bianca as an equally valued and loved member of The Magnificent Seven. The deafness caused her no pain or discomfort and, being a herd animal, it wouldn't typically affect her because she could take cues from the others. I saw no reason why she couldn't live a full and happy life at Willowdale Hall.

We left the alpacas to join Lizzie for a coffee in the farmhouse, after which I returned to the enclosure on my own. I took some more photos and a video and sent them to Killian to show to Lyla and Elsa. A little later, a video from Killian appeared.

'Hi, Emma,' Killian said. 'The Magnificent Seven's Fan Club want to say something.'

He moved away from the screen and two blonde-haired girls appeared, waving frantically.

'I'm Lyla,' said the oldest one, 'and I'm nine years old.'

'I'm Elsa and I'm six,' said her sister, holding up one hand, fingers splayed, and the index finger on her other.

'We love your alpacas!' they shouted together, before collapsing in a fit of giggles.

Killian's face appeared again. 'There was more but, as you can see, they've got the giggles. We just wanted to say thanks for the photos and videos. They're—'

But he didn't get to say any more because Elsa launched herself across his lap.

'My friend Courtney says they spit,' Lyla said, appearing close up to the screen.

'Urgh!' Elsa cried. 'They don't spit!'

'Courtney says they do.'

'That's yukky and the alpacas are cute,' Elsa protested, crossing her arms and pouting.

'I'm sure Emma will let us know the answer when she has time,' Killian said. 'Let's say goodbye and thank you.'

'Goodbye and thank you,' the girls cried, blowing kisses at the screen. The last thing I saw before the video disconnected was Killian looking apologetic and mouthing 'sorry'.

'Do alpacas spit?' I muttered to myself. 'Let's clear that up.'

I wandered over to the nearest alpaca – Jolene – and set my phone away recording us.

'Jolene, your fan club would like to know whether you spit.'

I bent my head close to her, nodding and smiling, as though listening to what she was telling me.

'Jolene says you're probably confusing her with her close relation, the llama. Llamas are more likely to spit but it's usually only when they feel threatened. Alpacas aren't known to be spitters but, as a last resort, if they're angry or scared, they might spit. If they do, it's actually more of a hiss with saliva and air coming out whereas when a llama spits, it can be quite nasty. We're talking regurgitated food and everything. Yeah, I know, that's really gross, isn't it?'

I adjusted the camera angle so they could see the rest of the herd in the background.

'Hope that answers your question. When they're settled in their new home at Willowdale Hall, you'll have to come and meet them all. Bye for now.'

I smiled and waved at the camera then sent the film to Killian. A few minutes later, a message arrived.

FROM KILLIAN

That video was fantastic. You could not be more of a hit with my girls. Thanks so much for that. Enjoy the rest of your weekend and I'll see you on Monday morning. And thanks for the link to the wellies. Hope you don't mind but, as suspected, they both chose the same ones as yours. Clearly you have excellent taste!

TO KILLIAN

We can be triplets in our matching boots. Glad they enjoyed it. Hope you all have a fabulous weekend too. See you soon x

I clocked the kiss just before I sent the message and hastily deleted it, replacing it with a smiley face. I really liked Killian but that was it and sending a kiss when we were only just starting to build a friendship was highly inappropriate.

As I slipped my phone back into my pocket, I reflected on his relationship status. He'd told me he had a fiancée at the time Patrick and Hattie died who hadn't stuck around but he hadn't mentioned there being anyone since then. I should have asked when he was talking about his family, although surely he'd have mentioned if a girlfriend was on the scene. Not that I'd told him about Grayson, but that was different. Grayson wasn't part of my family anymore.

It was half five and the temperature had dropped, so I said goodbye to the herd and walked over to the house.

'Do you have time for a cuppa before you go?' Lizzie asked when she answered the door.

'I'm a bit chilly so yes please and then I'll hit the road.'

'There's something we need to tell you,' Ruth said once we were settled in their lounge with hot drinks. 'Debbie rang yesterday.'

It took me a moment to register who Debbie was – the daughter of Mitch, the previous owner of the alpacas.

'How's her mum doing?' I asked.

'Not so good. Since the day of the rescue, her mum's had a couple more strokes and she's in a bad way. Debbie doesn't think she has much longer left and, as her parents aren't yet divorced, Mitch seems to think he's going to get the farm and has already made noises about getting his alpacas back.'

My stomach plummeted to the floor. 'Oh! Was she trying to get them back for him?'

Lizzie shook her head. 'Completely the opposite. She says Mitch made no attempt to find a new home for them when her mum kicked him out and he barely checked in on them so, as far as she's concerned, he's not the right person to care for them, but she wanted to give us a heads up in case he turns up here.'

'Do you think he will?'

Lizzie shrugged. 'He might try but he won't get anywhere. The handover documents are legally binding and we told Debbie to tell Mitch that we'd already passed them on to another sanctuary. She said it was better that she didn't know any details about where they'd gone so it couldn't slip out by mistake.'

'We're hoping he'll accept that he's too late,' Ruth said. 'We've updated our website with a picture of the herd and a spiel about their stay being short but sweet before moving on to another rescue centre elsewhere in the country so, if he doesn't believe her and looks us up, that'll back it up.' She gave me a gentle smile. 'Don't look so worried, Emma. It'll all be fine.'

Neither of them looked concerned, which reassured me a little, but as I drove home shortly after, a ball of anxiety swirled round my stomach. Mitch struck me as the act-now-think-later type, often without the latter. What if Debbie's mum passed away in the next couple of days and Mitch made it his number one priority to reclaim his alpacas? What if he turned up at Butterbea Croft in the middle of the night and stole them? I felt nauseous. There was no way I could risk anything happening to the alpacas or my new friends being vulnerable. I'd speak to Killian on Monday and see whether there was any chance we could speed up the building works so we could move the herd to Willowdale Hall even sooner. If that wasn't possible, I'd speak to Oliver and Rosie. There had to be somewhere we could keep them until their new enclosure was ready. It might not be ideal but it was far better they were with me than in danger of being snatched from Butterbea Croft by Mitch.

36

I woke up in the early hours of Sunday morning, heart racing, sweat pouring from me. In my dreams, I'd turned up at Butterbea Croft to visit The Magnificent Seven but Mitch was already there, trying to round them up. They were terrified, running in every direction. Maud jumped the fence and ran out of sight, Bianca took a nasty tumble and something cracked in her leg, and the others were screaming. I knew alpacas could scream when afraid, although I hadn't heard the sound and hoped I never would. The screaming in my dream – or nightmare – chilled me to the bones and, despite the sweat trickling down my back, I shivered as I wrapped the duvet more tightly around me.

Sleep was elusive after that and I lay on my side watching the room slowly lighten as dawn crept in. I was going to have to do something.

TO KILLIAN

I'm hoping your phone's on silent and you don't see this until a reasonable hour but can you give me a call as soon as you're awake? Thank you

It was shortly after seven when my phone rang and Killian's name flashed up.

'Are you okay?' he asked, sounding concerned.

'It's not me. It's the alpacas.' I ran through what I'd learned from Ruth and Lizzie yesterday. 'I know it's a big ask when we're only three days into a fortnight of work, but is there any way we could speed the shelter along and get the essentials ready so we can move them here sooner?'

'Give me ten minutes and I'll call you back.'

I waited impatiently, stomach churning, my heart pounding when he rang back.

'I can be at the hall for half eight.'

'I can't ask you to forfeit another day with your girls. That's your precious time.'

'It's not something I do often so they'll understand, especially when it means they'll get to meet the alpacas sooner, and I want to help. If you can rope in another pair of hands, we should be able to make good progress with the shelter today.'

'I'm sure my dad'll be willing.'

'Perfect. I'll see you soon and try not to worry. We'll take stock of progress at lunchtime but I'd like to think we can be ready with the basics by Wednesday. When are your deliveries due?'

Damn! I hadn't even thought about that. 'Not till the following week. I can call them tomorrow but I won't hold my breath for flexibility after I've already messed them around.'

'It's still worth a try. If it's not an option for the equipment, there's the water trough in the field already and we'll either be able to borrow some things from the stables or improvise. The food might be more of an issue.'

'I should be able to get supplies from Ruth and Lizzie.' I heaved a sigh of relief that moving my herd sooner was a possibility. 'Thanks for this, Killian. I really appreciate it.'

* * *

Dad was eager to help and we were able to call on Oliver's assistance too. Rosie was tied up with riding lessons although five of us trying to work in a small space might have been counterproductive.

Killian's project management skills were superb and I was impressed at how calm he was under pressure. We'd talked while we were working last week but it had mainly been about the work itself, my plans for the business, and the work Oliver and Rosie had asked him to do around the estate. Our lunchtime beach conversation on Friday had been the first time I'd found out any personal details and I remembered him saying he and his brother were both ex-army and I wondered what his role had been and whether his project management skills came from that.

He wasn't the only one with impressive skills. I was amazed at how good Dad was with the tools and how much he clearly enjoyed working with his hands.

Alice appeared at lunchtime with sandwiches, drinks and fruit for the workers and invited us to join her for a Sunday roast at teatime. Dad and I had originally planned to go out for Sunday lunch and had no food in so gratefully accepted her invite, but Killian declined, saying he needed to get home to relieve his mum from looking after the girls.

After I'd eaten my sandwich, I called Ruth to see if they could transport the herd on Wednesday. I thought she might protest and say I was worrying unnecessarily but the fact that she didn't made me think that the sisters shared the same fears as me that Mitch was a loose cannon who'd do what he wanted when he wanted. She also confirmed that they could bring sufficient hay and feed to tide the herd over if I couldn't change the delivery date for my order.

By the time Killian left, the shelter was complete and looked amazing. The old water trough had been thoroughly cleaned and we'd made a start on putting down the rubber matting. After a quick tidy of the site, Dad and I followed Oliver to the hall where we were greeted by the delicious smell of a joint of beef cooking.

The day had started with fear and panic but now I felt calm. How kind of everyone to have rallied around, giving up their Sundays to help me like this. Not that I'd had any doubts about Willowdale Hall being the right home for the herd but today's efforts had shown how important and valuable everyone thought the alpacas were. Couldn't be more different from Grayson's *you needn't think I'll be helping* attitude.

Dad and I arrived back home to Pippinthwaite shortly after eight. While he showered in his en suite, I ran a bath in the family bathroom, pouring a generous helping of muscle soak bubble bath under the running tap. I'd worked hard this week and my muscles definitely felt it.

The bath eased the aches and when I returned to my room feeling all relaxed, I found a steaming mug of hot chocolate on my bedside drawers. I pulled on a pair of fleecy pyjamas, brushed my hair and curled up on the bed with my drink. I'd already thanked Killian before he left this afternoon but wanted to emphasise how grateful I was so I messaged him.

TO KILLIAN

Thank you so very, very much for everything you've done for me and the alpacas this week and especially for today. Giving up your Sunday was above and beyond and I'm so grateful. Hope the girls were OK without you. Feeling a lot calmer now thanks to your kindness

My thumb hovered over the 'x' but, again, I was concerned about sending the wrong message. I meant it in grateful friendship but it could be misconstrued so I scrolled through the emojis and selected the smiling face with hearts.

A few minutes later, a reply came through.

FROM KILLIAN

You're so welcome. It's a great project and there was no way I wasn't going to help today. We'll soon have The Magnificent Seven safe and settled in their new home. The girls had an amazing time with my mam. They've been crafting and I think I might be finding sequins and glitter for the next two months! How was tea?

TO KILLIAN

Delicious. Alice is an amazing cook. She'd made apple crumble for pudding and it's the first time I've had it with more crumble than fruit. I think I might be spoilt for life!

FROM KILLIAN

Love it! Rosie has told me before about her family crumble:fruit ratio so I must try this one day. Have you just got back?

TO KILLIAN

About 45 mins ago. I've had a long bath to ease my aching muscles. Not used to the physical work but really enjoying it. Do you ever ache or have you been doing this so long that you're used to it?

FROM KILLIAN

I'm used to it. I've always done physical work but, if I've done something different that's used muscles I don't normally use, I can definitely feel it

TO KILLIAN

You mentioned being in the army like your brother. Is that what you did before you set up your own business?

FROM KILLIAN

Yes, but I never planned to join the army. Are you doing anything now? I can FaceTime you if you're free? If not, I can tell you the story tomorrow

My hand went instinctively to my damp hair and my fingers brushed against my make-up-free face before I shook my head for even thinking about it. Killian had seen me all week without make-up, face dripping with sweat, and my hair scraped back into a ponytail so what did it matter if he saw me fresh-faced from the bath?

TO KILLIAN

Just relaxing in Dad's spare room with a hot chocolate while he's watching TV so I'm free to chat if I'm not disrupting your family time

FROM KILLIAN

> The girls are in bed and I'm not much of a TV
> person. Give me 2 mins to make a cuppa and
> then I'll call you

I took that time to run downstairs to thank Dad for the hot chocolate and tell him I was going to be on a call. Back in the bedroom, I'd just plumped the pillows and made myself more comfortable when the FaceTime request arrived.

'You're sure I'm not interrupting your evening?' I said after we'd greeted each other.

'I'm sure. As I say, not a telly person.'

'Me either. I like films and I've binged the odd series but there's nothing I watch regularly. I've never watched the soaps and I've never watched any reality TV either.'

'Snap!' he said, smiling. 'You were asking about my career.'

'Only if you don't mind sharing.'

'I don't mind at all. Like I said, I was in the army, but there's a story behind that and it's the reason I ultimately wanted to settle in the Lakes and also why I do a lot of the things I do through my company and outside of work.'

I didn't know what the *things* he was referring to were but presumably that was the reason for a conversation rather than a message.

'I told you that my dad cleared off when I was eight. It was the best thing that could have happened to us because he wasn't a nice man. He drank too much, he did drugs and, if he wasn't happy about something, he let his fists convey it. I swore I'd never be anything like him. Mam discovered she was pregnant after Dad left but he wasn't interested in having anything to do with her. He's never even seen his daughter but that's his loss, not Aoife's. Mam had a lot on her plate with a new baby and Patrick was still young so she really needed my help. I stepped up and was a good kid. But a few years later when I started at senior school, I got in with the wrong crowd and that good kid lost his way.'

He paused, a frown across his brow.

'Go on,' I encouraged. 'I'm listening but I'm not judging.'

He smiled and nodded. 'Before long I was drinking and getting into fights. Our gang skipped school more than we attended it but we were soon bored of wandering round the streets of Barrow so we turned to petty crime – gave us a kick, gave us something to do. My poor mam was at the end of her tether with the school constantly on the phone and the police turning up at the door most weeks. I didn't want to hurt her but I couldn't seem to help myself. I finished school but I hadn't turned up for half my exams so there was little hope of me leaving with any qualifications. I'd done nothing about finding a job and Mam was scared for my future. She was also scared for Patrick. He'd be starting senior school in the September and he looked up to me so much that Mam was worried he'd go down the same path. Her health had started to deteriorate and she didn't think she had the strength to deal with two sons going off the rails so she decided drastic times needed drastic action. She'd heard about this two-week programme called ABSORB and enrolled me on it. ABSORB stood for Activities and Bushcraft for Students and Offenders to Reset their Beliefs.'

'A religious programme?' I asked.

'No. The beliefs part was about self-belief. It was a programme run in conjunction with the police and several charities – a couple of which were Christian, but religion wasn't the point of the programme. It was aimed at teenagers who'd lost their way and didn't believe that they could amount to anything so they were going down a self-fulfilling spiral to destruction. By taking them away from their negative influences – drink, drugs, friends and, in some cases, their home life – they could begin to reset and learn a stack of skills along the way.

'Honestly, Emma, it was the best thing anyone has ever done for me. Mam couldn't drive at the time and the closest thing we got to going on holiday was a day trip on the bus to Morecambe so just being in the National Park blew me away. And the things we learned...' He pressed his fingers to his forehead and drew them away, indicating that the activities had also blown his mind.

'What sort of things?' I asked.

'Everything. We covered a load of practical survival skills like lighting a fire, building a shelter and first aid but we did fun things like mountaineering, kayaking and raft-building. Every day was packed with something new but we also had discussions where we looked at how things had gone wrong for us and what we wanted our future to look like when we returned home. The big thing for me was looking at who or what was to blame. I threw it all out – my dad, my mates, my teachers – but, ultimately, my big learning point was that *I* was the one who'd made the decisions and behaved the way I did. At any moment, I could have said no and taken a different path. It was such an eye-opener.'

'It sounds like an amazing programme. I can think of several past students who'd have massively benefited from something like that.'

'I can well imagine. I left my fortnight determined to get my life back on track and be a better role model for Patrick and Aoife, which meant ditching the mates and getting a job. I didn't have qualifications but our next-door neighbour's brother, Norman, was a kitchen fitter and he'd been toying with taking on a trainee to help him with the heavier stuff so he took a chance on me. I learned so much from him in a short space of time but he collapsed on the job one day – massive heart attack – and had to give up working.'

'Aw, that's awful. You were with him when he collapsed?'

'Yeah. It was terrifying but, because of the first aid they'd covered as part of ABSORB, I knew what to do. Got his heart going again and he lived another twenty years after that.'

'So ABSORB not only changed your life. It saved his.'

'It did indeed, which makes it even more of a crying shame that the programme folded. So, with Norman taking early retirement, I was back to being jobless but I'd got a thirst for learning new things. I wasn't academic so there was no point contemplating going back to school – not then, anyway – but I was practical and full of ideas and that's when I decided to join the army. I did eighteen years, finishing as Lieutenant Troop Commander in The Royal Logistics Corps. Loved it. I learned loads, saw some amazing places, saw some shocking things, met some great people including my now ex-fiancée Danika. I'd have stayed in the army for longer but Danika was ready to settle down and have children and she didn't want to bring them up in the military. She came from an army family and had travelled all over Europe, changing schools frequently, and she didn't want that for our kids. The plan was to settle in the Lakes, establish ourselves in new careers, get married and start a family. We managed the first two and had been looking at wedding venues when tragedy struck and the having kids part happened a bit sooner than planned, except they were my brother's children and that wasn't what Danika wanted.'

I winced at the familiarity of it and bit my lip, trying to dislodge the thoughts of Matthew circling round my head.

'That must have hurt,' I said, gently.

'Yes and no. At the time, I was grieving for Patrick and Hattie, trying to create a new normal for a baby and a four-year-old, and battling with Ken and Joan. I thought Danika and I were on the same page about *not now* for the wedding and family meaning exactly that – not now rather than not ever. Patience was never one of her strong points. She liked to have a plan and execute it to the letter and bringing up someone else's kids was not part of that plan so she was out. I used to wonder whether I could have given her more time and attention but I was treading water as it was and, whether she liked it or not, Lyla and Elsa had to be my number one priority. I'd like to think that, if she'd truly loved me, she'd have understood but she'd probably argue back that, if I truly loved her, I would have continued with the plans we had.'

'But it's not like you did that on a whim. Something very unexpected happened and of course you had to deal with that first. It's funny how big life changes – especially unexpected ones – can bring some couples together but destroy others.'

'That sounds like the voice of experience.'

'Sadly, it is. The reason I suddenly needed a new home for the alpacas was that my fiancé decided he didn't want me living in ours anymore...'

'And this was only a couple of weeks ago?' Killian asked after I'd outlined what had happened with Grayson.

'It's been the proverbial rollercoaster recently.'

'I'd never have guessed. You're always so cheerful when I see you.'

'I'm generally a positive person but I didn't feel remotely cheerful after it happened – just really stupid and used. How could I not have seen that?'

'Sometimes people are really good at hiding things and

sometimes we don't see things because we don't want to see them.'

I pondered on that for a moment. 'I think it might have been a combination of the two.' I bit my lip again as I added, 'Both times.'

'Both times?' he prompted when I fell silent.

'Before Grayson – a lot of years before – I was married...' I took a deep breath and ran a hand through my hair. Was I really going to tell him what happened with Matthew? This wasn't how I'd planned to spend this evening. All I'd wanted to do was thank him for being so kind but he'd offered to call me and he'd been open about his past which had to have taken guts. But if I did open up about Matthew, was I brave enough to tell him the whole story? The story nobody – not even Mum or Rachael – knew?

'...but it didn't work out,' I finished.

Killian's brow was furrowed once more, as though he was waiting for me to continue and I couldn't do it. I felt really comfortable with him, as though I could tell him anything and he'd understand, but I just couldn't do it. I'd spent too many years telling an edited version of my story and it was too difficult to give the full truth.

I shrugged. 'Long time ago now, though.'

'If you ever want to talk about it...'

'I'm good, but thanks. Maybe another time.' I yawned and rubbed my eyes. 'I'd better say goodnight so we can both get our beauty sleep.'

I heard a noise and Killian looked off to one side. 'Sounds like one of the girls are up anyway. See you tomorrow.'

'Will do and thanks again for today.'

He smiled and nodded before disconnecting.

I sank back against my pillows with a sigh. Why was it so

difficult after all these years to tell the truth? But I knew why. I was embarrassed, humiliated, ashamed. Grayson had found a dream he didn't want me to be part of and everyone knew that. How could I admit that he wasn't the first one to do that to me?

37

SIXTEEN YEARS AGO

Matthew and I sat side by side in the waiting room at the private clinic. His head was dipped, his hands tightly locked between his legs. I'd tried to take his hand in mine but he'd shrugged me off, angry that I'd insisted he join me for the appointment.

'What's the point when we already know it's bad news?' he'd snapped.

'You don't know that for certain.'

'Six years of trying and nothing happening is a pretty strong clue.'

But the whole point of today wasn't just to find out what was preventing me from conceiving a baby. It was about exploring our options for what happened next.

A door opened down the corridor and a middle-aged woman stepped out. 'Emma and Matthew Holmes?'

I stood up and gave Matthew a nudge. He trailed behind me like a sulky child being dragged around the supermarket.

'I'm Susanna Hawkins,' she said, smiling at us. 'Do come in and take a seat.'

She closed the door and sat down on the opposite side of a large desk to us. 'I understand you've been trying for a baby for six years without success and today we're going to discuss your test results and potential options. Is that correct?'

Matthew's head was dipped once more so I nodded.

'We'll start with the results from your tests, Matthew. You have low sperm count and also low motility. Would you like me to explain what that means?'

'I know what it means,' he said, his voice low and gruff. 'Might have known it was my fault.'

'We find it's best not to apportion blame,' Susanna said gently.

'But you've just told me it's my fault we can't have a baby. I've got hardly any swimmers and those I have can't swim. Blame.' He pointed his thumb to his chest as he said the last word.

Even though I understood that he was hurting, it struck me as quite an immature outburst in front of a professional, but Susanna had clearly encountered all sorts of reactions and didn't flinch.

'I know it's frustrating and difficult to hear news like this but, remember, this is about exploring options. This news doesn't mean children can't be part of your future.'

I reached for Matthew's hand but he rejected my touch again. I hated the way he retreated into himself when he was in an uncomfortable situation, especially one like this in which we should be supporting each other.

'Onto your results, Emma. They're inconclusive but, as you spoke previously about heavy and painful periods, endometriosis is a possibility. Is that something you're familiar with?'

'I teach biology,' I said, nodding. Endometriosis was a

condition where similar cells to those lining the womb grew elsewhere in the woman's body such as in the ovaries and fallopian tubes. The cells reacted to the menstrual cycle by bleeding but, as the blood had no passage out of the body, they caused inflammation and formed scar tissue. It could be extremely painful and even debilitating with heavy and painful periods, fatigue, bladder and bowel problems but I'd never thought to look into it because I hadn't experienced most of those symptoms.

'It's not something we can confirm for definite from scans, blood tests or internal examinations so the next step would be a laparoscopy.' Susanna explained what that would involve – a small camera known as a laparoscope inserted into my pelvis which a surgeon would use to look for signs of endometriosis.

'Would you like us to arrange that for you?' she asked.

'What's the point?' Matthew muttered before I could respond. 'We've already established that I can't have kids so what's the point in doing more tests on Emma when it's not going to change anything?'

I glared at him, furious that he'd answered a question about *my* body on my behalf. What gave him the right to do that?

'It's not just about fertility,' Susanna said. 'Emma has spoken of experiencing pain and, if it is endometriosis causing that, we might be able to alleviate the pain with treatment.'

'Yes, please to a laparoscopy,' I said, my voice tight.

Susanna gave me a gentle smile. 'I'll get that arranged for you.' She tapped something into her computer then turned back to us both. 'Although I can talk to you about next steps today, I'd suggest it makes more sense to wait until we get the results of the laparoscopy before we have that conversation. Is that all right with you both?'

'Yes, that's fine,' I said.

'Matthew?' she prompted.

He nodded then pushed his chair back, the scrape across the tiled floor cutting through me, and left the room.

I closed my eyes briefly, drawing in a deep breath. 'I'm sorry about that,' I said to Susanna.

'No need to apologise. I've done this for a long time and I've seen all sorts of reactions to results. It can be difficult to hear.' She removed a leaflet from a display by her desk and handed it to me. 'This might help.'

The title of the leaflet was *Understanding Your Partner's Reaction to Infertility*. I wanted to ask her if there was an accompanying leaflet called *Understanding Your Partner's Reaction to Life, the Universe and Everything* because I really didn't understand anything that was going on with Matthew right now but, instead, I thanked her and left the room.

I'd expected to find Matthew in the corridor or even in the waiting room but there was no sign of him. I hung around for several minutes, wondering if he'd gone to the toilet. When a man exited the gents, I asked him if there was anyone else in there but he said he'd been the only one.

'I didn't know where you were,' I said, trying to keep my voice light when I finally found Matthew in the car. 'I've been loitering outside the gents. You could have texted me to say you were outside.'

'I'd have thought it was obvious.'

Ten minutes clearly hadn't calmed his mood. He turned on the ignition and put the car into gear before I'd even had a chance to put my seatbelt on, which I didn't appreciate.

'Do you want to talk about it?' I asked.

'Do I look like someone who wants to talk about it?'

'Please don't be like that,' I said, placing my hand gently on his thigh.

He pushed my hand away. 'Like what? How do you want me to be? We can't have children and it's all my fault.'

'It's *not* your fault. You heard what Susanna said. And it sounds as though it might be my body too. We'll know more after I've had—'

'Is this not talking about it?' he snapped.

'But we *need* to talk. I know you're hurting but it doesn't mean we can never have children. As Susanna said, there are still options.'

'Options? Oh yeah, there are loads of *great* options. Sperm donor, surrogate, fostering, adoption. Where in any of those options do I get to be the dad?'

'All of them! You might not be the dad biologically but you'd get to be it in all the important ways.'

'It's not the same.'

'I'm not saying it's *exactly* the same but—'

'There's no *but*. It's not the same. If I can't be the biological dad, I'm not interested.'

'But what about what I want? Doesn't that matter?' I couldn't keep the exasperation out of my tone now, and I winced at the volume.

'I could ask you the same question. I don't want children if I'm not the biological father and clearly you couldn't care less who the dad is. Cheers for that.'

'I didn't say that.'

'You didn't have to. I know you're desperate to have kids and I'm pretty sure you want them more than you want me.'

I turned my body so that he couldn't see the silent tears flowing down my cheeks as I stared numbly out of the window. What more could I say when he was in this mood? He couldn't be more wrong. Yes, I wanted children so very badly but I loved Matthew. I'd loved him since I was a teenager and, even though we were very different personalities, it worked.

Until it didn't.

And with the news from Susanna Hawkins that he was infertile, I feared that Matthew might believe we'd hit that point.

38

FIFTEEN AND A HALF YEARS AGO

My eyes burned with unshed tears as I sank down onto the stairs, staring at the suitcase and small backpack in the hall with Matthew's coat draped across them.

'It's only a fortnight,' he said, emerging from the lounge with his passport and travel documents in a zipped wallet.

'I know, but we've never been apart for longer than a week-end.' My voice came out all squeaky.

He crouched down in front of me and gently tilted my chin so he could look into my eyes. 'Term starts tomorrow and don't you always say time flies after the Christmas break?'

I shrugged. Maybe it did, but I could see it dragging when I was coming home to an empty house at the end of each day while my husband was on the other side of the world.

'I'll be back before you know it,' he added, his voice soft, 'and we'll go away for a few days together over February half term. I promise.'

I nodded and swallowed hard on the lump restricting my throat. A mini-break was no consolation for this.

The last few months had been really tough on us both. My

laparoscopy had indeed revealed endometriosis. Because the investigation was carried out under a general anaesthetic, it was usual for the surgeon to operate at the same time so I'd had endometriotic cysts and scar tissue removed. The advice for pregnancy was to try as soon as possible after surgery as endometriosis had an unpredictable reoccurrence rate, but Matthew's stance on considering other options hadn't shifted. If anything, he'd dug his heels in further and exploring IVF using a sperm donor was something he point blank refused to discuss.

Concerned that he was sleeping badly and hardly touching his food, I'd repeatedly reached out to him but to no avail. When something was bothering him, he typically stewed for several days before reluctantly letting me in so I gave him the space he needed to get his head together. It hurt when he pushed me away like that but I'd learned to accept that it was nothing to do with not trusting me and was purely about the way he processed things.

When he was finally ready to talk, he told me he thought we needed some time apart. *Not a break-up, definitely not that.* I wanted so badly to believe him. *Just some time to recharge our batteries.* Didn't couples usually take the time to do that together?

And then he revealed what that time apart meant for him and my heart sank even further. *Karl's invited me to visit him in New Zealand.*

Because we hadn't had a big wedding, we'd gone big with the honeymoon, spending a month in New Zealand. It was somewhere I'd longed to visit for the beautiful scenery. For Matthew it was the place where Peter Jackson's *Lord of the Rings* trilogy had been filmed, the first film of which had been released the year before our wedding.

He'd longed to return and had often mentioned an open invitation from Karl – a friend who'd been a game programmer, like Matthew, at the same company but who'd emigrated there a few years back. It seemed that now was the time to take him up on that invite. It spoke volumes that his idea of *time apart* meant a trip to the other side of the world.

'Are you sure you don't want me to drive you to the airport?' I asked, my eyes pleading with Matthew's. I realised I was grasping at straws but maybe a couple more hours together could help us reconnect.

He shook his head. 'We've already been through this. I fly back on a school day so you can't pick me up. It's easier for me to leave my car at the airport.'

He eased me to my feet and wrapped his arms around me. 'It's only two weeks,' he whispered into my hair. 'It'll soon pass.'

The two weeks didn't worry me so much as the horrible feeling in my gut that a fortnight apart was going to irrevocably change things for us and not for the better. I was normally really optimistic but I couldn't see the chink of light in this situation – only dark ominous clouds on the horizon.

As expected, the days sped by but the nights dragged as I lay on the bed facing the empty space beside me, thinking. Always thinking.

I'd always thought that Matthew and I were strong enough to get through anything. We might appear to be opposite personalities but we were more closely aligned than people thought. My job required me to be confident, enthusiastic and passionate, constantly interacting with others, and I typically ended the day devoid of energy. I needed a less frantic home environment to recharge my batteries and Matthew gave me that. In return, I lifted his energy after a day spent mainly in solitude working from home so we complemented each other's needs perfectly. When we first got together, he'd been terrible for keeping things bottled up but I'd been patient and encouraging with him and he'd eventually opened up about all sorts of things – being bullied at school, his difficult relationship with his family, his anxieties around strangers – and every hurt we addressed made me understand and love him even more. In return, he always built me up if I'd had a bad day, listened to me offloading about a problem student, and was so caring and attentive. He was quick-witted and had a gift for turning the ordinary – a trip to the postbox, feeding the waterfowl on the lake, a visit to the dentist – into hilarious tales full of witty observations. He might not like being around people but he was a gifted observer of human behaviour. There was barely a day went by without laughter.

Then one day I realised we rarely laughed anymore. Multiple negative pregnancy tests and hopes dashed weren't funny.

We'd been asked the question that all couples struggling with fertility must dread – *When are you going to start a family?* Nobody who asked that question ever meant it insensitively – it was just one of those natural conversations, especially when the couple in question had expressed a desire to have children at some point, which Matthew and I had.

I hadn't told my family about our visit to the fertility clinic last summer but going into hospital for surgery was different. Matthew wanted to keep the whole thing quiet but I insisted on my family and Rachael knowing about my operation. They'd have found out anyway because I needed some time off school and couldn't do that without Rachael questioning my absence.

Matthew made me promise not to tell them about his diagnosis or that the laparoscopy had been on the back of us exploring fertility issues. I reluctantly went along with his request but I didn't feel comfortable being so vague with the people I cared about.

With Matthew away, I longed to talk to someone about everything that had been going on, but loyalty to Matthew stopped me. Also, I was scared to voice my concerns that I might be losing him and convinced myself that, if I said nothing and tried not to think about it, I could pretend it wasn't true. I'd told them that a last-minute opportunity had come up to visit Karl at a good time for work and, as I had a weekend away with my best friend every year, I'd encouraged him to have a holiday to visit his.

Five months later

I arrived home from school one Friday afternoon in late June, expecting Matthew to be in his office working as usual, but he was sitting on the stairs, evidently waiting for me.

'Matthew! You startled me!' I cried, jumping at the sight of him.

'We need to talk.'

Those four monotone words cut right through me and I knew at that moment that he was going to tell me it was over. I'd known for months that the day was coming and had woken up so many mornings wondering if that would be the day he finally found the courage to destroy our world. I hadn't ignored the elephant in the room. I *had* tried to get him to open up on more occasions than I cared to remember but he'd developed a stock phrase, delivered with a smile that didn't reach his eyes – *Everything's fine. Why wouldn't it be?*

It wouldn't be because he didn't want to be here anymore. As soon as he'd returned from New Zealand in January looking tanned and relaxed and buzzing about the place, I knew I'd lost him. *More beautiful than I remembered. All that space. The people are so laid-back. I'd love to go back. The lifestyle is so much more relaxed.* But it was the unspoken words that I heard loud and clear. *I want to move there and start over. Without you.*

And now that day had arrived.

Heart pounding, stomach churning, I followed him into the lounge. The silence clawed at me, making me feel light-headed as I sank down onto the sofa where I always sat during an evening. Matthew perched on the edge of his favourite armchair. I'd never felt like that chair was far away from me until now when suddenly the distance felt as wide as the Grand Canyon – just like the gap between us since he'd returned from his January trip to New Zealand. We never had gone on that February mini-break he'd promised me.

'Karl's boss has offered me a twelve-month working visa.'

'And I'm guessing you want to accept it?' I asked when he didn't expand on his statement, my voice coming out wobbly as tears rushed to my eyes.

'Erm... the thing is... erm... I've already accepted it.'

I couldn't breathe for a moment. That felt like a punch to the stomach, completely winding me. I'd had no doubts about his love for New Zealand or his unspoken desire to move there but I'd never in a million years expected it to be presented as a fait accompli.

'You've already accepted?' I finally managed. 'We don't get to discuss it?'

'There was another candidate so they needed an answer quickly.'

'Twelve months?' I asked.

He nodded.

'What happens after that?' Like I didn't already know the answer. Like I hadn't known since January. Since the visit to the fertility clinic. Since way before then.

His eyes held mine. 'I'm sorry.'

Tears spilled down my cheeks and I hoped he wouldn't rush over to comfort me because I could hardly bear to be in the same room as him right now, let alone have him touch me. But he stayed where he was. I should have known – after all, distance had become our new normal.

'I know I've sprung this on you but I can't stop thinking about the place.' He smiled in the way he always did when he talked about New Zealand – eyes shining as though he was in the first throes of a new loving relationship which, essentially, he was. 'I feel so much more relaxed there, more alive. It's like home but different. What am I saying? You know what it's like. You loved it too, didn't you?'

A flicker of hope. Did this mean...? 'You're asking me to go with you?' I asked tentatively.

His smile slipped and my stomach plummeted to the floor. Of course he wasn't. It was a throwaway comment – a filler in a difficult conversation – and certainly not an invitation to be part of his new life.

'I didn't mean for... I don't know if I can... You wouldn't want to come. You'd probably have to retrain to teach out there. And there's no way you'd leave your family.'

Was that desperation I detected in his voice, grasping for ways to discourage me? I wiped my cheeks and shook my head. 'Maybe not, but it would have been nice to be given the choice.

And you're forgetting something. *You're* my family too.' My voice cracked as I said that, knowing it used to be the case but wasn't anymore.

I fixed my eyes on his, needing an honest answer. 'But the truth is that you stopped wanting me to be yours quite some time ago, didn't you?'

I could see sorrow but also guilt before he averted his eyes.

'I guess that answers that,' I said, pushing myself to my feet. 'When do you go?'

'At the end of next week.'

'That soon?' I frowned. 'Don't you have to work some notice?'

He stared at the floor. 'I've already worked it.'

'When?'

He kept his eyes down.

I rubbed my forehead, struggling to comprehend what he was saying. 'So when did you get offered the job?'

He met my eyes once more. 'Does it really matter?'

'It does to me.'

He sighed. 'I met Karl's boss when I was there in January and they wanted to offer me a job then but they didn't have the sign-off on the position. They got it a few months later and...' He shrugged. 'There was paperwork to sort and... I'm sorry, Em.'

Was he seriously telling me he'd interviewed for the role in January and had known for six months that he wanted to leave? That he'd been offered the job three months ago and had started the process of relocating without telling me?

The tears which had temporarily stemmed began flowing again. 'Why didn't you say anything?'

'I didn't know how to. I'm not you. You know I find it hard to open up about stuff.'

'Don't you dare! This isn't the same as a discussion about feelings and anxieties. This is a life-changing decision to bugger off to the other side of the world to start a new life without me.' I stormed towards the door and paused. 'Do I really mean so little to you?'

'No! It's not about you. It's about me. You know I've always struggled to fit in but something about New Zealand clicked for me. I feel like me there.'

'I thought I made you feel like you.'

'You did!'

I winced at the use of past tense. 'But I don't anymore. Is that what you're saying?'

'No! You're twisting my words. It wasn't you, it was those tests you made us do.'

'*Made* us do? I didn't *make* us do anything. We discussed it in depth and we *both* agreed that six years of trying for a baby was long enough and we wanted answers. I can't help it if you didn't like the answers.'

'You didn't get it. You didn't understand how I felt. You wanted a baby by whatever means.'

I wasn't having that. 'No, Matthew. I wanted *our* baby, just like you did, but neither of our bodies would let that happen and what I wanted to do next was talk about it – how you were feeling, how I was feeling and the options available. And then I wanted us to decide as a couple what, if anything, we were going to do next. But you know what? You wouldn't talk to me. Every time I tried to have a discussion, you closed me down. So don't accuse me of not getting it or not understanding when you have no idea what I'm thinking or feeling because you never bloody asked.'

I couldn't bear to look at him anymore. A scream was welling up inside me and, if I stayed for even a minute longer, I was going to completely lose it and say cruel things that could never be unsaid. I snatched up my bag and car keys and stormed out of the house, slamming the door behind me.

I had no idea where I was going – just that I needed space. My body was shaking and I felt sick as I took turn after turn, seeking out a place where people weren't. Somehow I ended up on an industrial estate where the roads were half-constructed in preparation for the next phase of development. I pulled the car up at a dead end, clutched the steering wheel with both hands and opened my mouth. At first, no sound came out but, when it came, it was the most agonising, heart-wrenching wail. I screamed, yelled and swore, banging my palms against the steering wheel until they were red and throbbing.

Energy gone, I collapsed over the wheel, gasping for breath, tears raining down my cheeks and dripping onto my thighs. How had it come to this? How had the man I loved chosen a new life on the other side of the world with a friend over our marriage? How had he lived a lie for the past six months? And how had I not realised that our marriage wasn't just broken but was actually completely over?

39

On Tuesday morning, I arrived at Willowdale Hall a little earlier than I'd agreed with Killian because I wanted some time to take in everything we'd achieved so far before the noise and activity of the day started.

Dad had offered his services again yesterday, which had been exceptionally helpful. We'd also had Rosie and Autumn's assistance after Autumn's riding lesson. There'd been plenty to keep everyone occupied with finishing touches to the shelter, laying more rubber matting, fixing the fencing round the paddock and starting work on the new fencing to create the holding pen between the paddock and the shelter.

The equipment supplier had been incredibly understanding about the situation and had managed to deliver my order at the end of the day but the food supplier was waiting on a delivery themselves and the best they could offer was Friday. I'd let Ruth know and she'd confirmed that she'd transport enough supplies for a week.

Today, it was just going to be Killian and me on site. Dad had offered to cancel his plans but I wouldn't hear of it. He'd done so much for me already and we were much further ahead than I could ever have hoped. Today we should get the holding pen finished, the food trough installed and possibly even make a start on some of the non-essentials like the customer seating.

Yesterday it had been incredible having so much help but the downside was that I'd wanted to follow up my FaceTime conversation with Killian, find out more about his inspiring personal story – how he'd found the motivation to completely change his life at such a young age and how his own story influenced his role as a parent. We'd hopefully have an opportunity to talk some more today between tasks.

I was sweeping the dust out of the shelter when Killian arrived.

'Look at you, all house proud,' he said, smiling at me.

'I know it's a bit pointless when we'll be creating more mess today but it gives me an opportunity to try out my new sweeping brush.'

'What's the verdict?'

'Best brush I've ever owned.'

'Good to hear. Nothing but the best for The Magnificent Seven. Right, how about we head to the gatehouse and make a cuppa and then we'll crack on with the holding pen?'

I grabbed my bag and followed him down the track, listening intently as he ran through the plan for the day.

'Do you know what time we can expect the herd tomorrow?' he asked as he unlocked the gatehouse a few minutes later.

'It was originally going to be after lunch because they were expecting a group of volunteers in the morning. Ruth says they've had an email from one of them to say they *might* need to take a rain check. *Might* is too vague so Ruth was going to ring them first thing and call me back as, if it's off, they'll bring the herd across first thing.'

I'd just placed my sandwiches in the fridge while Killian added coffee granules to a couple of mugs when my phone rang.

'That's Ruth now,' I told Killian before connecting the call. 'Hi, Ruth, did you manage to get hold of them?'

'It's not that. It's Mitch. Debbie's mum died last night and Mitch has found out. He's on his way to reclaim the alpacas.'

'Oh, my God! Did she tell him you don't have them anymore?'

'Yes, but he didn't believe her.'

Noticing Killian's concerned expression, I flicked the call onto speaker so he could listen in.

'He's on his way now?' I asked, my heart pounding.

'Yes, but Debbie says he'll need to borrow a horse box from someone which buys us some time. I can get four of them loaded onto the bigger trailer and bring them over now but Lizzie can't leave the farm. We've got some primary school children here and we can't think of anybody who could drive the other trailer to you.'

I threaded my fingers into my hair, desperately trying to think of a solution.

'Ruth, it's Killian. How far away from you is this Mitch?'

'Ninety minutes plus however long it takes to find a horse box.'

'How far to the alpacas from here?' Killian asked me, his voice calm.

'Forty-five minutes in good traffic.'

Killian gave me a thumbs up. 'Ruth, can you give me five minutes and we'll call you back?'

As I disconnected, he fished his phone out of his pocket and made a call.

'Hi, Rosie. Bit of a problem. Any chance I can borrow your horse box?... Big enough to fit three alpacas... Yeah, the mum's died and the dad's on his way to get them back... I know!... Yeah, I'm good. Covered to drive any vehicle of any size... Perfect. We'll see you shortly.'

He hung up and placed a reassuring hand on my shoulder. 'Rosie's preparing one of her horse boxes now. She's going to give it a disinfectant spray and lay some fresh straw. She needs ten to fifteen minutes if you want to give Ruth a call and tell her we'll be there in just over an hour. If she could get the supplies loaded up in the meantime, that'd be really helpful.'

I couldn't believe I didn't think of Rosie. It was so obvious. I called Ruth to relay the information while Killian made a flask of coffee. He was so calm and reassuring in a crisis, although I suppose that came from serving in the army where he'd likely dealt with crises all the time.

Fifteen minutes later, Rosie wished us luck and waved us off. My heart was still racing. Because we had only half the distance that Mitch had to get to Butterbea Croft, I felt confident that we'd beat him there, even if he was stupid enough to turn up without a transport solution for the alpacas. What worried me more was leaving Lizzie on her own to deal with Mitch, especially when she had young children there. I'd raised that with Ruth when I confirmed that Killian and I were coming over but she already had it covered. One of their regular volunteers, Alf, was a former police sergeant and he was already on his way over to help Lizzie and avert any trouble.

'Are you okay?' Killian asked, giving me another concerned glance as we pulled up at the hall's gates and waited for them to open.

'A bit shaky.'

'Sugar's good for shock. If you go into the side pocket of my backpack, you should find some boiled sweets. I've always got some on me.'

I leaned over into the back seat and grabbed his bag. Sure enough, there were a handful of orange sweets in the second pocket I tried.

'Barley sugar,' I said, sucking on one. 'I can't remember the last time I had one of these. Do you want one?'

'I'm fine for the moment. Now tell me, are you a sucker or a cruncher?'

At the same moment he said that, I bit the sweet into two.

'I guess that answers my question,' he said, laughing.

'Funnily enough, I'd have said I was a sucker but...' I continued to crunch the sweet, '...apparently not.'

'Aoife's a cruncher too. If we go on a journey together, she'll have scoffed half the packet before I've finished my first one so we have to divide up the sweets before we set off.'

'You do not!' I said, laughing.

'True story! It's a serious business, sweet-eating.'

We hadn't even left Willowdale and already I was feeling so much more relaxed but, to stay that way, I needed a conversation to distract me and I knew what would.

'I was thinking about what you told me the other night about the ABSORB programme. You said it was why you wanted to settle in the Lakes, which I completely understand, but you also said it was why you do the things you do through your company and outside work. What sort of things did you mean?'

'Through work, it's taking on work experience and apprenticeship students. I try to take on kids who've lost their way and would benefit from having someone who believes in them, like the ABSORB counsellors believed in us. Someone who hasn't written them off. Someone who understands what it's like to go off the rails and how to get your life back on track. My aim is to teach them some practical skills but also to try and give them some life skills around self-belief, communication, decision-making and so on. I never get them to do anything I'm not willing to do myself. They're not here to be my dogsbody, doing all the crap jobs. They're with me to learn, which might mean making the coffee and sweeping up but they'll also do the big stuff. I make them drinks and I clean up too, demonstrating that every job comes with a mix of the exciting and the mundane.'

'It's a good philosophy to have. I remember doing a week's work experience in an office when I was fourteen and all I did was make the drinks, do the filing and spend hours shredding documents.'

'And what did you learn?'

'That some people are extremely fussy about how they take their tea or coffee.'

'Exactly my point. You had a chance to learn something valuable about the world of work and to contribute something effective to that organisation but all they did was use you as free labour for the stuff they couldn't be bothered to do. How's that work experience? As I'm sure you'll know if your school offered work experience, schools have really tightened up on it since we were at school but, no matter how hard employers are quizzed about what's on offer, there'll always be someone who takes advantage and I refuse to be *that* employer. I want them to have an enriching and rewarding learning experience. I actually had a kid start on a two-week placement with me last year and it didn't take long before I realised he was exceptionally bright but had been written off by his teachers long ago because he mucked about so much in lessons. A bit more investigating and I discovered he was interested in what makes people tick so I told him there was no point me teaching him how to fell a tree when I had a sister at home studying a PhD in psychology.'

'Your sister lives with you?' I asked. 'I hadn't realised.'

'She moved in temporarily to help with the girls when Danika cleared off and she ended up staying so I'm outnumbered by women three against one. It works really well for both of us – Aoife doesn't have to worry about money while she's studying and I can work full days knowing I've got someone reliable to do the school run.'

'Must be nice for the girls to have their auntie around too.'

'It is.'

'I have a question. Killian, Patrick, Aoife – they're all Irish names but you don't have an accent.'

'My grandparents on my mam's side were Irish but they moved over and settled in Barrow when they got married. Mam was born there and she has a very mild accent but my dad was broad Barrow and all our friends were so none of us picked up the Irish lilt.'

'That explains it. I'm guessing you and Aoife must be close if she's lived with you for years.'

'Yeah, always have been, despite the nine-year age gap. She's amazing. Patrick and I were never academic but Aoife's off-the-scale bright. I couldn't tell you the specifics of her PhD. Something to do with social background and crime and...' He broke off laughing. 'It's a very long title and it doesn't matter how many times she tells me it...' He swept his hand over his head to emphasise his lack of understanding.

'You were telling me about your work experience student and I completely distracted you,' I prompted, remembering how the conversation had started.

'Oh, yeah! So, I had a word with Aoife and he switched his placement to working with her and is now at college studying psychology and loving it.'

'Sounds like you changed his life.'

'He's the only one who could do that, but Aoife and I were able to show him a different path. Up to him whether he took it or not but it's easier to do that when someone gives you a little push and tells you the only stop sign is the one you put there.'

'I love that. It's shocking how many kids I've taught over the years have those stop signs up and it's heartbreaking that it's often their parents and sometimes their teachers who caused them to do that.'

We talked about some of the students with whom I'd taken that bit of extra time after they'd been written off by other teachers. Not that I was perfect or a miracle worker. With a class of thirty, it could be really hard to separate out those who wanted to change but didn't know how to show it, those who might want to change if someone pushed hard enough and presented an alternative way, and those who genuinely couldn't care less. I didn't always get it right but it never stopped me from trying. Killian told me about some of the other teens and young adults he'd worked with.

'That's all work,' I said. 'What about the out of work part you mentioned?'

'I run a youth club a couple of nights a week. Anyone can come along but my target audience is the same as for work experience – kids who need a bit of guidance. One of the evenings is about practical skills and the other is life skills.'

He explained more about the programme and I was so impressed to discover that, despite leaving school with only two GCSE passes, he'd completed a part-time degree in counselling through the Open University while he was in the army, believing the skills learned would help him with his job and whatever he went on to do after leaving.

'I thought you said you weren't academic,' I said, smiling at him.

'I'm not. I had to work damn hard for that degree. I understood the subject no problem but writing essays the way they needed them was a nightmare to get my head around, whereas Aoife loves all that stuff.'

I'd given Ruth a quick call fifteen minutes ago to give her our ETA. When we pulled up by the alpaca enclosure a bit later, she was leading Maud onto the back of the trailer, watched by a horseshoe of wide-eyed schoolchildren. She'd have needed Lizzie's help to make sure the alpacas already in the trailer didn't escape so they'd evidently turned it into a learning experience for their visitors.

'Our friends have arrived to take the rest of the alpacas to their new home,' I heard Lizzie saying to the children as we exited Rosie's jeep. 'We're going to move on to another part of the farm now so we can leave them to get sorted.'

Lizzie waved at us as she ushered the children away with help from a handful of adults who were presumably teachers and parent helpers. There was a man with them who looked to be maybe in his late fifties to early sixties who I guessed was Alf – the retired police sergeant friend.

'I'm glad you're here,' Ruth said when they were out of earshot. 'It's been a fraught morning.'

'I'm so sorry you've had to deal with it all.'

'Gosh, not at all! If you hadn't been taking the herd, we'd have kept them so it would have happened anyway.'

I introduced her and Killian and she advised us that she'd gone for the same groups of alpacas as per the original move, with Bianca, Florence, Barbara and Maud travelling together.

'Maud was a lot less hesitant this time,' she said, 'and the other three were as compliant as before. I thought it best if the children moved away for the second load in case Camella, Charmaine and Jolene play up again.'

'Any more news from Debbie?'

'No, and I don't like to call her. Poor woman's just lost her mother and this'll be the last thing she needs to deal with. It was good of her to call this morning.' She glanced at the time on her phone. 'If Mitch does turn up without transport, we haven't got long.'

It was almost as though Camella, Charmaine and Jolene knew what was at stake as they were so much more responsive than last time. Jolene had a feisty moment when she decided to sit down for a bit but some treats soon got her shifting. The many walks they'd been taken on had likely helped greatly.

The whole time we were moving them, I felt on edge, constantly glancing down the track for any sign of approaching vehicles, but thankfully nothing came.

We agreed that Ruth would follow us but I got her to programme Willowdale Hall's postcode into her satnav just in case we got separated for any reason.

My heart was still pounding and I kept my eyes fixed on my wing mirror as we pulled off the farm track onto a minor road and then the main road.

'You might want another of those barley sugars,' Killian said after we'd been travelling for several minutes.

I nodded and unwrapped one, grateful for the sweetness on my tongue.

'They're safe now,' he assured me. 'We're not being followed. Well, we are, but that's Ruth and she's meant to be there. We've got the herd and they'll soon be settled at Casa Alpaca.'

After I'd sent messages to Dad and Rosie to confirm we were on our way back without incident, I finally relaxed into my seat.

'I can't thank you enough,' I said. 'Not just for today but for absolutely everything you've done. You know what you are? You're a fixer. You fix problems and you fix people and I'm so grateful you took the job with Rosie and Oliver because I honestly don't know what I'd have done without you.'

He glanced across at me and smiled. 'Always happy to help.' His smile was so genuine that I felt warm and fuzzy inside. He shifted his eyes back to the road. 'Anything else I can fix for you while you've got my undivided attention?'

Another glance at me and I knew I was ready. Whether I was still pumped full of adrenaline from rescuing the herd or whether it was just this feeling that I could trust him more than any other man I'd ever met, I'll never know.

'Can you fix broken hearts?' I asked.

40

Can you fix broken hearts? Had I really just asked Killian that? I wondered whether I should backtrack and say I was only joking, but the urge was strong to spill out what I hadn't been brave enough to voice on Sunday night.

'I can give it a try,' he said, his voice soft. 'Yours?'

'Yes.'

'The ex-husband?'

'Yes. His name's Matthew and he decided he'd rather move to the other side of the world than spend another minute being married to me.' I crunched my barley sugar and released a heavy sigh. 'That's the punchline, but I'd better start from the beginning...'

It was a longer story than I'd appreciated. I tried not to get too carried away with the details but I'd kept parts of it hidden for so long that, now I'd prised the lid off the box marked *things I don't talk about*, the words kept spewing out. I'd only got as far as Matthew leaving on his January trip to New Zealand by the time we reached the edge of the estate.

'Sorry, Killian!' I said, glancing at the clock. 'I've just talked at you solidly for an hour and I haven't even finished.' The journey back had been much slower with our precious cargo on board.

'You've got nothing to be sorry for,' Killian said. 'Matthew, on the other hand, has an extremely long rap sheet by my reckoning.'

'You're the first person I've told parts of that to.'

He glanced at me and nodded. 'I'm glad you did. I think you needed it.'

We reached the gates and Killian wound the window down to type in the entry code. As the gates clunked and slowly opened, he turned and fixed his eyes on mine.

'I hate pausing a big conversation like this, especially when you've been keeping it to yourself for such a long time. Are you going to be okay if we continue this later?'

I nodded. 'Thanks for listening so far. I really appreciate it.'

He placed his hand on my arm and gave it a gentle squeeze. He didn't need to add any words. That comforting touch told me he was here for me and that was more than Grayson or Matthew had been.

Ruth was right behind us and followed us through the gate and along the drive where Dad was waiting for us. As cutting back the bushes running alongside the track hadn't been the priority, we couldn't drive right up to the paddock so needed to release the herd here and walk them to their new home.

'What a beautiful setting,' Ruth said as we gathered on the drive. 'Those views of the lake as we drove through the village were amazing.'

I introduced her to Dad and shared the plan to empty her trailer first as those four alpacas had been inside for slightly longer, followed by our three and finally the supplies while The Magnificent Seven explored and grazed.

For the next half an hour, our focus was on moving the herd into the holding pen and then into the main paddock. As soon as we opened the holding pen gate, they dispersed into the field. I wondered if they'd head for the far end, eager to get away from us, but it seemed they were curious about their boundary and set off in different directions in two pairs and a three to explore. I headed over to the water trough and filled it up. They were intelligent and would have soon found the hay and water themselves but it did no harm making a show of where it was. Charmaine and Maud headed straight for the water trough and lapped on it before moving on to the hay while the others continued to explore the boundary.

While the trough filled, Dad put his arm round my shoulders and rested his head against mine. 'Congratulations! They're here! How do you feel?'

'Quite emotional,' I said, blinking back tears. 'I know it's a cliché but what a journey to get them here!'

'They look at home already,' Ruth said, smiling at me. 'Congratulations from me too.' She raised her phone to film them. 'Lizzie's going to want to see this.'

'Any news from the farm?' I asked when she'd finished recording.

'Mitch turned up about fifteen minutes after we left, demanding his alpacas back. Lizzie says he was driving a flatbed truck of all things. It had sides but that didn't make it any less unsuitable and dangerous. She told me she had a right go at him – which I can well imagine – about what an irresponsible animal owner he was and how his choice of transport proved that.'

'Good for her,' I said.

Ruth nodded. 'My sister won't stand for any nonsense. She thought it would inflame him but said it seemed to calm him and he looked at the truck as if suddenly realising how impulsive he'd been. He still insisted he wanted his alpacas back and would return with a proper animal trailer. Lizzie needed to return to the school children but she gave him a paper copy of the documents he'd signed relinquishing ownership and she got Alf to march him round the farm to prove that the alpacas had gone, exactly like he'd been told.'

'Did that finally get rid of him?' Killian asked.

'Yes. He wanted to know where they'd gone but there was no way he was getting that information. Alf told him it was none of his business and if he showed up at the farm again, he risked the police contacting him about stalking and harassment. That apparently shut him up and he toddled off, promising to leave it alone.'

I hoped that was the end of it. If Debbie didn't know where the herd had been taken and they all believed that it was another rescue centre, there was no way Mitch could track the alpacas back to me. He'd also been given a copy of the agreement and a friendly warning from a former police sergeant. That surely had to be enough.

Rosie appeared shortly afterwards on her lunchbreak. She advised us that Alice had made a batch of spicy parsnip soup and baked some bread rolls and we were all invited to Horseshoe Cottage for lunch. It sounded more appealing than my sandwiches so I was in. I thought Ruth might be keen to get back but she accepted eagerly, saying driving with a trailer always made her feel drained so a break and some sustenance was very welcome before she returned to Butterbea Croft.

* * *

'Well, that was quite a morning,' Killian said as we both rested on the fence a little later watching The Magnificent Seven grazing.

'Wasn't it? I hope I don't have to experience anything like that again, although it was worth it to get them here. I think they're happy in their new home.'

He smiled at me. 'That's because it's magnificent, just like them.'

After a delicious lunch, Rosie had returned to the stables and Ruth had headed home, promising me that she and Lizzie would come across one day to visit when the herd were fully settled and I'd found my feet, but to keep them posted in the meantime. Dad had offered to stick around to help but Killian and I had decided that, after the stress of travel, we'd let the alpacas relax rather than risk stressing them further with construction sounds. My aching muscles were grateful for the rest.

'You don't have to stay with me if you've got other things to get on with,' I said to Killian.

'And leave you to have all the fun with these girls? No way! I fully intend to spend the afternoon in alpaca heaven.'

'Alpaca heaven? I love that.'

'Also,' he said after a pause, 'there's part two of your story, whenever you're ready.'

'Now's as good a time as ever,' I said. 'If only we had a couple of deckchairs to sit in but I think we might have trashed those.'

'Nearly forgot! Back in a minute.' He ran off and appeared a couple of minutes later with a pair of wooden deckchairs. 'I brought these from home.'

He opened out both chairs. One had a red and white striped

lighthouse on it and the other had a puffin with a fish in its beak.

'The girls chose them,' he said. 'We've got two more at home – starfish on one and a mermaid on the other. Take your pick.'

I sat down on the puffin chair just as the sun peeked from behind a cloud, making me squint. 'This is the life,' I said, smiling. 'Relaxing in the sun with my new herd. Shame it's so cold.' I pulled my yellow bobble hat lower over my ears and zipped my coat up a little higher. A week today, it would be October and it certainly felt like it.

'Where were we? Oh, yeah! I'd got as far as telling you about Matthew's trip to New Zealand...'

I outlined everything that happened after Matthew returned, culminating in his shock announcement that he'd accepted a job in New Zealand and was hoping to emigrate.

'They say lightning never strikes twice but, for me, it did. I married Matthew and I was going to marry Grayson and both of them found a new dream that they didn't want me to be part of. And, not only that, but neither of them had the guts to tell me what was going on. In both cases, it was presented to me as a fait accompli and the end of our relationship. What does that say about me? I thought I was easy to talk to, to get along with, but obviously not.'

'I don't think it says anything about you,' Killian said. 'I think it says everything about them and you've already said why. *Neither of them had the guts to tell me what was going on.* Pure and simple, that's what it sounds like to me – selfish cowardice on their parts. Grayson used you when he had nowhere to live and continued to take advantage until he got the farm and Matthew pushed you away when things got tough. He made not having a baby all about him instead of it being about you as a couple, he shut you out when you tried to talk about it, and then he ran away. That's on both of them, not you.'

I thought about it for a moment. It *was* cowardice. 'I hated the way they just sprung it on me without warning.'

'If it helps, Danika did something similar to me. Obviously what happened to Patrick and Hattie was shocking and unexpected. Danika and Hattie had been really close and she adored the girls so she was as concerned as me about what was going to happen to them. When we found out about their wishes for me to take the girls, there was a lot to process alongside our grief, but Danika gave no indication that she wasn't fully on board. Her way of dealing with things was always to be very practical so she picked out paint colours and bedroom furniture. She was the one who suggested we put the wedding on hold and she was even the one who suggested we put our plans to have a family on hold too as supporting Lyla and Elsa needed to be our top priority. I agreed that it made sense to wait and then she turned that against me, accusing me of putting everyone else before her and making her feel like she didn't matter. I tried to talk to her but she'd already checked out. To this day, I don't know whether the wedding and family on hold thing had been some sort of test that I managed to fail. Aoife thinks it was but she was never Danika's biggest fan. She always thought Danika was too *me, me, me* and I guess she was right.'

'Sorry you went through it too. Being blindsided like that doesn't half hurt.'

'Too right. Danika had already had an estate agent round to value our house, presented me with a figure to buy her out, had found somewhere else to buy and had been moving some of her stuff out without me noticing. She actually had the audacity to throw that back in my face. I was grieving for my brother, his wife and the future of two little girls who'd just lost their parents, and she was pissed off that I hadn't noticed that a pineapple-shaped plant pot had disappeared from the kitchen window ledge.'

I laughed at how unbelievably petty some people could be and shared the battle of the cushion placement I'd had with Grayson.

'Sounds like Grayson and Danika would be well suited. They could out-petty each other.'

'Ah, but Grayson's a lone wolf. He doesn't need anyone.' I rolled my eyes at Killian. 'What a pair we are!'

We sat in companionable silence for a while, watching the herd.

'I know you've been badly hurt,' Killian said eventually, 'but has it put you off relationships?'

'No. I still believe in love and I still believe that the right one for me is out there somewhere. You know what I think my problem is? I'm like you – I'm a fixer too. I think I'm pretty good at it when it comes to confused and directionless schoolkids but I'm pretty useless at it when it comes to adults. I seem to be drawn to broken men who don't actually want or need me to fix them. They don't want or need me at all.'

'It's not specifically you they don't want or need. It's anyone. Some people don't want to be fixed. You can tie yourself into knots trying and you can blame yourself for saying or doing the wrong thing but ultimately what you'd consider a failure on your part only failed to work because it was never something you could succeed at. That's why, when we were talking before about what I do for lost kids, I told you I don't change anyone's life – I just present them with other options. I give them the tools – including self-belief – to realise that their life can be different, but *they* have to make those changes themselves and they're only going to do that if they really want to. Accepting that I can't fix everyone was one of my biggest life lessons.'

'That makes a lot of sense but where does it leave me? I'm the one still nursing the broken heart while they live happily ever after without me.'

'They both broke your heart?' Killian asked, no judgement in his tone.

I shook my head. 'No. Just Matthew. I thought Grayson had, but it was already broken when I met him and I don't think I truly gave him what was left. He hurt me – no doubt about that – but Matthew properly broke my heart. How are you supposed to move on when you don't understand how you can have got it so wrong about the kind of person they were? When you fully trusted someone only for them to let you down so badly? When you wholeheartedly believed in someone and didn't notice that they were feeding you a pack of lies?'

Killian's eyes were so full of empathy that I found myself on the verge of tears and had to look away to regain control of my emotions.

'You're making it about you again,' he said gently. 'The way you talk about both of them, particularly Matthew, is always led by what you consider to be your failings. *You* got it wrong about them, *you* trusted them, *you* believed in them. What you need to do is flip those sentences round so that the focus is on them instead. *They* treated you wrong, *they* broke your trust and let you down, and *they* lied to you. Believe me, you're not difficult to talk to, Emma. They chose not to talk to you because they didn't want to. It's not about what you did or didn't say or do. It's about their behaviour and it's about them choosing the path they wanted to travel without you, with no regard for your feelings. Don't beat yourself up for not realising what they were up to. Celebrate the good times you had, congratulate yourself on being free, and reflect on all the positive things you learned about what you want and don't want from future relationships.'

I looked at him, full of admiration for his wise words. 'It sounds so logical. I just wish it was that easy.'

'You and me both. I'm not going to lie and say it *is* easy because it absolutely isn't, but we can make it harder on ourselves than we need to. Grayson, Matthew, Danika, your former students and the kids I've worked with all made choices about their future, but the people around them are making choices all the time too about their impact. I chose to accept that my new life with my girls wasn't the right life for Danika and to invest my energy in them instead of focusing on regrets about what might have been with her. My mam chose to be the best single mum she could possibly be instead of trying to convince my dad to come back. You've refused to let a couple of really hurtful experiences make you stop believing in love. And if you need more evidence to prove that you've forged your own pathway without them, just look around you. After what Grayson did to you, it would have been easy to forget about My Alpaca Adventure, return to teaching, and continue with life as you used to know it but, instead, you kept going with your new dream. You hit a massive bump in the road and said *I'm still going that way, but I'm taking a different route.*'

I smiled at him once more. 'You, Mr Fixer, are worth your weight in gold. That has helped me so much, although it does feel like the kind of discussion we should have had over a couple of stiff drinks rather than sitting on deckchairs sharing a flask of tea.'

'Any time you want to continue the conversation over something stronger, just say the word.'

We sat there for a while, smiling at each other. A noise

behind us made us both whip round to see Alice approaching, holding a foil package in her hands.

'You two look comfortable,' she said.

'We are,' I said. 'A spot of alpaca watching definitely soothes the soul.'

'I have something else that soothes the soul.' She handed me the foil package and I opened it up.

'Flapjacks!' I breathed in the sweet scent of the golden syrup.

'Your dad said they were your favourites so I whipped up a batch. There are two pieces each. They haven't had a chance to set properly yet but I personally love them when they're squidgy and warm.'

I snapped off a chunk and slipped it into my mouth. 'Oh, Alice! Wow! You might just have spoilt me for all future flap-jacks. This is incredible!'

I removed the one I'd touched and handed the package to Killian so he could take a piece. He bit into it and enthusiastically agreed with my assessment.

'I'll leave you both to it,' Alice said. 'If you have any other favourites, just let me know. I love baking but I don't have many people to bake for.'

'You know what you should do when I open the walks to the public?' I said. 'You should run a pop-up café. We could find somewhere to put some chairs and tables and offer drinks and snacks after their walk.'

Alice's smile widened. 'That sounds like a wonderful idea, love. It's up to Rosie and Oliver, but I'd be happy to give it a go. It'd be nice to be part of all the exciting new things going on here.'

She said goodbye and headed back down the track.

'Did you see her face?' Killian said when she'd gone. 'I think you might have just made her day with that suggestion.'

'You don't think I should have mentioned it to Rosie and Oliver before I opened my mouth?'

'They won't have a problem with it. Ultimately they want to have a café here and the best businesses often start small and grow.'

My mind was whirring. 'The gatehouse kitchen could be used for making the drinks and the chairs and tables could go in the garden.'

'It's a brilliant idea and I'm sure Rosie and Oliver will think so too.'

A WhatsApp notification arrived from Mum on the family thread.

'It's my mum,' I told Killian. 'They're due back from their holiday today. Oh, no! Delayed flight. Give me a sec while I respond.'

FROM MUM

> Our flight's delayed. We won't be home until after midnight. Missing you all and eager to catch up on all your news. We'd love to have you all round for tea tomorrow night if you're free. See you soon x

TO MUM

> That's a shame. Hope you have a good flight. See you tomorrow x

I slipped my phone back in my pocket and looked at the open foil wrapper on my lap.

'Would you judge me if I had my second piece now?' I asked Killian.

'Only if you don't judge me for doing the same,' he said, winking at me. 'Hand it over, Wynterson.'

'Yes, sir, Lieutenant Buchanan,' I said, smiling as I saluted him.

* * *

Settling into bed that evening, I opened up a book but closed it again. No way could I read. My head was buzzing with the events of the day. It was hard to believe that so much had happened and that the alpacas were finally here. Twelve days later than originally planned for Bracken Ridge Farm, ten days earlier than the revised plan for Willowdale Hall and one day earlier than the revised revised plan. My head hurt just thinking about it! But they were here, safe and happy, and this really was the start of My Alpaca Adventure.

Opening up to Killian about what had really happened with Matthew had been like shaking off a heavy old coat that I'd been wearing for far too long. I couldn't have picked a better person to offload to as, not only was he an amazing listener, but he had personal experience of something very similar.

Everything he said about how I should view my past seemed so obvious now but I'd been so convinced I'd done something wrong that I'd been incapable of taking that step back and looking at it from a different perspective. I'd liked his various analogies about pathways and had found a way of extending that to reflect my life with Matthew. The pair of us had started out together travelling down the same road towards the same destination, enjoying the journey, holding hands. Like any couple, we hit a few small potholes here and there but they were easy to navigate round, even if we walked on different sides, without breaking hold. But then we hit an enormous pothole and I wanted to go one way round it but Matthew wanted to go the other. The hole was too wide for us to do that still holding hands so we let go and, when we found ourselves at the other side of that pothole, I wanted to take hold of Matthew's hand and keep going on the same road as before but he'd spotted a turning which he wanted to explore. He never took my hand again and that was where our journey together ended. It had been different with Grayson but I could still use a journey analogy. I'd thought we were heading for the same destination but really I'd been a hitchhiker who Grayson had picked up along the way – someone who served the purpose of some company and financial help on his journey but who ultimately was only there for the ride with us going our separate ways once he reached his destination.

After it ended with Matthew, I was left on the same road, still wanting to reach the original destination, but I no longer had my travelling partner and I'd lost my map. I wasn't off pursuing my exciting new dream. For me, life had to go on as normal when normal no longer existed and I'd never quite got over that. Now I felt like I had and I might just have Grayson to thank for that. He had his exciting new dream but I also had mine and despite life as I knew it being thrown into disarray, I'd actually never felt more settled.

41

It was so good to spend a couple of hours with my family the following evening. Mum and John looked tanned and relaxed after their holiday and were already planning their next one. They showed us their photos and told us all about the beautiful places they'd visited and amazing food they'd eaten. Laura and Dillon updated us on their wedding plans, Sawyer and Ashton told us about their return to school, and Eden shared a garbled tale about starting at nursery school which nobody really understood – not even her parents – but the way she told it was adorable with lots of waving of the arms and dramatic facial expressions. Everyone was eager to hear about the alpacas. I'd already sent photos and updates on the family WhatsApp but I hadn't told anyone about the big rescue dash yesterday so they listened, enthralled by the drama.

'Sounds like this Killian's your knight in shining armour,' Stacie said, her eyes sparkling with mischief, her tone teasing.

'He's not *my* anything,' I said, knowing full well what she was up to.

'Not even your friend?' she asked, feigning innocence.

'Okay, he *is* my friend but it's only been a couple of weeks since it ended with Grayson.'

Laura raised her eyebrows. 'Please don't tell us you're missing him.'

'I'm missing Monty a lot but not Grayson, so don't panic.'

'Is Killian single?' Stacie asked.

'I think so, but...' I tailed off, shaking my head at my sisters' exchange of scheming looks. 'Stop it, the pair of you! I've just come out of a long-term relationship and I'm not about to dive straight into another one. I like Killian as a friend and colleague. He's a fantastic fixer of things gone wrong and I'm very grateful to him but I have a new business to set up so a new boyfriend is the last thing on my mind right now.'

They didn't look convinced but Anna and Eden were both getting grizzly so they needed to drop their interrogation and head home. As they gathered their belongings together, my thoughts were on Killian. He really was an amazing human being and so different from Matthew and Grayson. Admittedly, he was good looking, but it wasn't his looks that drew me to him. It was that he talked, listened and understood. He had emotional intelligence – something my two exes had sadly lacked. Danika had been a fool to let him go when he really was the full package. I wondered whether he might think the same about Matthew and Grayson letting me go and my heart beat a little faster at the idea before I dismissed it as a daft little fantasy brought on by Stacie and Laura's teasing.

The goodbyes were loud with hugs all round and then it was just Mum, John and me with calm restored.

'Cup of tea or do you need to rush off?' Mum asked.

'I'd love another cuppa. There's something I want to talk to you both about.'

We settled down on the corner sofa in their lounge with

our drinks shortly after and Mum and John looked at me expectantly. Last night, I'd made the decision to tell my family the full story. Telling Killian some of it first had been what I needed – less emotive than admitting to my family that I'd kept some very personal issues hidden for over fifteen years – but it was only right that I opened up to them now about what I'd told him. And the part I'd kept back from Killian.

'I wasn't completely honest with you about what happened between Matthew and me,' I said. 'He, erm... he didn't ask me to go to New Zealand with him.' I took in their shocked expressions and drew in a deep breath before continuing. 'We never discussed emigrating together. It was something he did on his own without telling me. The first I knew of it was the day he walked out.'

Mum pressed her fingers to her lips, her eyes wide as she shook her head. 'Oh, Emma! I'm so sorry. You must have been devastated.'

I nodded. 'And completely blindsided.'

'Why would he do that without you?' she asked. 'I thought you two were happy.'

'We were for a lot of years but there'd been something slowly pulling us apart which came to a head about a year before he left. Remember when I had surgery for endometriosis? That was because Matthew and I had been to a private clinic to find out why I hadn't been able to conceive.'

I chewed on my lip as I waited for that second revelation to hit.

Mum gasped. 'You were trying for a baby? But I thought you'd changed your mind about wanting children.'

'It was easier to tell you that than admit the truth.'

She shuffled along the sofa and took my hand in hers,

curling her fingers round mine. 'Do you want to tell us the full story now?'

I took another deep breath as I squeezed her hand gratefully. 'I do. It's time.'

Mum kept hold of my hand and she and John listened in silence as I told them about the disastrous visit to the clinic, Matthew's refusal to discuss the outcome, never mind consider alternative options, my fears for our marriage when he went on his January visit to New Zealand and the difficult months that followed before he dropped his ultimate bombshell.

When I finished, Mum released my hand, shuffled closer and held me tightly. I'd somehow managed to get through the full story without any tears but the simple act of my mum cuddling me and stroking my hair without saying a word broke me and I sobbed in her arms. As much as the tears were about how much Matthew had hurt me, they were for how much I'd hurt myself by hiding the past from the people I loved, the people who'd have understood and supported me if I'd let them.

As the tears subsided and I relaxed my hold on Mum, I breathed in the sweet aroma of hot chocolate. Glancing up, I saw John placing a mug on the table beside me.

'I thought you might need that,' he said, softly.

I noticed the squirty cream and mini marshmallows and smiled at him gratefully. 'Never needed one more.'

'Are you okay?' Mum asked, settling back into her original space while I wiped my eyes with a tissue.

'I am now. I'm sorry I didn't tell you all that sooner.'

'Don't be sorry and please don't ever feel guilty,' John said, his voice gentle. 'You only ever need to share anything if and when you're ready for it.'

I smiled gratefully at them both. 'I thought it was all my

fault at the time for becoming so obsessed with having a baby that I'd lost sight of us as a couple. How bad must I be to live with if my husband could plan a move to the other side of the world and only tell me about it when he was about to leave? At first, I kidded myself that he'd feel differently once he got there and adjusted to the reality of living and working there rather than being on holiday. He'd realise what he'd left behind and return to the Lakes, begging me to take him back. I didn't want you all to think badly of him and for things to be awkward when that happened, which is why I told everyone he had my full support to take a sabbatical. It was only when I heard from his solicitor that I had to accept that he wasn't coming back, which was when I admitted we'd grown apart because we wanted different things.'

I'd let them think that, for Matthew, that was a new life in New Zealand and that I didn't share that dream, choosing to remain in the Lakes with my family, friends and career. Nobody questioned it because it was plausible.

'You do know it's not your fault?' John asked.

'I do now but it's taken me a long time to get there.'

'I can relate to that,' he said.

Mum nodded. 'Me too.'

Mum admitted that she'd felt for years that it was her fault things hadn't worked out. John had felt the same with his ex-wife, believing it was something he'd done wrong that had driven her to having an affair. It was only by sharing their stories with each other that they'd been able to see that they weren't to blame. They'd both worked hard at their marriages and had wanted them to succeed but the simple truth was that both partners loved someone else and there was nothing that Mum or John could have done to change that. If blame was to be apportioned, it was on the other person, but it wasn't helpful to go down that route. Relationships ended, people got hurt, and it was what happened afterwards that was important. For Mum and John, they'd gone on to find true love and happiness second time around but were both convinced that their marriage was all the stronger because of what they'd learned first time.

'I'm thinking about all the stories Sadie and I shared with you about the babies we delivered,' Mum said. 'They must have been hard to hear. If I'd known you wanted children, I'd never have—'

I grabbed her hand, stopping her mid-flow. 'I'd categorically told you I'd changed my mind. You weren't to know.'

It had started at a family get-together. Matthew and I had been trying for a baby for three years and Laura, age fourteen at the time, had posed the classic question – *Are you and Matthew going to have a baby soon?*

'No plans at the moment,' I'd responded, eager to deflect. And the next part just came from nowhere. 'We're not sure if we even want kids.'

Mum either overheard or Laura told her as she collared me in the kitchen later. 'Have you and Matthew changed your minds about having children?'

I could have admitted the truth but Matthew had already made a few comments about feeling under pressure from the family and I saw an opportunity to alleviate that so I made a joke about days spent surrounded by hundreds of kids being enough to put anyone off.

Over time, declaring an uncertainty about having children and later categorically saying we didn't want them wasn't just protecting Matthew. It was a great protective mechanism for me too just in case the worst happened, just in case there was something wrong and we couldn't have kids. Or, as it turned out, just in case my husband decided to leave me when that day came.

'I really appreciate how understanding you're both being,' I said after we'd discussed my throwaway deflective comment and how it sprouted wings. 'I was worried that you might be upset about me not telling you everything before. You were so supportive when he filed for divorce and I did want to tell you but I was struggling to get my head around it all and I just couldn't put the full story into words.'

'Whatever happens in your life, we'll always be here for you,' Mum said, 'but it's your life so, as John said, it's up to you what you share and when you choose to do that. Please don't worry that we'll ever take the huff if you don't fill us in on every aspect of your life the moment it happens. Tell who you want, when you want, if you want.'

We hugged tightly once more. Mum rubbed my back like she used to when I was a little girl and upset about something. When she released me, John took over.

'I'm going to tell Stacie and Laura too,' I said. 'I didn't want it to turn into some big family discussion earlier while the kids were here – not the time or place. I'll tell Dad too.'

'How are you feeling about things now?' Mum asked.

'Really good. I had a long talk with Killian earlier about some of it and he's the one who triggered the full confession. He helped me see things in a different way.' I smiled as I pictured his caring expression. 'It's lifted a lot of guilt.'

'This Killian sounds like a good man,' John said.

'He is. He's been a good friend and a great help.'

The clock on their mantelpiece chimed nine and I stretched my arms out. 'You two must be flagging after your flight delay so I'll say goodnight. Drop me a message tomorrow and let me know what day's best for you to meet The Magnificent Seven. I can't wait to introduce them to you.'

I hugged goodnight to John in the lounge and thanked him for the delicious hot chocolate which had been just what I needed. He headed into the kitchen with our empty mugs while Mum walked me to the door.

'I heard what your sisters were saying about Killian earlier,' she said as I pulled on my trainers. 'I know it's not been long since it ended with Grayson, but does it matter? Sometimes people come into our lives at what might seem the wrong moment but is actually the right one.'

'Like in the divorce solicitor's office?' I said, thinking about her and John.

'Exactly. Seeing someone else was the furthest thing from my mind but there he was in the midst of the world's greatest admin cock-up and we both grabbed at that chance. Life doesn't work to a timetable. It's messy, unexpected and chaotic but we only get one go. You might think you have all the time in the world to move on, but does Killian? What if he meets someone else while you're getting over a man you never even loved in the first place?'

'We're just friends,' I said, grinning at her. 'But I appreciate the pep talk.'

42

Driving home, I thought about what Mum and John had said about their first marriages falling apart and how they fitted into my hitchhiker analogy. Mum had definitely been the passenger on Dad's journey and the only reason they'd travelled so far was that they had a baby strapped in the back. I wasn't sure how things had started out with John and his ex-wife but it seemed he'd been the passenger too. And then they got into the right car and made the journey through life together.

The comments about Killian made me laugh. What were they all like, matchmaking like that? Mum's parting words ran through my mind and I tutted to myself. *All the time in the world!* I *still* hadn't returned to that conversation with Dad. If he was up when I got home and didn't look too tired, I'd tell him what I'd told Mum and John tonight as well as closing the loop on that conversation about Kathryn.

Dad was up and his reaction to the truth about Matthew was very similar to Mum and John's – so sorry I'd been through that and full of understanding as to why I'd found it too difficult to talk about at the time.

'You're talking to the man who kept an enormous secret for several decades,' he said. 'If anyone's going to understand, it's me.'

'Speaking of Kathryn, you were going to tell me about why you zoned out when I said *all the time in the world*. We've started this conversation a couple of times and keep getting distracted.'

Dad smiled and nodded. 'It's not just the phrase, it's the song. Do you know it? Louis Armstrong, late sixties?'

I nodded. 'It's in a James Bond film, isn't it?'

'Yes. It's in the George Lazenby one – *On Her Majesty's Secret Service*. It's an ironic song title because Bond gets married and his wife is killed in a drive-by shooting later that day so it turns out that they don't really have all the time in the world.'

'Plot twist!' I said.

'Exactly. You think he has his happy ending and then...' He pointed two fingers at me like a gun. 'When we were first together, Kathryn and I hired it on video. The story really moved her and the ending had her in tears. We got talking about our future and it was the first time we said we loved each other. *We have all the time in the world* became our saying and our song. When we started seeing each other again years later, we'd talk about how we still had all the time in the world and would eventually find a way to be together without Kathryn losing the hall. Except we *didn't* have all the time in the world. Nobody does.'

'I'm so sorry you lost her, Dad.'

'Me too. But now that Oliver's found me, there's part of her back in my life. I know he looks more like me but I can also see Kathryn in him, the way I can also see Liv in you. I know Kathryn was the love of my life but I loved your mum too – just in a different way – and I'm sad I lost them both.'

Dad took a deep breath. 'Always grasp at life, Emma,

because you never know how long you've got. Hold on to people you love, grab opportunities, really live every day.' He shook his head. 'I don't know why I'm telling you this when you're the one who's actually doing that. I love that you've dared to have a different dream – to do something new after so long in the same career. Keep dreaming, keep believing, live and love boldly. Don't let what happened with Grayson and Matthew keep you from letting anyone else in as a life without someone special can be a lonely one.'

I had to ask. 'Are you lonely, Dad?'

'I've got you for company.'

'I don't mean this minute. I mean in general, before I moved in, after Kathryn, after you retired.'

He seemed to consider it for a moment. 'After Kathryn, it was a dark time but I had work, I had you, I had Oliver – even though he had no idea who I was – and I just had to get on with it. After I retired, I'll admit to floundering for months. Maybe even a year. I soon realised I didn't have a big circle of friends. I used to go out for drinks with other teachers but it was more a case of *fancy a pint after school?* Once I retired, I never saw any of them again – not good friends after all. Oliver was long gone from my life, I barely saw you and I had no hobbies. I wondered if I should try dating but I looked at a dating app and it scared the life out of me so I knocked that on the head.'

'What changed?'

'I realised that nobody was going to come knocking on my door asking if I wanted to come out to play. If I wanted friends, I needed to find them myself so that's how I got into cycling and hiking. At first it was only seeing people at an organised event but now I have people I see outside of those who I'd properly call friends. I got into DIY and found I was surprisingly good at it, and I got myself an unexpected hobby, although it might have got a bit out of hand.'

'Sounds intriguing. What is it?'

'It's better if I show you but my workshop's a mess at the moment so give me some time to sort it and I'll show you at the weekend.'

'Okay. You're on. But one more question before I say goodnight. You say you looked at a dating app and it scared you off. Does that mean you'd still be open to the idea of meeting someone?'

He grimaced. 'I'm not sure. It's been so long.'

'How long since your last relationship?'

'My last relationship was Kathryn. I think it's too late for me.'

So he hadn't been keeping his girlfriends from me – he genuinely hadn't had any. 'It's never too late to let love in again, but let's talk about that another day. Night, Dad.'

'Night, Emma.'

A fortnight ago, I wouldn't have been on love's side but I was now. Nearly everyone I knew had it and I wanted to find it for my dad. And perhaps for me too. But not with Killian. As I'd told my family tonight, we were friends. I had no romantic inclinations towards him at all.

But as I laid my head on the pillow and closed my eyes a little later, the last image I recalled before drifting off to sleep was Killian's face.

43

By the end of Friday, the work on Casa Alpaca was almost complete. The hedge still needed cutting and we needed to make the storage locker but, otherwise, it was all smaller jobs like putting up hooks and holders for soap, hand sanitiser and paper towels.

I couldn't have been more delighted with how well the herd had settled in and adjusted to seeing me every day rather than Ruth and Lizzie. Seeing them here completely transformed the place. I was besotted with my alpacas and I wasn't the only one. Killian was clearly smitten too, Rosie and Alice had visited every day so far, and I knew from them that Oliver and Xander had dropped by on the evenings they were around.

Killian's girls were desperate to meet the alpacas. Alpacas were gentle, docile animals but they could also be skittish. Safety of them and the public was paramount. If the herd had come to me directly, I'd have wanted to spend a lot more time with them before exposing them to children but, as they'd already been introduced to several groups of children from schools and clubs during their stop-off at Butterbea Croft, I was confident that they'd be comfortable around Lyla and Elsa and that the girls would be safe around them.

Walks were a different matter. I wasn't ready for the alpacas to walk with adults they didn't know, never mind children. Even though I was excited about building that side of the business, I knew better than to rush. Ruth and Lizzie had made amazing progress with them but this was an unfamiliar setting with different distractions and a new owner so I wanted to ensure the herd were confident with me and the proposed route around Willowdale Hall as well as building my own confidence in handling them. Ruth had told me which alpacas were leaders versus followers and who liked to go on walks together but she hadn't had as much time to devote to them as I did and I wanted to be sure I agreed with her assessment. Killian had volunteered his services to take them on pairs walks so we'd incorporated those into the past few days and I had Dad and Alice lined up for some larger group walks next week. Ultimately I was going to build up to all seven walking at the same time and had Rosie, Autumn and her partner Dane eager to help with that as they all had some flexibility during the day around their work commitments. Evenings weren't viable now that we were heading into October and it was getting darker earlier.

When I was confident with the herd and believed they were comfortable with the route and being around strangers, I'd conduct several trial walks where I'd enlist friends and family to go through the same experience I was planning to offer to the general public – welcome, safety briefing, walk with information, photo opportunities and so on. I wanted their feedback on what, if anything, could be improved so that, when I did go live, My Alpaca Adventure was polished and professional. I wasn't short of volunteers for my trial walks with my family and

Rachael's all eager to help out as well as Laura's best friend Alisha chomping at the bit.

Having Stacie and Laura bringing Eden and Anna to Casa Alpaca would be a good opportunity to work with very young children but Sawyer and Ashton were in the same age group as Lyla and Elsa. I was keen to do a trial with over-tens and teenagers but I didn't know anyone with kids that age. Killian the fixer stepped in, organising a few mixed-age, mixed-personality groups from his youth club.

If everything went well, we hoped to launch a soft start for My Alpaca Adventure across the October half-term holiday, take the feedback from that, and actively promote the business across the winter months. It might appear unwise to kickstart an outdoor business at a time of year when we had the worst of the weather and fewer tourists but I actually saw that as a benefit. We could start small, constantly evaluating how it was going, and slowly build the business. It gave several months to build our social media presence and promote what we did in order to generate more bookings across the spring and summer. Staying with Dad, having the site rent-free and having the proceeds from the sale of Riverside Cottage took away any financial pressures for now.

It was funny how I often thought of 'we' in relation to the business. Even though it was mine, Killian very much felt part of My Alpaca Adventure, as did everyone who'd already done so much to help set it up. And, practically, it would need to become more than just me and seven alpacas. If it was as popular as I hoped it would be, I'd need to recruit staff and I'd also need to expand the herd and get the newcomers trained because, if I built up to several walks during the day, I couldn't keep taking the same alpacas out. It would be far too much for them.

As I drove home through Willowdale on Friday evening, I spotted Killian's van parked near The Hardy Herdwick. He'd mentioned earlier that he was taking the girls there for tea and had asked if I had any evening plans, which I didn't. I'd assumed he was just making conversation but he'd fixed his gaze on mine and there'd been such intensity in his eyes that my heart had started racing and my palms felt clammy. Was he about to invite me to join them? But he didn't. He said he hoped I had a good evening and he'd see me on Monday, and then he dashed off.

With no traffic behind me, I slowed right down, wondering whether Killian might have just arrived, in which case I'd wave at him if he spotted me. A tall, slim woman with long blonde hair was walking towards the pub and, next moment, the door opened and Killian exited. My heart unexpectedly leapt and I stopped the car, planning to wind the window down and shout across to him to have a great weekend. But he didn't see me because his eyes were focused on the blonde woman. He rushed towards her, arms outstretched, and they hugged. For a moment, I wondered if she could be his sister despite having a completely different build and hair colour, but they held on to each other for far too long to be siblings. Clearly Killian had a girlfriend.

I pulled away as quietly as I could, glad I hadn't made a fool of myself for shouting across to him at an inopportune moment. He hadn't mentioned a girlfriend in any of our conversations but she could be recent and he'd probably feel a bit strange blurting out, *By the way, I'm seeing someone now* when all I was to him was a colleague. Although I did think we were friends too. And, from the disappointment I was feeling right now, I had perhaps hoped for something a little more.

I sighed and shook my head wearily. Jumping into another

relationship was the last thing I needed. Whoever she was, she was welcome to Killian. I needed time alone to focus on my business, my growing family and my relationships with them. I didn't need or want romantic entanglements. Just a shame my heart might be thinking otherwise.

* * *

'You're sure you're okay?' Dad asked as we finished our tea a bit later. 'You're very quiet.'

'I'm fine. Honestly. Just a lot going on in my head right now.' *And my heart.* But I wasn't going to tell him that. Dad had already shown his meddling nature in getting the alpacas to Willowdale Hall and, while that had led to a positive outcome, I wasn't going to say anything that might give him cause to meddle in my love life.

'Anything you want to talk about?'

'No. Just thinking things through.' I felt bad for dismissing Dad. That wall between us had come down and no way did I want to start rebuilding it. I had been thinking about something earlier which he could maybe help with. 'Actually, you know how I've named their home Casa Alpaca? I'm thinking I might like to name the different parts of their home. Saying *shelter* is okay but saying *the part where I do the talks* sounds rubbish. Fancy a bottle of wine and a brainstorming session?'

'I'm up for that.'

So we shared a bottle of wine and tossed around some ideas which became increasingly silly the more we drank. Out came all the daft phrases incorporating the word 'alpaca' like *alpaca my bags* and *alpaca picnic* before moving on to jokes. My favourites were *Why don't alpacas enjoy singing with backing music? Because they prefer to sing alpacapella.* Try saying *alpacapella* with a few drinks inside you! And *Why's it the end of the world if you get kissed by an alpaca? Because it's the alpaca-lips.*

Despite all the hilarity, we did manage to come up with some sensible suggestions for the various areas of Casa Alpaca, all with a similar theme – Paca Pen for the holding pen, Paca Shack for the shelter, Paca Plaza for the area where I'd do my talks and Paca Pasture for the paddock. Killian had said he'd make me a pub sign for Casa Alpaca so I'd have to see if he could make me smaller signs for each area. Although thinking about Killian set off butterflies in my stomach... until I pictured him embracing that woman outside the pub and the butterflies sank.

44

I spent Saturday morning with the herd and joined Alice and Rosie for lunch at Horseshoe Cottage in between them running riding lessons. As I walked back to Casa Alpaca, I felt a little nervous. Killian was coming over with his sister and the girls to finally meet my alpacas. I was used to meeting strangers – a part of my teaching role every time the new school year started and at every parents' evening – so it didn't make sense to have butterflies about meeting them. It was possible the apprehension was because Lyla and Elsa were the first children I'd be introducing to the herd and I was keen for it to go smoothly. Or was I kidding myself and it was more about seeing Killian again rather than meeting his family? I couldn't stop thinking about that brief moment yesterday when I'd thought he was going to ask me out and the disappointment I'd felt after I'd seen him outside the pub.

I'd bought myself a pair of black wellies with thick linings in them – more practical and much warmer than my colourful sheep ones – but Killian had told me the girls were going to be wearing their new wellies and it would make their day if I matched them. I knew that Lyla's favourite colour was purple but Elsa's was pink so I'd also put on the pink boiler suit Rachael gave me, muttering *Bollocks to you, Grayson*, under my breath as I fastened the poppers.

When I heard voices from the track, my stomach did a loop-the-loop. *Deep breath, the herd are used to children, nothing's going to go wrong. If, indeed, that's what you're reacting to!*

Killian came into view with six-year-old Elsa holding on to his hand and bouncing beside him, looking adorable in her sheep wellies and a pink waterproof with her long blonde hair in a high plait, but there was no sign of Aoife and Lyla.

'Needed the toilet,' Killian said, evidently picking up on my confused expression. 'But *somebody* was too impatient to wait. Can't imagine who that might have been.'

'Me!' Elsa declared loudly.

'It's lovely to meet you, Elsa,' I said, crouching down beside her. 'Loving those welly boots.'

'We're twins,' she said, stamping her foot beside mine.

'And I'm loving that boiler suit,' Killian said, grinning at me. 'Is this a new purchase?'

'No. Rachael bought me it when I moved to the farm but somebody hated it – the same somebody who hated my wellies.'

Killian rolled his eyes and shook his head. 'We love it, don't we, Elsa?'

Elsa stroked her hand down the material and looked up at Killian. 'Can I have one, please, Daddy?'

'How about you add a pink boiler suit to your list for Santa?'

'You've got a list already?' I asked Elsa.

She nodded, grinning.

'The list usually starts on Boxing Day,' Killian said. 'But Santa finds it helpful to plan ahead. Oh! I hear the other two.'

Lyla came running along the track, dressed the same as her sister except her waterproof was purple, with Aoife not far behind and I did a double-take. It was the woman I'd seen hugging Killian. So that had been his sister after all, not a girlfriend or a date. It perturbed me how relieved I felt.

'I've been looking forward to meeting you so much,' Aoife said, drawing me into a hug. 'Thank you for letting us visit.'

She was exceptionally pretty with peaches and cream skin and warm grey eyes. A delicate nose stud caught the light and sparkled.

'It's a pleasure. And you must be Lyla,' I said, smiling at Killian's other daughter.

The confidence that had propelled Lyla down the track seemed to slip away and she looked at me wide-eyed before tucking behind Killian's legs.

'If you want to meet the alpacas, you can't hide behind me,' Killian said, his tone jovial. 'Do you want to meet the alpacas?'

Lyla stepped to the side and looked up at him, nodding.

'That's better.' He glanced at me and mouthed the words, 'Bit shy.' He'd already told me that she was the quieter of the two.

'Lyla and Elsa, can you sit on the benches for me with your Auntie Aoife while your daddy helps me round up the alpacas? We're going to bring them into Paca Pen which is this area here with the fences and two gates and we'll talk a bit about them before we bring them into this section – Paca Plaza – for you to properly meet them.'

The girls obediently sat on the benches, one either side of Aoife. I handed Killian a bucket of treats to shake – perfect for grabbing the alpacas' attention – and we headed into Paca Pasture. Typically, the herd were all at the furthest end.

'Your girls are the sweetest,' I told Killian as we wandered towards the centre of the field before trying to attract their attention.

'They've been so excited about today. Lyla just needs a little while to settle and then she'll be just as chatty as her sister.'

'It's fine. It can be daunting meeting new people at any age and she's got seven animals thrown into the mix too.'

We stopped walking and Killian shook the bucket while I released several short whistles and all seven alpacas were soon following us into Paca Pen.

'Lyla and Elsa, you've seen photos and videos of The Magnificent Seven,' I said as Killian and I moved into Paca Plaza. 'But can you tell me which alpaca is which? Let's start with the dark brown one.'

The naming game soon perked Lyla up. The girls had no trouble naming Jolene, Maud and Barbara as they each had an individual colour. Bianca and Florence, both being white, took a bit longer until Lyla remembered a photo of Bianca having blue eyes. It was therefore only the two light fawn alpacas – Charmaine and Camella – who provided a challenge but as soon as I pointed to a white stripe on one of their heads, they identified that alpaca as Charmaine.

'I'm going to bring them out for you to stroke two at a time but, before I do, it's important we talk about where they like being stroked and where they don't. Any guesses?'

It was a lively discussion about what they might and might not like. Both girls had assumed that they'd love their heads, ears and backs being stroked, just like dogs, but I explained that it was quite different for alpacas. Their favourite body parts for stroking were their neck and shoulders but they weren't keen on having their faces and heads, including their ears, touched so those parts were to be avoided. The reason for that was mainly because these were blind spots for the alpaca so it made them uneasy. Their back, tail and rear were definitely to be avoided. Because alpacas were herd animals, it wasn't unusual for them to jump on each other's backs to assert their dominance while establishing (or disrupting) the pecking order so having a human touch them there would put them on alert and in defence mode and they might kick out. A kick wouldn't do the same damage as a kick from a horse as alpacas weren't hooved animals – they had feet with two toes and, like cats and dogs, had soft paw pads – but it would still be a shock as well as distressing for the alpaca.

The next hour flew by. Both girls were a little hesitant about approaching the first two alpacas but me demonstrating how best to stroke them – a slow and calm approach with an open palm – soon reassured them that they were in no danger. I hadn't been sure whether we'd get as far as all seven of the herd being in Paca Plaza at once but we naturally built up to that and the alpacas seemed to be loving the attention as much as the girls. Maud, who'd been hesitant when I first walked her at Butterbea Croft, surprised me with how enamoured she appeared to be by the girls, gently nudging them for more attention and humming for most of the session. That sound, when I knew it was made in contentment, made my heart soar.

Lyla and Elsa were a credit to Killian and Aoife and it was such a pleasure to spend time in their company. They were so gentle and caring with the alpacas, listening to everything I told them and asking lots of great questions.

I'd already known that Killian would be a great father from how he talked about the pair of them and the videos he'd sent me, but seeing him interacting with them in real life was wonderful. It also tugged on my heart strings. Lyla and Elsa were not his biological daughters but it was obvious it didn't make a jot of difference. He loved them and they loved him as though they were. Matthew and I could have had that. Admittedly, Killian was Lyla and Elsa's uncle and we wouldn't have had that family connection if we'd explored other avenues for having children, but it wouldn't have mattered. They'd have still been *our* children and welcomed into a loving family. Why had Matthew been so unable or unwilling to see that?

By the time they were ready to leave, it was clear that Aoife, Lyla and Elsa were smitten with the alpacas but I was smitten with Killian's family too, especially when I had huge hugs from them all before they left.

'Can you take the girls to the car?' Killian asked Aoife. 'I just want a quick word with Emma.'

I waved them off and Killian waited until they were out of sight and therefore out of earshot before he spoke.

'Thank you for today. It was brilliant.'

'I've never worked with that age group before but they seemed to enjoy themselves.'

'You're a natural.'

'Thank you. I was thinking I could offer sessions like that as an alternative to the walks. They might appeal more to younger children and they'd be ideal for anyone with mobility challenges.'

'That's a great idea. I think they'd be really popular and you've already got the seating for it.'

'Thanks to you. How was your meal last night, by the way?'

'It was great. The girls love The Hardy Herdwick. They like to count how many sheep there are around the pub. Aoife joined us, which we weren't expecting. She'd had a tough day so it was great to take her mind off it.'

'Everything all right?' I didn't want to sound intrusive but, having now met his sister, I didn't feel I could ignore the comment.

'It will be now. She's been in an on-off toxic relationship for the past four years and yesterday she finally ripped off the sticking plaster and ended it for good. She got me to meet her outside the pub so she could have a hug and a cry before she saw the girls.'

That explained the extra-long embrace – a brother comforting his heartbroken sister. 'Relationship break-ups are the pits,' I said.

'Aren't they just? Anyway, the reason I wanted to stay back was so I could thank you properly without anyone interrupting and to let you know how impressed I am by what you've created here. I know it's going to be a huge success.'

'That means a lot to me.'

We stood there, smiling at each other and I found myself focusing on his lips and wondering what it would feel like to kiss him, which took me by surprise.

'You've got a bit of hay in your hair,' he said. 'Do you want me to...'

I nodded to indicate that he could remove it. His fingers brushed against my skin as he removed the offending piece, sending a pulse of excitement through my body. He showed it to me before dropping it to the floor.

'Well, thanks again for today,' he said, still holding my gaze.

'Thanks for introducing me to your lovely family.'

As everyone else had had hugs, it felt only right to give Killian one too. He wrapped his arms round me and it struck me how solid he felt compared to Grayson and Matthew.

'I can't believe this is the first time we've hugged,' I said, squeezing him tightly. 'I'm usually a big hugger.'

'Then we'll need to make it an extra-long one to make up for the missed ones,' he said, his voice sounding a little hoarse.

Standing there in Paca Plaza, arms wrapped round each other, I wanted to slow down time and never let him go. I closed my eyes and sank further into his chest, listening to his heart pounding. Was it my imagination or was it racing faster than it should? And was mine matching it?

45

The following morning, I drove to Willowdale Hall, prepared the food for the herd and called them in from Paca Pasture. While they ate, I scooped up their droppings and tidied around before returning to Pippinthwaite to spend the day drawing. Dad had also promised to show me the hobby he'd told me about the other night now that he'd had time to tidy his workshop.

He was at the breakfast bar with a coffee, scrolling through his phone, when I arrived back.

'How were they this morning?' he asked.

'Magnificent as always. Maud's definitely coming out of her shell. She was very attentive, which is lovely. I might draw her this morning.'

'Before you crack on with that, do you want to take a look in my workshop?'

He downed the last of his coffee and I followed him outside. The workshop was connected to the back of his double garage, increasing his storage space by one and a half times. The previous owner had built it to house his model railway and run a club there. I knew Dad used it to store his tools and saw wood but I had no inkling what his hobby could be.

'I've cleared my workbench and put a few examples on there.' He pushed open the door and I stepped inside.

'Oh, wow! Dad!' I glanced at him in amazement. 'You made all these yourself?'

'Yes. I started off simple and built up to more detail. I'm still experimenting with the style I like best but I think I'm about there.'

I moved closer and ran my fingers down the beautiful wooden chainsaw carvings. Most of them were owls, hares and bears in various sizes and styles but I spied a squirrel and a fox too.

'I had no idea you were so creative!' I gasped, completely captivated by their facial expressions.

'Neither did I until Yvonne asked me if the pile of wood in her garage would be any use for my DIY projects.'

'Yvonne?' I asked, the name unfamiliar to me.

'I probably haven't mentioned her before. She lives over the road.' He waved his arm in the vague direction, as though I wouldn't understand what *over the road* meant. 'Her husband, Cliff, died a few years back. He was a joiner so, when she cleared the garage out, she said I could help myself to anything I wanted and I was drawn to all these chunks of tree trunk. Cliff had apparently been building up his collection for years, intending to get into wood carving when he retired, except he died just a few months after retirement.'

'They're amazing, Dad. Have you tried selling any of them?'

'I wouldn't know where to start but I do need to do something with them as they're starting to take over.'

I followed his eyeline and my jaw dropped as I took in shelf after shelf laden with carvings.

'Yvonne gave me Cliff's chainsaws and tools too and, as you can see, I got hooked.'

'Not that I want to encourage you to add to your collection before you've had a chance to create some space but, if you could carve an alpaca, I'd happily buy one from you. There could be a market for selling alpacas through the business.'

'Funny you should say that...' Dad wandered over to a side table and removed a cloth, revealing a stunning carving of an alpaca's head.

'Is that...' I peered closer. 'That looks just like...'

'Barbara,' we said at the same time.

'Dad! I don't know what to say! She's incredible.'

'She's yours and I wouldn't dream of taking payment for her. I'm just flattered you like her.'

'I love her. I can't believe you're so good that I actually recognise her. It must have taken you ages.'

'I've been steadily working on her since you first sent me some photos and I've taken a stack of them each time I've seen her since.'

'I never noticed.'

'Stealth,' he said, winking at me. 'I could tell you had a soft spot for her and she has such strong features that she was the logical one to go for.'

'Thank you,' I said, hugging him. 'What else don't I know about you?'

'I think it's all out in the open now,' he said, smiling as we pulled apart.

Another thing I could be grateful to Grayson for. If he hadn't ended things, I'd never have discovered this about my dad.

* * *

With my beautiful Barbara carving watching me, I spent the rest of the day in creative heaven. Seeing the alpacas every day really helped my drawings as I now knew their quirks and personalities so much better and could capture those.

I missed having Killian to talk to and couldn't resist sending him a photo of my wooden Barbara.

TO KILLIAN

> Look at what my talented dad made!
> Recognise her? How's your Sunday so far?

A response arrived a few minutes later.

FROM KILLIAN

> Is that Barbara? Your dad has some impressive
> skills. I'm at Whinlatter Forest with the girls.
> Thought we'd better leave Aoife in peace to do
> some work. They're on the adventure
> playground atm & we're walking the Gruffalo
> Trail later. What are you up to?

TO KILLIAN

> A day of drawing. Have fun in the forest and
> say hi to the girls for me

I returned to my sketches, my thoughts frequently drifting to Killian. He was evidently thinking about me too as he sent me photos across the day of various things he saw that he thought I'd like. Every message made me smile. I definitely missed his company across the weekends. It would be very strange next week when we'd completed those final touches and there was nothing more needed at Casa Alpaca. I was excited to be moving forward with the business, but I was really going to miss his company.

Later that evening, another message came through.

FROM KILLIAN

Having spent the day having my ears chewed off by two under-10s, I'd love to talk to an adult. Don't suppose you fancy another FaceTime chat?

TO KILLIAN

Would love one. Give me five minutes to make a hot chocolate then I'm all yours

It was only after I'd pressed send that I realised what I'd written. Might he read something into that? So what if he did. I liked him. Possibly as more than a friend and that should probably scare me but it didn't because Killian didn't scare me. Everything about him was solid and safe but not in a boring way. He had a zest for life and bucketloads of energy and every moment in his company reminded me of the person I really was – the person I'd been with Matthew before trying for a baby became all-consuming and we lost our way, the person I'd found my way back to before I met Grayson, and the person who I was around my family and Rachael. The person I wanted to be always.

My chat with Killian was relaxed and lovely. He told me about his day out and how the girls were still buzzing about their afternoon with the alpacas, and I told him more about Dad's amazing talent before showing him the pictures I'd drawn that day.

'Creativity clearly runs in the family,' he said, when I closed my sketchpad. 'I'm so impressed.'

The conversation moved on to his youth club and the kids he was planning to use for my trial. Hearing him speak about their progress under difficult home conditions or after extreme bullying was heart-warming but I loved how he never took the credit – the emphasis was always on what *they'd* done, how deep *they'd* dug, how much strength *they'd* shown.

'I know you say it's all them, but none of that progress would have been possible without you,' I said. 'I hope you do give yourself credit for the important role you play in their journey, even though I know you don't do it for the thanks.'

'I don't, but I'd be lying if I said it isn't nice to be appreciated sometimes. It gives me a boost for those times when the stories don't have a happy ending – the kids who can't or won't be fixed.'

'But at least you know you've tried.'

He was so open and honest about everything. I loved the way he owned his past, taking responsibility for the bad decisions he'd made instead of trying to brush them under the carpet. Even though he'd turned his life around, he admitted he was still flawed and that he had personal issues with which he struggled. He had no time for Hattie's parents, especially after the recent memorial debacle, feeling unable and unwilling to forgive them for their self-centred behaviour which disrespected Patrick and Hattie's memories rather than honoured them.

'You can only give so many chances and they've used their last one,' he said, shrugging. 'They've repeatedly chosen the wrong path and the worst thing is that they aren't even willing to admit that anything they've done is wrong. I can't deal with people who'll never take ownership of their actions.'

He also refused to ever have anything to do with his dad, saying he'd made his choice long ago to abandon the family although, unlike Hattie's parents, that had actually been the right choice for everyone. None of them needed a violent man in their lives.

'He got in touch when I started progressing in the army,'

Killian said. 'He didn't write much in his letter but I wasn't born yesterday. It was so obvious that he was only making contact in the hope of wheedling some money out of me. I do have a few residual anger issues to deal with about that waster but I think I can be forgiven for that after what he did to us all. A grown man who uses their wife and eldest kid as a punchbag doesn't deserve a second chance.'

'I'm sorry you had a tough childhood. I do think forgiveness is important but I agree that there are people who don't deserve it. Hattie's parents and your dad definitely fall into that category.'

When I settled down to sleep a bit later, I was still thinking about forgiveness. If Grayson or Matthew got in touch out of the blue asking for mine, would I give them it? Clearly their behaviour was on a different level to Killian's dad's and Hattie's parents' but, nonetheless, they'd deceived, humiliated and hurt me and I wasn't sure they deserved my forgiveness. Perhaps it wasn't as straightforward as forgive or don't. I wished there was a third approach where I could hear an explanation and apology before calling them out on their bad behaviour and sending them on their way, dismissing them as lacking any further relevance to my life. I'd never get an explanation or apology from either of them but I could take that final step myself. From now on, Matthew and Grayson weren't relevant to me. I *didn't* have all the time in the world and I was going to live in the here and now rather than let the past bring me down.

46

Another full week passed and my concerns about missing working with Killian had come to fruition. We'd finished everything we needed to on the Monday and that was it. Project complete. He needed to fell some trees elsewhere on the estate, so the hedge trimming was put on hold and he wasn't even working nearby.

October had brought a drop in temperature and we'd had several windy days, blowing the autumn leaves from the trees to dance around Casa Alpaca. I had a cleaning, feeding and walking routine every day but there really wasn't any need for me to hang out with the alpacas all day, tempting as that might be.

Killian had suggested I use the lounge in the gatehouse as an art studio as it had huge windows which let in stacks of light. All the furniture was long gone and the laminate flooring was old and scratched so there was nothing for me to damage. I spent some of my time drawing – including developing my branding – and the rest of the time working on my website and social media platforms. I'd already posted several teaser videos on the socials and my following was steadily building. I hadn't committed to an official launch date yet because, as well as being sure the alpacas were ready, I wanted to be sure I had the booking and e-commerce systems working properly on my website before going live.

Across the week, Rosie, Alice, Dad and Killian had accompanied me on alpaca walks and they'd all commented on Maud's amazing confidence growth. Florence was still feisty but not quite as disruptive, and I'd learned so much about them all. Jolene, for example, couldn't get enough of going out on walks and was always nudging forward, eager to have her halter on. Charmaine, by contrast, only liked being walked first thing and would sit down, refusing to budge, if I tried to take her out on an afternoon. I'd never make them do anything they didn't want to so it was vital to have this time to understand their preferences and quirks. And the most adorable thing was on cold evenings when they cushed together in the shelter. Florence, Charmaine and Bianca had formed a strong friendship and cushed in a three with Barbara and Camella as a pair and Jolene and Maud as another pair.

Despite no longer working together, Killian did join me for lunch in the gatehouse every day so I at least got to spend some time in his company, sitting on the deckchairs he'd brought from home. We'd attempted a trip to the lakeside on Monday but it had been somewhat bracing and we'd hastily retreated indoors.

When Saturday arrived, I was acutely aware that I wouldn't be seeing Killian for two days and it felt really strange. However, I did have a visitor lined up, due late morning, and she'd be fantastic company as always.

'Oh. My. Gawd!' Rachael whispered, grasping my arm. 'They are the most perfect, beautiful, adorably cute critters I have *ever* seen. How do you do any work? How do you stop yourself from cuddling them all day?'

I laughed at her enthusiasm, especially when she continued to reel off a stack of complimentary adjectives in both French and Spanish, evidently having exhausted all English words.

'They are pretty special, aren't they?' I said, bursting with pride.

We went for a walk with besties Florence, Charmaine and Bianca along the route I intended to use with my customers. It was so encouraging to hear Rachael's oohs and aahs, especially with her being the first person to complete the route who wasn't already familiar with Willowdale Hall.

The highlight was the stop on the beach. A pathway took us through the woods, awarding tantalising glimpses of Derwent Water through the gaps in the trees, before sloping down to the water's edge.

'They love standing in the water,' I said, 'and Florence might... yes, there she goes.'

Florence sat down in the lake, looked around her and released a long, contented hum.

'Is Florence making that sound?' Rachael asked. 'It's lovely.'

'This is her happy place and she wants us to know that.'

Rachael turned in a slow circle, smiling. 'I think it's your happy place too, Em. When we were talking about your USP being the place you walked the herd, I pictured something special like the farm, but I never imagined anything quite so awe-inspiring as this place. You, my lovely, have struck gold.'

'Haven't I just?'

'And you know what else your USP is? It's not just your surroundings. It's you. This place has made you.'

'It has. You know when you confessed what you thought about Grayson and you said that, when we first got together, it was like a dimmer switch slowly being turned to brighter? You said it had dimmed again after I moved to the farm but I think that actually happened way before the move, only I never noticed. I feel like it's turned up again here.'

'I can see that. I should have noticed before, Em. I'm sorry.'

'Gosh, don't be. I hadn't realised I'd lost my way either. I thought I was happy with Grayson and it's taken me being here to realise I probably never was. Maybe he knew that. Maybe he'd realised that early on and that's why it was easy for him to say goodbye. Good luck to him, I say. I hope he's very happy all on his own.'

Rachael winced and I shook my head, laughing. 'He's not on his own, is he?'

'There's a new teaching assistant at school and she's best friends with Grayson's ex, Chrissie. Apparently they're back together.'

'Really? Wow! That was quick.' I grimaced as a thought struck me. 'Was he cheating on me?'

'No. They weren't in touch. Chrissie heard that it was over and she made contact a couple of weeks ago.'

'Good luck to the pair of them.' I shook my head. 'Wow! I sounded really bitter when I said that and I'm not. I'm glad for him. He really did love her and I hope it works out for them second time around. What's weird is that, just now, when you said they were together, I felt nothing. No sadness, no regret, nothing at all. It was only the thought that he might have been cheating that bothered me.'

We walked the alpacas back to Casa Alpaca.

'I've got a gift for you,' Rachael said, pulling me down beside her on the benches once the alpacas were back in Paca Pasture. 'I was going to save it for your birthday but I couldn't wait.'

She removed something from her bag, covered in bubble wrap, and handed it to me.

'Aw, Rach! It's gorgeous!' I cried once I'd unwrapped it. 'Thank you.'

The wooden ornament was clearly made by the same person who'd made the farm Rachael gave me as a house-warming gift. This time, in place of the farmhouse and sheep were a shelter with stable doors at each end and a pair of alpacas. Instead of *Our New Adventure*, the plinth read *My New Adventure*.

'I wanted to get you a replacement to reflect how things are now,' she said. 'Funnily enough, I nearly had *my* instead of *our* put on the original one but, even if I'd done that, the farmhouse and sheep wouldn't have fit anymore. You have permission to give the other one away or chuck it in the bin.'

I smiled at her. 'I'll keep it. In fact, I think I'll display them together. Everything happens for a reason and, without that dream, this one would never have happened. No regrets, only lessons learned.'

She hugged me. 'Welcome back, my friend.'

We joined Oliver, Rosie and Alice for lunch in the hall. It was only a quick catch-up before Rosie and Alice returned to the stables, but I was pleased that everyone got on well. My sisters knew Rachael well and I wanted my brother to have a relationship with her too as she was like another sister to me.

Back at Casa Alpaca after lunch, I was surprised when Killian turned up.

'I've just dropped the girls off at a party in the village hall. It wasn't worth driving home and back again so I thought I'd see if you need a hand walking the alpacas, completely forgetting you have company today.'

Rachael shook his hand as they exchanged greetings.

'We've walked three of them but we can take another couple out if you're up for a second walk, Rach.'

'Hell, yeah! Best thing I've done in ages. Can I have the brown one? I swear she's been winking at me.'

'Jolene? Of course. I'll just get her, and Maud for Killian.'

* * *

As we headed back down to the beach with Jolene and Maud, Rachael complimented Killian on the amazing work at Casa Alpaca.

'I couldn't have done it without Emma,' he said, smiling at me. 'We made a great team.'

'That's because she's fabulous – something certain people never appreciated.'

'Well, she's surrounded by people who fully appreciate her now.'

The warmth in his voice stirred the butterflies in my stomach and I knew Rachael would pick up on it and see an opportunity to stir.

'Emma tells me your sister lives with you,' Rachael said. 'Is it just the four of you or partners too?'

I had to stop myself from groaning out loud. *Not very subtle, Rach!*

'No, we're both single. Aoife's just come out of a relationship, although her partner never lived with us, and I've been single since it ended with my fiancée five years back.'

The butterflies flapped their wings at the absolute confirmation that he was single.

'Not even a few dates?'

If Killian was bothered by the interrogation, he didn't show it. 'The girls were my number one priority at first and I was dealing with a massive bereavement and a broken engagement. A couple of years back, Aoife convinced me to get out there again and I did go on a few dates. The women were nice but I soon realised dating wasn't just about me anymore – it was about all of us. If I couldn't see them fitting seamlessly into my new family, or they didn't want that sort of responsibility, what was the point? So I stopped dating. It would take someone incredibly special to make me reconsider.'

I looked down at my feet, cheeks burning, praying Rachael would leave it there. I bet Killian wished he'd stayed at the village hall after all.

* * *

'I think you've found yourself another USP,' Rachael said after Killian left to pick up the girls. 'He is amazing. So what's going on between you two?'

There was no point trying to be coy with Rachael. 'I do have some feelings for him but I don't know what to do about them. You know I'm no good at this sort of thing. What if I say something and he isn't interested and it's all awkward because we work at the same place?'

'Believe me, he *is* interested. He could barely take his eyes off you and I think you have way more than *some* feelings for him. You're besotted with the man and I can't say I blame you. He's hot, interesting, funny, caring...' She rattled off more words in French and Spanish, making me laugh.

'Seriously, Em, you like him and he likes you and that's all you need to know. Did you not see the way he looked at you when he said it would take *someone incredibly special* to make him date again?'

My heart leapt. He'd looked at me? 'No, because I was staring at the ground, mortified by your line of questioning.'

'It had to be done. I spotted the chemistry between you the second he showed up and I knew you wouldn't have done anything about it so I thought I'd lay some groundwork.'

'It's too soon.'

'Rubbish! I understand why the gap between Grayson and Matthew was enormous – especially now you've told me the full story – but you weren't truly in love with Grayson so there's no need for a big gap. He's moved on. You should too. Ask Killian out.'

'I can't do that!'

'Of course you can! What decade do you think this is? Ask him out for a drink. What's the worst that can happen?'

'He says no?'

'He's not going to. He's definitely interested but he's probably wary about asking you out. You're the one who's just come out of a long-term relationship, not him. You're the one who's just started over with a new home, new business and new family. I bet he's wanted to ask you out for ages but is waiting for the right time. If you don't want to make the move, then you need to give him the green light that it's okay for him to make it.'

'You make it sound easy,' I said, shrugging.

'It's only complicated if you make it complicated. I know! While we're away next weekend, we'll do some role plays. You can pretend I'm Killian and let me know you're interested.'

'We'd need a lot of wine to do that.'

'We *always* need a lot of wine. Are you up for it?'

I winced. 'I might regret this but, yes, I'm up for it.'

'Yes!' She punched her fist in the air. 'Bring on the birthday weekend!'

* * *

After Rachael left, I put Barbara's and Camella's halters and leads on to give them a walk too. I'd not long passed the house when I heard Oliver calling me.

'Can I join you?' he asked when he caught up with us.

'Absolutely. Who would you like?'

'Tough decision, but I'll go with Barbara.'

I handed her over and we set off.

'It struck me we've never had any time on our own so, when I saw you passing, I thought this might be a good opportunity.'

'It's perfect,' I agreed, smiling at him.

'How's the training going?'

'Really well. I'm so pleased with them all. We should be ready to start trial walks soon.'

While Barbara and Camella paused to graze on a patch of grass past the hall, I told Oliver more about my trial plans and all the work I'd been doing behind the scenes to develop my website and social media presence.

'When do you think you'll do your first walks with the public?' he asked when we set off walking once more.

'Hopefully during half term. I'm offering a small discount to the first twenty people who book a winter walk and have already got more than a hundred newsletter subscribers who want to hear from me as soon as I'm ready to take bookings.'

We reached the beach and, while Camella stood in the water looking around her, Barbara sat down in the lake, humming contentedly.

'I don't think I'll ever get tired of that noise,' Oliver said, stroking her neck.

'Me neither. I've heard them all doing it but Barbara is definitely the karaoke queen. They're really happy here. I can't thank you enough for giving them a home.'

'It's a pleasure having them here. And you, of course.'

'Of course!' I said, teasingly. 'I was just saying to Dad this morning that it's hard to believe I only met you three weeks ago. Feels like you've been part of my life for a lot longer.'

Oliver's smile widened. 'Rosie and I were saying the exact same thing last night. We both feel like you've been part of the family forever and we're very grateful to you for making it so easy.'

I knew what he was referring to there. Rosie had told me that Xander had two children, Evan and Angelica, both in their twenties. Evan had welcomed the news and Rosie had met up with him, his girlfriend Courtney and their baby son Jaxon several times, but she still hadn't met Angelica.

'It was a heck of a surprise,' I said, 'but I've always wanted to be part of a big family so discovering I had more family was never going to be bad news. I'm sorry it hasn't been as easy for Rosie and her half-sister.'

'It's been seven months so far but Xander says she's back on friendlier terms with him now so we're hoping she'll come round eventually.'

Oliver's phone rang. 'It's Rosie,' he said, connecting the call. 'Hi... On the beach with Emma, Barbara and Camella... Okay, we'll see you soon.'

'Everything okay?' I asked, noticing the frown as he disconnected the call.

'I think so. She said she has big news but she wouldn't tell me what. She's coming to find us. Are the alpacas okay for another ten minutes?'

Camella had changed position and was looking towards the broken jetty but Barbara hadn't moved an inch.

'I think they're pretty content where they are. Who wouldn't be when surrounded by this? What was it like growing up here?'

Oliver stared across the lake, chewing his lip, as though working out how best to answer the question.

'This place is the perfect playground for a child and I have so many happy memories of times when it was for me...' His shoulders slumped and his head dropped to this chest.

'But those memories are blighted by Hubert Cranleigh?' I suggested gently when he showed no sign of continuing.

He nodded, sighing. 'It was bad while Mum was around but after she died...' Shaking his head, Oliver stroked Barbara's neck and I watched the tension leave his body. Alpacas truly did have healing powers and they were at work right now.

'When I walked out at eighteen, I vowed never to return,' he continued. 'In my mind, this place represented everything bad, but Rosie helped me see that the hall had never been the enemy and I fell in love with it – and with Rosie – all over again.'

Rosie's ears must have been burning as she appeared on the woodland trail above us, waving as she followed the path down to the beach.

She kissed Oliver, hugged me and gave the two alpacas a quick stroke before turning back to us, eyes shining.

'Sorry for interrupting but I had to tell you the news. Evan just FaceTimed me and I'm going to be a half-auntie again.'

'That's great news,' Oliver said.

'Congratulations!' I added, loving how excited she looked and sounded. I recalled the same feeling myself when my sisters announced their pregnancies, despite the moment being tinged with sadness, knowing I'd never been able to make such an announcement myself.

'Courtney's fourteen weeks, due on 3 April, and it's another boy but that's not all the news. They've decided they want to get married before he's born so that's on 18 January. Xander was at the cottage and he was acting all cagey because he knew Evan was going to call with the news and had promised him he wouldn't say anything first. He's dead excited about having another grandson, although, of course, that got him and Mam both raising their eyebrows at me.'

Rosie turned to me. 'Mam and Xander have made no secret about how much they'd love for us to have kids sooner rather than later.'

'As soon as we start with the building work, it's going to be non-stop for years so we know there's never going to be a *right* time,' Oliver said, adding air quotes over the word *right*. 'We do want a family, but we'd like a bit more time for it to be just us first.'

Barbara stood up so we set off back towards Casa Alpaca.

'You never had kids, Emma?' Rosie asked.

'Matthew and I both had fertility problems and he wouldn't even discuss other options which became a wedge between us and led to him walking away. Or flying away in his case – he moved to New Zealand to get away from me.' Even though I said it flippantly, I felt the familiar tightness in my throat. It still hurt after all these years.

'I'm sorry,' they both said together.

'What about Grayson?' Rosie asked.

'I was forty when I met him and I'd already accepted that I wasn't going to be a mum. He made it clear from the start that he didn't want kids and it was actually a relief because it meant no chance of repeating what Matthew and I had been through. I couldn't have gone through that again.'

* * *

In bed that evening, I thought about the conversation I'd had with Oliver and Rosie about children. After we dropped Barbara and Maud back at Casa Alpaca, I joined them in the kitchen at Willowdale Hall for a coffee and shared more about what had happened with Matthew. They'd been really sympathetic about it and Rosie had asked if I'd ever considered going it alone after my split with Matthew. I'd told her the truth – that it genuinely hadn't entered my mind – but I now wondered why. Why hadn't I explored fostering or adoption? Why hadn't I considered IVF using a donor, especially after the successful procedure on my endometriosis?

I stared at the wall, my frown deepening. All I could think was that throwing myself into my career – specifically aiming for the headship – had been my way of coping with the hurt. Having a baby in my life would have meant maternity leave and I might have needed to take some time off depending on the age of a fostered or adopted child. If I'd taken that time – no matter how short – I was sure I'd have crumbled. All the hurt would have stifled me along with the bitterness that I should have been doing it with Matthew.

'I'd have been a good mum,' I whispered into the darkness, a tear trickling down my cheek and soaking into my pillow. I'd been a patient and caring teacher, a good godmother and I was a great auntie. But a few days out and the occasional evening babysitting my sisters' kids never quite filled that ache inside me to be the one to pick up my own son or daughter after a fall and kiss them better, to snuggle up on their bed creating silly voices for their storybook characters, to feel proud of each step they made towards becoming the person they were meant to be.

An image of Lyla and Elsa pushed into my mind. Last weekend when they'd visited the herd, Elsa had taken a tumble and, being closest to her, my motherly instinct had kicked in and I'd picked her up, swung her in the air and had her giggling instead of crying. Killian often talked about taking them to Whinlatter Forest and an image sprung to mind of me being there with the girls and Killian, the four of us laughing as we cycled along one of the gentle trails, enjoying a pub lunch together afterwards, a happy family unit. My heart began to pound and I swallowed hard. Where had that come from? I'd developed some slight feelings for Killian and suddenly I'd turned us into a family. Talk about jumping ten steps ahead!

Despite Rachael believing my feelings towards Killian were reciprocated, I wasn't convinced he felt anything stronger than friendship towards me. Those couple of moments we'd had might have been in my imagination. Killian's priority ever since the tragic loss of his brother had been those two girls and, from what I could tell, he'd been an incredible father to them. He'd had his sister to help him navigate unexpected parenthood and I doubted either of them wanted anyone interfering with what they had going. Killian's girls were not the answer to the ache inside me and neither was Killian. I'd filled that void before with work and art and I'd do that again now. No complications.

47

Rachael and I had booked a two-bedroom cottage in Bamburgh, Northumberland for our forty-eighth birthday weekend. We'd stayed in the same cottage before so we knew what to expect – plenty of places to eat within easy reach, beautiful scenery, and miles of sandy beaches to wander along.

I collected Rachael straight from school on the Friday so that we could make the most of our first evening. It was strange being back in the car park. So much had happened since my final day in July that my time as a teacher felt like another world away.

In the rear-view mirror, I spotted Rachael approaching the car and got out to give her a hug. 'Happy birthday weekend!'

'Happy birthday weekend to you too,' she said, squeezing me tightly.

'The Birthday Bangers are on shuffle and I'm stocked up on sweets,' I said as she loaded her case into the boot. 'I'm so ready for this.'

'It'll be fabulous. It always is.'

I pulled out of the car park and we sang along very loudly

to the first couple of tunes, after which I turned down the volume so we could talk.

'What's your dad doing this weekend?' Rachael asked. 'Has he got a date lined up?'

I'd managed to convince Dad to sign up to another dating app specifically aimed at over-fifties which had less to do with swiping and more to do with matches based on compatibility. He'd been filling in the details while Rachael and I FaceTimed a couple of days ago to finalise our weekend plans and had interrupted me a couple of times to ask for my advice.

'I wish!' I said, shaking my head. 'He bottled it and removed his profile after an hour.'

'What a shame, although I do get the wobble. It can't be easy after such a long time being single.'

'That was his biggest barrier at first – *too long, out of touch, don't know what to do.* But now he's doubting his suitability as a partner for anyone and thinks he'll ruin someone's life if he gets involved.'

'Oh, no! Why would he think that?'

'He'd been reflecting on his relationship history and decided it didn't read particularly well. Kathryn left him to travel the world, he married his best friend even though he didn't love her in a romantic sense, they divorced when she had enough of being second best, he got back with Kathryn, who'd married Hubert in the meantime and she never actually left Hubert to be with Dad even though she hated him, he treated her badly, and he wasn't really Oliver's father.'

Rachael turned the music down a little further. 'Why's he focusing on the negatives? Your dad would make someone a great partner.'

'I kept telling him that but I've never seen him quite so down. He became fixated on Kathryn. Kept saying things like,

Maybe her leaving Hubert was a big lie. Maybe I'm remembering how good it was between us through rose-tinted glasses. Maybe she never truly loved me. I told him there was only way to get to the truth – to read Kathryn's diaries and, for a moment, I thought he was going to agree, but he shook his head and said he stood by what he'd said before.'

'Aw, I want to give your dad a big hug,' Rachael said after I'd told her about his reaction to Oliver offering him Kathryn's diaries to read. 'It's so sad that he's believed for three-plus decades that Kathryn loved him only to start doubting it now. Would you consider looking through her diaries to find proof that she really did love him and was definitely going to leave her husband?'

'Look on the back seat,' I said.

Rachael twisted round. 'Are those diaries I spy in that crate?' she asked, excitement in her voice.

'They might be. Rosie and Oliver didn't mind me taking them, especially when I told them why. They said I'd be in no doubt of Kathryn's true feelings for my dad after I read them and there were plenty of passages I could show him for reassurance. I've got the scrumpled and ripped-up pages too so there's some sticky tape in there to help reassemble them if we need to.'

'I love a good jigsaw,' Rachael said, turning back to the front. 'Haven't we got an exciting weekend ahead of us? Reading someone else's diary, sticking pages back together and role-playing how to let Killian know you're interested.'

I groaned. 'I was hoping you'd forgotten about that.'

'It's our priority. I think we should do that tonight and read the diaries tomorrow.'

* * *

The role-playing was a disaster but extremely funny. Rachael had brought a joke beard with her and she scraped her hair back into a bun like Killian's. It had us both in hysterical laughter, especially when she forgot she was wearing the beard, tried to drink her wine, and the moustache part came off and floated in her drink.

Fortunately, our second task for the weekend was far more successful. We had breakfast and a bracing walk along the beach before returning to the cottage to flick through Kathryn's diaries. I felt a little uncomfortable at first as reading someone else's diary was an absolute no-no, but reminding myself it was done for positive reasons rather than malicious intentions helped.

Rachael was sprawled out on the sofa and I had my legs dangling over the side of the armchair as we read. Every so often, we'd read a passage aloud to each other which emphasised how awful Hubert Cranleigh had been or how much Kathryn had loved my dad. As Rosie and Oliver had said, there was no doubting that Kathryn's feelings for Dad were deep and genuine and several of the entries had us in tears.

'I've found a great one,' I said after a while, passing the diary up to Rachael.

Tuesday 24 May 1994

I planted my birthday sunflowers today, like I always do, and it made me cry, like it always does. Each time I push those seeds into the soil, it's a metaphor for how my life was with H in the beginning – dark, lifeless, trapped. Then the miracle happens – the shoots appear and life begins, just like it did for me that day on the jetty when C came back into my life. When the sunflowers finally bloom, it's how life should be – beautiful and vibrant. It's how life is with C, how he makes me feel, how I hope I make him feel. One day, I'll be able to tell the world how much I love him but, for now, I pour it out to my sunflowers instead as I name them, water them, talk to them. I think that's why they grow so tall. It's not the sun that does it. It's my pure, enduring love for the person who gave me them.

'She definitely loved him,' I said after Rachael put the diary down.

'I suspect he knows it but he's scared.'

'Of trying again?'

'And of getting hurt again. The heart's a fragile thing.'

'But what if he doesn't get hurt? What if he finds pure, enduring love the second time around, just like Mum and John did?'

Rachael raised her eyebrows at me. 'What if you substitute the word *he* for the word *I* in those two questions?'

It was a fair point. I thought about what Killian had said about the kids he worked with putting up stop signs. I was the only one holding up mine. Was I brave enough to put it down? I really wanted Dad to give the dating app a go and it would be hypocritical of me to encourage him to date again if I wasn't willing to take that same leap of faith.

48

It was nearly 8 p.m. when I got back to Pippinthwaite after an amazing weekend in Northumberland. Rachael and I had found a few more great entries in Kathryn's diaries and I couldn't wait to share them with Dad, giving him reassurance that Kathryn's love for him was deep and genuine.

'Good weekend?' Dad asked, helping me inside the house with my luggage.

'Fantastic one. It always is. How was yours?'

'Really good. Went on a couple of bike rides and spent a bit of time in my workshop. It was strange not having you here. I've got used to the company.'

He spoke the words with a smile but there was a sadness in his eyes, as though he'd acknowledged how lonely he'd been for all of these years. Our relationship had changed beyond recognition and I anticipated that we'd continue to become closer as our bond strengthened, but I wouldn't be staying forever. Once My Alpaca Adventure was generating a reasonable income, I'd need to look for a place of my own and I wanted to leave knowing that Dad had found love again or was at least exploring that possibility.

I took my suitcase up to my bedroom, leaving the crate of diaries by the front door, while Dad made mugs of tea. On my way back down, I retrieved the diaries with the best entries. We'd found a gorgeous passage after Dad gave Kathryn Sunny – the soft toy Highland cow – and another after he'd bought Angus the Westie for Oliver in which Kathryn lamented how sad she was that she couldn't tell Oliver who it was really from. She talked about how cuddling the dog made her feel closer to Dad and how she longed for it just to be Angus, Oliver, Dad and her together forever. Her love for him had poured from the pages but so many entries had mentioned Hubert – always in a negative light – and I only wanted Dad to feel her love rather than her sadness.

'What's that you've got?' Dad asked, nodding at the small pile of notebooks on my knee as we settled in the lounge with our drinks.

'Some of Kathryn's diaries.'

He immediately stiffened. 'Why?'

'You were so down last week and I thought that, if I could find some diary entries where Kathryn wrote about how much she loved you, it might give you a boost and help you move on.'

'By move on, you mean get me signed up for a dating site?' His tone was gruff with an edge of sarcasm and it was obvious he was annoyed with me, but this was important so I was going to persist.

'That would be great, but that wasn't the main motivator. It was about showing you that you had no reason to doubt Kathryn's feelings for you. There's this lovely entry where—'

'What did I say when Oliver asked me if I wanted to read Kathryn's diaries?' he demanded.

'That you didn't want to read her words without hearing her voice. But I just thought—'

'That you knew better. Why, Emma? I was very clear that it was a strong no from me. You should have left it alone.'

'But what she says is so—'

'Enough!' he cried, jumping to his feet. 'Know when to let go! You can't be distant for forty years and then think it's okay to start controlling my life the minute you move in.' His eyes widened and he pressed his fingers to his lips, shaking his head. 'I'm sorry. I shouldn't have said that. That wasn't fair.'

'No, it *was* a fair comment. You're right. I shouldn't have interfered but please know that it wasn't because I'm trying to control your life. It's because I care.'

'I know you do.' Dad sank back down onto his chair, his voice catching. 'If I could take those words back...'

'Let's just forget about it.' I reached for my tea and stood up. 'I'm shattered so I think a bath and early night is calling. I'll take the diaries back to the hall tomorrow.'

'You don't have to go to bed because of me.'

'It's not that. I honestly am shattered after a busy weekend and the drive back. I'll see you tomorrow.'

I placed the four diaries in the crate with a sigh. I should probably take them upstairs but the crate was heavy and I'd only have to bring it down again in the morning. If I left them there, Dad would see them and it would be further fuel. Placing my mug on the stairs, I pushed open the dining room door and moved the crate into there where he'd be unlikely to spot them. That hadn't gone at all as I'd planned. What a sad ending to a wonderful weekend.

49

The following morning, I was up early, a knot in my stomach after last night's heated words. I felt awful about what I'd done. While it genuinely had come from a place of love, I'd meddled in something I shouldn't have. Dad and Kathryn had a long and complicated history and it had been a huge thing for him opening up to me about what had happened between them without me pushing for even more, especially when he'd specifically said he didn't want to read her diaries. My relationship with Dad had being going from strength to strength and I was so annoyed with myself for placing that great progress in jeopardy.

I crept around the house getting ready for work then slipped outside before Dad stirred. It was only when I turned off the main road into Willowdale that I realised I'd left the diaries behind. If I'd left them by the door, I'd never have remembered to pick them up but moving them to the dining room had taken away that visual reminder. I slowed down, wondering whether to go back for them, but Dad would likely be rising now so I kept driving.

Florence, Charmaine and Bianca were cushing in the Paca Shack when I arrived. Just being near them, sinking my fingers into their soft fleeces, I felt much calmer. It was a bit early to feed them, especially when I had a routine established, so I sat on the bench watching them, trying not to worry about how much I'd upset Dad.

'You're early!' Oliver's voice made me jump. He was leaning on the main gate with Toffee and Chester beside him.

'You startled me!'

'Sorry. I spotted your car after walking these two and wanted to check everything's all right.'

I shrugged as I wandered over to join him. 'The diaries were a bad idea. I found some great entries to share with Dad but I didn't get a chance. He reiterated what he'd said to you about it being a hard no and a few other things that hurt, but which I deserved.'

Oliver winced. 'I'm sorry it didn't get the reaction you'd hoped.'

'I should have sounded him out and got his approval instead of diving in. Hindsight, eh?'

'You can't blame yourself. Rosie and I both thought it was a good idea. Is that why you're here so early?'

'Yeah. I wanted to give him some space and, truth is, I'm embarrassed. I'm forty-eight but I think I might have acted like a teenager.'

'I disagree. You acted like a daughter who cares and wants to help although, looking back, we probably could all have benefited from putting ourselves in his shoes and thinking about how hard this all is for him. It's not easy raking up the past. I've had so many uncomfortable and difficult moments doing that this year and I wanted to walk away rather than face it so many times, but, with Rosie's help, I braved it. If I hadn't gone there, so many people's lives would be very different. Rosie and I wouldn't be together, Alice wouldn't be on the road to recovery, Xander wouldn't be in her life, I wouldn't know who my dad is, I'd never have met you, you wouldn't have found the ideal home for your herd, there'd be no alpacas here to make everyone happy and Willowdale Hall would be up for sale.'

'That's a lot of lives changed for the better,' I said, a little shocked that one person's bravery to face the past could have such a positive impact on so many others.

'Exactly! So any pain on my part was worth it a hundred fold. It takes a lot of courage, people around you who care, and a giant leap of faith where you focus on flying instead of falling. The past can be a scary place but the future doesn't need to be. If Dad can take that leap of faith, I reckon he'll find the best is yet to come.'

The best is yet to come. Rachael had said that to me when we met up after Grayson ended things. At the time, it hadn't felt like it but she'd been right. I hadn't realised that I'd lost myself while I was with Grayson but I clearly had because, current situation with Dad aside, I hadn't felt more relaxed or alive in years.

'I need to get the dogs back and head to work,' Oliver said, apologetically. 'Will you be okay?'

'I'll be fine. What you said is really helpful. Thanks, Oliver.'

'If you want to talk again, just give me a shout. I'm here for you.'

We hugged each other over the gate and I watched him disappear round the bend in the track with Toffee and Chester.

Spurred on by Oliver's words, I grabbed my bag and

returned to the car. It was wrong of me to leave this morning without speaking to Dad so I'd grab some pastries from the bakery in the village and take them back as a peace offering.

* * *

Dad was in the kitchen making a coffee.

'Morning!' I said, tentatively.

He smiled. 'Good morning! You were up and about early.'

I lifted the paper bags. 'Peace offering?'

He shook his head. 'There was no need to do that. You did nothing wrong.'

'I did and you were right to call me out on it. You said no to reading the diaries which wasn't a translation for *but Emma, you can read them and pick out the best bits for me.* I'm sorry.'

'I'm not annoyed with you. You were only doing what you thought was best for me. And, when I think about it, I can hardly be mad with you for going against my wishes when I'd already gone against yours.'

I narrowed my eyes at him, not sure what he was referring to.

'About a home for the alpacas,' he said, evidently noticing my confusion. 'You wanted time to adjust to your new life and get to know your brother without mentioning the alpacas but I took you to Willowdale Hall and, even though I had no idea we'd see Rosie there, I spilled out your land issue when you'd asked me not to. Except you took the whole thing in good grace and didn't have a go at me. So if anyone needs to apologise, it's me. I'm sorry, Emma.'

'I obviously got the meddling gene from you,' I said. 'Your meddling, although uncomfortable at the time, turned out to be the best thing you could have done. What if the same could be said for mine?'

He opened his mouth to protest and I cut him off.

'I'm not going to tell you what the diaries said so don't panic, but I'd like you to hear me out.' I paused and waited for him to nod his consent before continuing. 'Like you, I did it from a place of love and concern. You had questions which Kathryn can't answer in person and doubts that she can't address but I thought it was possible her diaries could do both. I know delving into the past is scary but it's cathartic too. Oliver had to do it when he returned to Willowdale Hall and so many great things have happened since then including him reconnecting with you. I've done it by telling you all what really happened between Matthew and me and I feel so much lighter for doing so. You could have similar success. So what I'm going to do for you is leave Kathryn's diaries here for a week. They're in the dining room. The passages I found for you are in the top four and marked with Post-it notes. You could just read those entries, you could read all the diaries, or you could decide not to look at anything. Next Monday morning, unless you ask otherwise, I'll return them to Oliver. Agreed?'

'Okay, but I can tell you now that it doesn't matter how long they're here, I'm not going to read them.'

'The easy choice and a somewhat stubborn one at that.'

His eyes widened. 'Easy? Stubborn?'

'Yes! I think it might be your default mode and it hasn't got you anywhere in the past.'

'Like when?'

I cringed at the high pitch of his voice. This was turning into another confrontation which absolutely wasn't what I'd planned. 'Forget I said it. I don't want us to fall out over it.'

He softened his tone. 'We won't. I'm genuinely interested.

When do you think I've taken the easy choice or been stubborn? I promise not to get defensive.'

I sighed. 'Okay, but bear in mind I don't have the full story around any of this – I'm only sharing observations based on what you and Mum have told me. So we have breaking up with Kathryn when you were in love with her, sticking it out in a marriage with Mum that wasn't going anywhere, turning Kathryn away for a couple of years because she was married, not telling Oliver the truth in case he reacted badly but losing contact with him anyw...' I tailed off as Dad's whole body seemed to deflate. 'Sorry. I've gone too far. You *did* ask.'

'I did and you're right. I've tended to go for the path of least resistance and it hasn't taken me anywhere good. Maybe I am stubborn.'

'It's not always a bad thing,' I said with a shrug. 'I'd strongly encourage you to reconsider the diaries but I know you need time which is why I'm suggesting a week with an extension if you need it. I promise I won't mention them until the week is up and I'll respect whatever decision you make at that point. Okay?'

'Okay.'

'For now, there's a really important decision to make. Almond croissant, pain au chocolat or one of each?'

'One of each, please,' he said, smiling at me. 'You know who you reminded me of just now? Your mum. She was always good at taking that step back and seeing things for what they really were. She was a good friend. I miss that.'

It was on the tip of my tongue to suggest he invite her out for coffee and see if there was any way of rekindling that friendship but I stopped myself. I'd done enough interfering for now and Mum might not appreciate me pushing Dad back into her life after everything they'd been through. I didn't want to upset

John either. I'd leave that one well alone and, for now, I'd enjoy my breakfast with Dad, relieved that he wasn't angry with me, and I'd hope that he ventured into the dining room at some point across the week and pick up one of those diaries because he deserved to know how much he'd been loved. And how much he could be loved again if he was willing to take that chance.

50

When I arrived at Casa Alpaca on Tuesday – my actual birthday – there was an envelope sitting on the benches with my name written on it. I thought it was maybe a birthday card from Rosie and Oliver so I opened it but it was a note from Killian:

When you've finished your morning routine, please come to the gatehouse x

The kiss sent the butterflies in my stomach soaring and I found myself speeding through my morning routine, anxious to see Killian.

'I'll be back soon,' I told the herd. 'I need to see someone first.'

Killian was in the kitchen and the butterflies went wild at the sight of him. He'd had his beard closely shaved and it made him look younger and hotter.

'Happy birthday,' he said, hugging me.

'Thank you.'

'I wanted to give you a card but I usually struggle to find the right one. The verses can be a bit much but it feels a copout to pick one without a verse, so I've made you one. Hope you like it.'

He passed me an A5 envelope and I removed what was more like a small booklet than a card. On the front was a cartoon picture of a broken heart with a very sad face and the caption:

On your birthday, I'd love to give you everything you need to fix your broken heart...

I opened up to the first page:

A mug of hot chocolate.

He'd drawn a steaming mug of hot chocolate with cream and marshmallows in it and I noted that the mug itself was the shape of an alpaca's head.

'Wait a second,' he said, opening a cupboard and whipping out a gift bag. 'The card comes with gifts.'

Inside the bag was the alpaca mug he'd drawn, some sachets of instant hot chocolate, a bag of mini marshmallows and a can of squirty cream.

'Aw, that's so sweet of you. The mug's amazing.'

'Glad you like it. Keep reading...'

I flicked onto the next page:

A piece of flapjack.

'Sticky and squidgy, courtesy of Alice Jacobs,' he said, producing a container full of flapjack.

'That's elevenses sorted,' I said, smiling at him.

At Killian's request, I turned the next page. *Lilies* was accompanied by a beautifully drawn bouquet. He surely hadn't... but he had.

'I wasn't sure whether they were a good idea after the argument you told me about,' he said, presenting me with the flowers, 'but I took the chance anyway because you said they were one of your favourites.'

'They are and it *was* a good idea. But you're really spoiling me.'

He smiled. 'I promise there isn't a gift for every single entry because, as you'll see when you read on, some would be a little more challenging than others.'

The next page had *Good friends* on it and I glanced around the kitchen, half-expecting Rachael to jump out on me but knowing it was impossible when she was at school.

'There's no gift for that one or the next,' he said. I turned the page to see the word *Family*. Both entries were accompanied by beautiful cartoon drawings of my friends and family which must have taken him ages.

On the following page was *Alpacas* and he'd drawn a fantastic cartoon of The Magnificent Seven.

'Obviously I wasn't going to bring one of the herd into the kitchen, but I do have something for you to represent that entry. I need you to read the next page first.'

I turned over and smiled at *Kayaking*, loving how he'd listened when I'd told him how much being on the water used to mean to me.

'You haven't bought me a kayak, have you?' I asked. I was only joking but my eyes widened when he nodded.

'I don't think it'll be very water-safe, though,' he said, passing me another gift bag. Inside were two items wrapped together and I laughed when I removed the tissue paper – Christmas tree decorations of a kayak and an alpaca wearing a Christmas hat.

'These are brilliant,' I said, dangling one from each hand.

'Well, who doesn't need an alpaca in a Christmas hat on their tree?'

'Or a sparkly kayak?' I agreed. 'I can't wait to get the tree up and decorate it now. Is 15 October too early?'

'In our house, we start our Christmas lists on Boxing Day, so I say go for whatever feels right for you.'

I turned another page where there was an incredible caricature of me and the words:

Courage and self-belief.

I ran my fingers down the image. Wasn't that the truth? One more turn and I'd reached the end of the card with the words:

Hope these help fix that broken heart of yours. Wishing you the best birthday ever. Hugs, Killian x

'It's the best birthday card anyone has ever given me,' I said, feeling quite choked up by the effort he'd gone to. I held it to my chest, smiling at him. 'Thank you so much for doing this and for my amazing gifts.'

I'd expected him to smile back at me but he looked a little uncertain of himself.

'Everything all right?' I asked.

'There was going to be one more page but I bottled it before you arrived and now I'm kicking myself for removing it.'

'What did it say?'

He held my gaze for a moment before wandering over to

the cupboard and removing a single sheet of paper, but he didn't hand it over.

'If I give you it, will you promise to be honest with me about your reaction but not be weird with me if it's really ill-judged and removing it was the right thing to do?'

'I promise,' I said, intrigued as to what it could be.

'Read the front of the card again,' he said.

On your birthday, I'd love to give you everything you need to fix your broken heart...

When I looked up again, he handed me the piece of paper, face down. I turned it over and it was a brilliant caricature of Killian. My heart leapt. Did this mean Rachael was right and he was interested in me? Or did the picture symbolise the listening ear of the fixer? But, if it was the latter, he wouldn't have made that speech about me giving him an honest reaction and not being weird with him? I looked up questioningly and met his dark eyes. He ran his hands down his beard, looking incredibly uncertain and vulnerable.

I glanced back down at the page. He'd drawn himself surrounded by trees with a tool belt round his waist, a hammer in one hand and a *Frozen* storybook in the other and suddenly panic gripped me. That scene that had appeared in my head last week of Killian, Lyla, Elsa and me as a happy family unit filled my mind but, this time, the girls pushed me away and ran to their Auntie Aoife who shook her head in disgust at me for trying to infiltrate the unit of four they'd carefully established.

I'm not sure what Killian read from my expression but it clearly wasn't good.

'Too soon,' he said. 'Sorry. I should have left it in the cupboard or maybe not drawn it at all. Forget you ever saw it.'

I looked up at him and he was smiling but I could see the hurt behind his eyes and I willed myself to say something but I had no idea what.

'Happy birthday, Emma. I've got to...' He pointed over his shoulder with his thumb. 'Things to... you know... so, have a great time with your family tonight.'

Then he was gone and I closed my eyes, wishing the last couple of minutes hadn't happened or, rather, that I'd reacted differently. But what would that reaction have been? Killian had just presented me with all the ingredients to fix my broken heart but, with that final picture, he'd also presented me with the potential to break it all over again and not just once but three times because Killian came as a three-for-one package deal. If I became part of Killian's life, I'd become part of his family. He'd made those girls his sole focus for five years and he'd specifically told Rachael that the only women he'd dated hadn't come to anything because of that. *If I couldn't see them fitting seamlessly into my new family, or they didn't want that sort of responsibility, what was the point? So I stopped dating. It would take someone incredibly special to make me reconsider.* Which had to mean that he thought I was incredibly special and he believed I fit. But what if I didn't? What if the girls rejected me or I messed up trying to be a mother to them when that wasn't really my role? Killian had dangled a life I'd always longed for but it was too much, too risky, too terrifying. I couldn't put my heart on the line again for him or for his daughters because, if it went wrong, I doubted I'd recover.

I felt subdued all day. Even listening to Barbara and Florence humming did little to lift my spirits. I set off down the track several times, intending to seek out Killian, but talked myself out of it before I reached the end. I couldn't explain my turmoil to myself so there was no way I could even begin to explain it to him.

I'd arranged to meet my family for tea at a lovely pub in Grasmere and, even though I wasn't in the mood for celebrating, I pasted on a smile as I pulled into the car park.

I was running a little late so they were all at the table when I arrived to shouts of 'Happy birthday!' and bursts of party poppers.

'Dad?' I gasped, doing a double-take. He was meant to be going out with a friend tonight and taking me out for a birthday meal tomorrow.

'Surprise!' he said, hugging me.

It certainly was. I found out later that Mum had visited while I was away with Rachael for a long overdue talk and had invited him to join the family tonight but to keep it as a surprise.

Despite my misgivings about tonight, it was the tonic I needed. The kids were adorable and we had a laughter-filled evening but it was over too soon. My sisters headed off with their families first which gave me an opportunity to discreetly thank Mum for involving Dad.

'The hurt is long gone,' she said. 'He's your family which means he's our family and he's very welcome to be part of all our future celebrations. Laura wants to invite him to her wedding but I said she'd need to check that with you first.'

I was so touched by that, I couldn't speak. To see my parents laughing together this evening – and John being a part of that too – had absolutely made my day and pushed aside the mess I'd made of things with Killian. Or at least I thought it had.

'You were quiet tonight,' Dad said once we were home.

'Was I? I didn't mean to be. It was a brilliant evening and such a great surprise to have you there. I'm tired. I think a dramatic couple of months might be catching up with me.'

I felt bad for lying to Dad. Our new relationship was meant to be based on honesty so, in the morning, I showed him the card from Killian and talked him through my reaction and Killian's swift exit. Out tumbled all my fears and doubts. They were a bit garbled and inarticulate but I could tell Dad got the gist.

'I understand completely,' he said. 'Many of the questions you're asking yourself are the ones I've been asking myself about dating again but I need to show you something.'

He picked up his phone, tapped the screen a few times, and handed it to me. It was the dating app he'd previously removed, open on his profile.

'This is live?' I asked.

'It is and I've got a date lined up for Saturday.'

'Oh, my gosh! That's brilliant, Dad! But what made you change your mind?'

'I spent the whole of yesterday reading Kathryn's diaries.'

I gasped. 'You never did!'

He smiled ruefully. 'I was doing something on my computer and they were there and I thought maybe if I'd just read one of those entries you found. It was the one about the sunflowers and you were right. I needed to read it. So I read the others you'd picked out and that was going to be it but you'd piqued my curiosity. Obviously I didn't read everything – it would take far too long – but I read enough to know that it was true love. Thanks for challenging me and for leaving them here for me. You knew I'd be tempted, didn't you?'

'Not knew, but hoped. I can't believe you're back on the app and you've got a date.'

'It was time. Kathryn wouldn't have wanted me to spend decades pining over her. She'd have wanted me to get back out there and take a leap of faith with someone new so I took that leap and let's hope I fly.'

I thought about what Oliver had said about leaps of faith when I saw him on Monday morning. If Dad had been brave enough to take one, could I?

'I look forward to hearing all about your date,' I said, smiling at him. 'I'm so glad you did that.'

'I am too. You should know how grateful I am to you, Emma. You've told me I'm a lifesaver and have repeatedly thanked me for all the things I've done for you, but you've done just as much for me, if not more. Just because it didn't work out for Kathryn and me doesn't mean it won't for anyone else. Perhaps the best is yet to come but I'll never know unless I let it.'

* * *

All the way to Willowdale Hall, my mind was racing. Who knew how Dad's date would go on Saturday but he was finally giving it a try, which made me so happy. It wasn't a competition of whose heart had been most badly broken but, if it had been, I'd have to say that Dad's had been pretty badly mangled. And if he could be brave enough to take that leap of faith and try again after what he'd been through, so could I. But how?

While the alpacas ate their supplements and I cleaned up, I searched for the right words to convey to Killian how I felt. The problem was, it had tumbled out incoherently in front of Dad and it was still all jumbled in my mind. Maybe a big explanatory speech was the wrong way to go. Killian was a visual thinker who hated essays but he loved sketches. Could that be the way to go?

'I know what I need to do,' I told Maud who'd wandered out of the Paca Shack in search of attention. 'Let's hope it works.'

* * *

I was concerned that Killian might avoid the gatehouse at lunchtime after his hasty retreat yesterday so I'd sent him a message saying I needed to show him something and asked him to meet me there at one.

It was 12.55 p.m. now and I released a shaky, nervous sigh as I placed the lid back on my coloured charcoals box. The drawings were complete and the pieces I wanted to add to them were face down on a table, each with a number and a piece of sticky tape on the back. It had been a bit more rushed than I'd have liked but it was the message rather than perfection that was needed here. I just hoped it wasn't too much.

My heart pounded as I heard the door open and Killian call out, 'Emma?'

'In the front room,' I called back, rising from the stool and draping a sheet over the easel.

'Hi,' he said, hovering by the door, his body filling most of the gap.

'Hi. Thanks for coming.'

He was smiling but there was a definite air of awkwardness between us and I hated that I'd caused that.

'I messed up yesterday,' I said, 'and I want to explain.'

'You don't have to. I misread things and went too far.'

I shook my head. 'You didn't misread anything.'

His expression turned from uncomfortable to hopeful and he took a step forward. 'I didn't?'

'No, you didn't. That card was incredible and so was the page you'd bottled giving me and...' I stopped, shaking my head once more. 'I've been struggling to find the right words so I've taken a leaf out of your book and gone for drawings.'

At my invitation, he sat on the stool. I removed the sheet from the easel, revealing the first drawing of two alpacas – a male and female – who were gazing at each other through long eyelashes, clearly attracted to each other, but there was a big distance between them, pointed out by a large red arrow.

'What's in the gap?' I asked. 'All this baggage.'

I stuck on several colourful suitcases containing the words *broken heart, bereavement, exes, children, secrets.*

'All these pieces of baggage have one thing in common,' I said, before covering them with one enormous suitcase labelled in capitals: *THE PAST.*

Killian glanced up at me, nodding. He didn't say anything, not that I expected him to. For all he knew, this could be a presentation about reasons I didn't want to date him, although I hoped he knew me well enough to know I'd never do something so cruel.

I turned to my second drawing where the two alpacas were standing closer to each other. There were balloons in the top corners and a birthday card in the middle bearing the same words Killian had written on his.

I picked up my next addition – a think bubble containing red hearts which I added over the male alpaca. I added a matching one over the female and Killian's eyes met mine once more.

'Like I said, you didn't misread anything. But...' I added another think bubble over the female alpaca – a copy of THE PAST suitcase – and slapped several signs on top of it each containing one word emphasised by four exclamation marks either side of it – *PANIC, FEAR, UNCERTAINTY.*

'Because of everything that's happened in the past?' he asked, gently.

'I really, really like you, Killian and I do want to be with you but I'm scared.'

I turned over to the final page – a circus scene where the female alpaca was balanced on the edge of a high podium holding onto a trapeze with the male already on another trapeze, swinging towards her.

'I want to take that leap of faith,' I said. 'I'm holding on to that trapeze and I'm ready to jump and the only reason I hesitated yesterday is not because of all my baggage – or at least not directly.'

'Then what is it?' he asked, taking my hand in his and gently pulling me closer so that our legs were touching and my eyes were level with his.

'It's that it's not just you coming towards me on that trapeze.'

I twisted round and grabbed the final addition – two little alpacas which I added either side of the male.

'You don't want the girls,' he said, releasing my hand, his legs tensing against mine.

'Exactly the opposite,' I said, grabbing his hand. 'What you have is what I've always dreamed of having. I *want* to be part of your family. I *want* to be with you and help you raise your gorgeous daughters. My hesitation is how I'd ever recover if you let me go because I wouldn't just be losing you. I'd be losing all of you.'

'Oh, Emma. I never thought about that!' He drew my hand to his lips and brushed them against my fingers, sending a fizz of delight through me. 'I should have, especially when I know what you went through with Matthew. Of course you're going to be scared of finding a family and losing it again.'

He brushed his fingers through my hair and rested his forehead against mine for a moment. My heart pounded with longing for him and I could tell from his rapid breathing that he was feeling the same. He dipped his head back and looked deep into my eyes once more.

'Your friend Rachael asked me about dating. I told her I hadn't found anyone I could see fitting seamlessly into my family and that it would take someone incredibly special to make me reconsider. I meant it, but do you know why I shared that with her?'

'Because she's pretty intimidating with her interrogation techniques?' I suggested.

'She is that!' he agreed, returning my smile. 'But the real reason I told her was that I took the question as an enquiry on your behalf – presumably without your consent, given your reaction – and I wanted you to know that I was single but also that I thought you fit the brief. I looked at you as I said it...'

'But I wanted the ground to swallow me up and I missed it.'

Killian took my other hand in his and ran both thumbs lightly over my wrists which did nothing to ease the urge to kiss him.

'Nobody can guarantee a happy ever after,' he said, 'but I can reassure you that I would never have asked you out if I didn't care deeply already and if I didn't think the girls would want you in my life which, believe me, they do. I've had dating advice from a six- and nine-year-old for the past week or so. They took a real shine to you – haven't stopped talking about you since you met – and Aoife thinks the world of you too.'

That horrible vision I'd had of them turning against me faded into oblivion.

'The girls really like me?' I asked, my voice catching in my throat.

'Yes! So if you're willing to take us all on, we're ready for you but we can wait if you're not ready to take that leap just yet. We're not going anywhere.' He laughed lightly. 'We'll just be hanging around on our trapeze. In fact, I've got something for you. Wait here a second.'

He returned to the room moments later holding out a slim gift box.

'I know you've been hurt badly and, even though my card might have come across as light with all the cartoons, I do know that broken hearts take a long time to heal which is why I have one more gift for you. I was going to give it to you yesterday with the final page.'

I lifted the lid to see a beautiful wooden heart with clock hands on it but no numbers.

'This is me giving you all the time in the world,' he said.

My eyebrows shot up. That phrase! I glanced back at the second hand on the clock and back up at Killian. Time was already ticking by and I thought about Dad's advice to me: *Keep dreaming, keep believing, live and love boldly. Don't let what happened with Grayson and Matthew keep you from letting anyone else in as a life without someone special can be a lonely one.*

'The clock's beautiful,' I said, 'but I don't need all the time in the world.'

Love boldly!

I shuffled a little closer to him. 'My own personal fixer has already worked his magic and given me heaps of reassurance and courage. There's only one more thing I need right now. It wasn't in your card but it's something I'd like very much and I think it might mend the final piece of my broken heart.'

'What is it?' he asked, his eyes fixed on mine, his voice barely a whisper.

My heart pounded. 'A kiss?'

He ever so gently placed his hands on my cheeks and lowered his lips to mine with the softest of kisses.

'Was it just the one?' he whispered, still holding me.

'Plural. Definitely plural.'

His lips pressed against mine once more and I melted against him as his second kiss took my breath away. If this was living and loving boldly, I was ready for a lifetime of it.

52

Dad dropped me off in Keswick that evening to meet Killian, who took me to what he said was his favourite pub. There were lots of hidden nooks and crannies and, after ordering our drinks, we chose a small table tucked away in a corner – lovely and private.

'You look stunning!' he declared as I removed my coat, revealing a deep pink wrap dress.

'Thank you. Grayson would have said something like *That's very bright* and I'd stupidly think he was giving me a compliment.'

'Just as well I'm nothing like Grayson,' Killian said as I sat beside him on a padded bench.

'Nothing like him at all,' I agreed. 'And that's the last time I mention his name tonight.'

Killian shook his head. 'You talk about whatever you want or need to talk about. I'm just happy to be here. Thanks for taking that leap.'

'You're worth leaping for.'

He placed a soft kiss on my lips, leaving me longing for more.

'I've been thinking about your amazing card and the guts it took to put yourself out there like that,' I said.

'Right back at you with your trapeze-artist alpacas.'

'Did you really remove that page just before you gave me it?'

'Literally two minutes before you appeared. I'd asked you out a couple of times before and got no response. I kicked myself for both times being too soon and I realised that very little time had passed since then so the *too soon* thing probably still applied.'

I narrowed my eyes at him, confused. 'When did you ask me out?'

'The first time was the day of the alpaca rescue after you'd told me about Matthew. I said to give me a shout any time you wanted to continue the conversation over something stronger than tea.'

'That was asking me out?'

He wrinkled his nose. 'Yeah, I should probably have been a bit clearer. I'm not good at this sort of thing.'

I smiled at him. 'Believe me, you're doing brilliantly and it was more likely me not taking the cue than you doing it badly. I'm appalling at this sort of thing. So, when was the second time?'

'When I was taking the girls to The Hardy Herdwick for tea. Actually, scrub that one because it was an even worse attempt. I asked if you had evening plans and I so badly wanted to ask if you'd join us but I realised that a pair of under-tens in tow wasn't the stuff of first date dreams.'

I couldn't help laughing. 'I've got a double confession for you. Firstly, I thought you were about to invite me and felt really disappointed when you didn't. And, secondly, I saw you outside the pub hugging Aoife but I hadn't met her at the time—'

'And you thought she was my girlfriend,' he finished for me, shaking his head.

'Exactly. Which disappointed me too and that's when I knew I started to think about you as more than a friend and Rachael picked up on that as soon as she met you, which is why she put you under the spotlight. And I might as well confess something else...'

I told him about Rachael's role-play attempts with the fake beard and the moustache in wine incident, which had him laughing heartily.

As we held hands and talked for the rest of the evening, sharing the occasional kiss, I couldn't remember feeling this happy, comfortable or completely me with Matthew or Grayson. There'd been good times and laughter with them but Killian was different. Just from that card and the way he'd reacted to my drawings, I knew he already understood me more than they ever had but it worked both ways. I felt like I understood Killian more too. It felt like we were equals when before I'd always felt like I was the one pushing and having to take the initiative, which was pretty ironic when ultimately both my exes had ended up being the ones in control.

Was it really only a fortnight ago when I'd shared my story with Killian and asked if he could fix broken hearts? He could and he had – or, as he'd say, he'd given me the tools, including the self-belief, to fix my own. And that was another thing that made him so different and so special. He saw people and he helped them help themselves. Some were unwilling, some were unable, but the ones who wanted to be fixed could do it through their own courage, belief and determination.

As he kissed me goodnight a couple of hours later, I had a

very strong feeling that I'd finally found something that was real and enduring because neither of us needed to pretend about anything. Killian was who he was and I was who I was. This wasn't just the start of My Alpaca Adventure. It was the start of *our* new adventure together. The Magnificent Seven and the flawed but fabulous two, united by one dream to make Willowdale Hall a place of healing. It had already worked its magic on me and I couldn't wait to see what would happen next in that stunning setting nestled between the fells and the lake as winter approached and the alpacas met their public.

Rachael had told me that she was convinced that the best was yet to come for me. This was it. It had arrived because, thanks to my brother and my dad sharing their leaps of faith with me, focusing on flying rather than falling, I'd found the courage to fly too and it felt amazing.

ACKNOWLEDGEMENTS

Thank you for choosing *The Best is Yet to Come*. I hope you enjoyed reading about Emma's fresh start at Willowdale Hall and those gorgeous alpacas. There's lots more to come from the hall and village as Escape to the Lakes is planned as my longest series yet – potentially 12–15 books. So you can hum contentedly as this won't be the last we've seen of The Magnificent Seven!

This is the third book in the Escape to the Lakes series and I've been delighted with how quickly readers have embraced this new setting, making it my fastest-selling series so far. Book I – *The Start of Something Wonderful* – was one of five finalists in the Romantic Novelists' Association's Contemporary Romance Novel of the Year 2024, which was such an honour.

As always, there are so many people to thank for the inspiration and support while writing this book. Thank you to David and Jane Seymour, owners of The Lingholm Estate – the inspiration for the creation of Willowdale Hall. David and Jane kindly welcomed me into their beautiful home for a tour and shared more about its amazing history. I'd always intended for Oliver and Rosie's vision to be about creating a place where people can relax, heal and find happiness. In my original pitch to my publisher, I'd stated that Willowdale Hall would have been used as a place of convalescence for soldiers injured during World War I and II. Spookily enough, the Seymours shared that The Lingholm Estate had actually served that exact purpose during World War I but had been a school for evacuees from Newcastle upon Tyne during World War II. I loved this so much that I tweaked Willowdale Hall's history to reflect this.

It was lovely bringing Beatrix Potter into the story again, this time through one of her tenant farms. Thank you to Orla and her colleagues at the National Trust's North West Lettings Team who gave me a detailed insight into the process and answered my many questions. To keep the story moving, I couldn't include everything I'd discovered but I'm so grateful for the fascinating detail. Bracken Ridge Farm is fictional but the appearance of the farmhouse, the fells and the setting near Coniston is inspired by the fabulous Yew Tree Farm which is one of Potter's fifteen farms.

My biggest thanks go to the team to whom I've dedicated this book – the wonderful social enterprise, Alpacaly Ever After – found at https://alpacalyeverafter.co.uk

Enormous gratitude to the founders Emma and Terry for sharing their knowledge and passion for alpacas with me and answering copious questions on anything from shelter sizes to feed to cushing. Thanks to John for organising my meeting with Emma and my morning volunteering with the Lingholm Team. Huge thanks to fabulous guides Nicole and Jade for looking after me while I volunteered as well as taking me out for the most delightful walks with Jebediah, Ralph, Howard and Billy. If you live near the Lake District or have a chance to visit, I'd urge you to book yourself a meet and greet or a walk at one of Alpacaly Ever After's many sites. You won't be disappointed.

We ran a competition for readers to name three of The

Magnificent Seven. There were lots of brilliant entries, many of which made us laugh. Congratulations to Claire Gosney who named Jolene, Jane Woodcock who suggested Barbara, and Amanda Ward for the very clever name of Camella.

I turned to my lovely Facebook group, Redland's Readers (you're welcome to join us!) for some inspiration around what to name The Magnificent Seven's new home and was delighted with the suggestions. Credit goes to Kay Hamilton (Casa Alpaca), Helena Phoenix (Paca Shack), Jen Michel (Paca Plaza) and Jessie Porter (Paca Pasture).

Before I move onto my final thank yous, I wanted to add a note about endometriosis. It's a small part of this story so I haven't gone into depth about it. I appreciate that diagnosis can be slow so I've speeded this up by having Emma go private and, as with all medical issues, the experience I have shared for Emma might not be reflective of someone's experience or that person's ability to have or not have children.

Which brings me onto a final thank you. It takes a single author to write a book but a village to bring it to fruition. Eternal gratitude to my incredible editor, the wonderful Nia Beynon, for being a joy to work with and for providing so much advice and encouragement. Thank you to our Head of Marketing Claire Fenby for fabulous promotional ideas and boundless enthusiasm every time I have animals in my books. Thanks to my copy editor Cecily Blench, proofreader Shirley Khan, cover designer Lizzie Gardiner for another stunner, Rachel Gilbey for organising the blog tour and all the amazing bloggers/reviewers taking part, Boldwood's production team, and the vocal talents of Rebecca Norfolk in bringing Emma to life in the audiobook.

I look forward to bringing you more from Willowdale very

soon. Thank you once more for choosing this story, whether it's your first or twenty-fourth one of mine (have I really written that many?!). I'm so incredibly grateful.

Big alpaca-shaped hugs

Jessica xx

ABOUT THE AUTHOR

Jessica Redland is a million-copy bestseller, writing uplifting stories of love, friendship, family and community. Her Escape to the Lakes books transport readers to the stunning Lake District and her Hedgehog Hollow series takes them to the beautiful countryside of the Yorkshire Wolds.

Sign up to Jessica Redland's mailing list here for news, competitions and updates on future books.

Visit Jessica's website: www.jessicaredland.com

Follow Jessica on social media:

 facebook.com/JessicaRedlandAuthor

 x.com/JessicaRedland

 instagram.com/JessicaRedlandAuthor

 bookbub.com/authors/jessica-redland

ALSO BY JESSICA REDLAND

WHITSBOROUGH BAY

Welcome to Whitsborough Bay

Making Wishes at Bay View

New Beginnings at Seaside Blooms

Finding Hope at Lighthouse Cove

Coming Home to Seashell Cottage

Christmas on Castle Street Collection

Christmas Wishes at the Chocolate Shop

Christmas at Carly's Cupcakes

Starry Skies Over The Chocolate Pot Café

Christmas at the Cat Café

The Starfish Café

Snowflakes Over the Starfish Café

Spring Tides at the Starfish Café

Summer Nights at the Starfish Café

Standalones

All You Need is Love

The Secret to Happiness

YORKSHIRE WOLDS

Hedgehog Hollow

Finding Love at Hedgehog Hollow

New Arrivals at Hedgehog Hollow

Family Secrets at Hedgehog Hollow

A Wedding at Hedgehog Hollow

Chasing Dreams at Hedgehog Hollow

Christmas Miracles at Hedgehog Hollow

The Bumblebee Barn Collection

Healing Hearts at Bumblebee Barn

A New Dawn at Owl's Lodge

THE LAKE DISTRICT

Escape to the Lakes

The Start of Something Wonderful

A Breath of Fresh Air

The Best is Yet to Come

LOVE NOTES

LOVE IN EVERY CHAPTER

WHERE ALL YOUR ROMANCE
DREAMS COME TRUE!

THE HOME OF BESTSELLING
ROMANCE AND WOMEN'S
FICTION

 WARNING:
MAY CONTAIN SPICE

SIGN UP TO OUR
NEWSLETTER

https://bit.ly/Lovenotesnews

Boldwood

Boldwood Books is an award-winning fiction publishing company seeking out the best stories from around the world.

Find out more at www.boldwoodbooks.com

Join our reader community for brilliant books, competitions and offers!

Follow us
@BoldwoodBooks
@TheBoldBookClub

Sign up to our weekly deals newsletter

https://bit.ly/BoldwoodBNewsletter

Printed in Great Britain
by Amazon